SKINNER'S QUESTS

In which a young B.F. Skinner traveled
to Europe in 1939, met Sigmund Freud,
Ludwig Wittgenstein and Alan Turing,
and warned the White House of Nazi
plans.

To Linda, with very best wishes,
Richard.

RICHARD GILBERT

Borden House Press
Toronto

© 2016 by Richard Gilbert

This book is a work of fiction. Names, characters, places, and incidents portrayed in the book are the product of the author's imagination or are used in a fictitious manner. Resemblance to the activities of actual persons is coincidental.

Produced and published by Borden House Press
1106-297 College Street, Toronto, Ontario, Canada M5T 1S2
www.bordenhouse.info
Tel. +1 416 923 8839

Library and Archives Canada Cataloguing in Publication

Gilbert, Richard, 1940-, author
    Skinner's quests / Richard Gilbert.

Issued in print and electronic formats.
ISBN 978-0-9919562-4-1 (paperback).—ISBN 978-0-9919562-2-7 (pdf).—
ISBN 978-0-9919562-3-4 (html)

    1. Skinner, B. F. (Burrhus Frederic), 1904-1990--Fiction. I. Title.

PS8613.I3986S55 2016   C813'.6   C2016-906118-3
                                        C2016-904119-0

To Rosalind

Contents

The map continues on the next page.

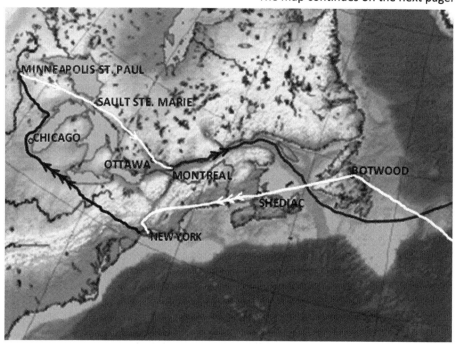

Left half of map showing routes and means of transportation taken by B.F. (Fred) Skinner during his fictional odyssey in May and June 1939, beginning with a rail trip from Minneapolis-St. Paul to Montreal.

The map continues from the previous page.

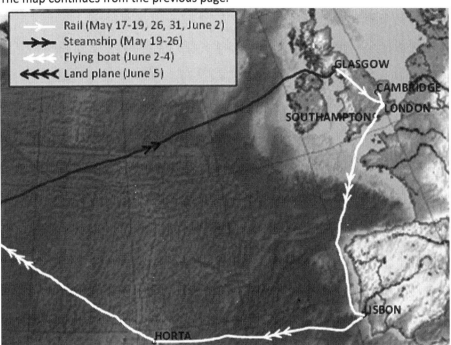

Right half of map showing routes and means of transportation taken by B.F. (Fred) Skinner during his fictional odyssey in May and June 1939, beginning with a rail trip from Minneapolis-St. Paul to Montreal.

Author's note

THIS NOVEL WAS INSPIRED by the play *Freud's Last Session*, by Mark St. Germain, which Rosalind and I – with Laura Simich and David Gurin – saw at New World Stages, New York, in February 2012. The play is about a fictional meeting between Sigmund Freud and C.S. Lewis on September 3, 1939. It was the day World War Two began and twenty days before Freud died at the age of eighty-three.

In the play, Freud, founder of psychoanalysis, debates religion, love, sex, and war with Lewis, a forty-one-year-old Irish scholar, novelist, poet, and prominent Christian. Their discussion is punctuated by radio bulletins about the German invasion of Poland and declarations of war on Germany.

I'd been writing another novel for some time, set in the spring of 1939. Freud was an early but incidental character. Thus, I was already immersed in one of modern history's most unsettling periods and in the circumstances of Freud's last year. After seeing Mark St. Germain's excellent play, I put the other novel aside and imagined a 1939 encounter between a young B.F. Skinner and Sigmund Freud. They were ranked first and third in a list of the ninety-nine most eminent psychologists of the twentieth century. The list had been compiled by Steven Haggbloom and colleagues and reported in the *Review of General Psychology* in 2002. (Jean Piaget was second. Anna Freud was ninety-ninth.) On the face of it, Skinner and Freud seemed as potentially antagonistic as Lewis and Freud, although on different topics, notably the role of mind in human behavior.

I'd long been an admirer of Skinner's writings, and had much respect for Freud. Several decades ago, I used to give a lecture comparing and contrasting Skinner and Freud as part of a course taught at Aberdeen University in Scotland. Subsequent diverse careers kept me at a distance from these interests. I saw writing a novel about their meeting as an opportunity to reenter the fray. Two other considerations quickly emerged.

One was my surprise and dismay at discovering how far Skinner's star had fallen in the twenty-first century. Freud's star had fallen too, but his best work was more than a century old. Some of Skinner's best work was only a few decades old.

The other was my concern that Skinner's contribution as a philosopher had become almost entirely neglected. He was never well regarded among philosophers; he was not one of them. He's been given little credit, for example, for his independent provision of a similar but more substantial analysis of language than that of Ludwig Wittgenstein. This was in Skinner's 1957 book *Verbal Behavior*, which had the misfortune to be adversely and influentially reviewed by Noam Chomsky, a technical linguist with a persuasive style and odd views about inheritance and infant development. Skinner compounded the damage by declining to reply to the review, which had hardly addressed the substance of *Verbal Behavior*.

Largely as a result of the analyses of language in his book *Philosophical Investigations,* published posthumously in 1953, Wittgenstein has been designated the "greatest philosopher of the twentieth century." This was in an informal poll conducted by University of Chicago philosopher Brian Leiter. In this assessment, Bertrand Russell was second to his former student, in spite of or because of their many disagreements dating from the 1920s.

It wasn't long before I contemplated including a meeting between Skinner and Wittgenstein, as well as the one with Freud. Wittgenstein and Freud were both in England in 1939. The challenge became how to get Skinner across the Atlantic with some plausibility. As it happened, near the beginning of 1939, Skinner actually met Bertrand Russell, who was spending a year at the University of Chicago. The eminent philosopher and political activist visited Minneapolis, where Skinner was teaching at the University of Minnesota. Russell then had reason to believe, mistakenly, that Skinner could have a positive influence on his errant protégé.

I soon understood that in 1939 Wittgenstein had had and was having an extraordinary life. Among the remarkable features of his history was attendance at the same high school as Adolf Hitler, who was a few days older than the philosopher. Like Hitler, Wittgenstein was more bizarre than can ordinarily be contemplated. Was it possible that their shared high school experience could provide clues as to Hitler's likely behavior? I imagined that Russell thought so, and that he persuaded U.S. President Roosevelt of this possibility. As it also happened, James Roosevelt, the president's son and former secretary, was near Minneapolis at the time. It wasn't hard to conceive of a role for him as an emissary.

Thus, I had Skinner embark on an odyssey with two quests, both inspired by Russell and both focusing on Wittgenstein. The intellectual quest was to redirect Wittgenstein's analysis of language toward something Russell would find more palatable. The political quest – undertaken for the White House – was to provide insights through Wittgenstein about Hitler's likely behavior. Skinner, who had little interest in Wittgenstein, undertook the odyssey chiefly for the chance of meeting Sigmund Freud. In his work on language, Skinner cited Freud more than any other writer, usually with admiration although not always with agreement.

Three more real characters of significance completed my picture: Anna Freud in London, Alan Turing in Cambridge, and Edward Bernays in New York. Anna Freud was her father's closest associate and would likely have been involved in any meeting with the father. Alan Turing was a mathematician who was part of Wittgenstein's Cambridge scene. He became famous for devising computers as we know them and for wartime decryption. Edward Bernays was Sigmund Freud's double nephew and his American publicist and benefactor. He was known to the White House as a prominent public relations expert, and could plausibly have been recruited to help bring Skinner's odyssey to a conclusion. Bernays (but not Skinner or any other psychologist) was among *Life* magazine's "100 Most Influential Americans of the 20th Century."

During his fictional odyssey, I gave B.F. (Fred) Skinner an important encounter with journalist Raimund Pretzel – known later as Sebastian Haffner – a German émigré who lived in Cambridge in 1939. I kept off-stage two other real characters of importance to the plot: the already-noted Bertrand Russell and the underestimated William Bullitt, then U.S. ambassador to France.

Special mention should be made of Fred Keller, Skinner's best friend and closest academic associate. During Fred Skinner's fictional odyssey, I had him write eight letters to "the other Fred," all unsent. These letters summarized and sometimes elaborated on the progress of Fred Skinner's intellectual quest and his meetings with Freud, Wittgenstein and Turing. Readers with limited tolerance for discussion of behavioral issues may well choose to skim or skip the letters, an option aided by how they are set out in the novel.

This note has focused on imagined versions of people who existed in May and June 1939. In the novel, Skinner also had numerous encounters with entirely fictional characters. Some of the encounters were romantic. Some were merely social. Some had a sinister edge that reflected the time of his travels, one of modern history's most fraught periods.

In July 2010, Ken Jaworowski wrote in the *New York Times*, "At its core [*Freud's Last Session*] is a discussion of ideas rather than a true dramatic work. At it unfolds, you may find yourself lamenting the lack of tension. But at the same time, you can't help but admire all the clever talk." I suspect readers of this novel will lament the lack of dramatic tension as much as audiences of the play that inspired it. But if readers get even half as much pleasure and elucidation from this novel's "clever talk" as those audiences evidently did, I'll be gratified.

Many family, friends and colleagues undertook reviews of drafts of the novel and made invaluable comments on them: Felix Gill, Rachel Lewis, Lory Rice, Ellen Richardson, Máirín Wilkinson, Helen Breslauer (and the late Bob Frankford), Timothy Hurson, Ron Ginsberg, Magdelene Winterhoff, Walter Fisk, Toni Howard, David Gurin, Gord Brown, Michael Miloff, and last but certainly not least, Evalyn Segal and Edward Morris. I'm deeply indebted to all these readers, and to Rosalind Gilbert, a skilled and tolerant psychotherapist, for enduring what must have been the tiresome obsessions of an aspiring novelist.

Richard Gilbert
Toronto, November 2016

Part I

Minneapolis
to
Montreal

B.F. (Fred) Skinner late in 1936.

ONE

Meeting Roosevelt

St. Paul, Minnesota, Thursday May 4, 1939

Fred Skinner was near the end of the streetcar ride from his home in Minneapolis to downtown St. Paul. He was thinking about thinking, something he did often. Just now, he was thinking about how novelists deal with thinking. How many have done what he and other psychologists have tried to do: focus on people's behavior rather than their thoughts and feelings?

Fred was also wondering about the four-o'clock meeting he was on his way to. Was yesterday morning's telephone call a hoax? Or was it really from the son of the U.S. president? The call seemed authentic, but he knew some students to be notorious pranksters. They were quite capable of setting him up for embarrassment. He'd seen in yesterday's *Minneapolis Tribune* that James Roosevelt was indeed to stay at the St. Paul Hotel. That didn't rule out a practical joke. If it was Roosevelt who called, what did he want to meet about? Fred had asked this of the caller, but his question was not answered. Perhaps he should have declined to meet, but curiosity got the better of him.

The *Tribune* article had reminded Fred that James Roosevelt had been on the cover of *Time* early last year. He was then his father's principal secretary and chief adviser. He was known as the "Assistant

3

President of the United States." In September, the son had been operated on for a stomach ulcer at the Mayo Clinic, not far from Minneapolis. The president himself had arrived at the Clinic on a Sunday morning, after a thirty-six-hour train ride from his Hyde Park summer home.

A few days later, continued the *Tribune* article, there was almost as long a trip in the presidential train to the White House. All the while, the president was dealing with the diplomatic turmoil following Adolf Hitler's threats to invade Czechoslovakia. They'd been bellowed out to a million supporters at a Nazi party rally in Nuremberg. For the first time, one of Hitler's speeches was broadcast live across the Atlantic. It was listened to at the Clinic by an attentive president who understood German well. He'd visited Germany often as a child and had even been to school there.

James Roosevelt had left the White House in November, perhaps for health reasons. He went to work in Hollywood. Fred wondered whether Roosevelt could be seeking his advice about a movie. It seemed improbable, but the thought was intriguing.

Fred's musings returned to the matter of thinking. Some psychologists – known as behaviorists – have ignored thinking because it's not observable. A person couldn't know another's thoughts, only what the other person said about the thoughts. There was no way of confirming whether such reports were accurate. Psychologists who've ignored thinking have argued that it was not a proper subject for a science of psychology, which should consider only what could be observed, including what people said. Fred was supposed to be a behaviorist, but he'd become unhappy about ignoring thinking.

Fred spent much of his time thinking. He suspected other people did too. A science of psychology should embrace rather than ignore such large amounts of human activity. This didn't have to mean that introspection was a valid scientific method. Introspection – looking inward and talking or writing about one's thinking – was a favorite practice of some of the early giants of psychology. The problem was that what people thought, what they said about it, and how they otherwise behaved didn't have to bear any relation to each other.

Along with other behaviorists, Fred believed that the first places to look for important causes of behavior were in a person's present and past environments, not in their thoughts. Two things preoccupied Fred. One was whether thinking was no more or less than talking to oneself covertly, without audible speech. The other was how children got to think. Was it related to how they learned to speak?

Fred was so engrossed in thinking about thinking he didn't notice that the streetcar had reached its East Fifth Street terminus. He walked the few blocks to the hotel, gave his name to the doorman, and asked for Mr. James Roosevelt. He was directed to a suite on the twelfth floor.

Fred knocked and the door opened immediately. "Come in, Professor Skinner. I'm James Roosevelt. Pleased to meet you." Fred recognized the genial face from photographs he'd seen in the press. He was surprised by Roosevelt's height – a good six inches more than his own five-foot-ten – and by how bald he was. He knew that Roosevelt was only in his early thirties, a few years his junior. He followed the well-dressed figure into an evidently opulent suite.

Roosevelt said, "Meet Calvin Cooper and Romelle Schneider. Mr. Cooper works with my father at the White House. Nurse Schneider is looking after my health while she's on leave from the Mayo Clinic."

Fred went to shake their hands, but Roosevelt continued speaking as if further introductions were unnecessary. "I'm glad you found us and we have this brief opportunity to chat. You should know that I must leave in about thirty minutes to talk with Governor Stassen – another errand for my father." He pointed to the well-stocked bar and a gently puffing coffee percolator, "Can we get you something?"

Fred declined and said, "I'm glad to meet you too. Until just now, I'd thought your invitation could be some kind of student prank. If you're here for your father, I'm especially honored, and even more curious as to why you want to talk with me." Fred felt his first words were spoken well. Unusually, he felt small. The three of them were all taller than average; the woman was almost his height.

Roosevelt gestured and they all sat down on facing sofas. Fred was across a coffee table from the two men. Roosevelt was elegant and comfortable with himself. Cooper was bespectacled, unsmiling and fidgety. Romelle Schneider was at Fred's side. He was aware of her perfume, and had to resist looking more than twice at her pleasing calves and ankles. He tried to remember what she was like when she was standing, but could not.

Roosevelt said, "You may have heard that I now work in Hollywood and no longer at the White House; but I'm still helping out behind the scenes. What I want to discuss with you is very much behind the scenes. We want it to stay that way. Can I have your word that you'll not share what we are to discuss?"

Fred paused before replying. "I guess I'll have to agree if my curiosity about the reason for this meeting is to be satisfied. If what we talk about makes me uncomfortable, I'll tell you. I'll leave, and never mention whatever I've heard or said."

"I'm glad you understand. What I want to talk with you about is the invitation you've received to go to Cambridge University in England. Would you mind telling us where that stands today?"

Fred paused again. "How do you know about the invitation?"

"We think we know how you were invited. Please tell us what happened, so we're sure?"

"You'll know of Bertrand Russell, the English philosopher. He was here at the University of Minnesota in January. He and I had a long talk about verbal behavior – about speaking, listening, writing, and reading – all the things you do with words. He seemed upset about the direction being taken by his protégé Ludwig Wittgenstein. Alfred North Whitehead, Russell's one-time teacher and collaborator, had suggested to Russell that some exposure to my approach could put Wittgenstein on a surer path. I'd often discussed such matters with Whitehead at Harvard. Russell said his discussion with me had led him to agree with Whitehead. I'm not sure why. I'd heard of Wittgenstein, but know nothing of his current work. Nevertheless, I was pleased Russell thought I might have something to contribute. It was something he wrote many years ago that first stimulated my interest in studying behavior."

Roosevelt intervened, "If we had more time, I'd like to know more about these ideas. Please continue about the invitation."

"Last week I received two letters. One was an official-looking invitation to attend the inaugural lecture by Dr. Ludwig Wittgenstein on June the first. He's been appointed Professor of Philosophy at Cambridge. The other letter was from Mr. Russell. I believe he should be called Earl Russell or Lord Russell. He wrote that he hoped I'd go to Cambridge. He'd persuaded the Carnegie Foundation to contribute two hundred and fifty dollars toward the cost of the journey. Before I continue, please tell me how you knew about the invitation."

"Well," Roosevelt said, "I know only what I've been told by my father's people. Mr. Cooper may be able to say more."

Cooper said, "Mr. Russell wrote to the president last month applauding what he described as the president's 'peace plea' to Herr Hitler. We sent a routine note of thanks. It provoked another letter from Russell. This suggested that more understanding of Adolf Hitler could be beneficial. Russell felt Wittgenstein could be a source of useful knowledge about Hitler. The two Austrians went to the same high school and they are close in age. Wittgenstein could also be useful because his well-connected Jewish family is now negotiating with the German government to secure exemption from Germany's Race Laws. There are other possible links between the two. They both spent prewar years as young men in Vienna. They both fought, bravely by all accounts, on the German side during the Great War. Russell said you'd be receiving an invitation to Wittgenstein's inaugural lecture. If you went he'd arrange that you meet Wittgenstein in person. Through him you could perhaps learn something about Hitler that we don't know. What you learn could be of use in our assessment of the European situation."

Roosevelt interrupted, "Let's be frank. We know that using you to find out anything new about Hitler through this fellow Wittgenstein would be a shot in the dark. The truth is, the United States government doesn't have good enough intelligence on Hitler, or on much else to do with Germany for that matter. My father's now thoroughly convinced that Hitler's Germany is a major threat to world peace. He's short on ideas as to what can be done about it. He's quite uncertain – especially given our political situation – as to whether and how America could intervene. More knowledge could enable us to anticipate what Hitler will do. It could put us in a better position to figure out what *we* should do."

"Russell's musings may well be pie in the sky," Roosevelt continued. "But, they come with the interesting suggestion that you can help us. We know you're a well-regarded, up-and-coming psychologist. You're a Harvard graduate no less, like my father and me. We've heard you're good at reading people. You had an interesting piece on Gertrude Stein's personality in *Atlantic Monthly*. We've heard too that you speak some German, which may be useful. My father's people think they could learn something from what you might discover."

"Could I add something before you respond?" Cooper said to Fred. "We don't have a properly functioning embassy in Berlin any more. We've had Mr. Kennedy, our ambassador in London, check out this Wittgenstein person, who is of course now living in England. We didn't tell Kennedy why we are interested. His partiality for Hitler is public knowledge and we didn't want the Germans to hear about our inquiries. Wittgenstein seems to be both a famous philosopher, whatever that means, and some kind of maniac. His family is one of the richest in Europe, but he himself seems to be friendly with the communists in Russia, or the Soviet Union as we must now call that country. Getting Wittgenstein to spill some beans about Hitler, if he has any to spill, may take the skills of a psychologist."

Fred was able to speak at last. "I'm impressed by the research you've done on me, and I'm flattered by what you think I could do. However, you should know that Yvonne – my wife – and I have discussed the matter and we're pretty much decided that I won't go to England. It would mean leaving her alone for a month with a one-year-old child in a still unfamiliar city. Also, I'm committed to teaching my course on the Psychology of Literature in the summer school. It's to begin on June the tenth, and I wouldn't be back in time. The course will be broadcast by radio. Thus, it's especially important. We need the money that teaching the course will bring in. On the matter of money, the offer from the Carnegie Foundation is generous but I'd have to use some of my own funds for the trip. As I said, we're already short."

"I'm interested enough in visiting Cambridge University to have looked into it," Fred continued. "I went as far as figuring out how best to get there. I even made a provisional booking for a crossing from Montreal leaving on May the nineteenth. I have until Monday, four days from now, to confirm the booking with the travel agent or it's cancelled. The way things stand now, I'm not going to confirm it." Fred wondered how they knew he could speak a little German, and how this might be useful.

Roosevelt said, "Can I say two things that could change your decision? The first is that it's not often that a professor in a Midwestern university gets a chance like this to serve his country. The only example I can think of just now is the University of Chicago's Bill Dodd, who was our ambassador in Berlin until 1937. The second is that we have a way around your concerns about money and timing."

"We can get you back here well before June the tenth," Roosevelt continued. "You would fly back. The *Clipper* flying boats cross the Atlantic in a day and a half instead of the six or more days it takes by sea. Test flights are under way. Regular airmail service starts soon, and passenger service is to begin in late June."

9

Fred moved to interrupt. Roosevelt gestured that he should wait.

Roosevelt said, "The head of Pan American Airways, Juan Trippe, is indebted to my mother for the publicity given Pam Am when she launched the first *Clipper* test flight in March. We asked him because we'd want you back quickly. He's agreed that a seat can be made available on a return mail service flight on June the second, at no charge, no questions asked."

Fred again moved to interrupt. Again, he was waved back.

Roosevelt continued, "The *Clipper* would get you back in plenty of time to recover from the trip and to teach your course. It would reduce your expenses because you wouldn't need to pay for the return trip. There's no procedure for giving you actual money while keeping this matter under wraps. Mr. Trippe has kindly offered something more that will also shorten your travel time and reduce your costs. Through his connections with other airlines, he'd have you flown without charge from New York, where the *Clipper* will land, to Minneapolis."

There was a long pause, and then Fred spoke. "The offer of the *Clipper* ride and the flight from New York could make a difference. It's an exciting prospect. I'd need to convince Yvonne."

He paused. The other three regarded him closely. Fred continued, "Can we have until tomorrow to decide? If the answer is yes what would happen next?"

Cooper said, "I'd visit you and Mrs. Skinner with a federal judge. He'd swear you both to secrecy for as long as this president and later presidents see fit. In fact, we might like to have a judge swear you even if the answer is no. You and I would meet again before you leave. This would be to discuss the kind of thing we'd like to learn about Hitler. We'd also meet as soon as you return. Then you'd resume your normal life. You'd be with your family, teach your course, and have a nice summer knowing you'd done something good for your country."

Roosevelt interjected, "Miss Schneider and I must go now. We must attend to my other reason for visiting the Twin Cities: to see if your new governor, young Harold Stassen, is as much an internationalist as the press makes him out to be. We've read that Stassen wants to deal with the worsening world situation rather than just keep America out of it. If true, he could be the kind of Republican whose support will be needed during the coming years. We'll call you at your office tomorrow afternoon to learn of your decision. I do hope you'll agree to go and talk with Professor Wittgenstein."

They all stood. Fred felt small again. Leaning down a little to shake Fred's hand, Roosevelt continued, "Thank you for coming here, and good-bye. Mr. Cooper will see you out."

Romelle Schneider spoke for the first time. "Goodbye, Professor Skinner. It's been a pleasure meeting you." Fred's usual courtesy left him. He muttered an inaudible, "I've enjoyed our meeting," and overlooked offering his hand.

They left. Fred pondered the relationship between patient and nurse. He hoped but doubted she'd be the one to call tomorrow. He wanted to hear that voice again. He chatted with Calvin Cooper for a few minutes, mostly about the baseball season ahead. Then he left the room and the hotel for the streetcar ride back to Minneapolis.

"Romelle Schneider," he said to himself as the streetcar moved from stop to stop along University Avenue. He'd not heard the name Romelle before. Perhaps it was an Italian name, like Roma, although the one Roma he knew was from Scotland. *Schneider* is German for tailor. Italian and German, Fred reflected, a troubling combination in these perplexing times. He resumed his thinking about thinking.

James Roosevelt in February 1937.

TWO

Objections at Home

Minneapolis, Minnesota, Thursday May 4, 1939

Fred Skinner left the University Avenue streetcar at the Oak Street stop and walked toward the duplex where he, Yvonne and Julie lived. Could he persuade Yvonne to agree to what would now be a three-week rather than a four-week absence? She'd been opposed from the moment she read the letters. He'd wanted to go, but not for the obvious reasons. He'd little interest in Ludwig Wittgenstein. He'd little interest too in making the long journey across the Atlantic and back, at least until the offer of the *Clipper* flight came up. He'd many things to keep him here. The timing had been quite wrong for the summer school course. Moreover, Europe seemed poised for war. He saw many reasons to stay an ocean away.

Until the meeting at the St. Paul Hotel, going to England had appealed to Fred for one thing only: the possibility of meeting Sigmund Freud. He'd thought of getting to London even before the letters came. The wish had been inspired last fall during a Sunday morning sessions with the airplane edition of the *New York Times*, one of his and Yvonne's few extravagances. It was their alternative to church, keeping them in touch with the society and culture of the East Coast. Yvonne would have preferred the *Chicago Tribune* so she could know about happenings in her home town, but only day-old copies of the *Tribune* were available.

The *Times* article had described a frail wisp of a man, sick but still alert, beginning the late evening of his life in London. He was an exile from Vienna where he'd been prominent for decades until the Nazis took over. Fred had figured out that the coming Saturday, May the sixth, would be Freud's eighty-third birthday, likely his last.

The possibility that he might be able to use the visit to meet Freud had stopped Fred from agreeing wholeheartedly with Yvonne. She knew about his wish to meet Freud. She had little sympathy for the notion that the slight chance of a meeting with an unfamiliar, dying man, however famous, would be enough to offset her being left alone for so long. Fred doubted whether the shortening of the trip and its new mission would sway her.

Fred had read much of what Freud had written. Some was in the original, challenging German. Most was in translation. He applauded Freud's frequent insights but disagreed with him as to the location of important causes of human behavior. Freud believed behavior resulted from the interplay of elements of mind: id, ego, and superego. Fred saw human behavior as mostly a product of people's interactions with their past and present environments.

There were several things Fred admired about Freud's work. He endorsed Freud's belief that human behavior can be explained, rather than being hopelessly complex or obscure, even as he disagreed with Freud's explanations. He admired Freud's ingenuity in attending to such verbal oddities as slips of the tongue and preoccupations with phallic symbols. Above all, Fred liked the way Freud went about things. He liked Freud's reliance on detailed case studies of individuals. He liked how Freud pulled together large numbers of instances often replete with surprising parallels and analogies. Fred's high regard for Freud was reflected in his half-finished book on verbal behavior. In it he cited Freud more than any other author.

Now he had another reason for going to England: flying back on a *Clipper*. He hadn't done much flying since he was in Europe eleven years earlier. Among the high points of that trip were the numerous short flights that took him on a roundabout route from Venice to Paris in what often seemed to be barely serviceable aircraft. Fred now had a yearning to fly in a *Clipper*, which must be a pinnacle of human skill and ingenuity.

As he opened the door to the duplex he heard Julie scampering on hands and knees toward him. "Dada," she called out, "Dada." Fred remembered one of the main reasons for not wanting to go to England. It was his fascination with the daily language and other development of his daughter, not long past her first birthday.

"Well," said Fred, "I've only been away a few hours and you've already grown some more."

"Dada, look, look." She reached for Fred's hand, fell over, grabbed his leg, said "Julie fall, Julie up," took his hand and led him to the sitting room. "Dada, Dada, look." She showed him the mass of round shapes in a riot of colors she'd crayoned on to a large sheet of paper.

"That's beautiful, my big button," Fred said. "Can you do another one for me in this space here?" "Where's Momma?" he added.

"Where's Momma?" Julie imitated him, and then said, "Kitchen." She added, "Stay. Watch."

Fred watched her draw. A month ago, Julie was using many fewer words, although she was beginning to imitate sounds. She didn't understand so much of what was said to her. Now she seemed to understand just about everything. This lag of speaking behind understanding could offer important clues about how language developed. But, he asked himself, what do I really mean when I say that Julie understands a word? Is it just another way of saying that she acts appropriately when the word is used in her presence, and then comes to use the word correctly?

He'd re-read the article by Bertrand Russell that stimulated his interest in language as behavior. Russell had noted how infants' understanding of words came before their using them. He suggested that explanations of language learning should begin with listening to words rather than with speaking words. Fred had puzzled over this. If language was to be treated as behavior then speaking – which was evidently behavior – should have priority over listening, which could be something else.

Julie interrupted Fred's musings about speaking and listening, "Momma, look, look."

Yvonne had walked in from the kitchen. She took Fred's hand, looked at Julie's drawings and said, "Which one is Dada and which one is me?"

Julie pointed to the large mass of shapes she had just finished when Fred returned. "Dada," she said, and continued working on the small set.

"Well," said Yvonne, giving Fred a peck on the cheek, "What was the meeting all about?"

Fred hesitated, still wondering how to say what he wanted to say. "Roosevelt didn't come here to offer me a movie part. It had to do with the invitation to England."

"I thought so. How did he know about it? And what could he possibly want?"

Fred explained the interest of the president's staff in Ludwig Wittgenstein, emphasizing how he, Fred, could serve the national interest. He mentioned the *Clipper* flight back.

"That all seems far-fetched," Yvonne said. "I suppose you've now decided to go."

"Momma, drink," Julie said. She stood and took Yvonne's hand.

"I think we could all do with a drink," said Yvonne. "Let me get

Julie some milk and you get something for us."

Minutes later they were settled in chairs with vodkas and tonic. Julie was on the floor between them contentedly drawing again. Fred didn't know how to continue. He waited for Yvonne to speak.

"I don't care that the president himself wants you to go, or that you'd be away for three weeks rather than four. I can't face being alone here with Julie. I can't face being stuck in this dull city where I know nobody and nobody cares about me."

"Could you and Julie stay with your parents in Flossmoor?"

Julie looks up from her drawing. "Gamma Boo?" she said.

Fred marveled at his daughter. She could be intent on drawing and still listen to what was being said – not only listen but understand. What triggered her mention of Yvonne's mother, Grandma Blue? It must have been an association with Flossmoor, the Chicago suburb where Yvonne's parents lived. But how? Julie's one trip there was when she was just a few months old. Yvonne's mother had been to Minneapolis a few times since. It must have been because she, or Yvonne, had been talking about Flossmoor.

"I've thought of that," said Yvonne. "That's what I think I'll do if you decide to leave me like this. Don't be surprised if I stay there."

Fred felt queasy. Thinking about the trip had increased his desire to go to England. Discussing the trip with Yvonne was making him more fearful of the consequences of going. "If I had all the money in the world I'd make this an adventure for all three of us," he said.

Yvonne bristled. "That would be worse than staying here. Imagine dragging a one-year-old across the Atlantic to a place on the brink of war. Image what it would be for us, waiting in cramped, damp hotel rooms while you have your important meetings. Imagine flying back in an aircraft under test – if they would permit a young child on board. It would be miserable and foolhardy. You're losing your senses."

"Let's sleep on it," said Fred, now feeling a little tipsy as well as queasy. "Let's make a decision in the morning."

"We should decide now, and not have it hang over us. You go to England, as you clearly want to do. Julie and I will go to Flossmoor. We'll see what happens then."

"Look, Dada. Look, Momma," Julie cried out. Yvonne and Fred joined her on the floor, both a little tearful.

They watched Julie for some minutes. Yvonne said, "Why would you want to help Roosevelt? Your parents wouldn't like it. Nor would mine for that matter. As far as I know, you've only ever voted Republican. What on earth would your father think if he knew you were working for a Democrat? Remember, he despises Roosevelt so much he rushed away from our wedding to be home in time to vote against him."

"I don't see it as helping Roosevelt as much as helping our country in a time of growing difficulty. If things in Europe get worse, we're going to have to put aside some of our differences." Fred mentioned the reaching out to Governor Stassen. "I'll still want to vote against Roosevelt, but there'd have to be a Republican candidate – like Harold Stassen – who sees America as having international responsibilities."

"Stassen's too young to be president," said Yvonne. "He won't be thirty-five before next year's election. In any case, since when have you been so interested in these things?"

"Well, I'm surprised at you, for knowing Stassen's age and for remembering how old you have to be to run for president. As for me, I'm becoming concerned by what's happening in Europe. I think America may need to take a stand against Hitler's and Stalin's dictatorships. Their systems stifle excellence and creativity as well as freedom of speech and movement. Any spread of their ideas here will add to our woes."

"Getting involved in Europe will add to America's woes, especially if it means supporting England, its king, and all that empire nonsense. That's a part of why I'm against you going."

Fred was enjoying their first political discussion for more than a year. Now, not knowing what to say next, he watched Julie absorbed in her crayoning.

"The main reason is still that I don't want to be left alone," Yvonne continued. "I really don't know how to cope. I'll go to my parents, but I warn you Fred, I may stay there."

Fred almost capitulated, but said nothing and attended to Julie

The Century Psychology Series
Richard M. Elliott, *Editor*

THE BEHAVIOR OF ORGANISMS

An Experimental Analysis

BY

B. F. SKINNER

ASSISTANT PROFESSOR OF PSYCHOLOGY
UNIVERSITY OF MINNESOTA

APPLETON-CENTURY-CROFTS, INC.

New York

The title page of the first of fifteen books written by B.F. Skinner, published in September 1938 to mixed reviews. He'd already produced more than thirty academic articles and was to publish almost two hundred more before his death in 1990. For a full list, visit www.bfskinner.org.

THREE

White House Questions

Fred sat in the front-facing seat of his sleeping section. He looked occasionally at an English edition of Hitler's *Mein Kampf*. From the window to his right, through the dark forest, he caught glimpses of Lake Huron's North Channel, bright in the late afternoon sun. Across the Channel he could see Manitoulin Island. This was what he understood from a map in the weighty *Canadian Pacific Railway Guide* he'd bought in Sault Ste. Marie. He was dipping into the *Guide* as often as into *Mein Kampf*. The train had just moved out of Blind River, a small community dominated by a huge saw mill. It had left the station at six thirty-five, just as the *Guide* said it should.

On the same page as the details for Fred's train was the timetable for trains passing through Swastika, farther north in Ontario. In *Mein Kampf* he'd seen Hitler's account of his design of the flag of the National Socialist Party in 1920. Fred found the words describing the flag: "... the embodiment of our party programme. The red expressed the social thought underlying the movement. White the national thought. And the swastika signified the mission allotted to us – the struggle for the victory of Aryan mankind and at the same time the

21

triumph of the ideal of creative work which is in itself and always will be anti-Semitic." Fred had no clue as to how the swastika signified these things. Another mystery was how the community of Swastika had acquired its name – and why it kept it.

Fred was in Canada for the first time, the great "up there" on the map. So far it had seemed similar to Minnesota and northern Michigan. This is what he'd imagined Canada to be: a blander version of the northern United States, perhaps more formal on account of the British influence. Montreal and Quebec could be different, being French and possibly more European.

The only Canadian Fred had known well was T. Cunliffe Barnes, physiology instructor at Harvard. His affectation of wing collar and cravat was among the least of his eccentricities. Barnes, no older than Fred, was the senior author of Fred's first scientific article. Now at Yale, Barnes had cited their article in his recent *Textbook of General Physiology*. Fred wondered whether Barnes continued to be so interested in the behavior of ants. He considered what Barnes might think of his own *The Behavior of Organisms*, if he knew about it.

Fred was feeling homesick. It was the usual hour for Julie's bedtime story, the second day without their early evening ritual. He imagined lying with her on the bed next to her crib. He saw their heads together, both looking up at the picture book he was holding open. During the day she was enormously active, moving from one thing to another, jabbering almost without stop. At their reading time she lay still, attending to the pictures and sometimes pointing to and naming one of them.

The routine they'd settled into was that Fred first read *The ABC Bunny*. He could tell how tired she was by whether she pointed and said "Bun" when the page is turned to "B for Bunny snug a-bed." Julie was usually asleep before Fred reached "L for lizard – look how lazy." He would then lift her ever-so-gently into her crib. The rare time she was not asleep by "Z for zero – close the book" he'd move on to *Snippy and Snappy*, also by Wanda Gág. Fred and a heavily pregnant

Yvonne had bought the books at the Minneapolis Institute of Arts. They were at an exhibit of the work of Minnesota-born Gág, now a prominent graphic artist in New York. A student with a child a little older than Julie had recommended two new books by a Dr. Seuss. He'd track them down. Perhaps he'd find good reading books in England. He was already regretting going there.

He could see patches of snow among the trees even though the summer solstice was only a few weeks away. The sun was higher in the sky at than at the same time in Minneapolis. He figured that this must be because he'd had to move his wristwatch forward an hour when crossing into Canada. It was now only five hours behind England. Fred had asked the passing train conductor why there had been a two-hour stop this morning at Sault Ste. Marie, Michigan, before crossing the long bridge into Sault Ste. Marie, Ontario. The answer made no sense. Now he saw from the *Guide* it was a scheduled stop. He surmised that the wait provided slack to allow for delays caused by operation of various parts of the bridge. One section could be lifted and another section could be swung to the side. Both allowed passage of the large ships he'd seen moving between Lake Superior and Lake Huron.

Whatever the reason for the two-hour wait, it had been a long day, too much of it spent unraveling the turgid prose of *Mein Kampf.* Fred suspected that his difficulties with the book were not the fault of the translator. The original book was likely also a badly written hodge-podge of polemic and mysticism. He regretted not bringing along the other English version Calvin Cooper had given him. It could have provided a different perspective on what was in the original. It might have confused him more.

Fred asked a passing steward about having a drink before dinner. He was told that beer was served in the lounge car, and beer and wine in the dining car with a meal. These were Ontario regulations. Fred was surprised. He knew Canada had avoided Prohibition. He'd expected alcoholic beverages to be as available here as they'd become on many American trains. Instead, Ontario was more restrictive. Quebec by all accounts should be freer, but the train wouldn't reach there until the early morning. Fred decided to wait for dinner to have a drink. He wasn't sure as to the scene in the lounge car or whether he wanted to talk to strangers.

If there was any possibility that Romelle Schneider would be in the lounge car, he mused, he might already be there. She'd telephoned Fred at his office on the day after the meeting at the St. Paul Hotel. Her manner was efficient and remote while they negotiated a time for Calvin Cooper and a federal judge to visit him and Yvonne. Fred had almost asked if she would be part of the visit, but he didn't. And she wasn't.

The visit was the following Tuesday evening. "My, this must be important," said Judge Eustace Hopkins after the introductions. "We judges don't usually make house calls."

Cooper confirmed the importance of the visit when he showed the judge the oath that was to be sworn. Fred and Yvonne asked to affirm their oaths, but the judge talked them into swearing on the Bible he'd brought along. Fred asked what would happen if they violated the secrecy oath. Judge Hopkins replied that they could be convicted of a serious crime and spend time in a federal penitentiary. Yvonne looked alarmed and became tearful. Fred wondered what he had got himself into.

The visit lasted less than twenty minutes. This included time for Cooper to take Fred aside and give him two English editions of Hitler's *Mein Kampf*. "This book was published in Germany in 1926," Cooper told Fred. "It set out the plans of its author, now the most dangerous man in Europe. It's hard to believe a complete translation into English has only just appeared."

Cooper explained that the early months of 1939 had seen the publication of two English translations of *Mein Kampf*, one in America and one in England. He handed the thicker of the two editions to Fred. "This is the American translation."

Fred cracked open the pages of the weighty red-jacketed tome, sponsored by the New-York-based New School for Social Research. He knew that the School had been founded by Thorstein Veblen, whose *Theory of the Leisure Class* had stimulated his own thinking about evolution and behavior. He noted the book's almost one thousand pages including its extensive explanatory notes, and also the lack of an index. The sponsor's Introduction claimed that *Mein Kampf* "is probably the best written evidence of the character, the mind, and the spirit of Adolf Hitler and his government."

Cooper handed over the second, more compact book, which had a dark blue jacket embossed on the front with a gold swastika eagle. He said, "This translation was first commissioned by the Nazis. They hired an Irish translator whose wife gave a draft of his work to a London publisher." Fred knew immediately that he would take only the lighter book with him, but resolved to use the American version as much as possible before he left.

The week before Fred's departure had not been pleasant. Yvonne continued to make clear her unhappiness about his trip. Yesterday evening, she'd refused to kiss him goodbye at the Milwaukee Road Depot, where the overnight train taking her and Julie to Chicago left a few hours before his train to Montreal. Fred gave Julie several kisses in compensation. He said he would have something nice to give her when she returned from the visit to her grandparents. They could all have traveled to Chicago together, and he could have continued on to Montreal via Detroit and Toronto. Yvonne didn't want him there when her parents met her and Julie. So, he was taking the northern route via Sault Ste. Marie and Ottawa.

Fred did not meet Calvin Cooper again before he left. Instead, Cooper telephoned Fred at his office and asked him to remember without writing down three questions the president would like answered. They were questions to which Ludwig Wittgenstein might be able to help with providing answers:

1. Will Hitler order a German invasion of Poland?

2. Will the Soviet Union cooperate in such an invasion?

3. How far will Hitler go in ridding Greater Germany and German-controlled territory of Jews?

Cooper added that there was a fourth question Fred might answer. To what extent do British people accept the need for another war with Germany? Fred didn't have to rely on Wittgenstein for answers to the questions. Any relevant information could be of value.

Fred was astonished and a little alarmed. He had expected to be asked to provide answers to questions about Hitler's personality and character. These were terms he'd used in the *Atlantic Monthly* article on Gertrude Stein that had caught James Roosevelt's attention. He protested to Cooper that he had no more than an everyday newspaper reader's knowledge of the topics of his questions.

"We felt it would be better if you were to understand what we're really after, and fill in the gaps yourself," Cooper replied. "You don't have to engage Wittgenstein in discussion about Poland, for example. However, you might well touch on matters to do with Hitler that you consider relevant to Poland. Use your judgement about any information you come across. I hope I don't need to stress that the real reason for your inquiries must not, repeat not, be revealed."

Even though his stomach had turned a little at the reminder of the seriousness of his mission, Fred began to feel comforted. He wasn't being asked to provide answers about nebulous matters such as Hitler's character and personality. Also reassuring were recollections of the coffee-time discussions of some of his students, who showed a surprising political awareness. He rarely contributed, but listened with interest to their comments on Roosevelt, Chamberlain, Stalin, Hitler, Franco, and others. Japan was a focus too, although Fred couldn't remember the names of any of the Japanese rulers.

"I'll do what I can to answer your questions," said Fred. "May I ask one myself? Where does Japan fit in? I believe she was Nazi Germany's first ally, particularly against the Soviet Union."

"Your question suggests that you may be better informed than the average on international matters," Cooper said. "We don't think Wittgenstein will have much of relevance to say about Japan. In any case, we're not particularly worried about Japan, even though the Japanese army seems to be doing terrible things in China. America supplies Japan with almost every drop of oil she uses. We can turn that tap off pretty quickly."

"If you'll forgive me," continued Cooper, "I must end our discussion here. This evening, a messenger will deliver to you in person at your home an envelope containing instructions for your trip. Please confirm that you'll be at home at about seven o'clock." Fred said he would be there.

Cooper continued, "Please confirm too that you'll memorize these instructions and then destroy the envelope and its contents. As well, you must not mention these arrangements to anyone, including your travel agent." Fred said he would do and not do these things.

Cooper added, "We're to meet again shortly after the flying boat you'll be on has landed in New York, as you'll see from further instructions you'll get in England. We'll be looking for answers to our questions, and your rationale for the answers. I wish you the best for your journey, for your reasons and for ours."

Before Fred could say goodbye, he heard the click indicating that the call had been terminated. He wondered if the conversation had been moving into matters Cooper did not want to discuss, such as Japan. On the other hand, the call could have been ended abruptly simply because Cooper was busy. He rehearsed the four questions a few times, still bemused by the burden that had been placed on him.

Black and white version of the colorful front
cover of *The ABC Bunny* by Wanda Gág.

FOUR

Refugee from Vienna

Between Minneapolis and Montreal, Thursday May 18, 1939

A short, slight man stopped in the aisle by Fred's seat and asked if he could take the seat opposite. Fred guessed he was his own age or a little older. He gestured to him to sit down. As the man sat, Fred placed *Mein Kampf* on the table between them in a way that its title would not be obvious.

"My name is Lukas Glaser," the man said. He offered a business card indicating he was a dentist. "I should explain why there is no address on my card."

"I'm afraid I don't have a card," said Fred. "I'm Fred Skinner, a college professor in psychology. We're not in the habit of carrying them, at least not yet."

"Professor Skinner, I could not help noticing that you are reading *Mein Kampf*. This book upsets me whenever I see it, which I also want to explain. You are reading it in English. Perhaps it is less upsetting when not in the original German." Fred noticed that the man spoke near-perfect English with a slight, unplaceable accent.

"German is my mother tongue. My family is Austrian," Glaser

29

SKINNER'S QUESTS

said, "but much of my education was in England. I would like to be there now. When I managed to get out of what is now Greater Germany a few months ago I decided to go to Montreal. I have family there, but I was denied permission to settle in Canada. A Jewish dentist from Austria is more welcome in St. Paul, Minnesota, where there are many people who have fled Hitler's Germany. I have been exploring the possibility of joining a dental practice there, which I believe I will be permitted to do. I am staying in temporary accommodation until things are settled. I hope I am not boring you with the story of my life."

Fred said to himself "a wandering Jew," unsure as to the origin of the phrase and its likely reception. He'd known Jewish families as a child, and had Jewish friends at Harvard. Now, in Minneapolis, he knew no Jews at all. He signaled the talkative man to continue. Fred was interested in what he might say about *Mein Kampf* and about Austria and Germany. He was glad he was not being asked to talk about himself.

"Before I say more," Glaser continued, "please satisfy my curiosity as to why you are reading *Mein Kampf*. This book is well known in Austria and Germany but, I regret, hardly at all elsewhere, perhaps for lack of translations. If it were better known, people would not be so astonished by what Adolf Hitler and the Nazis have been doing." He picked up the book, flipping through it delicately at arm's length as though it might erupt in his face.

Fred didn't reply immediately and then said, "I'm going to England for reasons to do with my academic work. I can't help but be interested in Europe's political turmoil. A knowledgeable colleague said reading the *Glaubensbekenntnis* of the Nazi party could be insightful."

Glaser responded in German, slowly, "I see you know a little German, though perhaps not enough to read *Mein Kampf*?"

"Only very little German," Fred replied in English, "and certainly not enough to read a book like *Mein Kampf* without much use of a dictionary. *Glaubensbekenntnis* – which I believe means 'statement of belief' or 'creed' – may be the most impressive German word I know. I learned it from my colleague."

"You are reading a translation of *Mein Kampf* that was published in England only a few months ago and, I believe, not yet in America. May I ask how you have it so soon?"

Fred responded carefully, "The colleague who suggested I read it had just returned from London. He brought a few copies with him and gave me one." Fred hoped it was not obvious he was bending the truth as to how he had a copy of *Mein Kampf*. He was going to have to become a better liar.

"Your colleague was correct to say it would give you insights as to what is happening in Europe, Professor Skinner. The translation you have may not give the full flavor of the original. It is well known that this translation was originally commissioned by the Nazis. The mode of expression may have been," he paused, "*aufgeweicht* – I mean diluted, watered down – for English tastes. I have read much of *Mein Kampf* in German, but not in an English version."

"I've done no more than dip into it during this rail trip," said Fred. He glanced at the business card. "Dr. Glaser, could you help me by providing a summary of what you found in it?"

"I will be delighted to help you if I can. I will be brief. For all its words, *Mein Kampf* expresses only a few ideas or, more accurately, goals. First, what Hitler calls Aryan people, especially Germans, should be ruling the world. Second, Jews, who may not be human, are ruling it now or are trying to and should be challenged and even exterminated. Marxism-Bolshevism is also to be exterminated. According to Hitler, it is a manifestation of Jewishness. Third, all lands occupied by Germanic peoples should be integrated. Germanic peoples include Austrians, of whom Hitler himself is one. Fourth, Germans need more living room to the East, replacing the present occupants who are mostly Slavic and inferior to Aryans."

"Living room?" Fred interrupted. "Please tell me what is meant by this term." Fred noticed that he is beginning to use Glaser's formality and word order. He hoped he was not seen as being impolite.

"The German word is *Lebensraum*," Glaser replies. "Another translation could be 'living space.' *Lebensraum* is the word the Nazis use for their policy of moving the borders of Germany to the east to provide more space and resources for the German people. Yet another English translation of *Lebensraum* is the term 'habitat' used in biology. However, because the Nazis have taken over *Lebensraum*, biologists in Germany use the English word 'habitat' more often."

Fred sensed that Glaser was a compulsive talker who used interruptions as an opportunity to talk even more. He thanked Glaser for the explanation and asked if he had further points to make about *Mein Kampf*.

"My last point, and not the least important, is this. In Hitler's view, Germany did not lose *den großen Krieg* – the Great War – but agreed to a truce. This armistice was interpreted by enemies outside and inside Germany as a surrender. Defining the end of the war as a surrender allowed the imposition of unjust conditions and reparations. These injustices must be remedied."

Fred wondered whether the last view was that of Hitler or Glaser, or both of them. He held his tongue.

Glaser continued, "These five goals are popular in Germany, and also – I say with much regret – in Austria. Hitler has led the German people and now also the Austrian people some of the way toward achieving all five of them. He is on a path that can only lead to a major war. This aspect of his policies, to the extent that it is understood, is not so popular."

Fred found Glaser's summary of *Mein Kampf* useful. He began to welcome the possibility of continuing the discussion. He said, "Your helpful summary clarifies points in the book I was having difficulty understanding. Herr Hitler's pursuit of the second and third of these points – concerning Jews and Germanic peoples – has been much in the news. I imagine the fifth point, about the Great War, must be particularly appealing inside Germany and perhaps Austria."

Glaser interrupted, "You must understand that my country is often more German than Germany itself. At the end of *den großen Krieg*, Austrians wanted to join Germany, but this was not allowed by the treaties that ended the war. When *der Anschluss* occurred last year – when the *Wehrmacht* marched into Austria – it had almost complete support from Austrians, according to a plebiscite held soon after."

Fred said, "On another of your points about *Mein Kampf*, may I ask a very elementary question: what is a Jew? And another: why do you, as a Jew, believe there is so much prejudice against Jews, whether in Germany or here in North America?"

Glaser seemed pleased to have Fred's attention. He said, "A Jew is a descendant of a people who inhabited the eastern coast of the Mediterranean Sea several thousand years ago. Rabbinical Law, which Jews should observe, holds that a Jew is a person whose mother is a Jew. Some rabbis say that both parents must be Jews."

Fred said, "Is it possible to become a Jew though conversion?"

"Yes, it is although many rabbis oppose this practice. Of more practical importance in Germany are the Nuremberg Race Laws, which now apply to Austria and, presumably, to much of Czechoslovakia. They say that a Jew is a person with one or more Jewish grandparents. The Race Laws do not actually define a Jew."

Fred interrupted again, "So, Jews themselves and the Nazi government say Jewishness is mostly a matter of inheritance – although not in the same way. Where does the religion of Judaism fit in?"

"Judaism is a belief that there is one god and Jews have a special relationship with that god. This special relationship requires them to follow numerous dictates in the Jewish Bible, which is essentially the Christian Old Testament. To practice Judaism is the clearest sign of Jewishness, but many Jews are not religious. Many are atheists or agnostics, as are many people of Christian origin. Jews who do not practice Judaism may be difficult to recognize as Jews. The German government has armies of clerks going through baptismal and other records seeking to identify Jewish ancestors."

Glaser wiped his moist brow with a stained handkerchief. Fred said, "Is the German government's goal to identify as many Jews as possible, or just to establish who's a Jew and who's not?"

"It is usually the first. Nazi theory holds that Jewishness is a kind of disease that can be checked only by identifying and containing *all* cases of the disease. A recurrent story in Austria is that a diligent clerk found evidence that Hitler himself had a Jewish grandfather. The clerk then disappeared. The 'Aryanization' of Germany and now Austria has produced many surprises. There is no question that some of the decisions about Jewishness are political."

"What about cases of conversion away from Judaism, or is it a question of once a Jew always a Jew?"

"Jews and Nazis seem to agree that identity as a Jew cannot be renounced. There is an interesting case in Vienna just now concerning one of our best-known families: the Wittgensteins. They are Catholics, like most Austrians, but three of the grandparents of today's generation were Jews. Today's generation, by the way, includes Paul Wittgenstein the pianist and Ludwig Wittgenstein the philosopher. According to the Nuremberg Race Laws, the whole family is classified as Jewish, and all that means in today's Greater Germany."

Fred hid his alarm at the mention of the Wittgenstein family.

Glaser continued, "There is a small loophole through which the family is attempting to wriggle. Success would have one of the three Jewish grandparents – born as early as 1802 – reclassified as an Aryan. Then, today's members of the Wittgenstein family would be *Mischlinge*. I believe half-breed is the English word. *Mischlinge* are still Jews, but are not treated with as much harshness as *Volljuden*. There is a rumor that Hitler will grant *Mischling* status if the family hands over most of its huge fortune to the Nazis."

Fred asked himself if the mention of Ludwig Wittgenstein could be other than a coincidence. "What an extraordinary state of affairs," he said. "Jews of any kind are evidently under great strain. What about your own position?"

"Let me add that there are aspects of Jewishness other than Judaism. Two are the use of the Yiddish and Hebrew languages and the maintenance of particular dietary preferences. My own identity as a Jew is clear, as I will explain. First let me try to answer your second question, about prejudice against Jews."

A steward passed through the sleeping car announcing dinner. The train had stopped at a station named Cutler that seemed to have no associated community. The track ran close to the north shore of a wide bay. The bay's entrance was sheltered by a string of islands that were yellowy bright against a darkening sky. The sky was now lighter to the north-west. There the sun was behind distant low hills seen through gaps in the forest, its position clear from where the orange sky was brightest.

"Shall we eat together?" Glaser said. "Then I can answer your question about anti-Semitism."

Fred agreed and followed him to the dining car, passing through another car with sleeping sections. He noted Glaser's inexpertly cut hair and threadbare shirt collar. His worse-for-wear suit could at one time have been of a good style and quality.

The lights in the dining car gave it a romantic air. Fred thought he'd rather be eating with Romelle Schneider, nurse, than with Lukas Glaser, dentist. He conceded to himself that Glaser might be a useful source. He wondered again whether their meeting was a coincidence.

They sat at one of the tables for two. A steward gave them menus and pencils and asked that they mark their choices. Fred said he might want to return to the matters of inheritance and Judaism, after hearing about prejudice.

Fred looked for wine on the menu. Finding none, he asked a steward and was told there were four types on offer, all by the glass. They were a Canadian and a French red wine and a Canadian and a Californian white wine. Fred asked for more details. There were none. He asked Glaser what he would drink.

"As a rule, I do not consume liquor. Like many Jews, I get bad hangovers. Intolerance of alcohol is a part of our physical inheritance, although many Jews are not afflicted. Some people say that alcoholic beverages are forbidden to Jews, as they are to Muslims, but that is not true. Many of the rituals of Judaism involve wine."

Fred asked the patient steward for a glass of the Canadian white wine as an aperitif, curious to know how a Canadian wine might taste. Glaser asked for lemonade.

Fred had become keen to know more about his dinner companion. "Before you explain prejudice against Jews to me, do tell me more about yourself."

The drinks were served and the menus collected. The foxy odor of the wine struck Fred before he took a sip. It tasted like the foul white wine from New York State that could be bought cheaply in Minneapolis. He resolved to have the French wine with the roast ribs of beef he had ordered for dinner.

Glaser seemed pleased to be asked so many questions. He said, "I was doing well as a dentist in Vienna until last year. I had always lived there, apart from seven years in England in the 1920s. I went to London with my family, when my father's business took him there for a few years. I stayed to attend university and begin my dental training. My wife and I should have left Austria soon after *der Anschluss* in March last year, or even before. We did not want to abandon our ageing parents, who needed help."

Glaser paused. Fred was unsure whether to say something. He remained silent. Glaser continued in a more strained voice, "In November, during the madness known as *Kristallnacht*, my wife and our parents were burned and crushed to death. They were caught in a synagogue that was set ablaze by a Nazi gang and its doors barred shut. I arrived just as the roof was collapsing."

Fred gasped. "That's dreadful," he said softly.

Glaser dabbed his eyes with the table napkin and continued, "A few days later I was taken into what was called 'protective custody' and sent to a concentration camp. It was Dachau, near Munich. There, I and other Jews were offered the opportunity to leave Greater Germany – if we paid money to the government. I had no good reason to stay. I very much wanted to leave. Perhaps too easily, I agreed to hand over our three apartments in Vienna and their contents, and my dental practice. I agreed to order that five thousand pounds sterling be wired from our family's bank account in London to an account in Berlin. In return, I was given a new passport."

He pulled a document from an inside pocket and passed it to Fred. "Here it is. You can see it is clearly marked with a 'J' for '*Jude*.'" He pointed to a page, and then to another. "There is my exit permit and Italian transit visa to Trieste. I was able to return to Vienna and pack just one suitcase. At Trieste, I boarded a ship for a terrible journey to New York across seas stirred up by March storms."

He paused again. Fred almost interjected, but Glaser continued, "I was allowed to land in New York because I had evidence I was *en route* to Montreal and needed only a transit permit. I felt I would be welcome in Canada because my uncle and his family are there. However, at the border I was given a permit allowing me to stay for two weeks only. The permit required me to report to the Montreal police every two days."

After dabbing his eyes again, Glaser smiled and continued, "Then I had the most remarkable good fortune. A sympathetic official at Montreal's American consulate, who may himself have been Jewish, authorized my immigration into the United States. He offered the excellent advice that St. Paul could be a good place for a Jewish dentist to find work."

Fred wondered why Glaser was giving him so much detail. He wondered too whether an official in Montreal would be empowered to grant such permission. He said, "I'm astonished. I heard about *Kristallnacht* but not about the later extortion. I'm also puzzled. Surely if the Nazis don't like the Jews, and want them to leave, why not make it easy for them to go?"

"I think the Nazi view is that the Jews are leaving anyway. They believe that Jews are usually quite wealthy. The state and the party can use their money. Why not take the most advantage of the situation? Nazis believe too that Jewish wealth has been acquired through the exploitation of other races, especially Aryans. Thus, the confiscation of Jewish assets is a remedy for past abuse. Also, if Jews take their wealth with them, they will have more resources with which to combat Germany from abroad."

Fred reflected to himself that Glaser may understand the Nazi position perhaps a little too well, but said, "Thank you for telling me your distressing story. The loss of your family must have been almost unbearable."

Glaser thanked him for his commiseration. They stopped talking while the steward brought their bowls of vegetable soup. Fred was also given a small jar containing celery sticks. He returned the unfinished white wine and asked for a glass of French red wine.

After they had finished the soup, Fred said, "Perhaps now is the time to explain to me why there's so much prejudice against Jews, particularly among Nazis."

Glaser said, "Concerning prejudice, the simple answer is that Jews have been pariahs and scapegoats for centuries. It has been convenient for the Nazis to exploit this as a way of strengthening the identity of their cause with that of Germany. *You*, a psychologist, can perhaps tell *me* how a scapegoat can bind a group together better. Whatever is involved, there is no doubt that the Nazis' anti-Semitic practices have been popular in Germany and even more in Austria."

He continued, "There have been two main suggestions as to why Jews have been pariahs and scapegoats for centuries. One has to do with blame for the murder of Jesus Christ. The other, proposed by many including Dr. Sigmund Freud – a Jew who must be known to you as a psychologist – concerns resentment at Jews for considering themselves to be a chosen people and superior to gentiles."

Fred felt more unease. Apart from Hitler, Glaser had mentioned only three people by name. Two of them were the two people Fred was travelling to visit and the third was a brother of one of them. This couldn't have been a coincidence.

"A belief in specialness is one of the things that Jews and Nazis have in common," Glaser continued. "This may explain the ferocity of the Nazis' *Judenhass* – Jew hatred. Nazis believe in a leadership position for Aryans. Jews also see themselves as leaders, in that they are a people chosen to be an example to others. As well, Nazis and Jews are both preoccupied with biological inheritance and the avoidance of *Rassenmischung*."

Fred did interrupt. "I'm guessing that *Rassenmischung* means race mixing?" he asked.

"You are correct, and you have a good North German Accent."

"Thank you. And so both Nazis and Jews promote racial purity?"

"Yes, but they go about it in very different ways. To continue with matters we have in common: Nazis and Jews both emphasize families. They invest in the education of young people as a means of ensuring adult adherence to particular practices and beliefs. Both advocate – more than what is normal in liberal democracies – subordination of the interests of individuals to the demands of the group. One might speculate that Nazis hate Jews so much because, even though they may see themselves as Germans first, Jews often seem to want to set themselves apart from a people with whom they have so much in common."

Fred's unease was compounded by his growing puzzlement at Glaser's sympathy for the Jews' greatest enemies. Before he could interject, Glaser said, "In case I seem to be making too much of possible similarities between Nazis and Jews, may I hasten to point out some important differences. The most obvious one is that Nazis are militaristic and disposed to violence. Jews are not. There are important differences between Nazi and Jewish views of separateness. Nazis believe that the people they call Aryans should subjugate other people and even eliminate them. Jews favor their own kind but beyond that have little interest in worsening the position of others."

Fred felt he must interrupt again. "I thought you'd say that Jews are disliked because they are often more prosperous than non-Jews. They even seem to be preoccupied with acquiring wealth."

"There is truth in that, but the stronger factor could be that Jews have become more successful than the average because we have been ostracized. The separateness of Jews caused us to focus on a few professions. The closeness of our communities allowed us to work well toward that end. My parents decided what might work for me in a way that gentile parents did not need to. They chose my career as a dentist, and guided me toward that goal. Such are the successes of Jews, which have also attracted envy and a resulting vicious cycle. Ostracism – because Jews killed Christ or because we think we are special – causes separation, success, envy, and more ostracism."

"But," Glaser held sway, "there are almost as many types of anti-Semitism as there are Jews. To be sure, there is prejudice against us for economic reasons, but there are many other types of prejudice against Jews: racial, cultural, religious, and political. In *Mein Kampf*, you will read that Hitler's major grievance against Jews is that they are behind a Marxist-Bolshevik conspiracy to convert Germany into a soft-centered democracy."

Fred interjected, "That does seem absurd, when Hitler also credits the Jews with running big business in America."

"You are right, my friend. I could try to resolve this paradox for you but I have done enough talking for one dinner conversation. I know almost nothing about you and the journey you are making."

The main courses arrived. Glaser had ordered from the less expensive of the two table d'hôte menus: the dollar-thirty-five meal rather than the dollar-sixty meal. He was given an unappetizing plate of watery boiled fish with potatoes, carrots, and creamed cauliflower. Fred had ordered from the meat menu. His plate had the same vegetables but they seemed brighter next to the roast ribs of beef, bathed in steaming gravy. The ribs were arranged with the bones pointing upward. They reminded Fred of the Nazi salutes he'd seen in newspaper photos and newsreels.

They ate in silence for a while. It was now dark on the south side of the car. Fred wondered whether the moon would show. He thought about how to explain his journey, alert to the possibility that the encounter with Glaser might not be an accident, however farfetched that prospect seemed. The dining car was full and had become quite noisy. The air was thickening with tobacco smoke.

"I'm going to England chiefly in the hope of talking with Dr. Freud, whom you've just mentioned," said Fred. He'd decided that almost complete honesty may be the best policy. "I heard that he's now in London, and not in good health. I'm an admirer of his work, although I find myself quite critical of it. If he's well enough to discuss our differences, I'd be delighted to spend a little time with him. I'll also be participating in a conference and a few other meetings, but Dr. Freud is the real target of my visit."

"I met Professor Freud once, a few years ago," said Glaser, "and have had an interest in him ever since. I was an assistant to Dr. Joseph Weinmann at Vienna's Institute of Oral Pathology. Weinmann was a physician, not a dentist, but he had all the skills of a dentist. He was able to make necessary adjustments to Professor Freud's massive oral prosthesis. Professor Freud wears it to correct for the surgery he has endured on account of recurrent oral cancer. Weinmann took me along once to show me what was required, in case I might be called on, which I was not. I remember in particular Weinmann's liberal application of orthoform, a version of cocaine, to the inside of Professor Freud's ravaged mouth. I presumed this was done for orthoform's anesthetic effects."

Fred was pleased that Glaser's almost compulsive talking has taken over the discussion again, saving him from having to dissemble further about the purpose of his trip.

"Could I say just one more thing about prejudice against Jews?" said Glaser. "In Germany, as in the United States, Jews have often done well, usually in cities, and are on average more prosperous. In Poland, which may have the largest Jewish population in the world, there are very many poor Jews mostly in *shtetlekh*."

"*Shtetlekh?*"

"Forgive me for using a Yiddish word. *Shtetlekh* – the plural form of *shtetl* – are small towns throughout Poland and other parts of central Europe where Jews are usually in the majority. During the last century, when Poland was part of the Russian empire, many of these Jews were killed during pogroms. But the Russians, while anti-Semitic and cruel, are poor administrators. The main effects of their rule were to keep most Jews in poverty and encourage the more adventurous among them to emigrate to America."

"If Germany invades Poland as she has invaded Czechoslovakia," Glaser continued, "the Nazis will have millions of poor Jews to conduct their race war against rather than the few hundred thousand much more affluent Jews who remain in what is now Greater Germany. Germans are capable of doing whatever they choose to do. Thinking about what could happen to Polish Jews under Nazi rule makes me feel sick."

Fred wondered again whether their meeting was a coincidence. He decided against asking Glaser whether he thinks Germany will invade Poland. Instead, he took the bull by the horns. "Dr. Glaser, I appreciate what you've told me about these matters of great interest and concern to you. I'll be much better informed when I'm in England. I can't help feeling that our meeting may have other causes than your curiosity about my reading *Mein Kampf*."

Glaser gestured as if protesting. He looked around the dining car and said, "I think I will change my mind and have a glass of wine after all. Perhaps the red wine you seem to be enjoying will go well with the coconut cream pie my Viennese sweet tooth has prompted me to order. I will sip the wine slowly, between mouthfuls, in the hope of reducing its aftereffects."

Fred said, "The red wine was pleasant. I'll have another glass. I'll be having the cheese and crackers instead of a sweet dessert."

Glaser looked around again, called the steward, and asked for their next courses and two glasses of French red wine. Fred waited for him to speak.

Only after they have been served did Glaser continue, and then only after looking around once more, as if confirming that there was no one within earshot. He said in a low voice, "You are correct to doubt the coincidence, and I may be putting myself and my family at risk by telling you so. I engaged you in discussion, Professor Skinner, because I need to know why you are going to Europe."

Fred was now truly alarmed, but said nothing.

"There is an active German-American Bund organization in the Twin Cities, as elsewhere in the United States. It is an organization of Americans of German descent. Its main goal is to promote a favorable view of Nazi Germany."

Glaser continued, "When you and your wife attended the showing of *Confessions of a Nazi Spy* at the University Film Club last Saturday,

Bund members were monitoring who attended. I think they were trying to identify potential recruits and possible adversaries. The Bund organizations, as you will know from the movie, are fronts for the activities of the Nazi party and the German government in North America."

"I do not know why you were targeted for further investigation," Glaser said. "Bund members discovered that you were going to Britain via Montreal – perhaps from your travel agent, I am not sure. They knew I would be travelling to Montreal to visit my relatives. They told me to be on this train with you and find out more about you and your trip. I resisted, but was told the well-being of my cousins in Vienna could be at stake as well as my prospects for work in St. Paul. Having already experienced the strength and ruthlessness of the Nazis, I agreed to do what they wanted."

Glaser paused when the steward arrived with the wine and desserts, and their checks. They both declined coffee or tea. The steward took their American five-dollar bills away to convert to slightly less valuable Canadian dollars and bring change.

Fred reflected on the outing last Saturday. His favorite student and editorial assistant, Marian Kruse, had looked after Julie. Marian described herself as the "babysitter," a word Fred heard for the first time. It was also the first time Julie had been left in the care of someone other than her grandparents. The Film Club had procured a copy of *Confessions*, released in New York only a week earlier and not due in a regular Minneapolis theatre for another month. He'd taken Yvonne to the showing to try and engage her more in what he would be doing. The compelling portrayal of Nazi espionage in America had had the opposite effect, which he might have anticipated if he'd thought more about it.

The steward brought their change. In both cases it consisted of a colorful Canadian bill and coins bearing the heads of one or another king. Fred examined his coins and banknote. He was unused to two-dollar bills, but also wanted to avoid speaking and sidetracking Glaser's extraordinary confession.

The steward left and Glaser continued, "I believe that there may be more to your visit than you are revealing, but I don't need to know any more. When I arrive at Montreal, I will report to the Bund people in Minneapolis and tell them I was able to have a long discussion with you on the train. I will tell them that you are going to meet Professor Freud in London and other people of consequence to a psychologist. The Nazis are not likely to believe that a meeting with such an old and sick man could be threatening in any way. I will tell them too that you and your wife are admirers of the acting of Edward G. Robinson, and there was nothing more to your attending a special viewing of the movie *Confessions of a Nazi Spy*."

Glaser rose suddenly, leaving his pie and wine untouched. He bade Fred a restful night, and moved toward the dining car exit before Fred could say goodbye.

For the first time since he left Minneapolis, Fred yearned for the comfort of his pipe. He saw that only cigarettes were being smoked in the dining car, and imagined there might be a rule about pipe-smoking. He thought of asking if the steward had cigarettes for sale. Then he remembered his concern about smoking, prompted by a compelling article he'd read in *Science*. Males who smoked cigarettes died earlier than non-smokers. The effect seemed strong. Non-smokers had a fifty-percent greater chance of living beyond the age of sixty-five than heavy smokers. Fred didn't smoke often. He did want to be a grandparent to Julie's children.

Fred finished his second glass of red wine and then exchanged his empty glass with Glaser's full one. He hadn't read any serious studies showing that life was shortened by moderate alcohol consumption, in spite of the claims of many temperance campaigners.

If Glaser engaged him in discussion only to develop a story to relay back to the Bund people, why did he talk and disclose so much? Perhaps he felt that revealing so much of his own views and circumstances would stimulate confidences on Fred's part. As well, Glaser could just be a lonely man who'd grasped an opportunity to be companionable. Were his mentions of Wittgenstein and Freud deliberate, perhaps to flush out specific intentions for the journey? And did his story about the consular official in Montreal hold water? Could Glaser be working for the American government in return for permission to reside and work in the United States? Could Glaser have been sent to test how loose Fred's lips were? Fred was puzzled and uneasy, but the wine was dulling his concern. He was unaccustomed to being suspicious of people and did not like the feeling.

Fred was now the last passenger in the dining car. The steward asked if he could leave the car soon. It had to be prepared for disconnection from the train at Sudbury, where they were due to arrive at 9:30 p.m. As he finished Glaser's wine, he tried to read more of *Mein Kampf.* He'd brought it to dinner in case there'd be more discussion of it. Not remembering where he'd reached in the book, he turned to the end hoping to find a simple conclusion. He saw: "A State which, in an epoch of racial adulteration, devotes itself to the duty of preserving the best elements of its racial stock must one day become ruler of the Earth." The words made little sense but seemed to fit with Glaser's point about Germany's aspiration to rule the world. Thinking back to Calvin Cooper's questions and Glaser's comments about poor Jews, he wondered whether there is much in *Mein Kampf* about Poland. At his next reading he'd try and find words there about a country he knew almost nothing about.

Fred returned unsteadily to his sleeping section, now made up for the night. The upper berth was empty. He barely remembered to close the heavy curtain separating his berth from the aisle before he lay down without undressing. He fell asleep wondering whether Glaser was in a sleeping section or was spending the night on a seat in the coach part of the train.

Black and white version of the front cover of the itinerary of the 1939 royal visit to Canada produced by Canadian National Railways and Canadian Pacific Railway.

FIVE

Royal Presence

Ottawa and Montreal, Friday May 19, 1939

Fred woke with a thick head, and then closed his eyes to avoid the daylight streaming in at the edges of the window blind. He remembered waking in the middle of the night and visiting the pungent toilet. The train was stationary at the time. It was likely stopped at North Bay. He remembered being sober enough to wait until it had started moving before operating the flush mechanism. He was also sober enough to recall that the famous Dionne quintuplets were born in North Bay or somewhere close to it. He must have undressed at some point because now he had to dress before making another, urgent visit to the repugnant toilet.

His wristwatch said it was almost six-thirty. According to the *Railway Guide*, the train should be approaching Ottawa. He moved the window blind a little and was amazed by what he saw. The train was passing slowly through what appeared to be a movie set for a railroad station, bedecked with bunting, red carpets, and regal paraphernalia. It was as though the Prince of Ruritania – perhaps played by Leslie Howard – was about to return to his realm by train.

Fred walked to the solarium car where a breakfast buffet was being prepared. He asked a steward about the movie set and was told that it was temporary station set up for the arrival in a few hours of the King and Queen of England, also of Canada. They are to alight there rather than at the regular station in the center of the city. Then they would be driven in state for several miles through Ottawa streets. Breakfast would be served after this train has left Ottawa. Fred waited, sipping a coffee. He watched the passing show of river traffic, houses more suited to small-town Massachusetts than a nation's capital, a pulp and paper mill, and government buildings.

Ottawa newspapers were available with breakfast. They had page after page about the royal visit. Fred read the *Morning Citizen* first and then, summoning his French, *Le Droit*. He had expected French Canada to be less enamored by the English king, and found that the reporting in *Le Droit* was indeed more restrained than the effusive coverage in the *Citizen*. However, the great enthusiasm yesterday of the almost entirely French-speaking crowds in three Quebec cities was evident from both newspapers. Montreal seems to have given the king and queen a welcome beyond what the best-known film stars receive, and beyond what America's president has encountered in many cities. Fred wondered how their reception compared with the kind of adulation that newsreels have shown Hitler receiving in Germany and Austria, and Mussolini in Italy. He suspected that, on this measure, the dictators might be even more adored.

After picking up speed to leave Ottawa, the train slowed to a crawl. The steward said they were about to pass what he and the newspapers called the royal train. This train, with the king and queen on board, has spent the night in a siding near Caledonia Springs, a few miles south of the Ottawa River. Trains had to pass the siding at less than ten miles per hour to avoid disturbing their majesties.

There were two trains in the long siding, set back some twenty yards from the main track. The first train carried the media, said the steward. It traveled thirty minutes ahead of the royal train, ostensibly so that reporters could be ready at each arrival of the royal party. In reality, everyone knew it traveled ahead to detonate bombs that anti-monarchists and anarchists might place on the track. Fred wondered about the time it would take to place a bomb on the track in a remote location. He found it hard to believe that such an evidently popular couple would have enemies.

The second train in the siding was extraordinary: a magnificent streamlined locomotive and twelve cars, all in blue and silver, burnished and glinting in a brief appearance of the morning sun through the clouds. Every part had been polished, even the wheels. The train gleamed as if it was a new toy that has just been unwrapped. As extraordinary was the train's escort: men in smart blue uniforms trimmed with red, ten paces apart, all around the train.

The train for Montreal trundled slowly by. There was a cry from the front of the solarium car. "It's him, it's the king."

Two men stood on the viewing platform at the end of the royal train. The one farther away was older and sported a fedora and overcoat. The younger man, without coat or hat, turned to him and said a few words before leaning again on the railing and gazing vacantly at the passing train, all the while smoking a cigarette. Fred pulled out the Canadian coins in his pocket, found a new one and confirmed for himself that the man leaning on the railing was indeed the king. The face on the quarter continued to gaze at the passing train, and then looked down to light a new cigarette from the glowing end of the last one. Most passengers in the solarium car were waving but the king appeared not to see them.

Fred pondered the very un-American premise of royalty – that inheritance made a person fit to lead – and realized more strongly than before that he was now in a different country. The status of Canada seemed especially strange. Not only did Canadians accept the puzzling premise of royalty, they also seemed content that the inheritance was managed in a faraway place across the Atlantic.

He finished one too many coffees and noted an item on the front page of the *Citizen* suggesting that Canada might still be in essence a colony. "As a service to Their Majesties the King and Queen, the leading editorial from this morning's issue of *The Times* appears herewith." Inside the paper, the actual editorial from England's newspaper of record was devoted to assessing the implications of the results of three parliamentary by-elections held in what must be obscure corners of Britain. Fred surmised that the topic could provide no interest of any kind to the newspaper's regular readers. It appeared only as an expression of fealty.

As the train gathered speed, clouds covered the sun and the windows of the solarium became flecked with rain. Fred thought about the impact of the rain on today's events in Ottawa. He returned to his sleeping section, now made up for daytime use.

The train conductor, different from the one who had boarded at Sault Ste. Marie, advised Fred in accented English that the train was to arrive late in Montreal because of the disruptions caused by the royal tour. Fred should not worry because the sailing of the *Duchess of York* would, if necessary, be delayed beyond ten o'clock to accommodate the train's late arrival. Fred said in French that the possibility of such coordination must be a benefit of having the train and the ship run by the same company. The conductor asked him in English if he would mind repeating what he had just said. Fred thanked him in English for the information about the delay. He concluded to himself that he should probably forgo any opportunity to practice his French during his brief time in Montreal.

Fred had had his fill of *Mein Kampf* and German issues yesterday. He'd not seen Glaser since the man's abrupt departure from the dining car, and hoped not to see him again. For the remaining hour or so of the journey, Fred took out another book he'd brought with him: *How to Win Friends and Influence People*. A student who knew of his interest in controlling behavior had said that Dale Carnegie's popular book contained more wisdom on this topic than any other she'd encountered.

Before he got into *How to Win Friends* he remembered a discussion he had had on the train yesterday morning – which seemed days ago – on the way to Sault Ste. Marie. He was talking with an appealing young woman about F. Scott Fitzgerald's latest novel, *Tender is the Night*. How did that discussion begin? She, like Fitzgerald, happened to hail from St. Paul. Fred had not read the book, but resolved to do so on learning that it was mostly about a psychoanalyst. He didn't mention that he might be on his way to visit Sigmund Freud. Was he hoping he would encounter the young woman when he returned to the Twin Cities?

If anything, Fred was more uncomfortable to be seen reading *How to Win Friends* than *Mein Kampf*. A psychology professor known for having some expertise in the finer points of literature should not be seen with a popular self-help book. Reading *Mein Kampf* could at least be explained in terms of an interest in world affairs. Opening *How to Win Friends* he was surprised to find he liked what he read, beginning with the list of changes the author sought to bring about in the reader's behavior: "12 things this book will do for *you*."

Fred then read more that he liked. He saw that the first three chapters were essentially an argument that positive reinforcement is a more effective tool than negative reinforcement for getting people to do what you want them to do. As for what to use as a positive reinforcer, Carnegie had written "arouse in the other person an eager want." He used the example of an underweight boy who refused to eat properly and was bullied by a neighbor. The boy didn't eat more when nagged. He didn't respond to negative reinforcement, which involved following behavior with criticism or a slap or another punishing event. He did eat well "when his father told him he could wallop the daylights out of the bigger kid someday if he would only eat the things his mother wanted him to eat." Carnegie then went on to describe how the same boy was cured of bed-wetting, again using positive reinforcement.

Skimming through *How to Win Friends*, Fred noted other things he had already concluded from his own research with rats. Three of Carnegie's rules for changing human behavior were these:

1. Let the other man do a great deal of the talking.

2. Get the other person saying "yes, yes" immediately.

3. Praise the slightest improvement and praise every improvement.

These rules for producing desired behavior in humans were similar to those he had figured out for rats. They were: First, to the extent feasible, create situations in which the desired behavior or something close to it was likely to occur. Second, if necessary, achieve further changes by reinforcing successive approximations to the desired behavior. Changes in behavior are best achieved in small incremental steps that involve a lot of positive reinforcement.

Fred reflected on a satisfying exercise that had given him the added pleasure of modest popular fame. It involved training rats to perform complex sequences of behavior. The performance of one rat, Pliny, had been the subject of an article in *Life* magazine. Pliny pulled a chain that operated a mechanism that rolled a marble into his cage. The rat then lifted the marble into a slot. There it operated another mechanism that produced a pellet of food. The sequence of behavior was put together step by step, by adjusting the apparatus that was Pliny's environment. First, almost anything the rat did with a marble was reinforced with a small amount of food. Then only moving the marble near the slot was reinforced, and then only pushing the marble into the slot. At this point, delivery of a marble could be used as a reinforcer. Delivery of a marble was used first to reinforce movement towards the chain, then touching the chain, and then pulling it.

Fred wondered, as he had done before, whether Pliny's sequence of actions could have been induced equally well by starting with the first step, pulling the chain, and then adding the second step, putting the marble in the slot. This is often how humans are taught, first things first.

Whatever the training method, Fred could not imagine achieving the same degree of control over Pliny's behavior using punishment. An electric shock or a loud noise following unwanted behavior would only elicit a built-in emotional response that would interfere with the careful assembly of the complex behavior. Punishment might be good for temporarily suppressing an action, but that is about all. He could not imagine guiding the rat toward the desired act other than by providing frequent positive reinforcement of successive approximations to the final task. When Pliny's complex behavior chain had been assembled, Fred could keep it going without reinforcing every instance of it. He could even get Pliny to accumulate marbles during periods when the slot was closed off. *How to Win Friends* was indeed a "real-life" expression of his own lab findings.

He was about to begin reading *How to Win Friends* with more care when the conductor passed through the car again saying, in French and English, that the train would be arriving at Montreal's Windsor Station in thirty minutes, about twenty minutes late. Fred figured out from the *Guide* that he must be at the west end of Montreal Island, where the Ottawa River meets the St. Lawrence River. Passing through Ste.-Anne-de-Bellevue Station a few moments later confirmed this.

Fred packed his briefcase and small suitcase and readied himself for leaving the train. He saw mostly fields, with small communities around each of the several stations along the track. They had a jumble of French and English names: Baie-d'Urfée, Beaurepaire, Beaconsfield, Cedar Park, and more.

Now he was in Montreal. The rain had stopped, but it was still cloudy. He could see large buildings ahead on the right and, if he bent down and looked out of the window to the left, the big hill that must have given the city its name. As he began to count whether he saw more French or English signs, the track began to descend below street level. A minute later it stopped, the end of the long train trip.

It was nine twenty-five. The train had arrived at Windsor Station twenty minutes late. The *Duchess of York* was to leave at ten o'clock. Fred alighted, unsure where to go. The station was busy. He heard French spoken around him, in the accent of the train conductor. Like most indoor railroad stations, the predominant odor was coal smoke.

There was also the smell of truck exhaust. Fred noticed that the train he had just left was being pulled by one of the new diesel-electric locomotives. This must have replaced the steam locomotive at North Bay or Ottawa. He joined the departing passengers leaving the platform for the concourse.

The scene in the concourse reminded Fred of the Hollywood set at the edge of Ottawa. It was dominated by a large temporary sign *"Vive le roi. Vive la reine."* A red carpet had been laid from the main station entrance to the stairs that led down to the platform. On the ground were many discarded small flags, mostly British union jacks. Fred saw a more permanent bilingual sign "CP Ship Passengers Assemble Here" and joined the small, growing crowd beneath it. Their steamship tickets were checked. Fred asked about the temporary sign, carpet, and flags. He was told that the royal train departed from this station yesterday evening at eleven o'clock. A few minutes later, the group was escorted outside. Many of the group had porters in tow. They were led to a waiting bus with a luggage van behind it.

Sitting in the bus, Fred realized that he was at the front of a magnificent building, but had little memory of the architecture inside. As the bus began to move, he saw Glaser leave the main entrance, come close to the bus, wave, and walk away. The man seemed in no way sinister, but his reappearance made Fred anxious.

Fred once more regretted he'd undertaken this adventure. He also felt concern for Glaser. Fred still doubted that Glaser's portrayal of recent events was entirely accurate. He thought again that Glaser might be working for the United States government in exchange for permission to immigrate. Perhaps the White House was using Glaser both to infiltrate the German Bund and to test him, Fred, in some way. Fred's imagination was unusually active. What Glaser said about his fate and that of his family in Europe rang true. He did seem to be a casualty of the chaos in Europe. Would things would have been worse for him if he had stayed? Of course they would. Americans seemed blessed in being able to stand apart from the chaos. Perhaps Yvonne had more of a point than he admitted when she said that America should not become involved.

As the bus pulled away from Windsor Station, a Canadian Pacific attendant told the passengers that the journey to the port would take about fifteen minutes. The scene is unusual, she said, because they will be moving along parts of the route taken by the king and queen yesterday. Fred saw barricades and occasional viewing stands. He saw litter everywhere, including many more small British flags. Yesterday's events had turned the city upside down, confirming the magnitude of the reception he had read about in the Ottawa newspapers. As the bus passed through the morning-after chaos, the architecture and several narrow streets reminded Fred of a European rather than a North American city.

At the port, the bus moved along the quay where the *Duchess of York* was being readied for departure. The ship was much larger than any Fred had seen before, including those in which he'd made his previous trip to Europe and back a decade ago. It was many hundreds of feet long. The two massive funnels, already belching smoke, were the height of ten-story buildings. A small crane had just loaded supplies into a hold at the side of the ship. Seamen were loosening the ship's hawsers from bollards on the quay. The bus and luggage van drew up at the single gangway. Passengers and luggage were quickly moved aboard. As the gangway was pulled away from the ship, there was a huge blast of ship's horns. The remaining hawsers were pulled aboard as the gap between ship and quay widened.

Fred stayed close to the gate for the gangway. He and others near him waved to people on the quay. A minute later, the ship was moving down the St. Lawrence River. Looking ahead, Fred saw a tugboat cast off the ship's tow line and turn back towards the port. The next part of his strange odyssey had begun.

Part II

Montreal
to
Glasgow

Black and white version of a painting of the passenger steamship *Duchess of York*. She was owned and operated by the Canadian Pacific Steamship Co. and had been built in Scotland in 1928. The ship was sunk off the west coast of France in 1943 after an attack by *Luftwaffe* aircraft.

SIX

Biology and Psychology

A man in what seemed to be a naval officer's uniform inspected Fred's steamship ticket and, with a "Welcome aboard, Professor Skinner," directed him to Cabin 107 on Deck A. Fred took the stairs up one flight and found his interior single cabin. It was close to the men's washroom. Fred stood at the open door of his cabin while a steward worked inside.

"*Bonjour Professeur Skinner*, Good morning," said the steward, emphasizing the last syllable of Fred's name. "I am your cabin steward for this voyage. *Je m'appelle Jean-Paul.*"

"*Enchanté de vous rencontrer, Jean-Paul,*" replied Fred. He was unsure whether to use te or vous when speaking to the older cabin steward and continued in English. "The cabin seems comfortable, although it is rather close to the washroom."

"That could be an advantage, sir. In any case, you'll appreciate the cabin's position in the ship when we meet the open ocean two days from now. The *Duchess of York* is one of the 'drunken duchesses.' These are four Canadian Pacific ships we know for their lively perfor-

59

mance in heavy seas."

"I'm surprised," said Fred, "the ship seems large and sturdy."

"They were built with quite a flat bottom to do what this *Duchess* is doing now. She sails the shallow St. Lawrence above Quebec City providing big-ship service between Montreal and Britain. The flat bottoms make the *Duchesses* unstable in anything but calm seas. The *instabilité* is felt more near the stern and at the sides of the ship. This cabin's forward position near the ship's center makes for a more peaceful voyage. Also, there is less vibration here because we are far from the engines. They are at the bottom of the ship near the stern."

The steward joined Fred in the narrow passageway outside the cabin. "I've finished now. I'll make sure you have a good journey across the Atlantic. Lunch is served at noon or at one o'clock in the cabin class dining saloon on Deck C. That is two decks below where we are now. Your ticket will tell you whether you are for the first or second sitting. By the way, there is an envelope on the chest of drawers in the cabin. It probably contains an invitation to sit at the captain's table at dinner this evening. If you need anything pressed, leave it on the bed during the next hour."

Fred thanked Jean-Paul, noting that his accent was a milder version of what he'd heard on the train and in Montreal. He saw from his ticket that he had been allocated to the second sitting for all meals. He was hungry, but even more in need of stretching his legs after the long train journey. He asked, "Can I move throughout the ship, or only in areas designated for cabin class passengers?"

"*En principe*, you must stay in the cabin class section. No one will stop you visiting the tourist and third class sections, although you may receive *des regards impolis* – what do you say in English?"

"Rude stares?" Fred offered.

"Yes, some rude stares from the passengers in those sections. Until the crew knows you, take your ticket with you, so that you can return to the cabin class area. Please stay out of places that are only for the ship's crew."

"Thanks for this information," said Fred. "I haven't seen many passengers. Is the ship full?"

"No. This is our fourth eastward crossing of the Atlantic this season, the second from Montreal. For each one I doubt we've had more than a half of our permitted number of passengers. For our four westward crossing, every berth has been taken. As the situation in Europe becomes more tense, people are leaving there rather than going there. Goodbye for now, sir."

Fred had been tempted to try his French, but felt intimidated by Jean-Paul's fluency in English. Bilingualism was a remarkable skill and he should find a place for it in his account of verbal behavior.

He went into the small cabin, navigated around his large suitcase, and opened the envelope on the chest of drawers. Inside was a printed card with his name added in handwriting: "Captain Charles Richardson takes great pleasure in requesting the company of – Professor B.F. Skinner – at his table for dinner at 8PM on Friday May 19, 1939. Dress: business suit or more formal. RSVP by 2PM to your cabin steward or to the Purser's Office on Deck A." Would the invitation have been in French if he had a French-sounding name?

Fred unpacked the large suitcase, which had been picked up from his home on Tuesday. He laid out his business suit and a shirt on the bed, and stowed the remaining items in the wardrobe and the chest of drawers. He left a pair of shoes conspicuously by the bed, hoping that Jean-Paul would shine them.

He had almost two hours to explore the ship before lunch. First, he went to the purser's office, near his cabin. There he told a young man with a British accent that he would be pleased to have dinner at the captain's table. He asked why he had been chosen for this honor and was told he should ask the captain. Fred noted from a plaque on the wall of the office that the *Duchess of York* was registered in Britain, not in Canada as might be expected of a ship owned by Canadian Pacific Steamships Ocean Services Ltd. He imagined this was a further aspect of Canada's colonial subservience. Another item on the office wall asserted that although the steamships were run by a separate company their operations were well integrated with those of the Canadian Pacific Railway.

Fred climbed two flights of stairs past the promenade deck to the boat deck. There he spent several minutes looking at a large poster that presented plans of the ship's seven decks, and how the three classes of accommodation – Cabin, Tourist, and Third – were distributed among them. A few cabins were on this deck. Most cabins were two decks below on Deck A. Some cabins were further below on Decks B and C. Tourist Class berths were on Decks B, C, and D. The evidently cramped Third Class berths were further down on Decks C, D, and E. The Cabin Class dining saloon was on Deck C, linked to this deck and the decks between by the ship's only elevator.

There seemed to be few opportunities to move among the areas for the three classes. Fred couldn't remember such clear demarcation as a feature of his previous transatlantic trip, made on American ships. Keeping the lower classes firmly in their place might be sign of the Britishness of this shipping company.

Fred was both offended and pleased by the class arrangements. He would like everyone to have similar levels of comfort, recognizing that some cabins must be better located than others. If there had to be differences, he was pleased to have the more comfortable arrangements. He'd been booked in Tourist Class at first. Then he'd used some of the funds freed up by not having to buy a return ticket to pay for the much higher cost of Cabin Class. Yvonne might have approved, but he didn't have a chance to discuss it with her.

He walked out to the open deck. It was cool and mostly cloudy, but bearable without his coat if he avoided the strong headwind. The ship was following the river downstream, mostly towards the north He stayed on the right side of the ship – port? starboard? – which was a little warmer. A sandy shore was near. When he fought the headwind and moved to the deck rail, between the lifeboats, Fred could see from looking ahead and behind that the river had narrowed. The height of the deck allowed him to see over treetops to what must be another branch of the river with farmland on the far side. He could make out two horse-drawn plows working the fields and a stationary tractor with a group of people around it.

Fred returned to the top of the stairwell to warm up. Near the deck plan was a map of the St. Lawrence River. He figured that the ship has travelled about twenty miles from Montreal and must have just passed between Île Sainte-Thérèse to the left and La Grande Île. He should now be able to see Varennes to the right of the ship. Walking out to the deck, he had a good view of this small busy river port.

He took shelter at the front end of the deck (he must learn the correct nautical terms) and found himself at the entrance to the gymnasium. On the door was a notice that the gym was reserved for a yoga class from two-thirty to three-thirty each afternoon. Cabin Class passengers were welcome. Fred was intrigued by yoga because of the reported control its practitioners could achieve over their bodies. He'd like to know more about how that happens.

Fred walked down to the promenade deck. There was a walkway all the way around the ship, much of it sheltered overhead by the boat deck. With better weather, this could be truly pleasant. He walked through several elegantly appointed interior spaces. There was a smoking room with a well-stocked bar, a lounge, a gallery, a card and writing room, and an observation room. Three stewards were chatting at the bar, in French. There seemed to be no one else at this level. Perhaps the other cabin-class passengers were at lunch, or in their cabins recovering from their train trips.

It was now twenty minutes to his lunch sitting. He walked down to his cabin on the deck below. There, to read in case he had no company at lunch, he picked up photostats of British scientific articles he'd made before he left. He walked down two more levels to the dining saloon.

The saloon was sparsely occupied, with fewer passengers than waiters – or should they be called stewards? Some of the passengers were stragglers from the first sitting. Others, like him, were early for the second sitting. The assistant maître d' – so said the lapel badge – told Fred that seating for the voyage had not yet been assigned. It would be posted at the saloon entrance before dinner. He was asked if he would like to sit alone and was directed to a small corner table with a good view of the rest of the saloon. The menu was lavish. He ordered a chicken salad and began reading the articles, occasionally looking up to see who was coming and going.

Two of the articles were on natural selection, a key process in the evolution of species identified eighty years earlier by Charles Darwin and Alfred Russel Wallace. Fred wanted to know more about the process because of its many potential points of relevance to animal and human behavior. He'd also chosen these articles to give him more of a feel for the British academic style.

The great insight of Darwin, in particular, was that the kind of selection practiced by animal breeders acts in nature too. He concluded that it's pervasive in nature and is powerful enough to account for the evolution of life forms. Natural selection is a fairly simple process that – according to Darwin, Wallace and many biologists since, together with a few other processes – can account for the emergence of all creatures great and small, each little flower that opens, each little bird that sings.

Fred realized he was echoing the words of a famous hymn to himself, but he was using the words to deny a role for a supreme maker rather than to proclaim one. Perhaps God made natural selection possible and let things run on as they will. But, reflected Fred, the beauty of natural selection is that it needs nothing special to explain it beyond the processes of physics and chemistry. God didn't have to prescribe natural selection, only the basic laws of matter.

God didn't even have to infuse living things with the spark of life. Life could have begun, Fred had heard, as a result of the fortuitous occurrence of complex molecules in a primordial soup, perhaps shocked into combination by lightning. He surmised that life might have begun when, for whatever reason, molecules became complex enough to become part of a process of natural selection. They had to be capable of three things. The first was replication. This could have meant no more than simply splitting into viable halves. The second was variation. The replication was not always precise – the offspring could vary among themselves. The third was selection. In a particular environment some varieties were favored: they were more likely to reproduce than others.

Fred's thoughts turned to the role of natural selection, if any, in the everyday activities of humans and animals. He saw several possibilities for involvement. Natural selection and evolution set limits on what a particular organism can do. No matter how he tried, an experimenter was never going to get a rat to press a lever that required a force of a few pounds weight. Nor for that matter, could the experimenter himself ever be trained to lift several tons. Natural selection and evolution also set limits on which stimuli could be used to control behavior. Humans could never be trained to distinguish among stimuli having different ultraviolet wavelengths. They didn't have receptors that made this possible. Natural selection and evolution had caused some stimuli to be reinforcers – food and water, for example – although the effectiveness depended on degree of satiation, presumably another consequence of evolution.

Perhaps most important of all for Fred's purposes, another result of natural selection and evolution was the process of reinforcement itself. More specifically, what was inherited was the capacity of behavior to be reinforced. Another inherited process was the transfer of the effect of one stimulus to another by pairing, as when a tone came to cause salivation in one of Pavlov's dogs, and, in his own work, when a stimulus that signaled arrival of reinforcer acquired something of the power of the reinforcer.

While Fred was musing on these matters, he had an insight that he quickly recognized as being of great potential importance. It was that natural selection resembled the process of positive reinforcement he had been focusing on in his laboratory. In the former, a particular environment favors particular varieties that flourish in that environment. In the latter, a particular environment favors particular behavior that increases in frequency in that environment.

The waiter removed his plate. It was empty, but Fred had been so absorbed he remembered eating none of it. Absorbed by what? He could only conclude that he had been engaged in a very intense private monologue. The monologue must have been occurring without actual speech because none of the people at nearby tables seem to be paying attention to him. The dining saloon was now about a third full. He had not noticed people arriving. The private monologue – or what it a dialogue? – seemed to have been productive, even profound. He was not sure it would be useful unless he were to write it down. Perhaps he'd write a letter to his friend Fred Keller about its important point: that natural selection and reinforcement resembled each other.

The steward brought dessert – apple pie and ice cream – which he must have ordered but did not remember doing so. He asked for a pencil. While the ice cream melted, he attempted to recapitulate his thinking about natural selection and reinforcement in notes on the back of one of the photostats. It was almost as hard to remember the flow of his thoughts as it was to write on the paper's shiny surface.

Fred wrote down as much as he could remember. He left the pie in its pool of ice cream and resumed reading the three articles. One was a compendium of a dozen short items under the title "A Discussion on the Present State of the Theory of Natural Selection," published in the *Proceedings of the Royal Society*. Fred was struck by the extent of disagreement among eminent biologists about the importance of this process in evolution. This was even though eighty years have passed since Darwin and Wallace made it clear.

Fred was disheartened by the thought that another eighty years might have to pass before his own notions about the importance of reinforcement in behavior would be accepted. It would be well into the twenty-first century, which he does not expect to see. If he were to publish these notions now, psychologists – or whatever they will be called then – could still be arguing about them in 2019.

He was then uplifted, for a while, by the second article, "Natural Selection and the Evolutionary Process." It was the text of a 1936 speech by Julian Huxley to the British Association for the Advancement of Science. Huxley's elegant message spoke to the power and subtlety of natural selection. He argued that natural selection is capable of generating the richness of life, and that there is no other plausible mechanism. He argued too that growing acceptance of the importance of natural selection allows for the synthesis and unification of the biological sciences under the umbrella of evolution.

Towards the end of the article, Huxley's argument took a strange turn. He'd grafted several questionable assertions on to sensible arguments about the origin of species of plants and animals. The assertions were about progress and the need to enhance human superiority. He'd written, "If we were to adopt some system for using the gametes of a few highly endowed individuals, directly or from tissue-cultures, to produce all the next generation, then all kinds of new possibilities would emerge. Man might develop castes … ."

Fred had encountered similar sentiments while skimming through *Mein Kampf*. The difference was that Hitler believed that human perfection has already been achieved, in the form of Aryans, who are mostly Germans. The main challenge, according to Hitler, was to preserve perfection, chiefly by preventing dilution of Aryan stock, especially dilution by Jews.

Fred had made a photostat of the third article because it was the text of a recent speech by a grandson of Charles Darwin, the physicist Charles Galton Darwin, director of Britain's National Physical Laboratory. He'd been invited to address Britain's Eugenics Society more for his lineage than his biological expertise. His article suggested that civilization prevents natural selection from operating. This, C.G. Darwin said, "must inevitably lead to degeneration, which for men means decay of the intellect, and such decay must surely lead to a collapse of the civilization." This struck Fred as being similar to Hitler's argument that Aryans need frequent wars to maintain their form. He remembered Hitler's words as being something like this: "Mankind has become great through perpetual struggle. In perpetual peace his greatness must decline."

Eugenics provided another point of similarity among the views of Huxley, C.G. Darwin, and Hitler. They all wanted to achieve differential breeding. Huxley wanted intelligent people to reproduce more. C.G. Darwin wanted rich people to breed more, and would give governments the power to make that happen. The Nazis' program of what they call "racial hygiene," Fred had read, was now well established as a means of reducing the breeding ability of what are regarded as defective or inferior people. Could such similarities in views explain why the Nazis were getting away with so much?

The steward told Fred that the second lunch sitting was to end soon, at two-thirty. The dining saloon was now almost empty. Fred gathered his papers, walked up the wide staircase to his cabin, and then up to the boat deck. The scene was exhilarating. The sights displaced the disturbing similarities he'd just encountered. Beyond the blue, green, and brown hues of the wide river, a bright sun, at times behind white clouds, bathed a breath-catching landscape of newly plowed fields and early spring greenery. The air was clear and cool, uncomfortably so where there is no shelter from the headwind.

Fred returned to the top of the stairway and consulted the large map of Canada next to the deck plan. The ship must be approaching Trois-Rivières, half way to Quebec City. He went outside again. Braving the wind, he could just make out the small city far ahead on the river's left bank. He believed this was the port side of the ship. However, he was confused because the buoys on the right of the channel they were passing along were red, which he thought was port, and those on the left side were green. He had much to learn about nautical terminology.

Fred took shelter by the gymnasium door. Through the door's window, he saw the yoga session in progress. The leader was a thin, bearded man, perhaps from India, perhaps Fred's age, wearing only a pair of dark tight-fitting shorts. Doing the routines with him were two light-haired women wearing voluminous white robes that didn't restrict their movements. They seemed to be sisters. Fred entered quietly, leaned against a wall by the door, and watched.

The three continued as if he were not there. Fred now saw that although the women's faces had an evident family resemblance, one was more youthful. It had softer features and even a hint of adolescent pimples. He was misled by the older woman's grace and suppleness. The creases in her neck suggested she was close to his age, perhaps older. Her companion could be her daughter. The leader murmured directions and the three began a new routine, now on their backs, clearly coordinating their breathing with curls into their knees and arching of their spines. The robes fell back as they arched, giving Fred a sense of the shapes of women's bodies, which seemed as similar as their faces had first appeared.

The movements were hypnotic. Fred left the gymnasium, aware that he might have fallen asleep standing up if he had stayed. He looked forward to meeting the two women again during the voyage. Back in his cabin he saw that his suit and shirt had been pressed and his shoes shined. Afternoon tea was to be served in the lounge on the promenade deck between four o'clock and five-thirty. He lay on his bed and was soon fast asleep.

Fred slept for half an hour and woke refreshed, thinking about letters he should write. He should write to Yvonne, but he might well arrive back before his letter. He hesitated about sending a letter when he didn't know how it would be received. A letter to his good friend Fred Keller would involve no such complications. It could be an aid to getting his thoughts straight, although he'd have to be careful about what he said. He poured some water, sat on his bed, opened a fresh page in his notebook, and began writing.

Dear Fred,

I'm not sure whether you'll receive this. If you do, you'll be surprised to know that I'm making a brief trip to England. The ostensible purpose arises from a wish of A.N. Whitehead – remember him from Harvard? – and Bertrand Russell to bring me and Ludwig Wittgenstein together, which I can elaborate on. (I believe I told you I met B.R. when he was in Minneapolis in January.) I'm to attend Wittgenstein's inauguration as Professor of Philosophy at Cambridge University. My real reason for this trip is the chance to meet Sigmund Freud, who is now in London and on his last legs.

I've been thinking about evolution and natural selection and have become interested in the parallel between natural selection and our concept of reinforcement. The parallel is striking. Consider the darkening of moths in industrializing regions of England as a case of natural selection. Coal-burning spreads soot over a wide area. Darker moths are more likely to breed because they are less visible to predators. Before industrialization, dark moths were in a minority. In the sooty environment, they become a majority.

Now consider a rat's lever-pressing. We place a rat in a box equipped with a lever. Initially, lever presses are rare. If the environment changes so that a lever press produces a food pellet, the frequency of lever pressing increases. If only presses of more than one hundred grams produce food pellets, such presses, initially rare, become more frequent.

In each case, we have something that varies, an environment that favors one variety rather than others, and a mechanism for retaining the effect of the selection. In the case of inherited characteristics, the retention mechanism is to do with genes and chromosomes. We don't need to know the details to understand the importance of the retention process, although knowing the details could be useful. In the case of the behavior of a rat or even a human, the retention mechanism is in the brain. Again, we don't need to know the details to rec-

ognize the importance of the process.

By the way, you'll know that, although Charles Darwin is given all the credit, the notion of natural selection had two fathers. The other was Alfred Russel Wallace. Their reports were published together. Wallace's insight was soon overshadowed by the appearance of Darwin's magnificent On the Origin of Species. *Their views of natural selection differed a little. Darwin focused on competition for resources and reproduction. Wallace focused on adaptation to the environment. If I'm remembering correctly, reinforcement is therefore more like Wallace's view, although the similarities between the two were more important than the differences.*

I may not be the first to notice the parallel. I believe your neighbor at Columbia, Professor Thorndike, used it in his book Animal Intelligence. *My account above may have made the parallel clearer than he did. (I must write to Thorndike apologizing for not acknowledging his work in* The Behavior of Organisms. *And I must look at his new book on language.)*

But it's not only the parallel in itself that excites me. If, as many biologists believe, the natural selection is the overarching process in biology, could reinforcement not similarly be the overarching process in psychology? Could not reinforcement be as significant for the evolution of an organism's behavior as is natural selection for the evolution of the inherited characteristics of a species?

Increasingly, the first question many biologists ask about a particular feature of a species is this. What in the environment has favored and continues to favor the feature? Biologists no longer look for causes elsewhere: inside the organism or in heaven. Similarly, should not the first question psychologists ask about a feature of a person's behavior be this: what is it in the environment that has favored and continues to favor the behavior? The question should be asked for both normal and pathological behavior.

Biologists seem increasingly comfortable with the notion that the fairly simple-to-explain process of natural selection can in large measure account for the complexity and variety on life on Earth. Would it be too much to hope that psychologists will become com-

71

fortable with the notion that the fairly-simple-to-explain process of reinforcement can in large measure account for the complexity of the behavior of organisms? And I mean all behavior that is not inherited, including human verbal behavior.

This does not mean that reinforcement is the only *mechanism at play in changing and maintaining behavior. Natural selection is certainly* not *the only mechanism accounting for the evolution of species. But natural selection is becoming accepted as the most important process. It's taken eighty years for this to happen. I'd like to think it won't take another eighty years for reinforcement to be given similar standing.*

And then there is the matter of causality. Natural selection is a causal process. But it's different from the simple causality of the physical sciences, such as when one pool ball pushes another or a large object pulls smaller objects towards it as a result of gravitational attraction. Through natural selection, a change in the environment – e.g., more soot on the barks of trees – causes moths to change color. This doesn't happen through a simple push or pull process but through a more complex process of replication, variation, and selection. The complex process can no doubt be boiled down to a large number of simpler push and pull processes. However, the causality of natural selection is evident only when the whole process is considered.

The causality of natural selection even appears to involve intention or purpose. Giraffes' necks grow longer thereby allowing access to the leaves of trees on the plain, which are growing taller. It's almost as if the presumed purpose caused the change, somehow acting backward in time rather than forward. People's usual experience of causality is of the simple, forward type. That may be in part why natural selection as the basis for the origin of species remained hidden for millennia. It was hidden even though the effective techniques of plant and animal breeding were in plain sight. That may be why, in looking for simple forward-acting causes, people invoked supernatural forces acting purposefully.

Behavior often appears to be the result of the actions of a purposeful mind or will. In reality, it could be the result of a past history of rein-

forcement under particular environmental conditions. People are prone to invoke a purposeful mind or will because they are used to explaining things with forward-acting causes. As in evolution, the key process in behavior change has been hidden for millennia. It was hidden even though effective techniques for changing animal and human behavior were in plain sight.

Natural selection is the causal process that distinguishes biological sciences from the physical sciences such as physics and chemistry. Physical scientists can account for the phenomena they study without invoking natural selection. Biological sciences have to take natural selection into account. Indeed, nothing in biology may make sense except in the light of natural selection.

I'm wondering if the process of positive reinforcement may similarly be the most fundamental process in the psychological or behavioral sciences. Could it be that changing or maintaining particular actions by their consequences is the defining process of a third level of phenomena, alongside physiochemical and biological phenomena? Put another way, perhaps nothing in the behavioral sciences makes sense except in the light of reinforcement.

I'm so excited by these grand ideas I want to go and proclaim them from the top deck of this splendid ship. But there are many questions I need to ponder first. Here are some:

- *Why did the importance of natural selection not become apparent for thousands of years after the discovery of selective breeding, and what might prevent the importance of reinforcement from languishing in similar obscurity?*

- *Why, in spite of logic and accumulating evidence, are many biologists still unsure about the overarching importance of natural selection?*

- *Is concern about natural selection fostered by yesterday's and today's politics, notably concerns about eugenics and assertions of racial superiority?*

As you can see, my dear Fred, I am buzzing with half-baked implications of our lab work for the world at large. And I've hardly touched

*on my continuing preoccupation with verbal behavior as behavior.
I'm seeing it as a form of social behavior changed and maintained by
its consequences, which are usually other people's verbal behavior.
Watching and being a part of Julie's acquisition of verbal behavior
has been a truly productive experience. My main regret in making
this strange odyssey is that I am separated from her development for
a few weeks. I hope that what I gain from my travels will compensate
for this loss.*

Your friend,

Burrhus

As he wrote his first name, which he used for few other purposes
than to end letters to Fred Keller, Fred Skinner realized that the letter
would never be sent. He hadn't asked Calvin Cooper whether he could
send letters while he was away. Fred was pretty sure it would be
frowned on if not explicitly forbidden. The less he said about this trip
to Fred Keller or anyone else the less likely he would be to reveal its
purposes or provoke awkward questions.

It would not be a wasted letter. Writing promotes useful thinking
and clear expression of arguments. Fred asked himself how. He ran
through features of writing things down rather than just thinking or
talking about them. Writing's a slower process. This might aid clarity,
although Fred couldn't see how the clarity is achieved. Writing is often
for other people, so it needs to be clear. But much writing is in the
form of notes to oneself. Making the notes still seems to help with
achieving clarity as well as with aiding memory. Talking is usually to
other people and is usually more muddled. He should follow his own
dictum and look for answers in the environment.

Notes written for one's own use can be quite unclear, but they do
offer the possibility of editing. This can result in improvement of what
might otherwise be a train of muddled expression. It might be easier to
build on a thought captured on paper than on the elusive memory of a
thought. Fred found himself using terms – such as "the elusive memory
of a thought" – that would fit more comfortably in the vocabulary of a

psychologist committed to introspection. He blamed this on the lack of adequate terminology. He resolved he'd help the cause of behaviorism by providing better ways of talking and writing about such matters.

Fred's mention of Thorndike in the letter to the other Fred reminded him to pursue his interest in Alexander Bain. A history of psychology had described Bain, a Scot, as "the first psychologist" on account of two books published in the 1850s, even before Darwin's *On the Origin of Species*. Fred had skimmed through them. He'd been struck by an account of a lamb's first few hours of life. At first there were only random movements. Then, after chance contact with the mother's wooly skin, touching the skin became more frequent. The more frequent contact with the skin led to chance contact with a milky teat. Soon suckling became frequent. Fred was fascinated by the possible roles of behavioral variation and selection by reinforcement in what was commonly thought of as an instinctive – which is to say, inherited – pattern of behavior.

For a few moments Fred entertained the idea that elaborating the similarity between positive reinforcement and natural selection could be what would make his mark as a scientist. Could he become the Darwin of the twentieth century? Pavlov had won a Nobel Prize – in physiology – for his work on conditioned reflexes. Could there be a Nobel Prize – in what? – for a program of work on positive reinforcement conducted by this century's Darwin? Fred worked hard to stop this appealing but far-fetched train of thought.

It was time for afternoon tea. Fred recalled from his last trip to Britain that this meal was a high point of the daily meal arrangements. Perhaps this was also true of a British-registered ship. For the moment, he'd have to put aside consideration of the behavior of writing. He'd have to focus later on how writing might promote useful thinking and clear expression of arguments.

Fred Keller and Fred Skinner in 1937.

SEVEN

Yoga and Psychology

On the *Duchess of York*, Friday May 19, 1939

fternoon tea was available in the drawing and observation room. There, a few dozen passengers were being served by attentive waiters. A dark trim man in a business suit, sitting alone, stood and beckoned Fred to sit with him. It was the yoga instructor. Fred took a moment to recognize him as the man who was in the gymnasium wearing only shorts.

"Will you join me?" the man said. "My name is Kovoor Behanan." He spelled it out. "I saw you in the gymnasium today and believe you are Professor Skinner of the University of Minnesota. I have seen you before. You gave a talk at one of Professor Clark Hull's seminars at Yale. It was late in 1934 or early in 1935. I used to attend his excellent Wednesday seminars. You were at Harvard, but I heard that you then moved to Minnesota."

Fred was alarmed again. Was this another plant by the Bund? He said, "I am indeed Fred Skinner. I remember the seminar and Professor Hull's generous hospitality, but I'm afraid I don't remember you." Fred offered his hand. It was shaken firmly. They sat and were plied with the paraphernalia of afternoon tea. Two stewards laid out pots of tea, jugs of hot water and milk, a bowl of sugar cubes, tiered stands burdened with crustless sandwiches and small cakes, and silver-plated cutlery accompanied by stylish cups, saucers, and plates.

"My," said Fred, "this is indeed a treat. May I ask what you were doing at Yale?"

"I had just been awarded my Ph.D. in psychology, and had a fellowship there for another year. You may not recognize me because I did not have this beard then. Also, I was much too shy to say anything at your seminar."

"What was the topic of your thesis?"

"At its heart was an attempt to provide a scientific appraisal of the effects of some of the practices of yoga. It also endeavored to present yoga in the terms of western philosophy and psychology."

Behanan continued, "After I saw you in the gymnasium, I hoped to have the pleasure of meeting you here. In anticipation, I brought from my cabin a copy of the book based on my thesis. I am pleased to present it to you in honor of the occasion of our meeting."

Fred reflected on the man's perfect English, albeit accented and a little wordy. He had thought much the same about the dentist's English, although the accent was different. He began to reflect on what sustained accents, but was checked by the sight of the proffered book. Fred accepted it and thanked him. His alarm had subsided, although he continued to wonder about yet another coincidence: that he should encounter someone who knew him. He was becoming too suspicious for his own comfort.

Fred noted the book's title, *Yoga: A Scientific Evaluation*. He said, "I look forward to reading this. I know almost nothing about yoga. Before seeing you and the two women in the gymnasium, I'd seen only photographs of yoga practitioners in unusual poses. I presume the exercises you were doing there are a part of yoga?"

"They are a small part of yoga. If it will not be inconvenient, I will

78

be very pleased to discuss yoga with you during the voyage. For the moment, let me say that yoga is several things, as you could discover from my inadequate book. Yoga is chiefly a body of philosophy, but it is also a program of mental and physical therapy."

"I'll be pleased to learn more about yoga. I'll help our discussion by reading at least some of your book first. For now, perhaps you could tell me how you organized this afternoon's session so quickly after the start of our voyage?"

"The other two participants and I had travelled together by train from Toronto. They are a mother and daughter on their way to Germany: Sophie and Anna Graydon. I knew Mrs. Graydon well ten years ago. We were both graduate students in the philosophy department of the University of Toronto. I even met Anna then. She was about nine years old."

There was a pause while each busied himself with pouring tea and arranging sandwiches and cakes on his plate.

Fred bit into a cucumber sandwich, sipped a little tea, and asked, "I imagine Canadians who are going to Germany at this time must have a good reason to do so?"

"Mrs. Graydon has a most interesting background. She is originally from Germany and does have a good reason to go there just now. I would feel uncomfortable telling you more of what I know about her. She is very easy to converse with. You should take the opportunity to ask her about her intriguing life."

Fred paused before continuing, wondering yet again whether this encounter is merely a coincidence. "May I ask about you, Dr. Behanan? Are you also on your way to Germany?"

"No, Professor Skinner. I am returning to India where I am now living again, as a student and teacher of yoga. I have been lecturing in North America for three months. My tour ended in Toronto. I looked up old friends, including Mrs. Graydon. I discovered to my delight that she and I were to travel by the same steamship across the Atlantic, and Anna too. I learned as well that they had both acquired an interest in yoga, and I offered to help develop that interest."

Fred glanced at the book cover. "Dr. Behanan, I look forward to our further discussions. Should we include the ladies in them?"

"Perhaps we might see you in the yoga class, which is to be held at two-thirty on each day of our voyage?"

"I will have to think about that," Fred replied. "What I saw this afternoon resembled calisthenics, which has never been among my preferred activities."

"It was not ordinary calisthenics but an exercise designed to help achieve control over the diaphragm and other muscles involved in breathing. As you will see from my book, yoga attaches much importance to breathing. You would understand *how* the control occurs if you were to join our afternoon sessions. However, I can see, Professor Skinner, that perhaps you would prefer to learn about yoga more from reading and talking rather than from doing."

Behanan continued, "If you do care to read some of what I have written, may I recommend one chapter of my book in particular? It is Chapter 8, which has the title 'Yoga and psychoanalysis.' It provides a critique of Dr. Freud's system. It argues that his work has contributed little or nothing to the problems that occupy most academic psychologists. From what I remember of your talk at Professor Hull's seminar, you may be in agreement."

Fred's alarm level rose again. The conversation had moved too quickly to Freud and thus to one of the purposes of his trip. He said, "I agree that his contribution to our understanding of human behavior may be overrated. However, I remain an admirer of Dr. Freud, more for what he has tried to do than for what he has achieved. Perhaps that can be a topic of a later discussion. For the moment, please tell me more of what you wrote about yoga and psychoanalysis."

80

"I can say this very briefly. Both yoga and psychoanalysis focus on the unconscious. Both have a therapeutic component. However, the approach of yoga is deeper and more comprehensive. Moreover, the goals are different. Psychoanalysis aims to help with adjustment to everyday life. Yoga helps its practitioners achieve pure consciousness. This is consciousness without thoughts. It is consciousness without the distraction of the external world."

"Does the exercise you were doing in the gym lead to pure consciousness?" Fred hoped he was not appearing insincere.

"Indeed yes. Control over breathing is an aid to the liberation of consciousness from its normal activities. If you join us tomorrow you may better understand what I mean."

"You're very persistent. I certainly appreciate the invitation."

Behanan moved to leave. He said, "I must apologize for burdening you with my talking. I hope we will continue our discussion, and that I will be allowing you more opportunity to speak. I must take my leave. Thank you very much for sitting with me."

Fred watched him weave elegantly towards the exit through the spaces between the chairs of other passengers and the waiters and their trolleys. He was pleased he had said so little. He would feel silly in a yoga class, but the closeness of the two women could make it worthwhile. And he might even learn something about how to control his own behavior.

He looked at the photos in *Yoga: A Scientific Evaluation* and was struck by a pair captioned "Isolation of the right/left rectus abdominus." Each showed a thin, heavily bearded man – wilder-looking than Behanan – bending forward slightly with hands on upper thighs and flexing one or the other side of his abdominal muscles. The abdomen was mostly a cavity, but with a pronounced ribbon of muscle running from the right or the left of the ribcage to below the waist. The ribbons of muscle disappeared within the sparse white cloth the man wore folded about his loins. The wrapping reminded Fred of one of Julie's diapers.

Fred moved a hand inside his jacket to feel his own abdominal muscles, barely identifiable below the layer of fat that had thickened over the last few years. He could flex these muscles but only both sides together. He wondered how he might train himself – or be trained – to flex just one side or the other..

He searched the text around the photos for clues as to how this might be done. He learned that isolation of the two muscles is a requirement for a purificatory exercise involving washing of the colon and rectum. How isolation could be achieved was unclear. He read that it is a continuation of a diaphragm-raising exercise. Perhaps it is a stage after what he saw in the gymnasium this afternoon.

He read further, "When the diaphragm has been raised, with the practitioner in a standing position, a downward and forward push is given to the abdominal portion above the pubic bone. After considerable practice, sometimes running over several months, one is able to isolate the two muscles. Next the attempt is directed to isolating either one, keeping the other one relaxed. If the isolation of the left rectus is desired, the body is bent a little to that side and a corresponding change is introduced for isolating the right muscle."

Fred supposed that in everyday language this would be described as practice resulting in control by the mind over the body. He would prefer to talk of behavior – in this case, flexing both or one abdominal muscles – coming under the control of stimuli emanating from that area. He remembered a book that had much influenced him as a student: *The Integrative Action of the Nervous System* by Charles Sherrington. He wondered whether these stimuli would be similar to those from nerves in or near the muscles of the arm. Or were stimuli from abdominal muscles less conspicuous? Would the English physiologist Sherrington still be alive? Might he be in London or Cambridge?

Fred's thinking moved on to the mechanism of how these stimuli, whatever their nature, might gain control over the left or the right abdominal muscle. The mechanism could be similar to what happens in his laboratory when a rat comes to press a bar only when a tone sounds. This happens because delivery of a food pellet follows a bar-press only when the tone is sounding. The pairing of the tone with the food gives the tone some of the properties of the food. But, what is the equivalent of the food pellet when a person is acquiring control over his abdominal muscles? It could be kind words from an instructor or changes in the appearance of the abdomen as viewed directly or in a mirror. It could even be other internal stimuli that indicate progress towards control, or some combination of all or any of these.

He began to read about how control of the two rectus muscles can used to achieve washing of the colon by taking in water through the anus. He found the description off-putting and stopped. He flipped back through the book to the chapter on psychoanalysis, but saw that afternoon tea was winding down. He resolved to walk several times around this deck and the deck above before returning to his cabin to change for dinner.

As he walked around the boat deck, Fred relished the views of the unfolding Quebec countryside from high above the river. Seeing this large ship from a field near the river must be an even more impressive sight. The air was becoming noticeably cooler as evening approached. It was too early to change for dinner. He retreated to the lounge on the promenade deck, preferring to read *Yoga: A Scientific Evaluation* there than in his small cabin.

He began reading the chapter on psychoanalysis. The first paragraph ended with the kind of assessment Fred would like one day to be made about his own work: "... psychoanalysis [as developed and refined by Sigmund Freud] has deepened our understanding of the social sciences more than any other intellectual movement of the last three decades. The result is a new way of looking at history, religion, social evolution, literature, and of late even politics."

But, in the third paragraph, Behanan characterized the same psychoanalysis as repugnant to academic psychologists. It was "somewhat like a religious cult," and an "unpardonably one-sided theory of human motivation." He suggested that "making sexuality the central theme of human motivation" is an "interesting line of thought ... which is not very different from that of yoga."

Behanan asked in his book, "How can there be any similarity between the materialistic psychoanalysis and the spiritual yoga, two disciplines which were born in different ages and bear the marks of different cultures?" He had touched on one similarity during afternoon tea: that "both ... are in the final analysis therapeutic systems."

Fred read that other similarities concern the unconscious. Both psychoanalysis and yoga divided mental activity into conscious and unconscious. Both assigned a stronger role in the causation of human behavior to unconscious activity. Both said that pleasure is "the guiding principle" of unconscious activity. Psychoanalysis and yoga both held that unconscious mental activity somehow included the experiences of previous generations as well as, particularly in the case of psychoanalysis, those of early childhood.

What were the differences? Two seemed to be important to Behanan. One concerned the antithesis of the instinct to sustain life. Freud characterized it as the death instinct. Yoga saw it as the condition of being liberated from the clamor of consciousness. The therapeutic goal of yoga is attainment of this liberation. Behanan described this goal as "release from the chain of existence" and as gratification of a "deep yearning for passivity."

Behanan noted that Freud initially proposed the existence of instincts concerned only with sex and self-worth, or protection of the ego. Then, after the horrors of the Great War, he introduced the death instinct. Some of Freud's followers claimed that the death instinct had no significance in clinical work. Others said it was a discovery of cardinal importance for the development of psychoanalysis.

The second difference between Freud's psychoanalysis and yoga, according to Behanan, was the greater profundity of yoga. He wrote,

"… therapeutic similarities exist between psychoanalysis and only the earlier phases of yoga. The higher stages of yoga are reached by psychophysical and mental exercises for which psychoanalysis has no parallel. Freud's 'depth-psychology' would not be considered deep enough by yoga."

Fred feared that a discussion with Behanan might not be productive. Behanan would want to argue for yoga's superior concept of mind, consciousness, and the unconscious. Fred might well respond in a way that Behanan could consider unkind. Fred would say that whether one or the other concept of mind is better is of little importance in figuring out why people do what they do. Only two factors matter: what a person has inherited, and his or her interactions with the environment since birth or even in the womb. There might have been unrecalled happenings in early childhood that contribute to current behavior. There might even have been happenings in the history of the human species that so contribute, through books, oral traditions, and other cultural features. But surely, if current behavior is to be changed, the current environment – which sustains most current behavior – offers the best opportunities?

There's no doubt that people engage in covert or private behavior – and experience private stimuli and events – that cannot be observed by others. Fred himself was doing it now: he was talking to himself inaudibly. He was experiencing words and images that no one else could directly experience. Acknowledging the existence of such covert behavior and private events is one thing. Concluding that they are part of a mysterious and powerful entity called mind is something else. Fred surmised that better understanding would reveal that overt behavior and covert behavior have only a frail relationship to each other. What people do is determined mostly by their interactions with the environment and only a little by their private events. Indeed, what people think might be as much determined by what they do as what they do might be caused by what they think.

Fred was consoled by the thought that a discussion with Behanan could at least provide the challenge of addressing these issues more clearly. And the discussion might cast light on how yoga practitioners can achieve such exquisite control over their bodies. He noted that the book's final chapter might provide some assessment of this control. He resolved to read it before tomorrow afternoon.

A steward told Fred there would be welcoming cocktails for Cabin Class passengers before the second sitting of dinner. The event was to be in the lounge and smoking room from six-thirty onward. Could Fred leave soon because the space must be prepared?

*   *   *

At the cocktail event, Fred found the first crowd he'd seen on the ship. How did all these passengers know about the event? He may have missed an announcement. If he'd not stayed on the promenade deck to read Behanan's book he might not have known about it.

He looked for Behanan and for the two ladies in the yoga class. Sophie was the mother's name, Anna the daughter's, but he couldn't remember their last name. Grayson? He didn't see them, but noted that nearly all the men were more formally dressed than he was. Most wore tuxedos. Some had more elaborate attire, associated with military or diplomatic service. Many wore medals. Most women wore evening gowns, often colorful. He felt out of place and quickly resorted to the bar for the comfort of a vodka and tonic.

When Fred was in Europe before, he'd carried his tuxedo every-where but wore it only during the return voyage with his parents, when they'd all traveled first class. The travel agent had said that because the *Duchess* didn't have a first class, a tuxedo wouldn't be required. The vodka was making him feel less out of place.

As he looked for someone to make conversation with, Fred saw an exodus, mainly of men, to the outside promenade. He followed and joined a group gazing at a magnificent cantilever bridge spanning the river a few miles ahead. The *Duchess of York* was reducing speed and finding the center line between the river's two banks, which now seemed a mile apart. The river narrowed as the bridge was approached, but was still over half a mile wide at the crossing point. The ship headed for the center point of the bridge's huge span, now moving at little more than a walking pace. The bridge nevertheless loomed too quickly for Fred's comfort, given how little space there was below the span's elaborate ironwork. He estimated that the ship's two funnels would fit under the bridge but wondered about the taller masts. Then the ship was under the bridge. The top of the front mast passed no more than few feet below the structure. Fred looked behind and saw the rear mast doing the same.

The crowd on the deck cheered. A man said to Fred, "Captain Richardson was taking a risk, going under the Quebec Bridge at high tide. The water level here rises by as much as fifteen feet, leaving hardly enough clearance for these *Duchesses*. There's talk of putting hinges on the masts, but the engineers are against it because they will be less able to stand up to heavy mid-Atlantic weather."

Fred was only half listening because he'd noticed that the bridge itself, now a few hundred yards behind them, was a place of considerable activity. A long passenger train was moving across it from south to north, silhouetted against a setting sun. Streetcars were moving in the other direction as were several automobiles and trucks. Many pedestrians and cyclists were using the bridge. Several people were leaning on the safety railing, watching the fast-receding liner.

He turned to his neighbor after what might have been an impolitely long delay and said, "That is all very interesting. May I ask how you come to be so well informed?" The neighbor appeared to be in his sixties, slightly corpulent, and neatly dressed although also wearing only a business suit.

"I used to work on these ships as an engineer, but I had to stop because of ill-health. Now I have a shore job, and travel only as a passenger. I never want to miss the sight of the Quebec Bridge. It's one of the world's engineering marvels. Nearly a hundred workmen died during its construction and during the aborted construction of a predecessor. There's still a whole collapsed central span at the bottom of the river. Turn around and look forward and you'll see another splendid sight."

Fred turned and saw above the steep left bank what must be the City of Quebec. First were several well-maintained fortifications. Beyond was an extraordinary structure that combined elements of a castle, a hotel, and a railroad station. Several upper windows caught the light of the setting sun that could no longer be seen from the ship.

"That's the Chateau Frontenac," his neighbor offered, "said to be the most photographed building in the world. My name is Samuel Brown, by the way, brought up in Scotland as you can probably hear, but resident in Montreal for more than half my life."

"I'm Fred Skinner, very much an American, living in Minneapolis and on my way to London."

"Ah! You must be the Professor Skinner who'll be dining at the captain's table. I'm glad you too are not dressed to the nines. Do you use that phrase in America?"

"Yes, we do. How do you know I am to be at the captain's table? How did most of the people here and inside know about this event?"

Brown answered the first question, "Very simple. I'm to sit there too. I asked the chief steward who else would be at the table. The captain usually humors me by including me once when I travel on his ship. Ginger Dick – as he's often called by his friends and, not to his face, by his subordinates – and I have a history together. His previous command was another Canadian Pacific ship, *Montrose*. I was the chief engineer."

Fred said, "Shall we go inside? It's quite chilly."

"Let's do one round of the promenade deck, and you'll see something more that may interest you."

"OK." They began walking and Fred said, "Tell me how a captain and his chief engineer get on."

"We got on well. As often happens, I had more seniority in the company than he did, and was paid more. This can be a source of friction because a ship's master is in charge and is always responsible. Had I been less senior when I had my heart problem I might have been allowed to continue as an engineer, but I was too expensive for the company. Now I work less and am paid much less."

Fred reflected that people talked to him more in Canada than he was used to at home. Was it because he was a stranger, a traveler, an American – or was it something that Canadians did?

Brown steered them to the side of the ship and pointed down to the water. The ship had stopped. Anchors were being dropped. He said, "This is the only stop on the way to Glasgow – more precisely to Greenock, a little farther west on the River Clyde."

The ship was close to the shore at Quebec City, just past the Chateau Frontenac. Two motor boats had already tied up to the ship's side delivering a few dozen more passengers and their baggage.

"Over there where the cranes are," said Brown, "you'll see the *Empress of Australia*, the CP ship that brought the King and Queen to Canada. They arrived two days late because of ice and fog"

"Och, what's gonnae oan?" Brown's Scots background showed through. He pointed at a small boat speeding away from the *Duchess of York* around the end of the jetty that sheltered the *Empress of Australia*. "I'm guessing that Ginger Dick has gone to say hello to the *Empress's* captain. I believe he's Archie Meikle, one of the princes of our fleet. Our captain may want a face-to-face account of the reasons for the delay." Brown had quickly reverted to more comprehensible English. "Expecting difficulties, they'd allowed two extra days for the crossing, but they were held up for almost four days."

The small speedboat returned some fifteen minutes later. The deafening horn sounded for several seconds, the motorboats moved away, the anchors were raised, and the *Duchess of York* resumed its stately progress down the St. Lawrence River towards the Atlantic.

The two men went inside and made for the bar. Fred had another vodka and tonic, Brown a scotch with a little water.

Brown said, "You are wise to travel via Montreal rather than New York or Boston. The journey is usually shorter by a day. It's probably less expensive, and certainly more beautiful."

"That is all true, Mr. Brown, and I'm also becoming more aware of the complex country to our north, about which I knew very little."

"There's no more complex part of this country than where I live. Montreal is English and Protestant at the top and French and Catholic at the bottom, at least in business and culture. Politics is another matter. It's French and Catholic through and through. Montreal's City Hall is a French-speaking place, as is the Legislative Assembly here in Quebec City – equivalent to your state legislatures."

"I've heard that the province of Quebec – Montreal in particular – is quite a liberal place compared with the rest of Canada and much of the United States?" ventured Fred.

"I haven't travelled that much in Canada and America, but I do believe you're correct as far as the consumption of alcoholic beverages is concerned. You might say it's a Gallic attitude, although the preference here is for beer. Roman Catholic priests don't get upset about drinking. They do much of it themselves. Occasional or even frequent excess can be forgiven in the confessional."

Fred said, "I take it the Catholic Church is strong here. Every town and village I've seen from this ship is dominated by a steeple."

"It's far deeper than that." Brown's rolling of his Rs at the end of "far" and "deeper" was appealing. "In many respects, the Roman Catholic hierarchy rules this province. There's another, odd way in which Quebec is liberal, in its federal politics. Quebec provides the solid core of the Liberal Party in Ottawa, which is similar to your

Democratic Party. But, there's a right-wing party in charge here at the provincial capital, the Union Nationale. In spite of its name, this provincial government is very much against trade unions. It spends as little as possible on social services. It's for farmers and the Church. Priests reward this support by telling their congregations that heaven is blue, the Union Nationale's color, and hell is red, the Liberals' color."

They stood by the one of the lounge's windows and saw that the ship was now well under way. It was passing to the right of a large, intensively cultivated island, beautiful in the evening light. "If you look over there," Brown says, pointing across the island and behind the ship, "you can make out the towers of the splendid new suspension bridge that links this Île d'Orléans to the mainland."

"They stand out well against the evening sky," said Fred. "Tell me, Mr. Brown, what happens next on this voyage?"

"We sail for almost two more days, some eight hundred miles, until we reach the Atlantic Ocean. We'll be seeing land for most of the two days – unless there's fog – but less and less evidence of man's work on the land. We'll meet the ocean north or south of the huge island of Newfoundland. It's not part of Canada but some kind of colony of Britain governed directly from London. Then we'll be roughly a third of the way through our journey. When we get to the ocean, perhaps before, you'll likely see one or another of two magnificent sights, even both of them: icebergs and whales. There are said to be a couple of dozen different kinds of whale there."

Brown added, "I expect Ginger Dick was advised by Archie Meikle to take the longer, southern route. This could add up to half a day to our voyage, although if the wind is with us and the ship's engines work well we'll make up the time. When we've passed Île d'Orléans the ship's speed is no longer limited to fifteen knots," Brown continued "We'll sail farther from fragile shorelines at our usual speed of eighteen knots, or even faster."

Fred was about to ask for a conversion of knots into miles per hour when a man in uniform rang a hand bell and asked for quiet. "The chief steward," whispered Brown. The man announced that dinner was to be served in a few minutes. Ladies and gentlemen were asked to make their way down to the dining saloon on Deck C.

The chief steward continued, "This may be a lot to ask after your refreshments but could you use the lift – the elevator – only if absolutely necessary. Then passengers who really need it will not be late for dinner. If you don't yet know where you are sitting, please consult the plan at the entrance to the dining saloon."

Fred Skinner and Samuel Brown made for the stairs. They pushed gently through the growing crowd of grumbling, jostling passengers waiting for the elevator. Brown said, "They'll realize quickly that it's much better to walk down the three flights, even if some of the ladies'll have to gather up their gowns."

"By the way," Brown continued as they walked down the stairs, "I think you may have wanted to know about knots. A knot is one nautical mile per hour. A nautical mile is just over six thousand feet, about fifteen percent longer than an ordinary mile. Thus, this ship's usual speed is about twenty-one miles per hour."

"Why do mariners use nautical miles? They must add to the confusion that already exists between regular miles and kilometers?"

"A nautical mile is one minute of arc – a sixtieth of a degree latitude – measured along any line of longitude. On a chart degrees latitude are all sixty nautical miles apart."

As they reached the dining saloon, Fred said, "You're a real mine of information, Mr. Brown. I'm glad we had the opportunity to talk."

"Thank you for that. Please call me Samuel. Most people do."

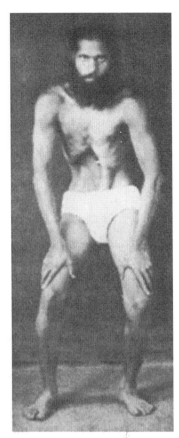

ISOLATION OF THE RIGHT AND LEFT
RECTUS ABDOMINUS

A pair of illustrations from Kovoor T. Behanan's *Yoga: A Scientific Evaluation* (New York, Macmillan, 1937).

EIGHT

Praising Hitler

On the *Duchess of York*, Friday May 19, 1939

T he dining saloon had been transformed since Fred was there for lunch. What had seemed then to be a utilitarian eating area had become a warm, inviting place. It was formal and elegant yet cozy and intimate, even when set for a few hundred people. The effect, Fred noted, was achieved with soft lighting and sparkling tableware. It was helped by a piano and string quintet that played versions of popular orchestral music barely audible above the chatter of the diners as they introduced themselves. The formal suits and dresses of almost everyone present added to the elegance.

Fred felt out of place in his business suit, yet he approached the captain's table with a light step. The plan at the entrance had shown that Sophie and Anna Graydon were also to be two of the captain's guests. Fred is to sit next to Anna and almost opposite Sophie. He might have preferred to sit next to the mother, but the daughter could be a good second-best. He recognized none of the other names of the captain's guests, apart from Samuel Brown, who was now chatting with the captain, both standing by the table.

Brown introduced Fred to Captain Richardson, whose graying red hair and beard were the obvious prompts for his nickname Ginger Dick. The Captain introduced Fred to the other guests at his table. Sophie and Anna Graydon were still to arrive. Fred made a point of remembering the name of the elderly woman to his right, between him and the captain. He then noticed a name card at each place setting. His read, "Professor B.F. Skinner." Hers read, "The Hon. Mrs. George MacDonald."

The quintet made a concluding flourish. The chief steward called for quiet. When it was mostly achieved, he introduced himself and welcomed the cabin class passengers to the ship on behalf of Captain Charles Richardson, who waved his hand in acknowledgement. The chief steward asked all to be seated for grace, to be recited by the Reverend Andrew Anderson.

A fierce-looking man wearing a clerical collar rose some tables away. He was short, but his voice was deep and loud. He intoned with what seemed to Fred to be a touch of anger, "Some hae meat and cannae eat. Some nae meat but want it. We hae meat and we can eat and sae the Lord be thankit."

Fred understood almost none of what was said. Mrs. MacDonald pointed at a slip of paper by his name card bearing the words just said. They came with a translation into regular English and a note on their presumed author, Robert Burns.

The Reverend sat noisily and conversation began gradually. Mrs. MacDonald said to Fred, "You're going to hear the grace at every dinner. You'll know it by the time we get to Scotland. It's the Captain's way of adding a little Scots flavor to our proceedings."

"Are you from Scotland?" Fred asked her.

"No, the name is my husband's. I'm originally Dolly Brown, as English as can be, although Brown seems a popular name on both sides of the border. If you'll forgive me, I must say a word to the Captain. I know he'll be leaving the table soon. He always does."

She said something to Captain Richardson, who listened with evident attention. The Captain then stood to welcome the two Graydon women, introducing them to the other table guests. Sophie Graydon offered apologies. Fred helped the daughter into her chair. Her ungracious manner suggested she'd been the cause of the lateness.

The men sat back down. Mrs. MacDonald resumed talking to the captain. Fred rehearsed to himself a few ways of opening a conversation with the young woman to his left, but she spoke first. "I can't stand my mother. I'm nineteen and she treats me like I'm nine."

Fred said, "Isn't that little outburst more in the character of a nine-year-old than of a beautiful young lady poised to be an adult?"

"If you're trying to say that I behave like a nine-year-old and thus should expect to be treated like one, you may be right. But *she* makes me behave like that."

"This is going around in circles, and you may regret saying any of it anyway. Are you looking forward to going to Germany?"

Anna snapped back, "How do you know I'm going there?"

"Your yoga instructor told me. I had tea with him today."

"Dr. Behanan's still in love with my mother, and you mustn't believe a word he says about us, although we *are* going to Germany, and I'm much looking forward to it – so much, I may stay there."

Fred would have liked to question her about Behanan and her mother but said, "Dr. Behanan told me that your mother was originally from Germany. Do you have much family there?"

"Only my grandmother, in Bonn. Her two daughters, my mother and my aunt, live in Toronto. As far as I know, my grandmother was an only child and never remarried after my grandfather was killed in the war. I've not met her. This may be the only time I do, because she's old and because there could be another war."

"Aren't you worried about going to a country that could be the instigator of the next war?"

"Germany won't be the cause of a war. There'll be fighting only if another country does something to harm German people. Other countries are envious of the progress Germany is making."

Soup was served by waiters each balancing eight or more bowls on a large tray. The movement of the ship down the St. Lawrence River was hardly noticeable. Fred wondered about service on the open seas. He tried to recall his previous trip across the Atlantic. The young lady next to him was enjoyably articulate. Did her pro-German views come from her mother? He sipped a spoonful of the minestrone soup and asked, "What is it about German progress that appeals to you?"

"Everything. Other countries seem helpless and unfocused. Germany knows where she's going. My aunt says the government has made sure there's no unemployment in Germany. Most other countries are plagued by it. She says too that there's no crime, and nobody goes on strike because there's no need to. Things go so well in the Germany led by *Führer* Adolf Hitler that other countries have begged to join Germany."

A waiter offered wine and other beverages. Fred was surprised to see Anna Graydon ask for white wine. He saw her mother frown as the wine was poured. Fred looked at the bottle. It was a sauvignon blanc from France. He took some too, and reflected on what might be the legal drinking age in Canada, in Quebec, and on board a ship.

Anna Graydon was attacking the soup and crackers with enthusiasm. Her mood had changed. Her tone had become friendlier. It was now more adoring than petulant, adoring perhaps of the aunt, of Hitler or of Germany, or all of them. Fred was not sure.

Fred surmised that some of her bad mood might have been the result of hunger, but the young woman was clearly happy to be talking about Germany. He said, "That seems a rose-colored view. Many people don't share it, particularly the Jews in Germany and Austria who are treated like second-class citizens, or worse. And Czechoslovakia

97

didn't seem so keen on joining Germany."

"Jews are second-class citizens wherever they live. They should have their own homeland where they can be at the center of things rather than at the edge. The *Führer* has been trying to give them a homeland in Palestine, but they seem to prefer to be second-class citizens in America, Canada or England."

"How are they second-class citizens in America and Canada?"

"I just know that in Toronto Jews are seen as second-rate and not suitable for the best jobs or the best clubs. They keep to themselves."

Fred said, "Why can't they stay in Germany, even if they are regarded as second-class citizens?"

"My aunt, who's been back to Germany a few times, says they're not wanted in Germany. She says many Jews are communists who work against the best interests of Germany. Even worse, they breed with unsuspecting German men and women and weaken the Aryan race. She says too that many American Jews are international financiers who stir things up so that they can profit from trading in armaments and other things needed during a war."

They stopped talking to listen to the captain, who was offering his apologies to his table guests for leaving so early in the meal. Fred feared that Mrs. MacDonald would turn her attention to him, but she moved into the captain's seat and began talking to the woman on the other side of her. Across the table, Samuel Brown and Sophie Graydon were chatting with their heads quite close together. Fred was envious. He resolved to be gentle with the daughter in spite of the outrageous things she was saying.

Fred said, "Communists *and* international financiers. Jews seem pretty versatile."

"You are so right. They're clever and wicked."

"I've heard that Adolf Hitler may have a Jewish ancestor."

"How could you say such a thing? The *Führer* could not be such a great leader if his blood were contaminated in that way."

"But you have to agree he's far from the Aryan ideal. He's neither blond nor athletic."

"You're joking with me. The *Führer* is restoring Germany's greatness. Only a pure-blooded Aryan could do that."

Fred wondered whether the young woman had become a little unhinged by her dedication to Hitler and today's Germany. He asked, "Does your mother share the views that you and your aunt have about Hitler and what is happening in Germany?"

Before she could reply, one waiter cleared her soup plate and another asked whether she would be having the fish course. She replied that it's Friday and she must have only fish. She'll have the meatless pasta dish, *gnocchi alla Piemontese*, at the time of the meat course.

Fred looked at the menu and puzzled over both "broiled shad" and its French equivalent "*alose grillé*." He asked about it and was told that shad is a very flavorful kind of herring caught in Quebec's coastal rivers. They go there to breed in the spring. He opted for the shad, to be followed by stuffed shoulder of veal.

Another waiter offered more wine, which Anna Graydon took. Fred was not half way through his first glass. The mother appeared not to notice her daughter's glass being refilled.

The daughter said, "I've now forgotten what you asked me?"

"Whether your mother shares your views of Hitler and Germany."

"Oh no! She and my aunt have had many arguments. They speak in German and some of it is difficult to follow. It's what my aunt says during their fights that has convinced me of the *Führer's* greatness and the wonderful example he and Germany are providing."

"What does your mother say?"

"My mother says that Hitler and the Nazi Party are trampling on

99

people's rights and freedoms. She says they bring out the worst in the German people on matters such as race and foreigners. She says Hitler and the Nazis are leading Germany to disaster."

"How does your aunt respond?"

"My aunt says that Germany was and should still be the center of European culture, even world culture. In 1919, Germany was tricked into accepting the role of loser of the Great War. The country descended into a pit of hopelessness that lasted more than a decade. In only six years, Hitler has revived Germany, restored the country's confidence and made the world pay attention."

"But what about his methods: the cruelty to the Jews and others, the suppression of political opposition, the total domination of the country by the Nazi Party?"

"I don't know too much about his methods, but they must be needed to get things done. What I do know is that the *Führer* has made things a lot better for most Germans."

They paused while the fish course was served. Fred was entranced by her youth and intensity. She was giving him a sense of the Hitler's strong influence over young people. Fred couldn't figure out how this could happen. He feared he will have little to say in response to the questions Calvin Cooper has asked him. His doubts were interrupted by Mrs. MacDonald, who had moved back to her seat when another ship's officer took the captain's place at the table.

What Mrs. MacDonald was saying was overridden by the new officer, who announced himself to the table as the ship's chief engineer. Fred exchanged a nod with Samuel Brown in acknowledgement of their earlier discussion. He was pleased to see that Sophie Graydon was now turned away from Brown and was talking with the frail-looking man between her and her daughter. Fred turned to resume the discussion about Hitler, but he was sidetracked by Mrs. MacDonald, who insisted on knowing more about him.

Fred realized she was tipsy and hoped he was not. He said, "I'm a college professor in Minneapolis, in the psychology department."

"How very interesting! Are you one of these followers of Dr. Freud who believes that everything is to do with sex?"

She was both tipsy and flirtatious. Fred wondered how he could extricate himself. "I've heard of Dr. Freud, but I'm afraid his ideas haven't had much of an impact at the University of Minnesota. I do know what might be called a Freudian joke, which may appeal to you. Why is psychoanalysis a lot quicker for a man than a woman?"

Mrs. MacDonald spluttered a few times but said nothing. The question had made her speechless.

"When it's time to go back to childhood, a man is already there."

Mrs. MacDonald could still find nothing to say. She gave Fred a cold, lopsided smile and turned to the chief engineer.

Fred turned to see that the daughter's wineglass was being refilled again. He had more too.

He asked her, "What will you and your mother do in Germany, apart from visit your grandmother?"

"We will stay with her for two weeks. The plan is that we then re-turn to Canada. That's what my mother will do. She has her position at the university to return to. During the two weeks, I'll explore staying longer in Germany, perhaps forever."

"How will your mother feel about that?"

"She'll be annoyed, even angry, as she is about many things I do or want to do. But she can't stop me if the German government allows me to stay, and I feel sure they will."

"Are you not afraid of war?"

"You've asked me that. There won't be a war unless Germany is harmed. Then I'll be pleased to give the Fatherland any help I can."

"If there is a war, Canada and Germany could be on opposite sides. You'll be on one side and your mother, and the friends you must have in Toronto, will be on the other."

"Your logical arguments are not going to change my mind."

The plates were cleared, the wine glasses topped up or replaced, and the main course served. After a few mouthfuls, Fred asked about her gnocchi.

"It's pretty tasteless," she replied. "I think I've already had enough of it. I envy you your meat dish, but the Catholic Church doesn't permit me to eat meat on a Friday."

"Your mother's having the veal. Is she not Catholic too?"

"My mother has rejected the Church, just as she's rejected Germany and everything to do with her youth."

"But she's going to see her mother. She must have some positive feeling about her upbringing, isn't that so?"

"She's going out of a sense of duty. And her mother could be a little too old to be upset about what her daughter now thinks."

Fred noticed that her words had become a little slurred. 'Sense' sounded more like 'senth.' Even more, he noticed that she had moved closer to him and was lightly pressing her knee against his. As he wondered whether to move his leg, there was a commotion to his right. Mrs. MacDonald had stood up, grabbed her purse hanging over the back of her chair, and immediately fallen down.

Fred and the chief engineer helped the fallen woman to her feet. The chief steward arrived. He said a few words to her and escorted her out of the dining saloon, evidently supporting her.

As Fred resumed his seat, the daughter said, "I'd like to go back to my cabin too. Could you help me?"

Fred stood and she took his offered arm. Her mother arrived and began scolding her. "You were drinking wine as if it was water. Let me get you to bed." Although her accent was strong, Fred had no difficulty in understanding what she was saying.

The three walked to the exit where Mrs. Macdonald had just been escorted. Fred saw that Samuel Brown had moved into Mrs. MacDonald's seat and was talking with the chief engineer. Fred did not know whether to continue with the mother and daughter to their cabin. Neither spoke to him. He continued because he sensed that if he were no longer supporting the young woman she too would fall.

Their cabin, No. 118, was near Fred's. It was identical except that the bed had an upper bunk. The mother said to the daughter, "I suppose you'll now sleep on the lower bunk even though we agreed I would sleep there." She began undressing her as if Fred were not there. Fred cleared his throat and asked if he should leave. She said her first words to him, "No. I may need your help. Stay."

Fred averted his eyes while the mother undressed the daughter. She then dressed her in elegant pajamas and began to arrange her under the covers of the lower bunk. The daughter said her first words since they were in the dining saloon, "*Mutti*, I need to pee-pee."

"You can brush your teeth too," said the mother, "your breath smells like *eine schmutzige Toilette*."

Fred sat on the lower bunk while they left the cabin for the toilets. He stayed there while the mother helped the daughter brush her teeth at the basin in the cabin. He stood and helped put the daughter under the covers. She fell asleep immediately. Outside, Sophie Graydon said, "I don't want to go back to the dining saloon. Will you walk on the deck with me?"

"We'll need coats," Fred replied, and waited while she retrieved one from her cabin. She came into his cabin while he was fetching his coat. The recent intimacy of putting her daughter to bed and her presence in his cabin heightened her appeal.

They climbed the stairs to the boat deck. Outside, they could see nothing beyond the ship except stars in a dark sky and a very faint glow on the horizon where the sun had set more than an hour ago. There was no moon and there were no lights from other ships or from the river banks they were passing. They walked back to the head of the stairs. There, they figured out from the map that the ship should have just passed the northern tip of Île d'Orléans and entered a long stretch where the river was ten to twenty miles wide.

"Shall we go outside again?" said Fred.

"Maybe for a few minutes, if we can be sheltered from the wind." She asked Fred to tell her his name, which he did.

They found a position leaning on the deck rail, sheltered by one of the lifeboat supports. Fred put his arm around her, to shelter her more, he said. She did not resist. She seemed taller than he had thought she might be when she was on the floor in the gymnasium. Perhaps her evening wear included shoes with high heels.

He wondered if he should say something about her daughter, but was unsure what to say. He told her he had learned she came from Germany and was making a visit there. He asked if that was a wise thing to do when there was so much talk of another war.

"I am frightened to go, but feel I should see my mother one last time. I have not seen her since I left Europe twenty years ago, and she has never met my daughter."

"This may be a silly question, but what led you to leave for Canada at the end of the Great War?"

"You want to hear the story of my life?"

"Yes, please," said Fred.

"Here it is. I was born Sophie Bauer almost forty-one years ago in Bonn, Germany, where my mother still lives. In my teen-age years – is that the right expression? – I spent several summers as the guest of a French pen-friend – again, is that word correct? – and became quite fluent in the language. In 1917, I was assigned to work as a clerk in

104

Mons, a French-speaking part of Belgium then occupied by Germany. Two things happened. I became appalled by what we were doing to the Belgians and I fell in love with a young Belgian man. I quit my position early in 1918. I assumed the identity of a Belgian woman displaced by the turmoil of war, and found work on a nearby farm. The Canadians liberated Mons on the last day of the war. I was given a job processing German documents they had captured."

"Weren't the Canadians a little suspicious of you because you were German? Was your French good enough for a French Canadian to think you were a Belgium?"

"They did not know I was German, only that I spoke, read, and wrote German well, as do many Belgians brought up near the border with Germany. I had false Belgian identity papers and several Belgian friends who vouched for me. I'd been in Belgium for more than a year and spoke French well, with quite a good Belgian accent."

"Please continue with your fascinating history."

"A little later, I became involved with a Canadian soldier, Captain Arnold Graydon. We married because we wanted to and so that I could return with him to Canada. Arnold was a lawyer. He took over his father's law practice when he died in 1926. Arnold himself died in 1927 from injuries received in an automobile accident. Anna was only seven and did not take his death well. Arnold left us a house and enough money to live on while I completed my graduate studies in philosophy at the University of Toronto. I now have a minor teaching position in that department. That is my story."

"It must have been hard, dealing with your and Anna's bereavements, and bringing her up by herself."

"She has a wonderful grandmother – my mother-in-law – and, for the last seven years, my younger sister Freda, who joined us. We are four women, three generations, living happily together."

"Anna said that you and your sister argue a lot about Germany."

She had moved closer to Fred, but when Fred mentioned arguing about Germany she moved away a little.

"Anna was speaking out of turn. Freda and I do disagree about Herr Hitler and some of the things happening there, but our disagreements are not serious."

"Your sister seems to have had quite an influence on Anna. I may perhaps speak out of turn when I say that Anna has been so strongly persuaded by her aunt she is thinking of staying in Germany."

"What an absurd idea! She must be really angry with me to have said that to you." She paused and continued, "If I am going to talk with you about my daughter, first I want to know who you are. Remind me of your name, and tell me the story of your life."

"My name is Fred Skinner. Please call me Fred. My life has been uneventful compared with yours. I haven't experienced a war, nor moved to another country, nor changed the language I speak every day. I had a conventional upbringing in a small town in Pennsylvania, went to a small liberal arts college in upstate New York, and was then a graduate student at Harvard. Now I teach at the University of Minnesota. Your story is much more interesting."

She seemed satisfied by this account. She said, "I have never been to the United States, except across the Honeymoon Bridge at Niagara Falls, which I have heard exists no more. I have a limited understanding of the geography of your country. I do know that Harvard is in the Boston area, but not where Minnesota is. But, even if you are a geography professor, please do not tell me where it is. Do tell me what you teach and why you are on this ship."

"I'm in the psychology department. I'm interested in a wide range of topics that includes animal behavior and literature. I am going to England to meet a philosopher and a psychoanalyst."

Fred felt her move back close to him, perhaps more for shelter and warmth than for intimacy.

She said, "I am a philosopher, in a very modest way, and so I cannot help being interested in knowing whom you are to meet."

Fred explained that he had been invited to attend Wittgenstein's inauguration, adding that he hoped to meet Sigmund Freud.

She said, "I know little about Wittgenstein, except that he appears to have been influenced by the philosopher whose work has been my special study: Søren Kierkegaard."

"I'm afraid I don't recognize your philosopher."

"Perhaps that is because of my accent, or because I am influenced by the way his Danish countrymen say his name, which can make it completely unrecognizable to someone who does not speak Danish." She spelled out Kierkegaard's name.

"I'm afraid I still don't know who this man is. Is he still living? Could you summarize his contribution in one or two sentences?"

"You sound like a professor! My philosopher died nearly one hundred years ago. He has been called the father of what is known today as existentialism. If you do not know what that is, perhaps we could talk about it another time. I would be happy now to return to the more difficult subject of my daughter."

"It's becoming cold out here. Perhaps we could find a place to talk inside on the deck below."

They walked down the stairs. Fred still had his arm around her, but somehow they became disengaged as they reached the promenade deck. They walked through the gallery to the drawing and observation room, where Fred and Kovoor Behanan had had afternoon tea some hours earlier. They took off their coats and sat in a corner, but then she said she must go and check on Anna. Fred felt she would not return, but her coat was there and she did return several minutes later. She said that all was as well as could be, given the amount of wine Anna had drunk.

Fred asked if Anna drank alcohol often.

"I do not think so. But I am never quite sure what she does with her friends. We had the biggest argument of our lives just before dinner. She told me for the first time she might want to stay in Germany with my mother. I think the idea is absurd, and I am annoyed that my sister Freda has had so much influence on Anna. Freda often talks as though she would like to be back in Germany. Anna and I agreed that we would continue to discuss it during the voyage. But then she told you, which has also annoyed me. Don't take offense. You are innocently caught up in a family argument."

Fred said, "From what Anna was saying, and how she said it, I couldn't work out how much her notion of staying in Germany is to spite you and how much it results from admiration for what she believes is happening there."

"Forgive me, my English has become pretty good, but I do not understand 'spite.'"

"It means to deliberately annoy or hurt someone."

"Thank you. It is probably some of both, hurting me and admiration for the Nazis. She has certainly been influenced by Freda's rose-tinted view of what is happening in Germany."

"That's what I said to her. I told her that many people, inside and outside Germany, find conditions there to be harsh and cruel."

"Anna is the center of my life. Even though we are having a bad time just now, I do not want to be separated from her yet. I do not want her to become caught up in the terrible things that are happening in Germany and the even worse things that could happen if there is another war. I know about the horrors of war. I saw Germans do unspeakable things to Belgian civilians during the Great War. Under the Nazis, the atrocities will know no limit. What can I do to bring Anna to her senses?"

"Perhaps when she sees Germany for herself, she'll not want to stay. Couldn't your mother help persuade her to return to Canada?"

"My mother may do the opposite. She is lonely. She would like to have a granddaughter living with her for more than two weeks. And, like many of her generation, she is a supporter of the Nazis."

"Why is that?"

"Older people remember the glory of Germany before the Great War. They respond well to the arguments that take up nine-tenths of Hitler's speeches. He says that Germany was tricked into being seen as the Great War's loser and has been held back since by the so-called victors. The older people also respond well to the remaining tenth: that the Nazis are restoring Germany's greatness and will do so even more."

"I am enjoying talking with you," she continued, "but I should go back to my cabin – in case Anna wakes up and needs my help."

They gathered their coats and walked back through the gallery to the stairs. The door to the lounge was open as they passed. They heard music, glanced inside, and saw a few couples dancing. They were accompanied by the band that had been in the dining saloon.

"Shall we have one dance?" she said.

"I'll be delighted," said Fred. "We can leave our coats here for a few minutes," he added, pointing to a chair opposite the stairs down to the decks below.

Inside, the band had stopped. Its leader was saying that on other nights the dancing would continue for longer but for tonight it was time to have the last waltz. They joined the few couples on the floor.

As the band began playing, they assumed the conventional almost arm's-length positions of practiced dancers and launched into a spirited waltz, whirling around the other couples. Fred pulled her closer and murmured, "Roses from the South?" She murmured back, "*Rosen aus dem Süden*," reminding Fred that this was a Viennese waltz, probably by one of the Strausses.

She stayed close to Fred, who was beginning to be aroused by her soft warmth. The tightness of his underpants forced his erection straight ahead. To avoid embarrassing contact, he made what he hoped was an inconspicuous adjustment so that his penis pointed upwards. After another minute or so of slower and slower dancing, she moved closer. Fred felt what must be the top of her pubic bone pushing into the base of his now much engorged penis. He looked at her quizzically, but her face was in his shoulder. Fred had an almost irrelevant thought: did she share his preference for using proper names for body parts – penis instead of schlong, dong, willy or whanger – or did she have her own words or none at all?

More minutes passed. Then, with a drum roll and flourish, the band stopped playing. They remained close while the band leader bade them all goodnight. Fred made to turn her head so that he could kiss her, but she stepped back, looked at him, and said, "Another time. I must go back to my cabin."

They did kiss fleetingly at the door of her cabin. Some minutes later, Fred was falling asleep imagining that her body was still against his, thinking that he would like nothing more than for her to be with him in his narrow bed. He woke during the night and became quite alert contrasting her warmth with Yvonne's recent coldness. To avoid dwelling on this, he began to go over the long day that had passed, and fell asleep again before his review had reached Montreal.

Black and white version of a color illustration for the cover
of the *Duchesses'* passenger lists in the 1930s.

NINE

Foot Inspection

On the *Duchess of York*, Saturday May 20, 1939

Fred woke wondering what Julie did each morning at Yvonne's parents' house. In Minneapolis, she and he had breakfast together on weekdays, Julie in her high chair pulled close to Fred. He read the *Minneapolis Tribune*, often sharing choice bits with Julie. She was otherwise content to play with and eat her Pablum and apple slices, occasionally saying things to herself or to Fred. Then they woke Yvonne with a cup of coffee. Julie stayed with Yvonne while Fred left for the office.

There was a knock on the cabin door. Fred put on the light above the bed and looked at his watch, which said seven thirty. Jean-Paul entered and told him that the official time on the ship was eight thirty because this was one of the five days of the voyage on which the time was advanced by an hour. He reminded Fred that service for the sole breakfast sitting ended at nine o'clock. He'd brought coffee (because Fred is American) and biscuits, which he pronounced "biskwee," which Fred remembered as the British – and perhaps the Canadian – word for cookies.

He thanked Jean-Paul and said he would skip breakfast today.

Jean-Paul said that tea, coffee and some little things to eat would be available in the lounge on the promenade deck at ten thirty. Fred drank some coffee and ate one of the cookies. He set his watch forward by an hour and went back to sleep. He woke hungry at ten fifteen, quickly shaved, showered, and dressed, and headed upstairs.

Kovoor Behanan was in the lounge. He could have been waiting for Fred. "Shall we take our refreshments outside?" Behanan said, "It will be quite pleasant if we are out of the wind."

Outside on the promenade deck they were sheltered a little by the boat deck above. They had to decide whether to sit on the sunny side and not see nearby land or sit in the shade and see the sunlit shore of the St. Lawrence a few miles to the northwest. They chose the sunny side, and accepted the offer of blankets by the steward who brought them coffee and pastries.

"This is blissful," said Fred, waving at the refreshments, the sun on the waves, and the forested south shore of the St. Lawrence, perhaps twenty miles away. "To add to my enjoyment, please tell me how yoga helps one do things that people cannot usually do. I'm thinking in particular of the photos in your book of a man flexing his left and right abdominal muscles, separately."

"I cannot do that very well, and this is not the place to expose my abdomen. But perhaps I could illustrate what you might call 'another little trick,' one that you may be unable to perform."

Behanan removed his shoes and socks, placed his feet flat on the deck, and began to move his toes in what for Fred were remarkable ways. He could move each foot's big toe and little toe quite independently of each other and of the three toes between. The big toes moved up, down, and sideways. Behanan could also move each set of middle toes together without moving the adjacent big and little toes. His brown toes were long and sinuous, as well as being unusually hairy. They were clearly toes, but they seemed to have some of the dexterity of fingers.

"I do not want to embarrass you or otherwise discomfort you," said Behanan, "but would you mind removing your shoes and socks so that I can show you something?"

Fred disliked being undignified. With much misgiving, he succumbed to his curiosity as to what might happen Compared with those of Behanan, his feet seemed cast from stone and about as immovable. Hairy toes were one of the few features the four feet had in common. Fred's dark tufts seemed stuck on his pallid protuberances. Behanan's almost stylish whorls of hair seemed natural accompaniments to his elegant brown extremities.

Fred's examination of the four feet was interrupted by Behanan's request that Fred raise first one then the other of his big toes while leaving the remaining toes on the deck. Behanan demonstrated by moving each big toe up quite far without a hint of movement of his other toes. Fred could not raise either big toe even a small amount without also raising all four neighboring toes. If he raised a big toe as high as possible, the other toes on the foot moved up almost as far.

"What's your secret?" said Fred.

"Nothing more than many hours of practice," replied Behanan. "You learned as a young child to move your fingers separately, which you could not do at first. I learned as well to be dexterous with my toes. I am from a culture in which feet are more than devices for support and locomotion. In India, feet are less often entombed in shoes than in America. There, it is not uncommon to see a man use his foot to transfer an object from floor to hand, or vice versa."

Behanan demonstrated by catching one of his socks between the toes of one foot and, with a mild flourish, putting the sock in his lap.

Fred moved the fingers of each hand up and down, one by one. In contrast to his lumpish toes, his fingers seemed agile and eminently controllable. Hours of practice at the piano and saxophone had probably helped. But he could not figure out how he achieved the control. Nor could he see how he could acquire the ability to move toes inde-

114

pendently. If his toes always moved together, repeating the movement hundreds of times would not necessarily help him to move them separately.

Behanan said, "Even with hours of practice, we cannot achieve as much dexterity with our toes as we have with our fingers. Two factors seem important. One is obvious: our toes are shorter and thus have a potentially smaller range of movement in relation to each other. The other is less obvious: toes seem to share nerves or muscles or tendons in a way that fingers do not. I have tried for years, but I cannot move either middle toe independently of the toes on either side of it. Look at what happens."

Fred looked again at Behanan's elegant feet. The three middle toes were rising and falling, first one foot then the other.

"Also," Behanan said, "I can move my little toes almost but not quite independently of their neighbors, whereas my big toes move quite independently."

Behanan's little toes seemed as long as Fred's big toes. Fred watched as the man's little toes were alternately raised and let fall, now noting that in each case that the next toe moved just a little along with it. Behanan then moved his big toes up and down with no evident movement of other toes.

Both men's bare feet were suddenly in the shade.

"My, my, what *is* going on here?" Fred looked up to see Samuel Brown flanked by Sophie and Anna Graydon. "I beg the pardon of you gentlemen," Brown continued, "but would not a cabin or the sick bay be a more appropriate setting for a foot inspection?"

"Mr. Brown is joking of course," said Sophie Graydon. She introduced Behanan to Brown, explaining how the others had met Behanan before. She and Anna had just met Mr. Brown again while walking around the deck.

Fred remembered the envy he'd felt seeing Sophie chat with

Brown at dinner, envy now sharpened by what might be jealousy. Anna seemed sulky again, but she could have been hung over.

Behanan began putting on his socks and shoes. "Professor Skinner is interested in how control is achieved over parts of the body. I was showing him what was possible, using my toes, and was about to explain how control might be achieved. I am hoping to recruit him to our yoga classes, where we will be exploring some of these matters. Would you be interested in attending the class, Mr. Brown?"

"Thanks for asking me. I think I must decline your kind invitation. I've been quite unwell and my doctor in Montreal has said I must not take on anything more without consulting him. Indeed, he advised me against making this trip to Scotland."

Fred had feared that Brown would agree to participate, meaning that he might also have to be there. He hid his relief by busying himself with replacing his socks and shoes. He wondered whether Brown's infirmity might make him less or more of a rival for Sophie Graydon's attention.

Anna said, "I'm getting cold standing here. Can we move on?"

"Let us all walk together," said Sophie.

"I think I need to sit down," said Brown, "and if Dr. Behanan would care to stay, I'd be interested in learning more about this business of yoga."

"I will be delighted," said Behanan, "and perhaps I will be able to help you understand that yoga has restorative properties that could be of benefit to you."

"By the way," said Brown, "have you noticed that while we've been talking the ship has been changing course towards the south east? This means we'll be going south of Anticosti Island, which you should soon be able to see ahead or from the port side of the ship. It's a big island, about ten by thirty miles. It's technically part of Quebec and almost uninhabited. There've been rumors that the Germans have their eye on it as a potential submarine refueling station."

"Why are we changing course?" asked Fred.

"I imagine we were to go by the more direct route through the Strait of Belle Isle, north of Newfoundland. I imagine too that the advice of the captain of the *Empress of Australia*, and continuing reports of heavy fog and icebergs, have led our Captain Richardson to go south of Newfoundland. It's a few hundred miles farther, but we're less likely to be held up. He'll be able to speed up across the Atlantic and keep to our scheduled arrival time on Friday morning."

"Thank you, Samuel Brown," said Fred, "you always provide such useful information."

Sophie, Anna, and Fred took their leave and began walking around the deck. Fred had felt brief excitement and fear at the mention of possible preparations for war, but his main sentiment now was delight at walking alone with Sophie and Anna. On reaching the other side of the ship, away from the sun, Anna said, "I'm not getting any warmer. Could you take me back to the cabin?"

"I'll take you," said Sophie, "but then I think I'll continue walking for a while. Please excuse me, Professor Skinner."

"By all means," replied Fred. He waited at the stairs down to the cabins. After a few minutes, he sat on the sofa facing the elevator, regretting he had brought nothing to read. After thirty minutes, he concluded that she would likely not return and resolved to wait no more than another minute. Just then he saw Behanan and Brown navigate the door from the deck. Fred ran quickly down the stairs to avoid explaining why he was waiting there. In his cabin he felt it was time to write another letter to Fred Keller.

Dear Fred,

This is another letter that you're not likely to receive. Like the first one I wrote during this trip, it will do me a world of good to write it.

117

A passenger on this ship is a Dr. Kovoor Behanan, a man from India with a Ph.D. from Yale. His thesis has become a book Yoga: A Scientific Evaluation. *He's given me a copy. It set me thinking about how control is achieved over the various parts of our bodies that are controllable.*

Behanan is a yoga practitioner and instructor. Perhaps like all yoga practitioners he has more control over his body than I have. Today, if you can believe it, we were outside on a deck examining each other's toes. Some of his toes can be moved independently. None of mine can. If I move one the others all move too. He says it's a matter of practice.

So far, I can't figure out what the practice involves. However much I wiggle my toes, they move together. Each toe seems firmly linked to it neighbors. I wish Julie were here, for this and many other reasons. If she can wiggle her toes separately I could conclude it's a skill I've lost. If she can't, I might be able to train her to do so. How would I train her? I'd use the method of successive approximations that got Pliny the rat to perform his complicated sequence of behavior.

You'll remember from the work with Pliny that I was able to use the delivery of a marble as a reinforcer, once the marble had become a signal for occasional delivery of a food pellet. The marble became a "conditioned reinforcing stimulus." It wouldn't have to be a marble. I could use a token she could put into a machine that sometimes delivered candy (rather like the contraptions at railroad stations that sometimes deliver a chocolate bar when you put in a nickel).

Maybe I could get away from the candy altogether. I've noticed that she likes to operate the light switch when I carry her into a room. Light onset could be a reinforcer. If so, I could operate a lamp switch when she moved her toes, then when she moved a big toe. If that worked I'd flash the lamp when she moved a big toe with progressively less movement of other toes. And if

118

that worked, we might get to no movement of other toes. If for some reason, the light onset stopped being a reinforcer, I could perhaps restore its effectiveness of by – in a separate procedure – flashing the lamp on just before I gave her a candy, or sometimes gave her a candy.

You might well ask why not just tell her what you want her to do and give her a candy (or a big hug) when she does it. This could work, but a positive result would beg the question as to how she did it. I could be back with the problem I started with, which is how I could acquire control over my toes. I can't just tell myself to move them independently.

I look at my toes as they move and see that sometimes they move with more independence. This gives me some satisfaction. There's no lasting gain and so the satisfaction doesn't appear to reinforce the independent movement. My toes continue to seem as much tied together as before.

It could be that stimuli other than visual stimuli are more important for this kind of muscular control. I can move my fingers independently. You probably can too. Moving them with my eyes shut seems to be a more intimate experience than moving them when I am looking at them. When my eyes are shut I can sense the position of each finger. This is presumably the action of sensory nerves in my fingers or in the muscles or tendons involved in moving my fingers.

My big problem is figuring out how the analysis set out in The Behavior of Organisms *can be applied to the differentiation of my toe movements so that one toe can move independently of the others. I need to figure out what can reinforce such independence and which stimuli – perhaps generated internally – are associated with the reinforcement.*

Two things may be important. Behanan cannot wiggle every toe independently, only his big and little toes. The three in the middle of each foot seem incapable of independent movement. He may not have practiced moving these toes enough. More likely they share muscles or tendons or nerves. Fingers, which we can move separately, may all be served by separate nerves.

The availability of musculature and associated organs, notably nerves, obviously sets limits on what can be achieved through reinforcement. In the same way, there are constraints on what can be achieved through selective breeding. Chimpanzees seem smart enough to speak. But they may lack important elements of vocal musculature that make it possible for the fine-grained control that speech requires.

Another important thing for controlling toes could lie in something that Behanan said. In India, shoes are worn much less than in America. It's not uncommon to see a man use his foot to transfer an object from floor to hand and even mouth, and vice versa. Perhaps experience of successful gripping and re-location of an object using one's toes is required for development of independent toe movement. This possibility adds what may be a more substantial opportunity to apply my analysis. You'll be able to figure out how to do it.

Your friend,

Burrhus

Fred felt famished. He realized he had hardly eaten since the interrupted dinner yesterday evening. He'd been so engrossed in writing this short but difficult letter he'd almost missed lunch. He ran down to the dining saloon and arrived just in time to see Sophie and Anna Graydon leaving with Samuel Brown and Kovoor Behanan. Brown was telling a story that the others were intent on. None of the four noticed Fred as he was directed to a table for six that appeared to have been unused for lunch so far. This was his allocated table for the voyage. He resolved to change it if he could. Most of the other passengers in the saloon seemed to be leaving or about to leave. He was to eat alone and, in his haste, had brought nothing to read.

Fred felt in low spirits. He wondered yet again why he had agreed to make this trip. Being on board this ship was pleasant enough, but it provided small compensation for absenting himself from his life in Minneapolis. His feeling of dejection reminded him of his dark year after receiving his B.A. from Hamilton College, when he tried fruitlessly to write a novel – a period that had ended with his previous trip to Europe. So far during *this* trip, he'd made little progress with preparations for his possible encounters with Freud and Wittgenstein. He'd made little progress toward answering Calvin Cooper's questions. He'd expected that a change in environment and meeting new people would be intellectually refreshing. He'd been expecting too much.

The compensations were Sophie Graydon – although she might have been avoiding him – and the excitement of exploring the parallel between reinforcement and natural selection. Even this excitement was being dulled by the possibility that natural selection was being tainted by some of the appalling things happening in Europe. He needed to work out whether embracing natural selection implied support for Hitler's cruel program or opposition to it, or neither. Could natural selection as a scientific matter be reasonably seen as being unrelated to the politics of the day?

Postcard image of a blue whale on its back outside a whale oil factory on St. Pierre early in the twentieth century. Note the size of the whale in relation to the worker standing near its mouth.

TEN

Freedom and Free Will

On the *Duchess of York*, Sunday May 21, 1939

After breakfast, Fred was leaning on the port-side rail at the edge of the boat deck, half listening to Behanan and Brown banter beside him about yoga and healing. More of his attention was on the passing show of land and water. He'd now remembered how during his previous trip he'd figured out which side was port and which was starboard: L (left) came before R in the alphabet and P (port) came before S. He remembered too that "the passing show" was a favorite phrase of his Harvard philosopher friend Willard Van Orman Quine. Why Van used it so much he couldn't remember.

The passing show was indeed captivating. In bright sunshine but cool air, the *Duchess of York* moved along the south coast of Newfoundland through gray, occasionally breaking waves. The ship had been moving away from land that had no sign of habitation. It was now passing inhabited islands at the end of a long peninsula. At the shore, occasional clumps of ice sparkled in the sunlight.

Behanan, on the other side of Brown, had been doing much of the talking, but Brown intervened in a way that now included Fred. "Those islands – Miquelon on the left and St. Pierre – are part of France, the remnant of her North American empire. I wouldn't be surprised to learn that the Germans have shown interest in them as well as in Anticosti Island. I've not been to these islands. I've heard they are very French – French as in France, not Quebec – even more than Newfoundland is British."

Fred said, "I can see houses on the island to the right, but I can't figure out how close that island is to the mainland peninsula."

"It's about ten miles as the crow flies from St. Pierre to the end of the Burin Peninsula. You can't see the town of St. Pierre from here. It's on the east side. You'll see it when we're past the island."

"Gosh!" Fred exclaimed, "Look at that! It must be a whale." A huge creature had broken the surface less than half a mile away.

"It's a blue whale," said Brown. "They're said to be the largest animals alive, up to a hundred feet long." He scrutinized the whale and continued, "This one seems to be half that or more. For all their size, they live on krill – small shrimp-like creatures – which are plentiful near this coast."

The whale let out a fountain of spray from its blowhole, upped its huge tail and dove out of sight. A minute later, it surfaced close to the *Duchess of York* and swam alongside, a little ahead of where the three men were standing. Fred wondered about the evolution of this huge mammal, whether it was descended from fishes or land mammals. If from fishes, mammals would have to have evolved at least twice, which seemed possible but unlikely. If from land mammals, there'd have to have been an extraordinary sequence of adaptations of form and function that could defy imagination. This kind of origin also seemed unlikely. The whale was an evolutionary impossibility and yet there it was, swimming alongside the *Duchess*.

Fred took comfort in the thought that these huge complex creatures were somehow the product of the rather simple processes of variation and natural selection. If so, it shouldn't seem so outlandish to suppose that complex human behavior such as speech could similarly result from the workings of simple processes of variation in behavior and reinforcement of some varieties.

In both cases, Fred said to himself, evolution of marine mammals and development of human speech, there are undoubtedly other factors involved. But each occurs within its overarching framework of one or the other kind of variation and selection.

"It's looking at us," said Behanan. The whale had slipped back so that its right eye was in line with the three men. "I discern intelligence in that beast," Behanan continued. "He or she seems to be wondering what kind of creatures we are."

"Blue whales have a lot of experience with ships and humans," said Brown, "much of it bad. Modern whaling ships catch tens of thousands of these huge beasts each year. Blue whales may have the largest brains of any animal, but they are not smart enough to keep out the way of the whalers."

"If you'll forgive me," Brown added, "I must go and change for the church service at eleven. Will either of you gentlemen be there?"

"That would be an interesting thing to do," Behanan said. "I am not a Christian, but I am interested in how Christians worship."

Fred wondered whether Sophie and Anna Graydon would be at the service, or at morning coffee in the lounge or walking outside. He said, "I think I'll give the service a miss and stretch my legs instead."

Brown and Behanan went inside. The whale dove out of sight. Fred walked for a while and then went to the lounge. He saw Sophie Graydon sitting alone and felt elated. He asked if he could join her. She smiled and said he could, adding that she had missed him.

"I saw you at lunch and dinner yesterday," Fred said, "but you were very much involved with the people you were talking to. You didn't seem to be at breakfast this morning. How is your daughter?"

"Anna has recovered from drinking too much wine the other evening, but not from her infatuations. She is busy with one this morning.

She is planning to go to the church service, even though it is for all Christian denominations and not only Catholics."

"Your daughter is a puzzling young lady. She is evidently obsessed with Adolf Hitler and perhaps also with Catholicism. Yet in *Mein Kampf*, as I understand it, Hitler wrote about replacing Christianity with Nazism, which suggests to me they are incompatible."

"*Mein Kampf* would be the last book on earth I would read. How do you know what is in that despicable book?"

Fred explained that a colleague had suggested he read a translation of it to help understand what is going on in Germany. He added, "To be more precise, I think Hitler wants to ensure that Germans adopt the *Weltanschauung* of Nazism rather than that of Christianity. *Weltanschauung* is untranslated – and misspelled – in my English version of *Mein Kampf*. It means world-view, does it not?"

"Let me answer that later. Do you have more to say about *Mein Kampf?*"

"I was going to say only that Hitler made positive comments about Christians but then berated them for fighting among themselves rather than working to protect the Aryan race against its chief enemy, the Jews."

"I agree that Nazism and Christianity are not compatible. I have not been a Christian for many years. I was nevertheless shocked when the Pope signed an agreement with Germany soon after Hitler assumed dictatorial powers. It aligned the Catholic Church with the Nazis and helped legitimize the Nazis' odious regime."

Sophie Graydon continued. "Just now my daughter is more concerned to oppose me than to be consistent. I am against the Nazis and so she supports them. I no longer attend church, or even believe in God, and so she embraces her family's Catholicism more strongly."

"Is your sister Freda a factor in her infatuation with religion? She seems to have encouraged her infatuation with today's Germany?"

"She has encouraged both infatuations, but I don't want to talk about her." Sophie Graydon paused while the waiter set out tea, coffee, and things to eat, and then said, "I would be interested in learning more about you: whether you are married, for example."

Fred poured coffee for both of them. He said, "Yes, I've been married for two and a half years, and we have a daughter, Julie, the apple of my eye. She's thirteen months old."

"You mention your daughter more than your wife. Is there difficulty there?"

"No more than usual, but I'm intrigued that you might want to know about such a detail."

"I'm sorry if I was impertinent. Saying what is in my mind is one of my failings. Let me ask you a more polite question, Professor Skinner. You told me you were going to England to meet Sigmund Freud and Ludwig Wittgenstein. What is it about these two men from Vienna that interests you?"

Fred felt a now-familiar stomach twinge when the purpose of his trip was touched on. He said, "Please call me Fred. And may I call you Sophie? After our dance together I feel we know each other well enough to do that."

"Do let us use first names, but cautiously, when we are alone. When we not alone, especially when Anna is present, we should use Mrs. Graydon and Professor or Dr. Skinner, whatever you prefer."

"Professor Skinner would be the most formal," he said. The mild ache in his stomach had become a warm glow, fueled by the intimacy that Sophie had agreed to and the deception she'd proposed.

"I believe I told you that I've been invited to Wittgenstein's inauguration as Professor of Philosophy at Cambridge University," he continued. "I'm not sure why. I can only imagine that Alfred North Whitehead has something to do with it. You may have heard of him. He knew me at Harvard as a young scholar with great ambitions concerning the analysis of language. He continues to have influence at Cambridge. He may have orchestrated the invitation because he felt that bringing Wittgenstein and me together may benefit one or the other or both of us. I'm more interested in meeting Freud."

Fred had decided not to mention Russell, whose association with the adventure could indicate its political element.

"I have not heard of Mr. Whitehead," said Sophie. "I could tell you the little I know about Wittgenstein, but it would only be boring regurgitation of other people's speculation about the influence of Kierkegaard on him."

"Mentioning Kierkegaard does remind me that I was to explain *Weltanschauung*," she continued. "This German word literally means world-view or view of the world, as you suggested. However, it has come to mean the whole set of beliefs through which an individual or a society interprets the world. Thus, if Hitler says he wants to replace the Christian with the Nazi *Weltanschauung*, he is really saying he wants to replace the *Bible* with *Mein Kampf* and to put himself in the place of God and Jesus."

"So, Anna's two infatuations really are incompatible. What you have said raises many questions. Would it bore you if I asked them?"

"I would be delighted. I like talking with you. But you may ask your questions only if I may also ask you questions too. I would like to know, for example, what kind of psychologist you are and what you hope to get out of your meetings with Wittgenstein and Freud."

This time Fred did not feel alarmed when she mentioned the two men he was to visit. Perhaps his interest in her was causing him to drop his guard. He said, "I like talking with you too, Sophie. Here are my questions. Why did you stop believing in God? What was Kierkegaard to do with the concept of *Weltanschauung*? What was his influence on Wittgenstein?"

"Your first question is as impertinent as my question about your wife. Let me say that the cruelties of the war gave me doubts about God. The cruelty of my husband's death strengthened my disbelief."

"Then," she continued, "I was persuaded to write my Master's thesis on the philosopher Søren Kierkegaard. He opposed organized religion. He did not lose his Christianity, but he caused me to lose mine. His aim, above all, was to make sense of human existence. He focused on individual free will. He said it led to distress in the face of the choices that humans must make. I could go on but I can easily become confusing or boring, or both. So I will stop there, and say nothing about Kierkegaard's version of *Weltanschauung*."

"Oh, and you asked about Wittgenstein," she added. "I have heard is that his book with the pretentious Latin title – I forget what it is – owes something to the work of Kierkegaard. I cannot remember what. I heard this during a lecture in Toronto by your colleague at the University of Minnesota, Professor Swenson, originally from Sweden. He is an expert on Kierkegaard, possibly *the* expert."

"He must be in the Philosophy Department. I'm afraid I don't know him," said Fred. "I'm certainly interested in free will and human freedom. Would it bore you to talk about them more?"

"As I said, I like talking with you. I also like discussing philosophical questions, within reason. If talking about philosophy is how we get to know each other, I am for it. You may find me rather limited. I do not always understand what I have to teach and I often struggle to keep up with my students."

Fred said, "You're probably too modest. I guess the first thing to discuss may be whether free will and freedom are philosophical matters. By this I mean that they can't be, or haven't been, addressed by science. Surely we invoke free will only when there is no other obvious reason for a person to do one thing rather than another?"

"But humans are not predictable," said Sophie. "You and I may have many reasons to kiss the other again, but each of us can exercise our free will and choose not to."

Fred blushed. He had wondered whether there would be another opportunity to kiss. "I like your example, and hope you are not teasing me. I'd like to think that if I had enough information about your behavior, I'd be able to predict with some certainty what you would do. If I were always right, where would your free will come into it?"

"This is what the extraordinary Frenchman Laplace was perhaps the first to say. His life overlapped a little with that of Kierkegaard. In my lectures, I use Laplace's argument about scientific determinism as a counterpoint to Kierkegaard. What kind of information *you* would need to make a firm prediction about *my* behavior?"

"I must think about that. I presume you mean your kissing behavior. The information would certainly include how you have behaved in similar situations in the past, and perhaps in some not-so-similar situations. It would include information about relevant matters in the present – for example, whether we were in a private place. It could even include information about your monthly cycle. I have read that women are more amorous when they are ovulating."

"Well, we are intimate! I do not mind that. I *do* mind ruling out free will. When I am confronted by a choice, even though everything pushes me one way, I *know* I can to go the other way if I want."

"Could your feeling of freedom to choose be an illusion?" said Fred. "If it is, then we have the very good question as to how the illusion is sustained, what keeps it going? But that's a less important line of questioning. More important is what could possibly be the nature of free will? Is it a physical or biological mechanism? Is it subject to the laws of nature, or is it outside those laws?"

"Free will is surely a fundamental expression of self, working through mind. Is it not something fundamental like gravity? One does not ask whether gravity obeys the laws of nature. Gravity is part of the laws of nature, is it not?"

Fred was impressed by her example. Sophie Graydon had been modest about her ability. "I don't know much about gravity," he said.

"Einstein had something to say about gravity, but I think he is still working on a full understanding of it. What I do know is that when gravity is understood, it won't be in terms of things invented just to create the illusion of understanding."

"I do not understand what you mean."

"Gods were invented to explain the inexplicable, such as thunder, earthquakes, and the daily rising of the sun. Gods actually explained nothing. The only evidence for them and their handiwork were the things that were being explained, which is no kind of explanation. It's as if you explain the color of this cup by saying that it is white because of its white nature. As phenomena were investigated, more satisfactory explanations emerged. The most satisfactory were the ones that allowed accurate prediction of what had once seemed to be in the capricious hands of the gods."

Fred continued, "Mind and self were invented to explain human behavior. But we know about them only through behavior, and so the explanation is similarly circular and unsatisfactory. Moreover, if you think that what you do is a product of your mind or will, you are left with the challenge of explaining the actions of these entities."

Sophie seemed thoughtful for as much as a minute, apparently oblivious to how intently Fred was regarding her. She said, "I take as my starting point that I, a human being, am an individual who can make choices that can be expressed as words and actions. I do not need to explain my ability to do this, except perhaps in terms of evolution. It is my nature as a human being. For me, the question is not whether I am free to act, but *how* I act. How I deal with important aspects of my existence such as the meaning of life, the inevitability of death, and whether there is purpose in it all."

Fred noticed that her accent was stronger when she was making philosophical points than when she was merely chatting. He said, "Sophie, you have summed up well and appealingly how many people feel about these matters, perhaps most people. There are still important questions about the nature of this feeling of freedom of choice. Could the answers lie in how children acquire this feeling?"

"You are obviously some kind of mechanist. I forget the term given to psychologists who have no time for mind, or thoughts or anything to do with our rich interior worlds."

"I think behaviorist is the word you are looking for. Yes, I am a behaviorist but one who happens to be interested in what I call private stimuli. By these I mean events that I alone have access to, or you alone have access to. They include my thinking and feeling and your thinking and feeling."

"However," Fred continued, "this does not mean I believe that thinking and feeling are expressions of entities called minds that play important roles in what we do. Private behavior – for example, thinking – may play a role in some public behavior. It may not. I'm more concerned with how the environment molds our public behavior. I've also become concerned with how the environment molds our private behavior and the way we refer to private stimuli. How do we learn to think? How do we learn to describe how we feel?"

"Professor Skinner," said Sophie as her daughter arrived, "I would like to continue this interesting discussion but I know that my daughter wants help with what she is to wear this evening."

Fred stood and invited Anna to sit with them. She ignored him, took her mother's hand, and led her out of the lounge. As they left, Sophie turned and gestured weakly to Fred with a small shrug. He smiled at her, waited a few minutes and went to his cabin to fetch his notebook, pencils, and pipe. As he went to light his pipe in the smoking room he was told that cigarettes only were permitted. Pipes had to be smoked outside. He walked forward to the writing room and began his third letter to the other Fred.

Dear Fred,

I've been thinking more about freedom and free will and about a behavioral analysis of these two notions.

They're not the same. Freedom above all implies freedom from *something, usually an adverse environmental condition such as criticism, hunger, tyranny, and threats of disaster. Freedom also refers to the state of being free to act. This may be just another way of saying there are no constraints on action (such as criticism, hunger, prison walls, etc.).*

The simplest behavioral analysis of freedom could be that it is the condition of being controlled by positive reinforcers. A person is free if what he is doing pleases him. The positive reinforcers may exert strong control over his behavior. Nevertheless, the person feels free because he's not being coerced, that is, subjected to force or threats.

Further analysis is required to figure out how compulsion by positive reinforcement becomes associated with the desirable feeling of freedom while compulsion by force or threats becomes associated with a different, unpleasant feeling. Perhaps for there to be a feeling of freedom the positive reinforcement must not be too strong or too evident. Moreover, there should be no sense of bribery or enticement or seduction. All this requires even more analysis.

Free will is said to be what causes behavior that's different from what would be expected from known environmental circumstances. Fred – you or me? – is said to exercise free will when he doesn't pursue a charming lady even though conditions favor pursuit. Joan, the charming lady, is said to be exercising free will when she's being perverse. Both Fred's and Joan's behavior is said to be a result of activation of their free wills. But how are the free wills activated?

Perversity has been dubbed a hallmark of humanity. Dostoevsky wrote something like this: "... if you could prove that man is only a piano key [a mechanism that behaves predictably], he would still do something unexpected out of sheer perversity."(I think it was in Notes from Underground.*)*

There's a logical inconsistency here: unpredictable behavior would disprove the resemblance to a piano key. But logic is not the problem. The real problem with free will is that the evidence for it is what is being explained. If perversity is the evidence for free will, which in turn is the explanation of perversity, the explanation is circular and explains nothing.

What explains perversity? It could be a partially inherited response to strong environmental control. Perverse behavior could have been reinforced in the past by the private feeling of freedom. It could have been reinforced by parents, teachers or peers who gave it unusual attention.

Fred may not pursue the lady because of his history of failed pursuits, or of successful pursuits that have been subsequently punished. An observer may not be aware of Fred's history. As a result, the observer may attribute Fred's lack of pursuit to his strong free will rather than to his history.

Human behavior is astonishingly complex, as are its interactions with human environments. We may believe, as the French polymath Laplace was perhaps the first to believe, that everything about human behavior is in principle knowable. He posited a superhuman intellect (was it Laplace's demon?) that could amass and use such knowledge. In practice, knowing enough to fully predict human behavior may forever be beyond human capacity. For this reason, the comforting illusion of freedom, if that is what we hold, can be sustained.

However, It's a stretch to say that because we might never know enough therefore humans are free and exercise their freedom through an entity somewhere in the body known as free will. All we can say is that we don't know enough to predict the behavior of a complex organism in a complex envi-

ronment (which largely consists of other complex organisms).

My dear Fred, I know you don't like these digressions into speculation about the human condition quite as much as my emerging taste for them pushes me. Nevertheless, I hope that before too long you'll help me grapple with these issues by applying your special brand of pragmatism.

Your friend,

Burrhus

Fred wondered about including the last paragraph, and then remembered that this was another letter that would likely never be sent. He must focus on the tasks at hand: Freud and Wittgenstein; Hitler and Germany. Perhaps getting his thinking clear about freedom will help with the first two. As for Hitler and Germany, perhaps he can induce Sophie to say more about them; and Anna too, although that could result in complications. Maybe he should suffer reading more of *Mein Kampf.*

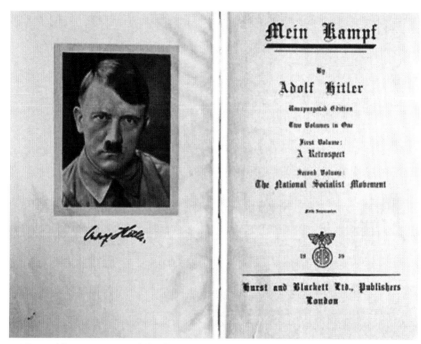

Title and facing pages of the first complete, unexpurgated English edition of the two volumes of Adolf Hitler's *Mein Kampf*, translated by James Murphy and published in London in March 1939. The title page of this English edition follows the main German edition's use of font and layout.

ELEVEN

Afterglow and Icebergs

On the *Duchess of York*, Monday May 22, 1939

Fred was holding the rail at the edge of the boat deck looking at the moonlit icebergs a few miles to the northwest. It was five-thirty in the morning and bitterly cold. Sophie had left his bed twenty minutes earlier. He still felt some of her warmth. The brilliant white icebergs set against the black sea and star-filled sky were an extraordinary and captivating sight. Fred was caught more by the memories of what had happened with Sophie.

The evening had been unremarkable. He had dined with the dull people at his table, seen no one he wanted to dance with, and retired to his cabin to read and sleep. He'd not been enjoying as much of Sophie's company as he'd have liked, and had wondered again if she was avoiding him. He'd fallen asleep after thirty minutes with *Mein Kampf*. It was a sure soporific.

He'd woken a few hours later just as a figure closed his cabin door from the inside, shutting out the corridor lights and restoring the cabin to darkness. It was Sophie. He recognized the smell of her even before he caught the sound of her voice as she gently shushed him while climbing into his narrow bed.

137

She told him not to say a word and pulled him to her. She pressed against him, held his face in her hands and kissed him gently on the lips. After a minute she suggested they take off what they were wearing. Fred remembered having difficulty believing what was happening. He followed her example and snuggled down with her under the blankets, skin against skin. As he realized he was not dreaming, he felt a strong need to talk, asking questions of her and of himself. Why have you come? What do you want? What do I want?

He cleared his throat to speak. She shushed him again and snuggled further down, taking his already erect penis in her mouth and then kissing it all over, applying copious saliva as she did so. Then she straightened up, kissed him on the lips and guided his penis into her – the culmination of what seemed to Fred to be a practiced series of moves. That was almost his last coherent thought for several minutes. He remembered hearing her ask him to slow down, and he did. She pulled away just a little and moved his fingers to her clitoris, showing him what she wanted. Again, she seemed practiced.

Fred still gazed at the icebergs, which were good competition for the clarity of his memory. He remembered the excitement of her orgasm, which caused him to come a few seconds later. Then they lay close together, with him still hard and deep inside her. He must have slept, and perhaps she did too. He remembered waking, his penis now soft but still inside her. It became hard and he could not stop himself thrusting. She moved with him. He waited for her to come but could wait no longer. She subsided with him, held him close and kissed his face and neck several times.

His memory of most of the encounter was clear. Reliving it at the ship's rail, detail by detail, was exquisite and arousing. He must have slept again. As he woke she was leaving the cabin. He dressed and went for a walk. He'd not thought of the cold and had to return to put on a pullover under his coat and jacket, and add a scarf and a hat, and – for holding on to the ship's metal rail – gloves.

The scene before him was changing quickly. The sky was brightening in the north east. The icebergs were gaining an orange tint. The sea was becoming gray. The sky now appeared darker.

The ship was speeding towards the rising sun, perhaps making up for the time lost when it had gone south of rather than north of Newfoundland. The excessively informative Samuel Brown had said that the *Duchess* has six steam turbines driving two propellers. Each engine must now be working at full power, thought Fred, rattling the ship in six different ways. The *Duchess* was rolling in the big Atlantic waves, but not enough to describe her movement as "drunken," not yet anyway.

Unless he had dreamed the whole thing, he'd been unfaithful to Yvonne for the first time. He felt virtuous in that he'd not taken the initiative, although he'd as good as done so by his attentiveness to Sophie and by what he had been hoping for. If he had to explain himself, not taking the initiative would be no kind of excuse. Was what happened last night a threat to his marriage? He didn't think so. Sophie was an appealing woman, and he wanted to see more of her, but she was mysterious and even disconcerting. Above all, she was not the mother of his precious Julie.

Fred then felt he was being foolish by even thinking that this could be more than a shipboard romance. He should, he said to himself, focus on how good he felt because of what happened last night. He should have no further thoughts beyond that, except to hope it might happen again before they reached Glasgow.

Is this what Sophie wanted, just a shipboard dalliance? She seemed more experienced in sexual matters than a long-ago marriage might suggest. She might do this often. If she did, she could well not expect a continuing relationship. But he hoped, just a little, that she would. What *did* she want? Perhaps it would be better if he didn't know. What did *he* want, beyond just being in bed with her again?

Then he had the gut-wrenching thought that he had taken no precautions against pregnancy. What if Sophie had become pregnant as a result of what happened last night? He remembered no concern on her part, and so he presumed she knew where she was in her monthly cycle. In any case, she might be too old to become pregnant. Fred knew she was past forty, but did not know much about menopause or how to recognize it. Sophie was certainly youthful in appearance and body, but she still might no longer be capable of becoming pregnant.

Could he talk about these things with her? He felt he could, but was uncertain as to whether he would. Could he also talk to her about her forthrightness in bed and how it might indicate considerable recent experience in lovemaking? Why would he want to do that? Just to be intimate, he supposed.

Clouds now obscured the rising sun. The icebergs had lost their brilliance. Beyond them, the sky was brighter. Quite far away there was mist or fog at sea level. Fred hoped the *Duchess* wouldn't encounter the combination of fog and icebergs that had marooned the ship carrying the English king and queen for several days. The *Duchess* now seemed to be heading in a more easterly direction, toward the sun and away from the icebergs.

Fred felt he had nothing more to agonize over on the matter of Sophie. His thoughts turned reluctantly to the four questions he had memorized and often rehearsed. He was hardly in a position to answer any of them, but perhaps he should try. The first was "Will Hitler order a German invasion of Poland?" Apart from Glaser's comments about Polish Jews, all he had learned towards an answer to this question came from *Mein Kampf*. There he had found little about Poland but many reasons for Germany to invade that country.

The first reason was Hitler's key objective of acquiring *Lebensraum*: new lands for the German people. *Lebensraum* was the word used by Lukas Glaser, the dentist. He had not found it untranslated in his English version of *Mein Kampf* – unlike *Weltanschauung* – but the goal was certainly expressed there, even numerically. Hitler wrote that in a hundred years Europe's German population would grow from eighty million to two hundred and fifty million. Germans would not be packed like coolies in Chinese factories, but would exist as farm and other workers supporting each other through their labor. They could thus require three times more land than now. These lands would likely be to Germany's east.

Such an expansion would involve appropriation of all of Poland and Czechoslovakia and all or parts of other Eastern European countries, including the Soviet Union. Poland had the longest border with Germany and was thus the easiest place from which to secure *Lebensraum*. Moreover, Poland lay between the separated part of Germany – East Prussia – and the rest of Germany. She could be attacked from the north east as well as from the west.

Germany had already taken over Czechoslovakia. The reasons were complex; acquisition of *Lebensraum* was surely among them.

Another reason for Hitler to invade Poland lay in his aim to overturn the *Treaty of Versailles*, the post-war settlement unfavorable to Germany. What became Poland in 1919 had been parts of Germany, Russia, and Austria-Hungary. In *Mein Kampf*, Hitler wrote about restoring the 1914 frontiers by force and even going beyond them.

Yet another reason to invade Poland found in *Mein Kampf* was as a step to ridding Russia of the scourge of bolshevism or communism, a philosophy inspired by Jews and one that threatens Germany.

Fred turned to the second of the questions he had to answer: "Will the Soviet Union cooperate in such an invasion of Poland?" At first sight, this was a paradoxical question given some of the reasons for Hitler to invade Poland. As well, near the end of *Mein Kampf* there were strong arguments against any kind of alliance with Russia. However, both the Nazis and the communists had a common enemy: international capitalists. In *Mein Kampf*, Hitler wrote that Jews were behind both capitalism and communism. Since then, he might have become more convinced by their role in capitalism than in communism.

Fred thought of another factor that might lead to an alliance between Germany and the Soviet Union. Both countries might want to

141

restore their 1914 boundaries. Each country might see a unilateral invasion of Poland by the other to be a threat and a reason for war. But if they agreed in advance to invade and meet at the 1914 boundary, the elimination of Poland could be achieved expeditiously.

In this line of thinking, Fred was going beyond anything in *Mein Kampf*. He had figured this out himself. For a moment he was much impressed by his own speculation about matters he'd thought little about. Then he remembered that the possibility of an alliance between the two dictatorships had come up during his students' coffee-time discussions. He felt a little deflated.

Fred asked himself whether the Russians had read *Mein Kampf* and knew of Hitler's designs on their land? If it had been translated into Russian, or if people of influence there read German, Soviet Union leaders must know about Germany aims. This argued against cooperation with Germany over Poland.

The second question was turning out to be very challenging. Fred thought he was getting out of his depth in trying to answer it.

The third question – "How far will Hitler go in ridding Greater Germany and German-controlled territory of Jews? – was easier to answer. *Mein Kampf* was full of invective against Jews: they were parasites, a type of bacillus, and public pests intent on polluting Aryan stock with their racial inferiority. The outcome of these sentiments could only be annihilation of Jews, in German-controlled territory and beyond. From what Fred knew of actions against Jews so far – terrorizing them and reducing them to non-citizens – Hitler and the Nazis seemed to be on a course towards the logical end.

The fourth question – "To what extent do British people accept the need for another war with Germany?" – should wait until he was in Britain. It was the most poignant question of all because in Europe only Britain could realistically restrain Germany. A faltering Britain could make America involvement more likely.

Fred surmised that talking with exotic central Europeans such as

Freud and Wittgenstein would give him little understanding of British views on this matter. When he was there, he'd have to read newspapers and, above all, talk to people about the prospect of war.

He'd become cold. The icebergs had disappeared into the haze that now linked the sea and sky. The *Duchess* was rolling with the steeper waves, enough to make Fred hold on tight with hands that were almost numb, even with gloves. It was time to go inside. There were two hours until the end of breakfast. He had time to retreat to the warm bed in his cabin and recapture what had happened there.

Tractatus
Logico-Philosophicus

By
LUDWIG WITTGENSTEIN

With an Introduction by
BERTRAND RUSSELL, F.R.S.

NEW YORK
HARCOURT, BRACE & COMPANY, INC.
LONDON: KEGAN PAUL, TRENCH, TRUBNER & CO., LTD.
1922

The title page of one of the two books by Ludwig Witt-genstein published while he was alive. (The other was a 1926 spelling dictionary for use in Austrian elementary schools.) *Tractatus Logico-Philosophicus* had appeared in 1921 in a German academic journal under the title *Logisch-Philosophische Abhandlung*. Both titles mean "Treatise on Logic and Philosophy." It was translated into English by Frank Ramsey, a 19-year-old Cambridge undergraduate with little more than a year's high-school German. The 1922 London and New York editions included the original German text on alternate pages.

TWELVE

Philosophy and Psychology

On the *Duchess of York*, Tuesday May 23, 1939

Fred was now spending most daylight hours on the promenade deck. He alternated between walking outside, occasionally smoking his pipe, and reading and writing in one of the public rooms. Yesterday, the *Duchess* passed the halfway point between Montreal and Glasgow. Today, the ship would be halfway across the Atlantic. He'd seen few other passengers since yesterday morning, even at dinner. The *Duchess* was living up to its reputation for rolling drunkenly. No doubt this was keeping most passengers in their cabins, near toilet facilities. Fred was unaffected, except that the erratic movements of the ship made writing and even reading difficult.

He had not seen Sophie since she left his bed yesterday morning, or Anna, or, for that matter, Behanan. If they were distressed by the ship's movements, he hoped that the two women and Behanan were suffering separately. He'd seen Brown, who was used to drunken *Duchesses*. Brown had kept him abreast of the ship's progress, usually with more detail than Fred needed. More than once Fred had excused himself, professing the need to prepare for the meetings he was to have in England.

There'd not been a storm and none was forecast. When he was outside, Fred could see the nature of the *Duchess's* erratic movements. The waves were huge and appeared to be moving in the same direction as the *Duchess*, but more slowly. The wind was from behind and must have had a speed similar to that of the *Duchess*. The ship was moving up and down as it moved ahead of the waves and rolling from side to side as it did so. Brown had explained that the captain couldn't make things better by going more slowly. Fred didn't fully understand why. Brown said that changing course so that the wind was not directly behind them was an option, but would add a day or more to the trip.

Fred liked to be outside watching the drama of the *Duchess's* movements. The sky was a uniform light grey as far as the horizon. The sea was a dull grey with occasional touches of dark green, all flashed with white where the wind blew across the tops of the waves. He knew that oceans were more than two thirds of the surface of the planet, which should perhaps be called Sea or Water rather than Earth. Land creatures named it Earth but that didn't mean that most happenings of significance for the evolution of humans had occurred on land. Perhaps they had. Again, Fred felt he should know more about evolution.

Certainly, Fred thought, oceans influence climate more than many people suppose. Minneapolis, thousands of miles from an ocean, is much farther south than the British Isles. Yet the cold February such as had just passed – with temperatures below -10°F on many nights – would be unheard of in Britain, kept warmer by Atlantic currents.

A small benefit of the ship's relentless movements has been a near cessation of conversation at dinner. Fred had been assigned to a table with a Mormon family of five: three earnest teenage boys and their even more earnest parents. He found little to discuss with them. Their mission had changed. They'd been going to Germany but were now going to France. The father spoke a little German and the mother a little French. Fred wasn't able to use this information as a step to a broader discussion about Europe.

Fred's first thought was to seek a change of table, but he decided to learn something about Mormons or enjoy not talking. As the rolling worsened, there were fewer people at meals. He had the table almost to himself yesterday evening. The youngest boy, the only member of the family to eat, was too tongue-tied to speak.

Today, Fred had focused on Wittgenstein. Before afternoon tea, he took his notebook and pencils to the writing room. There he collected his thoughts together in another letter that would not be sent:

Dear Fred,

As I wrote before, I'm on my way to England to attend Ludwig Wittgenstein's inauguration as Professor of Philosophy at Cambridge University. A.N. Whitehead and Bertrand Russell seemed concerned about some philosophical directions Wittgenstein was taking. They believed that exposure to my thinking might help steer him in other directions. I'm not clear as to the nature of their concerns, but have some suspicions that I'm setting out here.

You already know that it was Russell who first stimulated my interest in behaviorism when I read his review of Ogden and Richards' The Meaning of Meaning. *This was soon after I arrived at Harvard in 1928. Thus, right from the beginning of my interest, I was intrigued by what I now call verbal behavior. As you know, I had just turned away from unfulfilled literary aspirations and embarked on a new life as a graduate student in psychology. Russell's deft handling of words as behavior provided just the bridge I needed between my old life and my new.*

That time was equally important for me because it was the beginning of the intellectual and personal friendship that you and I have now maintained for more than a decade, for which I've never shown you enough appreciation.

I don't think I've told you about Whitehead's role in my in-

terest in verbal behavior. One evening in 1934, he and I were left alone with our glasses of port at the end of a dinner of Harvard's Society of Fellows. You'd long left Harvard for the teaching position at Colgate. Whitehead agreed that science could in principle account for human behavior but he made an exception of verbal behavior. He insisted that something else must be at work, and then issued a friendly challenge. "Account for my behavior," he said, "when I sit here saying 'No black scorpion is falling upon this table.'" The next morning I drew up the first outline of my book on verbal behavior.

I sat across the table from Russell at lunch when he visited Minneapolis last winter. I told him I had been converted to behaviorism by his review and by his book Philosophy. *He was aghast, explaining that he had hoped that the book had demolished behaviorism. I'd not read to the end of the book, where the demolition occurred, and so I let him believe he'd been effective. I've wondered what Russell imagined to be my qualification to help steer Wittgenstein away from his current concerns. I can conclude only that it's what Russell took to be my attachment to behaviorism and then my estrangement from it.*

Figuring out what Wittgenstein has been up to is quite a challenge. He's published just one item, a seventy-page book, Tractatus Logico-Philosophicus (TLP). *It appeared in German in 1921 and in English a year later. Russell wrote a long introduction concluding that TLP is a book that "no serious philosopher can afford to neglect." The challenge in 1939 is that Wittgenstein seems to have abandoned the direction he was taking in TLP. He seems to be replacing it with something else.*

I glanced through TLP before I left and read a little about it. It appears to be concerned with the logical relationships be-

tween what is said and what actually exists. In TPL, *Wittgenstein reduced what he considered to be meaningful language to a set of elementary statements. These statements and the words they comprise are pictures of the world, as are associated thoughts. He wrote that statements containing words that do not name (i.e., do not picture) objects in the world are meaningless. There's math in* TLP *too that I didn't try to grasp.*

Wittgenstein's ideas in TLP *seem to me to be mostly standard philosophizing of the kind engaged in by Russell and, to a lesser extent, Whitehead. I know that the Logical Positivists in Vienna were excited about* TPL. *Wittgenstein himself seemed to have been excited. He wrote in his preface that* TLP *had solved all the problems of philosophy.*

Don't worry if my summary of TLP *means little to you. The book didn't mean much to me, and I may well have missed some or many of its points. Understanding them is not important for what follows.*

What Wittgenstein has been saying recently is quite different from what is in TLP. *In a nutshell, he's been saying that language is a social phenomenon. Words have meaning only in relation to the speakers and listeners that use them. Put another way, he's been saying that meaning does not arise from the association of words with particular objects, or from any mental act. Meaning is a function of how words are used.*

How do I know what he's been saying? Because Russell sent me a copy of what is known as The Blue Book, *a hundred and twenty pages of type-written notes, double-spaced and bound in a blue cover, with no sections or headings. Russell told me that Wittgenstein dictated the notes to a few of his students in 1933-34 when too many people began attending his lectures. He stopped lecturing and asked would-be attendees to rely on the notes, which developed a fairly wide circulation. There's a later type-written book, also dictated to students, distributed in a brown cover. I haven't seen it, but I've heard that the big change in philosophizing is between* TLP *and* The Blue Book *and between* The Blue Book *and* The Brown Book.

I read most of The Blue Book *this morning. (A seven-day sea voyage is a good time to read; if you can put up with a lot of rolling from side to side.) I must say I like what I found. As a result, I may not be inclined to engage in the remedial behavior that Russell and Whitehead seemed to want me to engage in.*

Here's a sample quotation from The Blue Book *that appealed to me: "Is it possible for a machine to think? (whether the action of this machine can be described and predicted by the laws of physics or, possibly, only by laws of a different kind applying to the behavior of organisms)."*

It's appealing not only because of the reference to the "behavior of organisms" but also because of the mention of "laws of a different kind," which I would take to mean the laws of reinforcement (although Wittgenstein may not).

I won't go into Wittgenstein's answer here, which takes up several pages, except to say that it involved what I believe to be the fundamental point of The Blue Book: *that the meaning of a word is nothing more nor less than how it is used. According to Wittgenstein, meaning is not some kind of mental accompaniment to what is said or written. It is not "an occult connection the mind makes between a word and a thing." I strongly agree with his basic point.*

If language is a social phenomenon, how it is acquired is of profound interest. The Blue Book *touched on the general question of how children acquire language. On this, Wittgenstein noted the importance of "language games," a notion I didn't understand. He promised to say more about language games, although there's nothing more about them in* The Blue Book.

He also discussed how we learn to refer to private events such as a toothache or a feeling. His answer was long. I won't dwell on it except to say that I'm now even more convinced that we behaviorists must address the issues presented by private events such as thinking. We must figure out how private events are interwoven with our ways of using language.

Until dipping into The Blue Book, *I was not looking forward to my encounter with Ludwig Wittgenstein. Now I am. I believe our approaches to language have much in common. We may be able to help each other.*

But if I ever have to account for myself to Bertrand Russell – who after all made this trip possible – I may be in difficulty. After Russell's visit to Minneapolis, I read the rest of the book in which he claimed he demolished behaviorism. Of course, the behaviorism he addressed was that of J.B. Watson, which didn't allow consideration of private events. Russell didn't demolish behaviorism so much as deem it irrelevant because it didn't consider these events. He wrote that these events – in the form of "percepts" and "knowledge" – are the most important of all. He made a distinction between the data of psychology and those of physics. Both are private facts, but the former are not directly linked to facts outside the body whereas the latter are. Wittgenstein has moved a long way beyond this kind of thinking. I hope I will move further still. The key issue is how we learn to talk about private events. I can't see that Russell has even begun to grapple with that.

A child learns to say "red" when responding to the question, "What color is that car?" because saying "red" is rein-

forced – if the car is red – and saying anything else is not. But the verbal behavior "I have a toothache" cannot be consistently reinforced in this way. Nevertheless, I can think of several ways in which a child can learn to say "I have a toothache." Wittgenstein touched on one of them in The Blue Book. *He seemed to propose that the child's verbal community could make use of correlated public behavior such as holding one's cheek. I could suggest to him several more ways a verbal community could generate (teach?) verbal behavior associated with private events.*

By the way, "verbal community" is my term, not Wittgenstein's. I could have written "verbal environment." Both refer to the people who influence verbal behavior. They do this chiefly but not only by reinforcing particular behavior on some occasions and not on others. A speaker's verbal community normally comprises the people who interact with the speaker while using the language the speaker is using or acquiring.

And what is verbal behavior? It is behavior evoked and maintained by a verbal community. Is all human social behavior verbal behavior? I think not. If a man is making eyes at a woman and she at him, it may not be useful to call the eye-making verbal behavior. But perhaps analysis would show it is hardly different from verbal flirting. I need to think more about what distinguishes verbal behavior from other social behavior.

And what about thinking and reading? These are verbal behavior – to the extent that the thinking consists of words – but there is no immediate verbal community. I'd say two things in response to this question. One is that both thinking and reading depend on a history of interactions with a verbal community. The other is that participation in a verbal community involves two kinds of verbal behavior, speaking and *listening. Thinking and reading embrace private elements of both types of behavior.*

This may all seem a little tortured. What I am trying to do is position the use of language as no more nor less than a kind of behavior. This behavior is formed and maintained by the processes of variation and selection that form and maintain what I called "operant behavior" in The Behavior of Organisms. *This is essentially all behavior that an individual is not specifically born with.*

Once again, dear Fred, you have served the most useful purpose of helping me get my ideas in order. Even if you don't receive the letters I'm writing to you during this trip – and I doubt increasingly that you will – the letters are of profound value to me. As always, you are being superbly helpful.

Now I've got some of Wittgenstein and language out of my system, I can turn to Sigmund Freud, who I hope will be the topic of my next letter to you. But there's another letter I'd like to write too: about non-verbal thinking.

Your friend,

Burrhus

It was time for afternoon tea. Fred settled in the lounge enjoying the paraphernalia and delights of the British afternoon tea. Anna approached him soon after he had begun reading over the letter to the other Fred. "May I join you?" she said.

Fred stood, invited her to sit at his small table, and beckoned to a steward to bring tea things for her. "How are you feeling?" he asked.

"I found the motion of the ship very difficult yesterday, but today I'm more used to it. More than my mother, anyway. She's alternating between her bed and the basin."

"I'm sorry to hear that. If you haven't eaten much for a day or two, you may be very hungry."

"You are so right," said Anna, "I could eat all those sandwiches and more." She put four or five of the small, crustless triangles on her plate, began eating them with enthusiasm, and then paused. "It's even hard to eat properly with the motion of this ship. I've just bitten the edge of my tongue." She began eating again, more carefully.

Fred said, "I've been thinking about some of the things you said about Germany and Adolf Hitler when we sat at the captain's table at dinner on the first evening."

"Oh dear!" Anna replied quickly, "I'm trying hard to forget that meal, and my mother's anger about my behavior." "Oh dear too!" she continued, "I really don't want to have another argument about Germany. Can we talk about something else?"

"I don't think we did argue," said Fred. "I was asking you questions, and you gave me some answers."

"I felt I was being interrogated, and that you were hostile to what I was saying. Let me ask you a question, Professor Skinner. It is Professor Skinner, isn't it? My question is this: If the German people have found ways of doing things better – such as eliminating unemployment, poverty, crime, and strikes, and restoring self-esteem and national pride – why aren't they more admired? Why is not the person who made this possible, *Führer* Adolf Hitler, more admired?"

"Please call me Fred. Will you? And then I can call you Anna. You've asked a big question, a long question – in fact two questions. I wish I knew enough to give you a good answer. I'll take your word that these things are happening in Germany, and that they are not admired enough. If no one else felt threatened by them, I think there could be more admiration. But Jews in Germany feel very threatened, even Jews who risked their lives for Germany in the war. So do the Nazis' political opponents. And Germany's neighbors feel threatened. Look at what has happened in Austria and Czechoslovakia."

"I'd like to call you Fred, but my mother wouldn't approve. I now have to call Kovoor Behanan Dr. Behanan, even though years ago I used to call him Uncle K. She is concerned about what people may think, although more about what they think of her rather than of me. You may certainly call me Anna."

"Where were we?" she continued. "Yes, Austria and Czechoslovakia. Well, from what I've heard, Austrians wanted to be part of Germany even more than Germany wanted Austria. And the same thing happened in Czechoslovakia. The Germans there wanted to be part of Germany. Britain and France agreed, so my aunt said."

"Let's concede, said Fred, "that what happened to Austria and the German-speaking part of Czechoslovakia was a matter of rearranging Germany's boundaries to include more German speakers. What about the invasion by Germany of more of Czechoslovakia a few months ago? That seems to me to have been wholly unjustified."

"My aunt said that Germany was not the first to invade Czechoslovakia. Hungary and Poland had already taken over some of that little country, which was in any case falling apart. Some parts of it wanted independence. Germany needed to move in to bring some stability to that part of the world."

"Your aunt seems to be well informed." The ship rolled to a steep angle. Their almost empty teacups and saucers slid across the low table hitting its raised edge. The cups flew onto the carpeted floor. Fred and Anna retrieved their cups, with some difficulty because the ship had continued to roll steeply. A steward rushed to bring fresh cups and clean up the stains on the carpeted floor.

Fred and Anna smiled at each other while holding on to their seats. "Shall we go outside to see what is happening?" said Fred.

"I don't have a coat with me, and I don't want to go back to the cabin."

"You could use mine, and I'll get another pullover. Wait here for a few minutes."

"Let me come with you and see your cabin," said Anna.

155

"It's the same as yours, but with only one bed."

"Now I remember – a little. You helped my mother put me to bed after that frightful dinner. Why were you there? I am so embarrassed."

"I had helped her get you to your cabin. I was embarrassed too, but your mother asked me to stay in case she needed my help."

They were now walking down the stairs to the deck below. Anna was wearing his coat. Fred had somehow missed the opportunity to ask Anna to wait again. He needed very much *not* to meet Sophie just now.

Fred opened his cabin door and said to Anna, "Wait there, I'll be a few seconds." While he was getting his pullover from the chest of drawers, Anna came in, locked the door behind her, and, before he could turn round, enveloped him in his own coat.

"What are you doing?" said Fred. He extricated himself and turned, and she fell into him, kissing his neck. "You mustn't do this," he said, but found he was stroking her hair, not pushing her away as his words implied. "We must stop," he said, "or there'll be trouble."

"Why should there be trouble? I'm a woman, even if my mother treats me as a child. Before she became sick, I saw her leave our cabin at night, probably to spend time with Kovoor Behanan as she used to do when I was young. If she can do that so can I."

When she was not speaking, her body felt to Fred the same as her mother's had felt. She had the same height, build and odor, and moved in the same way. Fred began to be aroused. He grasped her arms above the elbows and moved her away from him. "Please stop now," he said. "Let's do what we'd planned to do: walk outside for a while."

"You're a mean and disappointing man and I don't want to walk with you. Take your coat." She disengaged herself from his grasp, re-moved the coat and handed it to him. "I'm going to do something else." She walked out of the cabin leaving the door ajar.

His cabin steward, Jean-Paul, appeared at the open door soon after Anna had left. Fred hoped he had not seen her. "*Est-ce qu'il y a*

156

quelque chose que je peux faire pour vous, Professeur Skinner?", Jean-Paul asked. Fred moved to the door smiling and gesturing that there was nothing Jean-Paul could do for him, and shut the door.

Fred waited for a few minutes, put on his coat, and went up to the promenade deck. His thoughts were racing. He could have been in his bed with Anna instead of fighting the squalls he encountered on deck. But Anna was a child, even though she resembled her mother so much. Sophie's German accent added to her allure. Anna's presumably Canadian accent reminded Fred of his women students in Minneapolis, especially his undergraduate students because she was about their age. The accent was not quite the same, but he couldn't pinpoint the differences.

But it wasn't only that Anna was a child, she was Sophie's child. Fred dreaded to imagine Sophie's wrath at discovering even what had happened between him and Anna just now. Anna's speculation – was it just speculation? – about her mother and Behanan suggested that the mother's and daughter's relationships were already a source of tension between them.

Fred then remembered the lack of precaution during the night with Sophie. He needed a trim anyway, and had time before dinner. He went in search of the barber shop, which he recalled as being on Deck B. What should he ask for? In Minneapolis he asked for rubbers or safes. But he had read somewhere that in Britain a rubber meant something else, and that might also be true of a Canadian ship registered in Britain. No doubt the ship had enough American passengers that a barber would know what was being asked for.

There was no problem. When his trim was complete the barber, who could have been Jean-Paul's brother, asked Fred if there was anything else he wanted, at the same time opening a drawer in his counter where there were familiar brands of condoms: Trojan, Sheik, Ramses. He left with a packet of Trojans in his pocket and the hope that he would have a chance to use at least one of them before the ship docked in Glasgow.

157

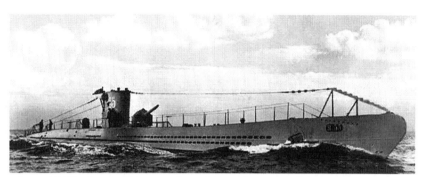

A pre-WW2 photo of *Unterseeboot* (U-boat) No. 35 of the *Kreigsmarine*, as the German navy was known in the late 1930s and early 1940s. U-35, with U-28, was the first German submarine to patrol the Atlantic, beginning with a trip to the Azores early in 1937. U-35 was also among the first U-boats sunk during World War Two. She was scuttled by her crew in November 1939 after combat in the North Sea. U-35 may have been the best known U-boat in the United States, a result of her appearance on the cover of *Life* magazine in October 1939.

THIRTEEN

Passing Ireland

On the *Duchess of York*, Thursday May 25, 1939

F red packed his large suitcase, to be picked up from his cabin and taken to the train he would catch the next day. He would see it again at his London hotel. Before that, he had spent some minutes testing whether the business suit and good shoes he was to wear for dinner this evening would, with the other things he would need, fit into the small suitcase he would carry with him on the train. His packing done, Fred dressed for his final evening on the *Duchess of York* and whatever that would bring.

He climbed the stairs to the promenade deck and joined the cocktail hour. Many people were outside. It was calmer and warmer. The sun was out for the first time since it shone on the icebergs after his night with Sophie. Fred asked for a vodka and tonic at the bar, went outside, and joined Samuel Brown at the rail. They exchanged pleasantries and Brown pointed out that land was visible about fifteen miles to the south, vivid green and brown in the evening sunlight.

"What you see there is the northern-most tip of Ireland," Brown said. "It's Malin Head, part of County Donegal. Even though Donegal is in the north, it's part of what is now called Eire, also known as the

Republic of Ireland. Everything east of Donegal is Northern Ireland, which remains part of Britain. It's confusing. It's even more confusing because Eire is still part of what is now called the British Commonwealth. And more confusing still because, for some purposes, Eire continues to recognize the British king as head of state even though it now has a president."

"You're bursting my head again with your facts," Fred said. "What you say is interesting, but I shall remember little of it."

"I'm sorry," said Brown, "I do go on, I must admit. I've been travelling this route for years as engineer and passenger. I've gotten to know things along it and assume too readily that others want to benefit from my knowledge. Our ships usually call in at Belfast, so I've kept an eye on Irish happenings. Let me say one more thing. That lighthouse you see on the hill there is not on the mainland but is on the eastern end of an island, Inishtrahull, halfway between here and Malin Head. The island was inhabited until ten years ago – we used to see smoke from the houses in the middle – but now the only residents are the elderly lighthouse keeper and his wife, or the young family that replaces them for a month each summer."

Fred could now see water beyond where the lighthouse stood. The island – what was the name? – seemed even greener than the mainland. It was fringed with a brown rocky coast. Hills at each end were separated by a low-lying area. There, he could see crumbled buildings and walls, and other signs of the former habitation.

A gray shape rose out of the water between the *Duchess* and the island. Given what he had seen off Newfoundland, for a moment Fred took the shape to be another whale. But it was much longer, and more rigid and metallic than a living thing. It was a submarine, with an oval conning tower sticking up from its center and a skywards-pointing gun in front of the tower. It had surfaced with its bow pointing towards the west and was soon moving quickly in that direction.

"Now I *do* want you to tell me about that," Fred said.

"It's what the Germans call a *U-Boot,* or *Unterseeboot.* We usually call them U-boats. The one you see there is U-boat No. 35. See the number on the conning tower. That means she's one of the class of attack U-boats the German navy is focusing on."

"What is it doing here? Or should you say 'she' for a submarine?"

"She and perhaps a few others nearby are likely on a training exercise in preparation for the war to come. U-35 probably surfaced because her crew hadn't noticed we are not far away or because her batteries were getting low. It's probably the latter because instead of going under again she's moving out of sight as quickly as possible. Somebody on the *Duchess* will surely be making a report to the Royal Navy about the sighting, if they're not already doing so."

"You may remember," Brown continued, "that German submarines played an important role in the Great War. The sinking of several American merchant ships by U-boats early in 1917 was the direct cause of your entry into the war. When America joined the war, Germany and its allies were bound to be defeated soon or later."

"I remember the sinking of the *Lusitania* by a German submarine. I must have been about eleven years old at the time. It's my earliest memory of reading a newspaper. The front page of the *Philadelphia Inquirer* had almost no other news."

"The *Lusitania* was a British passenger liner. Many American passengers went down with it, which no doubt contributed to changing public opinion. It took another two years for America to declare war, and it was the sinking of American merchant ships that did it."

Fred asked, "What were you doing then?"

"I was a junior engineer on several British merchant ships, mostly in the North Atlantic but I made two trips to Australia and back. I was fortunate. Both long trips were in the first half of 1917 when the U-boat menace in the North Atlantic was at its strongest. When I returned to North Atlantic duty, the convoy system had been introduced. A few naval escorts could protect many merchant ships, and things were a lot safer. I never actually saw a U-boat at sea during the war. Fear of them was instilled in us. We were taught a lot about them and I've kept up that interest."

The U-boat was almost out of sight. Fred asked, "So, that U-boat is in training to sink ships carrying supplies to Britain in the event of another war?"

"It would seem so. Germany has been investing heavily in a new U-boat fleet. I don't understand why Britain and America have not been more concerned. Another alarming development is the neutrality of Eire. This could make it easier for U-boats to operate just where we are now and also to the south of Ireland. These of course are the main shipping routes between North America and Britain."

"This is all very interesting," said Fred. "We should go inside. It's getting cold again."

Spread among the inside spaces of the promenade deck were many more passengers than Fred had seen since the first evening's dinner. When the *Duchess* had been lurching about in the Atlantic, dinners had become more and more informal as well as sparsely attended. Now, tuxes and elaborate dresses were on display again.

Soon after Fred and Samuel Brown had replenished their glasses, a hand bell rang. The chief steward announced dinner, reminding passengers that, as was the custom for the last evening of the voyage, they did not have to sit at their designated tables. If possible, he added, they should use the stairs rather than the lift – the elevator – to go down to the dining saloon on Deck C.

Brown said he had arranged to sit with the Graydon ladies and Dr. Behanan. He hoped that Professor Skinner would join them.

Fred agreed with many thanks. He wondered to himself how this arrangement had been made, and whether he would have been included if he had not met Brown on the promenade deck.

In the dining saloon, Brown guided Fred towards a table where Behanan was already sitting. They exchanged words about the weather and the U-boat, which Behanan had not seen. Sophie and Anna arrived. Fred almost gasped at the beauty of the two women. Their builds, their faces, and the styles of their blond-brown hair were almost but not quite identical, and their plain black dresses, although differing in detail, added to the similarity. As he felt when he had first seen them in the gym, they could have been sisters. Now they could even have been twin sisters, dressing slightly differently so they could be told apart.

Brown attempted to assign the five diners to seats at the table for six. Behanan intervened, proposing that the two ladies should not sit together. Fred took no part in the gentle jousting of the other two men and found himself between the two women, with Anna and Brown to his left and Sophie and Behanan to his right, with the unused place setting opposite.

The chief steward announced that the Reverend Andrew Anderson was still indisposed and asked former ship's engineer Samuel Brown to say the grace. Brown stood to say the words that Fred now understood. He had heard them from three different mouths at dinners since Sunday, when the Reverend was last seen. Brown intoned the grace in his pleasing accent, mostly Scottish but evidently softened by his time in Canada and elsewhere.

Behanan congratulated Brown on his rendering of the grace. Brown regretted that the ship's captain had not been present. After all, it was his wish for a little Scots flavor that led to the use of this grace. He asked if either of ladies had seen the U-boat.

"What was that?" said Anna. Brown explained. Sophie was evidently discomforted by the exchange.

"Why shouldn't Germany be able to protect herself?" said Anna.

"Surely," replied Brown, "sinking civilian ships with torpedoes goes beyond protecting oneself."

The discussion paused as the soup arrived and the diners were asked as to their choices of main course. The five busied themselves with passing bread, butter, salt and pepper. Behanan was the first to speak. "Does Anna not have a point? If there is a war, is it not fair game to attack your enemy's sources of supply? In the Great War, the British navy stopped food reaching Germany through a blockade that sometimes involved the sinking of merchant ships. Did not thousands of Germans die of starvation as a result?"

Brown answered, "I don't know how many starved. I do know that the Royal Navy almost never attacked without warning. U-boats almost always attacked without warning."

"The Royal Navy was all-powerful," replied Behanan. "Germany's only way of competing was to have U-boats. In practice, U-boats could give warning, but they are small and vulnerable. Giving warnings would have doomed them before they could achieve the goal of stopping the merchant ships."

"I'm surprised you are so sympathetic to Germany," said Brown. "In spite of our differences, I thought India was still a loyal member of our family of nations."

"That's a nice phrase and a nice sentiment," said Behanan, "but I think you will find that there is much pro-German feeling in India. And it is reciprocated. The swastika, you may know, is an ancient sign still in common use in India. It means something like 'auspiciousness.'"

"What does *that* mean?" interrupted Anna.

"A happening is auspicious," Fred said, "if it promises something good, such as success or happiness. You can say that auspicious means the same as promising – as in, she made an auspicious start to her career as an actress."

"Well, thank you, Professor," said Anna, moving her leg against his. Fred slowly moved his leg away.

Sophie said, "I was one of the Germans who became very hungry during the war, but I can understand why it had to happen. Germany did not behave well towards neutral countries such as Belgium and America, and Germany had to be stopped. Also, I don't like the *U-boote*. They are – what is the word? – sneaky. They hide in the water and don't give their victims a chance."

"*Mutti*," said Anna, "you are always so much against Germany. It's embarrassing."

"I'm even more embarrassed to be German now than when I was in Belgium during the war. Hitler is leading a gang of criminals who are causing what was my country to do shameful things."

"The *Führer*," Anna responded slowly, "has restored pride and dignity to a nation and people who have been unjustly treated. He has healed a nation that was and still is being undermined by international conspiracies. Germany is the only country, in Europe at least, that does not despair about its condition. And yet, at the end of the war, and for many years after, Germany was as low as could be."

Anna appeared to be reciting words she had read or heard somewhere and had committed to memory. Then she added in a less robotic manner, "Adolf Hitler made the difference. He's a genius. What do you think, Uncle B?"

Fred saw Sophie wince at her daughter's use of the former familiar name. Things would become quite tense between them if this line of discussion continued. He was relieved it was Behanan and not he who had been asked about Hitler.

"Herr Hitler's achievements are remarkable," said Behanan. "A downtrodden people needs a leader. He has been and is that leader. A leader must live simply and inspire his followers with his thoughts and his deeds. Herr Hitler does these things."

"I should say a word too about Britain and Germany from an Indian perspective," Behanan continued. "The British speak about their empire as a benign organization that has brought enlightenment to uncivilized peoples. The truth is that the empire has been a vehicle for the subjugation and exploitation of peoples the British regard as inferior. In many cases the subjugated peoples have far older civilizations than what passes for civilization in Europe. By many criteria, these older civilizations are more sophisticated."

"Germany had colonies before the Great War," said Brown.

"I do not want to defend Germany," replied Behanan. "I want to suggest only that Britain is no better."

"But you have praised Hitler," said Sophie, "a man who is making Germany a pariah among nations."

"You yourself said that Germany was doing unacceptable things *before* Hitler came to power," said Behanan.

The main course was served. Fred overheard Sophie decline wine. She asked the waiter not to give any to Anna. Should he help enforce this request? It was not his business.

After they had begun eating, Brown picked up the discussion again. "Two things concern me about the Nazi government. One is that it's provoking a war. The other is that it's ill-treating many of its own people, notably the Jews."

"I agree," said Sophie, "and I will add a third concern. Hitler has become a dictator and the *Nationalsozialistische Deutsche Arbeiterpartei* – to give the Nazis their full name – is the means for enforcing the dictatorship. Mr. Brown's concerns arise from two of the elements of the party's program: to achieve the goals of *Lebensraum* and *Rassenhygiene*. The first goal involves conquering new lands for Germans. The second involves protecting the purity of the German race by isolating and even annihilating other races, especially the Jews."

Fred remembered discussion of a party program in *Mein Kampf* but didn't remember seeing a program set out. He must look again.

Behanan said, "You are both – Mrs. Graydon and Mr. Brown – concerned about the persecution of Jews in Germany. But is it not the case that in many if not most societies there has been stratification according to birth, whether by family or race or whatever? In Britain there are rigid social classes. In India, we have our castes, a system that many say was strengthened by British rule. In America, you have had slavery and the continued subjugation of Negroes. Could it be that it is in the nature of societies to organize themselves in layers? Could it be too that within those societies people inherit their position just as they inherit hair or eye color?"

"Professor Skinner," said Brown. "You have been quiet. The rest of the table seems divided. Anna Graydon and Dr. Behanan are strongly or mostly on the side of Germany. Mrs. Graydon and I are strongly or mostly against Germany. Where do you stand?"

This is what Fred feared. He'd thought a little as to what he might say if pressed. He said, "If you insist on knowing, let me reply first as an American and then as a student of human behavior."

"As an American," he continued, "I have to be against Germany for two reasons and I have to step back from that opposition for one reason. I'm against Germany because I dislike inherited positions and because I believe in letting all adult citizens decide things rather than just an elite. Americans haven't always live up to these ideals, but we try. By inherited positions I mean both inheritance that puts you above people, such as royalty, and inheritance that puts you below people, as in a caste system."

"But also as an American, I have to say that I'm inclined to keep my country out of European affairs, indeed anyone else's affairs. Again, we haven't always lived up to this ideal, but there's reason for trying. However, I must say that the more I learn about what Germany is doing, the less inclined I am to stick to this isolationist position. But, isolationism is where I'm starting from."

Fred added, "As much as I'm repelled as an American by Hitler, the Nazis, and Germany, I must admit to some fascination with them as a student of human behavior. In almost everything they do, Hitler and the Nazis, and the German people in response to them, pose questions about and even challenges for our understanding of how and why people do what they do."

"I could probably be very boring about this," Fred said, "and talk as though I'm lecturing to my students. If I do, you must stop me. And in an attempt to avoid being boring, I'll be as brief as I can and focus on two things only."

"The first is something that Dr. Behanan touched on. He said it may be in the nature of societies to organize themselves in layers. If this is true – and I would question it – would it be something we mostly inherit or something we mostly acquire through the ways we are raised and through other early experiences? In either case, how might this happen?"

"Surely," said Brown, "if it's in our nature we must inherit it?"

"We may inherit a disposition – again, I doubt this – but it's clear from Dr. Behanan's examples that societies vary in *how* they are stratified. This suggests differences in the way children in different societies are raised. I'd go further and say inheritance plays essentially no role in stratification. It's entirely a matter of which kinds of behavior are favored in a particular society, among its children and even more importantly among its adults. Of course, this begs the question as to how a society might get to the point where it favors making odious distinctions among classes or castes or races."

Anna put her hand up, almost in front of Fred's face, as though she were in a classroom. She said, "I don't understand some of the words you use, 'stratification' for example. Could you explain it?"

"Anna, please do not interrupt with this display of your ignorance," said Sophie. Her German accent was stronger than usual. "Listen and learn from an adult discussion."

"It's not an adult discussion to be so disrespectful of the *Führer*."

"No one is being disrespectful," said Fred. "Stratification, as Dr.

Behanan put it well, means organizing a whole into layers, one above the other."

"Could I move on to the second thing that intrigues me?" said Fred. "It is how what might be called the *cult* of Hitler came about and continues. By *cult* I mean no more than the extraordinary admiration bordering on adoration that German people, and some outside Germany, have for Herr Hitler."

"I know what cult means," said Anna. "It's something to do with Devil-worship. You are being disrespectful of the *Führer* again."

"*Kind,* s*ei still. Lass den Mann sprechen,*" Sophie hissed across the table.

Fred replied to Anna, "I don't mean to be disrespectful at all. From newsreels and newspaper reports it seems that huge numbers of German people adore Hitler in a way no politician in America would ever be adored. Moreover, to an American, except in one way, he doesn't seem like the kind of person who would be adored."

Anna went to protest again and was given a warning shush by her mother.

"What is the exception that could help you understand why he is adored?" said Behanan.

"It's his oratory," replied Fred. "He's able to keep his huge audiences mesmerized for hours on end. If it is his oratory, I'd like to know how it works. I'd like to know how what he says and how he says it can produce such adoration and devotion."

"You are being too academic," said Sophie. "It is a simple matter of the German people being hoodwinked and intimidated by Hitler and his gang of crooks."

Anna stood and stormed out of the dining saloon. The three men busied themselves with eating, waiting for Sophie to say something or to follow Anna. She did neither of these things. Instead, she called for wine and drank it while looking at diners at other tables. Fred began to feel that the evening might not have the happy conclusion he had hoped for.

The silence was uncomfortable. Fred broke it by asking Behanan how the yoga classes went. He replied that he had kept them going. A few more people had come at first but for the last two days Anna had been the only participant. Mentioning Anna did not make the mood at the table more congenial.

Brown asked about plans for the next day. He said he'd be leaving the *Duchess* and going to stay in Glasgow with his younger sister and her family. The main purpose of his trip was to visit his mother, who lived with his older sister and was not in good health. After a week he'd return to Montreal on this very ship. He liked being at sea.

Sophie said, as if nothing unusual had occurred, "I think you all know we are going to visit my mother in Bonn. I will stay for a few weeks. I will not be happy to leave her – I will likely not see her again – but I will be happy to leave Germany for the last time." She paused, and then said with a stronger accent, "My silly daughter may stay there. A few days ago, that was the last thing I wanted. Now, I am not so sure."

This was another conversation stopper, thought Fred. But Behanan plowed on, "I think you said, Mrs. Graydon, you will be on this ship until Liverpool. Is that so?"

Sophie replied with less emotion, "Yes, we are getting a train from Liverpool Docks on Saturday that goes all the way to Bonn and beyond. We have a room. I think the British say sleeping compartment. Our rail car will actually be pushed on to a ferry at Harwich in England and pulled off at Zeebrugge in Belgium. We will be safe and sound in our room or in the dining car while this is happening, and we will be at my mother's house by lunchtime on Sunday. It seems remarkable."

Brown asked, "Are you not going to Liverpool too, Dr. Behanan?"

"Yes, and from there I will make a short trip to Manchester. I will stay there for a few days and give a lecture. Then I am going to London. I will be there for a few days and give two more lectures. I leave from London Docks for India one week from today. It is a three-week voyage. Except at the beginning, it will be very different from this trip across the North Atlantic."

"How different?" asked Fred.

"It will be much warmer and the seas will be calmer. On the way we will call in at what you would find to be increasingly exotic ports. They include Tangier in Morocco, Port Said at the entrance to the Suez Canal, and Aden at the southern tip of the Arabian Peninsula.

"You have an interesting month ahead of you," said Fred. "Then you will be far away from what appears to be an increasingly fraught situation in Europe."

"What are your plans, Professor Skinner?" said Behanan.

"I'll catch a train to London tomorrow afternoon, stay there for a few days, go to Cambridge for a few days, and then return to America. It's a short visit. I have to return to teach in my university's summer program." Fred didn't reveal that he'd be returning across the Atlantic by air. This could mean providing an explanation for how he was able to secure a flight on the *Clipper*.

"Perhaps we can both be glad that our visits will be short," said Behanan, "and hope that a war does not break out before our travels are completed."

"I think I'm going to leave now," said Fred. He looked at Sophie, but she was again looking around the dining saloon.

"Will you not stay for dessert?" said Brown.

"I have preparations to make for tomorrow. And, in any case, I've been eating too much on this ship." The three men exchanged wishes for a good night and safe journeys the next day. Sophie continued to survey the dining saloon. Fred said goodbye to her, but she ignored him or did not hear him. He left, wondering if she was looking for another man to dance with and spend the night with. He regretted leaving the table. He would have regretted staying more if he'd seen Sophie making a play for someone else. She made him feel younger, as young as when he was more concerned about such games. It was not a pleasant feeling.

The only place to read in the evenings was in his cabin, because of the dancing and other noisy activities in the public rooms on the promenade deck. And the only comfortable place to read in his cabin was in bed. So he undressed, got under the covers, and continued his reading of Freud's *Introductory Lectures on Psycho-Analysis*. He was re-reading these lectures in English. Several years ago, he had laboriously read some of them in their original German.

As well as preparing for his meeting with Freud, the re-reading was also preparation for reading, for the first time, Freud's *New Introductory Lectures in Psycho-Analysis*. The original twenty-eight lectures had been presented at the University of Vienna in 1915-1917. *New Introductory Lectures* was in the form of seven lectures published in English in 1933. Fred had figured out that the additional "lectures" were not actually delivered but were essays published in the same form to show developments in Freud's thinking.

After an hour with *Introductory Lectures*, Fred fell asleep with the reading lamp on. He woke to hear Sophie's voice saying, "Fred, please wake up. I need to talk with you." She was sitting on the edge of his bed in her nightclothes, shivering a little and gently moving his head from side to side.

Fred was quickly alert. His watch showed midnight. He said, "You'll get cold. Please come under the covers."

"But I want to talk."

"We'll talk. And be warm. Tell me what you want to say."

She got under the covers. In the narrow bed, their bodies had to press against each other. Fred tried not to be aroused. He imagined she wanted to talk about their relationship, but couldn't predict what she would say. Two possibilities seemed both welcome and unwelcome: she had come to say goodbye or to propose that their relationship somehow continue. He began to hope it was goodbye.

"It is about Anna," she said, not in distress but as though she knew he would be wondering what she would say. "I woke up to find that she has left the cabin. I thought she might be with you. Now I think she might be with Kovoor."

Both of Sophie's conjectures alarmed Fred. "Why would she be with anyone?" he said. "She may have just gone for a walk."

"That is not like her. In any case, she must still be in her night-clothes. She would be with a man to hurt or annoy me – I guess to spite me, to use that word you used – and you and Kovoor are the obvious possibilities."

"Why would you think she' be with me?"

"I saw her go into your cabin with you, a day or two ago. I am not sure exactly when. I was sick. I was making an undignified trip to the toilets."

Fred explained some of what had happened with Anna on Tuesday afternoon. He didn't say that she'd embraced him and certainly not that he'd responded briefly and then resisted her approaches. He told her that Anna believed she, Sophie, was with Behanan on Sunday night.

"This is becoming a farce. She probably knows that Kovoor and I were lovers when we were graduate students in Toronto. He was often at my house on Brunswick Avenue, although I do not think he ever stayed the night. Anna was only eight or nine, but children of that age know more than we think. Kovoor and I parted on good terms some weeks before he left Toronto. We have exchanged a few friendly letters since then."

"She must be with him now," Sophie continued. "I do not know whether to go and interrupt them."

"Why would you do that?" said Fred. He now didn't want her to leave his bed, ever. "Surely a young woman of her age can decide whom she wants to spend time with."

"She is making me angrier and angrier. Kovoor's support of her at dinner did not help. She may be doing something rash. I do not think Anna is suicidal but I hardly know her these days. Kovoor is twice her age, and she may need protection from him."

Fred wanted Sophie to stay, very much. He also realized he could become embroiled in relationships of unwelcome complexity. She moved to leave the bed and he didn't stop her. They sealed an exchange of goodbyes with a long kiss, and she left the cabin.

He tried to sleep, but couldn't, and returned to *Introductory Lectures*. He wondered what Freud had written about mother-daughter conflicts and found this: "The daughter finds in her mother the authority that hems in her will and that is entrusted with the task of causing her to carry out the abstention from sexual liberty which society demands; in certain cases also she is the rival who objects to being displaced." That seemed right on target.

But then, instead of clarifying matters such as the daughter's will and society's demands, Freud rooted the cause of the conflicts in early childhood: " … the little daughter sees in her mother a person who is a disturbing element in her tender relationship with her father, and who occupies a position she could very well fill herself."

Anna's father had died when she was about seven years old. Surely this trauma, and the multitude of intervening events, must be more significant in the mother-daughter relationship? If the intervening events included substantial romantic activity on Sophie's part, as with Kovoor Behanan, they could be especially significant. One of the *New Introductory Lectures* was on femininity. In the decade or two between the two sets of lectures, Freud might well have changed his views on mothers and daughters. Fred fell asleep before he could reach for the *New Introductory Lectures*.

Part III

Glasgow and London

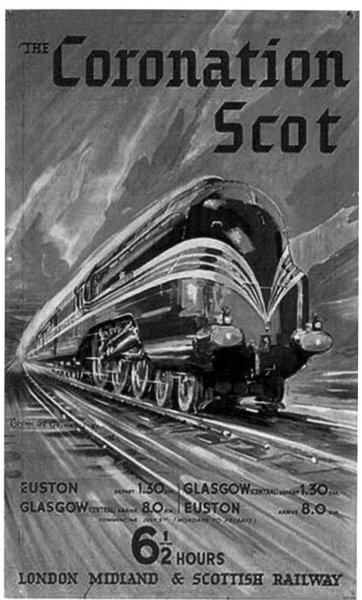

Black and white version of a poster announcing the *Coronation Scot*, which began service in July 1937, continuing until the start of World War Two in September 1939.

FOURTEEN

Meeting Mabel

Glasgow and London, Friday May 26, 1939

The *Duchess of York* anchored briefly off Greenock, a small port on the south side of the Firth of Clyde. Transatlantic ships stopped there rather than navigate eastward for some twenty-five miles up the narrowing River Clyde. A ferry carried disembarking passengers to Greenock's Princes Pier. A train then took them to Glasgow Central Station. By leaving the *Duchess* there, Fred would reach London a day earlier than if he stayed on the ship to its final port of Liverpool.

Brown was with Fred on what he called the boat train from Greenock to Glasgow. He talked almost continuously, excited to be in his native land. Fred tried to take in the scenery, enhanced by alternating sun and shade as puffy white clouds passed above. The grass and other vegetation were astonishingly green, more that Ireland's had seemed. Buildings were quaint except for the occasional industrial plant. Sometimes in view were the wide River Clyde and the farmland on its north bank, which seemed even more intensively cultivated than the fields they were passing through.

Then Glasgow began. A haze soon shrouded the sun. Every building had one or more chimneys sending dark smoke into the air. Fred felt it in his throat, harsher than the ever-present smoke from the boat train's locomotive. He remembered from his previous trip that the air of cities on this side of the Atlantic was almost always worse than in America.

Fred's next thought was the discomforting one that he'd not left a tip for Jean-Paul, the cabin steward. The matter hadn't come up between them. Fred had a hazy memory that the question of how much to tip had been much fretted about during the Atlantic crossing with his parents a decade ago. His father had taken care of things but Fred couldn't remember how. Now, he had barely sufficient cash for his estimated costs during this trip. Being frugal about tipping would help. Did the tipping system enhance employees' performance, or serve merely to keep employers' cost down?

The boat train arrived at Glasgow Central Station with two hours to spare before Fred's train to London was to depart. Brown insisted on taking Fred to lunch. He said the meals on the train would be expensive and in any case Fred should have at least one meal in Scotland. They had lunch in the restaurant of the Central Hotel, part of the station complex.

Brown explained that the hotel had played a role in the development of television, which would one day replace radio for entertainment and news. Fred had heard of television, although he had no experience of it. He knew only little about it but pretended to know more to avoid a torrent of information. Some came anyway. A Scot, John Logie Baird, had invented it. The hotel was where the first long-distance television broadcast had been received, from London, a dozen years earlier. Thanks to Baird, Britain was far ahead of America. The BBC was already providing daily television broadcasts in the London area that anyone with a receiver could enjoy.

Fred asked what he should eat for what might be the only meal he might ever have in Scotland. It was Friday. Fish dishes were prominent on the menu. Brown recommended the poached salmon. The finnan haddie – smoked haddock – would be good too although it would be better for breakfast. Whatever he had, Fred should try the black pudding, not a dessert but a delicious concoction of pig's blood, oatmeal, and onions encased in lengths of an animal's intestine. This was another breakfast food, but it should not to be missed when available, as it was now for lunch.

Fred had the lentil soup, and then finnan haddie, black pudding and peas, followed by hothouse strawberries and cream. He had not had a more delicious meal for a long time, including all the temptations on the *Duchess of York*. He felt guilty that he'd found Brown so often tedious. The man's huge store of information had some good points. Should he add to Brown's store as a reward for the splendid meal? What could he add? He could say something about natural selection and reinforcement. But what? And, in any case, what was guilt? He felt it often and needed to explain it, if not explain it away. Dr. Freud might be interested in discussing guilt. Would Brown?

Brown forestalled any enlightening discussion about evolutionary analogies or guilt by launching into a more challenging topic: their shipboard companions. What did Fred think of the exotic Indian, and the beautiful but prickly German and her crazed daughter? Fred said what he found the most difficult to understand was Behanan's favorable regard for Hitler and Germany. If he knew more about India, he would perhaps understand Behanan's views better. Anna's views were no more than a protest against her mother.

Brown didn't agree about Anna. "I've seen a few young people in Montreal who are more interested in Hitler than reason would suggest. There's genuine appeal there. For many years, young people in North America, and here in Britain for that matter, have not been given much in the way of hope. Hitler offers his people hope."

"As for Behanan," Brown continued, "I must say I've some sympathy for the independence movement in India. I saw some of the poverty there on my way to and from Australia. British colonial rule wasn't doing much to alleviate it. Many Indians may not like Hitler,

179

but they could be pleased if Britain were weakened by a war with Germany."

"What about Scotland?" said Fred, preferring not to talk more about Anna or Sophie. "Is it a separate country, or a colony or what?"

"Strictly speaking, Scotland has never been a colony of England, but she's becoming like one. Scotland is supposed to be an equal partner in the gathering of countries known as the United Kingdom, but she's always been a junior partner, ruled from London."

"An independence movement has been getting going here," Brown continued. "Indeed, a pal of mine in Glasgow convinced me to join the new Scottish National Party. At the moment, they're agitating only for a Scottish parliament concerned with purely Scottish matters, like Northern Ireland's. If they start talking about full independence, I'll have to think about my support. If England and Germany do go to war, I want Scotland firmly aligned with England, and not somewhere in the middle like Ireland."

It was almost time for Fred to board his train, the *Coronation Scot*. They went to the station's Platform 1 and walked the length of the magnificent train and back. The streamlined locomotive was getting up steam. The fireman was adding coal to the firebox. As they passed, Fred could see and feel the fierce yellow heat inside. The locomotive was a bright blue with four white stripes along the side. The color and stripes continued right to the end of the train.

"This train may be the fastest in Britain," said the ever-informative Samuel Brown, "but it's not as fast as many trains in American and Germany, and not nearly the fastest in the world." The fastest, he said, was an Italian electrically powered train running between Milan and a place whose name Fred could not catch. How did Brown know all these details? Perhaps he made them up.

They stopped outside the last of the nine cars, where Fred's reserved seat was. "It's been a pleasure to know you," said Brown. "I hope you do everything in England you want to do and your journey back – which I never asked you about – will be uneventful."

"All your information has much enhanced my trip," replied Fred. "I'm very grateful, and for the excellent lunch too. I wish *you* well, sir, in all your endeavors."

Fred quickly boarded the train, before Brown could ask how he would be returning to America. Just as he did so, the conductor sounded his whistle and waved a green flag. As the train began to move, the conductor boarded through the door Fred had used. The huge station clock showed exactly one thirty.

The third-class car had several compartments linked by a corridor that ran along one side of the train. Each compartment had eight seats. Fred found his compartment and his seat. It was the window seat that faced forward. He put his small suitcase and coat on the rack above his seat and kept his briefcase with him.

The other occupied seats were the two by the corridor. In each seat was an older man who had the appearance of a salesman of some kind. One man pointed to the cards above the seats. He said, "It looks as though we can spread out a little as there are only four of us: three now and one to join at Carlisle." Neither man spoke again. Fred wondered about British etiquette in such a situation. In America, the three men would already have introduced themselves and even shared a few personal details.

On Fred's seat was a slim booklet with a striking blue, gray and white cover, entitled *The Track of the Coronation Scot*. It was "a running commentary on the journey from London to Glasgow by the West Coast route."

Fred glanced through the booklet. He thought every rail trip should have one as a guide and souvenir. It was a commendable document of some thirty-two narrow pages, describing the communities passed through, the bridges and tunnels, and notable features of the terrain. It included a map, point-to-point mileages, running times, and speeds. It was written for passengers travelling to Glasgow, but easy to use for the trip from Glasgow to London.

They were nineteen minutes into the trip and Fred could see that the train was passing through Motherwell. The booklet advised that, since Glasgow, they had passed through Rutherglen, Cambuslang, Newton, Uddingston, and Fallside. There was as much detail all the way to London, with arrival scheduled for eight o'clock. Carlisle was the only stop, for just two minutes at three fifteen.

Fred slept for more than an hour, the effect of an early start on the *Duchess of York* and the two scotches that Brown insisted they have before lunch at the Central Hotel. From his watch and the booklet he figured the train was just passing from Scotland to England. It sped through Gretna Junction, just inside England, at what the booklet said would be more than seventy miles per hour. The booklet noted Gretna Green, just inside Scotland. Fred knew that, since the time of Jane Austen, runaway couples had gone to Gretna Green to taken advantage of Scotland's lenient marriage laws.

Fred wondered if Scottish marriage arrangements were a feature of a less formal society in which younger people had more responsibility. He should return there one day and learn more about the land of Adam Smith, David Hume and Alexander Bain.

A few minutes later, the *Coronation Scot* began a long deceleration to its stop in Carlisle. A woman and an elderly porter entered the compartment. He put her suitcase above her seat opposite Fred, took her tip with thanks and a touching of his forelock, and quickly left the train just as it was moving off. Fred had read about forelock-touching, but imagined it had died with the nineteenth century. It had not, at least not in Carlisle.

As the woman removed her hat and coat, Fred could see she seemed to be in her thirties, of medium height, with short black hair made striking by unusually pale skin. She was more interesting than beautiful. As Fred turned to the window, to avoid being seen looking at her, he noticed she had no wedding ring. She said "Excuse me, please" with a pleasant but unplaceable accent as she adjusted her feet in the narrow space between them. She took a small book out of her purse and began reading it in a way that precluded conversation.

Fred pulled out Freud's *New Introductory Lectures* from his brief-case, and a pencil and paper for the notes that would become his next letter to the other Fred. He read and made notes for an hour, often pausing to look at the scenery and check it against the booklet.

After Lancaster, a railroad official inspected their tickets. He looked at his watch and said, "Hold you seats, lady and gentlemen. The two *Coronation Scots* are about to pass, each travelling at over seventy miles per hour." He waited for a minute, looking at a large pocket watch attached by a chain to a buttonhole on his vest. Then, for a few seconds, on the track to the right, there was a whoosh and a blur and the train they were on rocked a little. The official smiled and added, "A steward will be around shortly to ask about dinner."

Fred noted that the official's accent was quite different from Brown's and from those of other people he had heard speak in Scotland. He'd read that there was a greater range of accents in the relatively small area of the British Isles than in the whole of America. He promised himself again he would think more about what caused and sustained differences in accents. For the moment, he must focus on Freud. He took out a pen and began his letter.

Dear Fred,

I'm now on a train from Glasgow to London, having had a brief taste of Scotland, which may warrant a further visit. I'll be in London a few days, chiefly in the hope of meeting Sigmund Freud. I wrote him asking for a meeting as soon as I knew I'd be in London, which was three weeks ago. I know that air mail service across the Atlantic is just being established. My letter would likely have gone by ship. But, there should have been enough time for the letter to have reached Freud by now. So I hope the people at his house will be expect-

ing a call from me tomorrow morning. I hope they'll respond positively to my request for a meeting on Monday.

An important consideration will be Freud's health. He is old – eighty-three earlier this month – and infirm. I wrote him an ingratiating letter, in my best German. I hope it "tickles his fancy," as they say. (You and I have agreed that Freud's work is mostly praiseworthy, although often misguided.)

Then there is the question of what to say to Freud. He may want to talk most of the time and I'll be content with that. I know he speaks some English. Last fall in Minneapolis, I heard a rebroadcast of a brief talk he'd given on BBC radio. This was undoubtedly well-prepared. It may not mean he can converse well in English. If we have to speak in German, we'll have a very limited discussion. Perhaps there will be someone else there who could interpret. His daughter Anna may be there, and she may speak English.

The steward entered to offer afternoon tea at their seats and ask about dinner, which would be at six o'clock in the car ahead. There was one table for four left. The two men by the door both said they would be dining in London. The woman said she would dine on the train, and Fred, who to this point was uncertain, said so too. The woman said she wouldn't have afternoon tea. Squeezing past the steward, she left the compartment. Fred followed the example of the two men and used the adjacent seat for his tea tray. After drinking some of the strong tea and eating what he now called a biscuit, he continued his letter to Fred Keller.

I've just read Freud's thirty-five Introductory Lectures. *I'm assuming you haven't read the last seven. If you have you'll know they were published years later. The first twenty eight were actual lectures given at the University of Vienna. The last seven were written in the same form but never presented.*

The last "lecture" is on the difficult concept of Weltanschauung. *You'll be able to figure out from your military service in Germany that it means something like "world-view." The word's not translated in my English version. Freud defined it early in the lecture, but not helpfully. I had a discussion about* Weltanschauung *on the ship with a philosopher from Toronto who said it is "the whole set of beliefs through which an individual or a society interprets the world."*

More specifically, Freud's last lecture asked whether psychoanalysis leads to a particular Weltanschauung. *His answer was that it does not. Psychoanalysis must accept the scientific* Weltanschauung. *He wrote that the scientific* Weltanschauung *was sometimes considered* not *to embrace the human intellect and mind. Such a* Weltanschauung *would be "paltry and cheerless." It "cannot be too energetically repudiated." He went on to say that "the intellect and mind are objects for scientific research in exactly the same way as any non-human beings."*

Well, Fred, if I could change some of the language, I'd find myself in one-hundred-percent agreement. As I wrote you before, I believe more and more that we behaviorists must deal with private events. We must deal with thinking and other manifestations of what is considered to be mind.

Freud began to lose me at this point. He asserted that only psychoanalysis can provide the means of dealing scientifically with private events. His goal was not to demonstrate the futility of other candidates for a scientific approach. It was to denigrate art, philosophy and, above all, religion as sources of knowledge and understanding.

Religion is his particular animus. It alone "is to be taken seriously as an enemy." Art and philosophy are illusionary and without influence, he wrote. By contrast, "religion is an immense power which has the strongest emotions of human beings at its service." Religion, Freud wrote, satisfies human

185

thirst for knowledge. It soothes fear of the dangers and vicissitudes of life. It directs how to live. Where does this all come from? Freud argued that the religious Weltanschauung *is determined by the situation of our childhood, a by-product of the family relationships and dysfunctions he'd already expounded. These are all mediated no doubt by the mental constructs he is well known for.*

The old boy knows how to tell a story. I wonder how he'd take to being challenged on his notions about a mental mechanism. The two main problems posed by such a mechanism are not specific to Freud. They are: how can its workings be observed and how can it be manipulated. I'm on shaky ground here. I want to explore thinking, on the one hand, and criticize ego, super-ego, and id, on the other.

There's more in the lecture. Freud said of science that its embrace of indeterminism could lead to intellectual nihilism and replacement by the religious Weltanschauung. *He said of Marxism that its aimed-for new order of society would require an improbable transformation of human nature.*

Near the end he wrote, "Strictly speaking, there are only two sciences: psychology, pure and applied, and natural science." Perhaps he and I could begin by talking about what these sciences have in common, and how they differ, or why psychology is not a natural science.

As always, writing to you is helping me sort out some of my thinking. I may write to you again over the weekend, after reading or rereading more of Freud's lectures. There's one I haven't read yet that I'll approach with considerable interest. The title is "Femininity." You know me well enough that I won't be writing much to you about it, whatever I may feel when I read it. I'm greatly missing the two women in my life – Yvonne and Julie – and I doubt whether Freud's inventions and speculations will help fill that gap.

Your friend,

Burrhus

It was five thirty. The railway booklet showed that the train must be between Warrington and Crewe. Fred read: "Crewe is entirely a railway town. The famous railway works cover 165 acres." He wondered how much of the works he would see. The woman had not returned. He left the compartment for the toilet, but also because he was curious as to where she might be. When he returned, she was in her seat, a little flushed. The train had passed Crewe.

At just before six o'clock, Fred asked the woman if he could escort her to the dining car. She thanked him and led the way toward the next car. He admired her trim body and shapely legs as she navigated the corridor and the difficult space between the cars where the floors joined and moved erratically. She seemed unstable. Fred wondered if she had been drinking while she was away. Perhaps she was simply not good at dealing with the train's movements. He resisted helping her. He didn't even know her name.

At the dining car, the maître d' showed them to the one vacant table and sat the woman at a window seat. Fred took the place diagonally opposite from her. She smiled and offered her hand. "My name is Mabel Miller," she said. "Please do sit opposite me if you would like. Unless you want to sit there and not talk."

Fred moved to the window seat. "I'm Fred Skinner," he said. "I'll be pleased to talk with you over dinner."

"You're an American, I think, and so you should call me Mabel. I could not ask someone from here to do that. It would be too forward. I would love to go to America, especially now. May I ask what you are doing here at this difficult time?"

He confirmed he was from America, asked her to call him Fred, and told her about his planned meetings with Sigmund Freud and Ludwig Wittgenstein. He said he could not place her accent, and asked where she was from.

"I'm from South Africa," she said, pronouncing the last word as Efrica, "but I've been working in London for a few weeks. I've just been in Carlisle visiting a great-aunt – my only relative here – before I return home to South Africa next week."

"What brought you to London all the way from South Africa?"

"I work for a department store in Cape Town, Stuttafords. Do you use that term, department store?" "You do," she said as Fred nodded. She continued, "I'm a buyer. Every year at this time they send one of us to Paris and London for six weeks to pick up design ideas and to make sure what we offer is not too far behind the leading edge. We don't buy from London or Paris. Their items are far too expensive. But we make drawings and even take photographs that we use with our suppliers in South Africa and India."

"I don't know much about South Africa except that it's part of the British Empire."

They were served soup in bowls deep enough to prevent spillage caused by the rocking train. Fred had brought the booklet to dinner. He told Mabel that the *Coronation Scot* was in its fastest stretch of the journey, the only time its speed was above eighty miles per hour.

"South Africa is a beautiful country but we have a lot of problems: between white and white, between white and black, and between people of mixed and other races and everyone else. Let's not talk about these problems. Avoiding them is the best thing about being away from home."

"Could I just ask about the white vs. white conflict?"

"Oh, it's between people of British origin like my family and the larger group of Afrikaners, people of Dutch origin who were there when the British forced their way in more than a century ago."

"How do South Africans feel about the situation in Europe, being so far away and yet, through Britain, potentially involved in what is happening?"

"I'm not one to keep up with the news at home, and in any case I know only what white English-speakers think. I guess there's not much interest in another war. I'm guessing too that the Afrikaners might be as partial to Germany as to England. I've little idea what the rest might feel. They seem to prefer the whites of British origin, but whether they would fight for them is another matter. I must say that here another war seems more and more likely."

"What makes you think that? I arrived in Britain only this morning and so I'm not up on things."

"Well, I can't explain exactly what's happening with Hitler, Czechoslovakia, Poland, and so on. I do know that over the three weeks I've been here, there's been more and more war talk and more and more signs of war."

The waiter took their soup bowls and served their main courses. Mabel had a layer of ground meat topped by browned mashed potato, accompanied by peas. She told him it was called Shepherd's Pie and the meat was lamb. It was a traditional English dish and very tasty. Fred had ordered the fish dish, hoping to recapture the excellent lunch. He was not successful. What was on his plate looked unappetizing: a piece of off-white and rubbery fish marooned in what appeared to be the milky water it had been boiled in. At the edge of the puddle were pale-green peas and gray mashed potato. He wished he'd asked for Shepherd's Pie.

Even more, Fred wished they had ordered wine. He hadn't suggested wine because the price seemed high. He was worried that the English pounds the travel agent had supplied would not be enough to last for his eight days in Britain.

"What are the signs of war?" he asked.

"You'll see for yourself in London. There are barrage balloons, trenches in the parks, and excavations for bomb shelters. The talk at tea breaks is more and more of war, especially what is to happen to children. They are being fitted with gas masks and taught what to do when a siren sounds. And practice sirens are sounding often, which is confusing. What upsets parents the most are the plans to send children away from London when war starts. The concern may all be in London. There was nothing like it in Carlisle. Look, there's a blimp!"

She pointed out of the window. Fred could see a large balloon in the sky a few miles to the east, bright in the evening sun. Like the submarine off the coast of Ireland, its shape brought to mind the whale seen on the other side of the Atlantic. The balloon seemed smaller than the submarine, perhaps close to the size of the whale. The wire that tethered the balloon to the ground glinted in the sun.

"Perhaps it's a test," Mabel said. "There seems to be nothing here that needs protecting from enemy planes."

They were passing through pleasant countryside, richly colored by the setting sun. Fred looked at the railway booklet. "It says here there's a military establishment over there." He pointed east. "It's a School of Equitation, which I think means horse-riding. I guess with increased motorization there's less need for horses. The space could be being used to test balloons. What did you call that one?"

"A blimp. That's what everyone called them. Barrage balloon is the other term people use. You see them occasionally over London."

They paused while the waiter cleared their plates and served dessert – cherry pie and custard, then a cheese plate and coffee.

"The people you talk to, are they for war, against it or just reconciled to it."

"You do ask a lot of questions. Are you some kind of agent for the American government sent to find out what is happening here?"

"Now *you* have asked *me* a question. I'll be pleased to answer it and any others you may have. I'm interested in what is happening here and in Europe. It's the big news of the day, and we Americans are not exposed to enough of it." Fred was pleased with his answer to the woman's alarming question, and the ease with which he gave it. He could be getting better at disguising his intentions.

"I'm sorry," she said, "I asked you a rude question. *You* asked about people's attitudes to war, a perfectly good question. As I said, even in the short time I've been here I've noticed more war talk. Part of this, I think, is growing acceptance of the need for war, if that is what is needed to stop Hitler, and to stop fascism."

"I arrived in Paris soon after the Spanish fascists won the civil war there with support from Germany and Italy," she continued. "As much as I was able to judge with my inadequate French, this victory caused many French people to switch from being against war to supporting firmer stands against Hitler and Mussolini. I've felt this more in London – where I understand everything. And there it wasn't only the Spanish matter. As my days in London passed, people seemed to be developing a stronger dislike for Hitler and the Nazis. They've been arguing more for the need to go to war to stop Hitler. No one in London seems much concerned about Mussolini."

"For someone who doesn't keep up with the news at home, you've become quite well-informed while you've been travelling."

"Thank you, sir. You'll find in London that people are now talking about little else, so it's quite easy to become well-informed. Can you remind me of your name – asked with many apologies for already forgetting – and why you are going to London?"

"Fred Skinner. Remember, you are to call me Fred and I am to call you Mabel. I'm going to London to meet Sigmund Freud, and then to a ceremony at Cambridge University." Fred was a little surprised she had already forgotten his name, if she had. There was something about her that urged caution, he was not sure what.

"Yes, do call me Mabel. Of course you said you were going to meet Freud. That is why you were reading his books so carefully back in the compartment. Why are you doing this?"

191

Fred explained again that he was a psychology professor and Freud was perhaps the best-known psychologist in the world. Freud now lived in London. He was old and might die soon. Fred hoped to be able to visit him on his way to Cambridge.

"Freud is famous enough that we've heard about him even in South Africa. Didn't he say that sex is at the root of everything?"

"Perhaps we should have some wine if we are to talk about sex when we hardly know each other?"

"You go ahead. I had two glasses before dinner, which is why I may have seemed a little light-headed and forgetful."

"Red or white?" Fred insisted. She threw her hands up in mock exasperation and agreed to a glass of white wine. Fred looked at the wine menu and asked for two glasses of Sancerre.

He continued, "Freud does say more about sex than many people feel comfortable with, particularly about sexual feelings in young children. He tells plausible stories about how these feelings give rise to adult problems."

"Does he make you feel uncomfortable?"

"A little, especially when I'm talking to a young lady about his ideas. As a scientist, I'm more concerned about whether the ideas can be tested and whether they apply to everyone or only to the kind of people he has had as patients."

Fred continued, "What I was reading just before dinner was something he wrote on femininity. He was obviously baffled by women. He wrote about 'the riddle of the nature of femininity.' He said it was something psychology is unable to solve. Do you think women are difficult to understand?"

"I must say I haven't given the matter much thought. Men, even quite intelligent men, do often seem to have simple-minded views of people, women and men. Was Freud baffled by masculinity too?"

"I don't know. He was writing only about femininity. He seemed to feel that women are an inferior version of humanity."

"Do you agree with him, that we women are baffling or inferior, or both?"

The waiter asked if they wanted two checks or one. Mabel asked for separate checks.

Fred said, "I think society is hard on women. Freud noted that little girls are smarter and livelier than little boys. My daughter Julie provides evidence of this. But women are usually not leaders of professions. Something happens during girls' upbringing that holds them back. Then there are all the domestic and child-rearing responsibilities that fall to women, even when there is no strong reason for it."

"You didn't say you were married and had a daughter."

"You didn't ask. I take it you are not married and don't have children."

"I've been married, now divorced. There are no children."

"I'm sorry to intrude. Please forgive me."

"There's nothing to forgive. I married young and, to say it in the politest possible way, I grew tired of my husband. He divorced me for what was called 'malicious desertion.' It was the best thing for both of us. The experience made me into an independent woman, capable of traveling alone and holding down an important job."

As if to emphasize the point she pulled what appeared to be a large white five-pound bill from her purse and put it on the table with one of the two checks left by the waiter. While Fred was fumbling with his wallet and figuring out what to leave, Mabel said, "I'll tell you what. This five-pound note is much more than enough for both of our meals. Let me pay today and you can take me for lunch tomorrow, if you are free."

Fred was taken aback by her proposal. He realized that he was surprised only because of the convention that men proposition women, and not vice versa. He said, "I'll be delighted to take you to lunch tomorrow. Where shall we meet?" He remembered for a moment that he should be cautious, but put that aside.

"I've been told that the restaurant at the Tate Gallery is a good place to eat. As good as the food, I've heard, is a mural that covers the restaurant walls. And if that's not enough art we can spend an hour or two in the Gallery proper. If you agree, I'll reserve a table."

"Thank you, Mabel. I would much appreciate that."

"Tell me the name of your hotel, and I'll telephone in the morning and leave the time we should meet at the restaurant. You'll have to find out from your concierge or doorman how to get to the Tate Gallery. You can always get a taxi, but going by bus will be much cheaper and nicer. Visitors often like going on the upper deck of a double-decker bus. I know I do."

Fred felt nicely enveloped by Mabel's thoughtful proposals. "Should we return to our compartment?" he said, "We've about forty-five minutes before we are scheduled to arrive at Euston."

"You Americans have such quaint ways of speaking. There's no 'k' in scheduled. Let's stay here a little while longer. May I look at your booklet?"

Mabel tried to read it, but the small print defeated her. She rummaged in her purse and pulled out a pair of glasses. Fred looked at her more closely than before. She was not a beauty like the Graydons, mother and daughter. In some ways she was the opposite: black hair, sallow skin, thin face. But Mabel had an animated smile. The glasses livened her up. The Graydons were statuesque and did not smile much. Mabel was certainly easy to talk with.

She said, "I see we're between Bletchley and Leighton Buzzard. What a name. I wonder where it comes from. In South Africa we have the jackal buzzard. It's a bird that catches and eats snakes."

For the first time since lunch, Fred regretted not having the company of Samuel Brown, who might well know the origin of Leighton Buzzard's name.

After a few minutes, Mabel continued, "So we've just passed the Buzzard place and now we're passing Cheddington. Here's something interesting. The next bridge, or the one after that, carries Icknield Way. You've heard of Roman roads. Well, this is a *pre*-Roman road. Imagine that."

"How far now?" said Fred.

"When we reach Tring, in a minute or two, we'll be twenty-nine miles from Euston. I know you were interested in speed. Well, the stretch just after Tring is," she paused, using a finger to examine the table of speeds, "is the second fastest stretch on the route, second to the one you pointed out earlier."

Fred noted that she was good with numbers, as well as being well organized and probably having a flair for clothes design.

"Now we really should be getting back to our seats," said Fred.

At Euston Station, Mabel had to take the Tube, as she called it, to Balham, which she pronounced "Bállam." It was some distance south of the river, she said, but she didn't have to change trains. Fred was staying at the Euston Hotel, within the station complex. He thought of inviting her there. Perhaps tomorrow night.

After she left, he looked at the Tube map on the station wall, trying to find Ballam. After a minute, he realized she had gone to Balham, but her 'h' was silent and her emphasis was on the first syllable rather than equally on the two, as he would say it.

From 1939 to 1945, Bletchley Park was Britain's main code-breaking center. The building and much adjacent land had been purchased in 1938 by Britain's Secret Intelligence Service because it was close to Bletchley station, fifty miles north-west of London, where the main rail line going north met the now-defunct line between Oxford and Cambridge. Fred Skinner and Mabel Miller may have glimpsed the building as they sped into and through Bletchley station at about seventy miles per hour. Alan Turing could have been there on the day of Ludwig Wittgenstein's inaugural lecture (see Chapter 22).

FIFTEEN

Tate to Balham

London, Saturday May 27, 1939

It was a fine spring day. Fred took the advice of the staff at the Euston Hotel and walked to the Tate Gallery. They gave him a route for sightseeing, marked on a small map. He had seen the British Museum, Piccadilly Circus, Green Park (where trenches were being dug), Buckingham Palace, St. James's Park, the Houses of Parliament, and the curving River Thames. The magnificent building that housed the Tate Gallery was just south of the parliament buildings, on the west bank of the river, which flowed from south to north at this point. Fred was told the walk would take an hour and a half but he did it in an hour without rushing.

Mabel had left a message at the hotel desk confirming that their lunch would be at one o'clock. Fred had more than half an hour to wait. He sat in the sun on a bench outside the main entrance. He admired the surroundings, watched the passing show of visitors to the Gallery, and reflected on things past and to come. The bench was against the plinth of one of the six Romanesque columns, about forty feet high, that supported the roof of the classical portico. It was a beautiful place to wait.

Earlier in the morning, Fred had mastered the quite different pay phone system and used two heavy pennies to call Freud's house: HAMpstead 2002. After attempts to explain who he was, in German and English, he was told to wait: *Bitte warten Sie, Herr Skinner*. After a few minutes, a woman who spoke an accented but understandable English came on the line and told Fred they had been expecting his call. Could he come to 20 Maresfield Gardens at four o'clock on Monday afternoon? He said he would be there.

He'd been inside the British Museum and the Houses of Parliament during his previous trip to England, the three days with his parents in 1928. What Fred remembered most about that visit was his father's shocked response to the amorous behavior of the couples lying on the grass in Hyde Park. He had seen none of that while walking through two other London parks this morning. Perhaps it was the wrong time of day. Perhaps such things happened only in Hyde Park, which he remembered as being larger and wilder. Perhaps the imminence of war suppressed amorous behavior, although he imagined it could have the opposite effect too.

Reading newspapers at breakfast in the Euston Hotel, Fred had learned that just yesterday Parliament had approved the introduction of conscription. It was for the first time during what was described as peacetime. Single men aged twenty and twenty-one were to be drafted for six months of military training and then transferred to a reserve. Several newspapers noted that a year ago most people in Britain opposed a draft. Opinion polls now indicated that a majority was in support, as were the editorial columns of the newspapers Fred saw. The change in support for the draft – known here as 'conscription' – was the strongest indication so far that British people accepted the need for another war with Germany.

He had a moment of guilt. He had not yet thought of Julie or Yvonne today. Usually his thoughts turned to Julie soon after waking, dwelling on their morning ritual together. It would be early morning in Chicago. He wondered whether she would like being with him at a gallery. She would. She liked doing anything with him. Freud had written about competition between mother and daughter for the father, but he had seen none of it. Perhaps Julie was too young. Perhaps this was just another of Freud's stories.

"Hello!" said Mabel, standing between him and the sun. "A penny for your thoughts?" She was wearing an appealing red and white summer dress and a dark shawl, an improvement, thought Fred, over the somber gray suit she'd worn yesterday

"If it's one of your big heavy pennies," he said, "I should reveal some big weighty thoughts. But I was thinking only about my daughter, and what we do each morning before my wife is up. I thought a little about Freud too. That thinking *was* on the heavy side."

"Hold the thought about Freud, and tell me more about your daughter while we go and find the restaurant."

Fred said a little about Julie as they walked inside and down the stairs. The restaurant was in a long room with a single arched window set into a massively thick wall. The overwhelming feature of the room was the mural that filled the upper two thirds of all the walls. On their table was a leaflet with a brief description of the mural. Its title was *The Expedition in Pursuit of Rare Meats*.

The mural had been painted a dozen years earlier by an art school student, Rex Whistler, over a period of eighteen months. It described a hunting party from the Duchy of Epicurania: a princess and her maid, a prince, a colonel, a captain, a pantry boy, and the son of an impoverished nobleman. The party set off on bicycles, carts, and horses. It traveled through strange lands and found foods that transformed the previously dull diet of the people of the Duchy.

Much of the mural depicted vegetation in different shades and textures of green, giving the restaurant a lush and soothing ambience. "I've been told the food they serve here is not as exotic as in the mural," said Mabel. "It's standard British fare, but nicely prepared."

"Remember," said Fred, "this lunch is on me, and I won't let you change our agreement."

"In that case I shall eat modestly, and certainly abide by my frequent resolution not to drink wine at lunch. I'm afraid drinking too much wine is an occupational hazard. And we have good wine in South Africa. It's hardly known elsewhere. It's a match for the French wine you get here and even in France."

They talked easily as Fred worked his way through steak and kidney pudding and Mabel her Lancashire hotpot. It was the first time Fred had eaten kidney, which he found tasty. Mabel explained that her dish was baked lamb under a layer of browned potato slices and onions. Fred said more about Julie. Mabel described her carefree life in South Africa, the pressure from her parents to settle down again, and her reluctance to do so.

"Once bitten, twice shy is the saying, I think," said Fred.

"That's what I say to my parents. They tell me I'll soon be an old maid, but that's not how I feel."

Fred was not sure of her age, but he felt she must be his side of thirty. She looked older than Sophie Graydon, whom Fred knew to be forty, but Sophie was exceptionally youthful.

They had dessert – pie and ice cream for Fred, ice cream alone for Mabel – and Fred asked for the check.

"A check is something else. The word here is bill," said Mabel. "I can see you don't understand the money. We have pounds, shillings, and pence in South Africa. They're our own, but they are worth the same as here and so I'm used to them. Let me help you." She took a one-pound bill from his small wad. "This one-pound note is worth about four of your dollars." She left it with the check. "The total was eleven shillings and sixpence, and you should leave a shilling or two as a tip." The waiter returned with three large silver coins and a smaller one. "Keep the three large ones; they are worth two shillings and sixpence each and are known as half-crowns. Leave the shilling as a tip and I'll add another sixpence."

"The basic thing to remember," she continued, "is that there are twelve pennies in a shilling and twenty shillings in a pound."

Fred was bewildered. He remembered none of this money nonsense from his previous trip here. His father must have paid for everything. How a country could function with such a complex money system was a real puzzle.

"You know," said Fred, "encountering your kind of money is a little like coming across Chinese writing. You want to know why on earth a simpler system isn't in use."

"We're used to it, and you haven't seen all of it yet. As well as pounds, shilling, pence, and half-crowns, there's the florin (which is two shillings), the guinea (twenty-one shillings), and the farthing (a quarter of a penny). And then we have the ha'penny as well as tuppence and thruppence, which are half a penny, two pennies and three pennies. It's a real mess, but we grow up with it, as they do here. Before you are eight years old you can add one shilling and sixpence and two shillings and ninepence ha'penny and in a flash know it is four shillings and thruppence ha'penny – and don't ask me how."

"I guess British kids, South African ones too, are good at math."

"We're all certainly quite good at mental arithmetic. Look, time's getting on. Are we going to look at some of the exhibits while we are here? It's all British stuff, and I'd heard some of it is quite good and there are very interesting early photographs."

The spent an hour looking at paintings, sculptures and photographs. Mabel said, "We shouldn't be indoors so much on a nice day like this, and there must be other things you want to do in London."

"I've nothing planned for this weekend. I'd certainly prefer to walk about than be indoors."

"It's too late in the day to go somewhere nice, like Kew Gardens.

Hyde Park is quite near, and Kensington Gardens too. Why don't we go and walk there?"

"Are you sure you don't have something better to do than spend time with an already married American professor who can be a bit of a bore given the chance."

"I've nothing else to do and I enjoy your company. And your being married doesn't bother me at all."

Fred wondered what she meant by that. They walked to Hyde Park through two neighborhoods of evidently expensive homes. She said the first was Pimlico and second was the even more well-to-do Belgravia. She said it was posher. They talked companionably, chatting about things they saw rather than the weighty matters that were Fred's usual fare or venturing into the complexities of their lives.

They came out of the maze of prosperous streets and gardens just by Harrods department store on Brompton Road. The imposing edifice reminded Fred of buildings in Vienna and other European cities he'd visited a decade earlier. Mabel said that part of her job was to spend time there in the women's fashion departments. She pointed out a café across the road where she would draw from memory what she had just seen in the store. Harrods people wouldn't let her draw in the store or take photographs.

They continued north to Hyde Park and joined the crowds watching workmen dig up vast grassy areas for trenches and air-raid shelters. They commented on the number of baby carriages being pushed or tended by uniformed nannies. Mabel called them prams – short, she said, for perambulators. At the north-east corner of the park, there were men, and a few women, on boxes and platforms, mostly orating about war. The audiences were larger for pro-war speakers than for pacifists.

One pacifist speaker had large crowds, and more attention from policemen in their tall helmets. The front of the speaker's platform bore the sign British Union. The speaker's words made it clear that he wanted peace because he was a supporter of Nazi Germany. Fred asked the man standing next to him if he knew the speaker's name. "It's not Oswald Mosley, but some other fascist," was the reply. The speaker was heckled often. Some in the audience tried to silence the hecklers. The policemen were quick to keep things calm. Fred was fascinated, but Mabel wanted to leave. She said the invective against Jews reminded her too much of Afrikaners' speaking about blacks.

Even though the sun had been out ten minutes earlier, it began to rain. Fred and Mabel took shelter in the entrance to Marble Arch Tube Station. "Perhaps I should now let you get on with your life," said Fred. "I've much enjoyed your company this afternoon, and want to thank you for showing me some of London."

"As I said, I've no plans," Mabel replied. "If you like, we could do something else, perhaps go to a cinema. One of London's best is near here." They walked there quickly and found long lines waiting in the rain for admission to the Regal Cinema. They did not even check which movie was playing and retreated to the station entrance.

"I have an idea," said Mabel, "I could show you my flat, which is in a part of London you'd otherwise never see. It'll take us a good half hour to get there, and the rain might have stopped by then, or it may not have rained there."

"What a nice idea," said Fred. But, just as he said this, he realized he was being incautious. He remembered his feeling on the train, during their dinner, that she might have not been quite what she seemed. He wondered if the encounter on the train had been other than fortuitous.

"But are you sure it would be a proper thing to do?" Fred said.

"I don't have designs on you," she replied. "I know you're married but I like your company. This may be a good way of seeing more of you."

Fred wondered if he should instead invite her back to his hotel, which was probably closer, and where he might be able to control things better. But then he thought he could control things more, what-ever than might entail, at her place. He could just walk out, which he couldn't do at the hotel. "How do we get there?" he said.

"It's simple. We get the Central Line to Tottenham Court Road, three stops away, and then the Northern Line going under the river for several stops to Balham." Again, she pronounced it Bállam.

They went down the steps to the ticket hall. All the ticket machines were out of order. There was a long line for the single wicket where tickets were sold. Mabel said, "I've a better idea. A bus goes from here to where I live. It's slower, but we won't even have to change. It goes past the Tate Gallery too. I came on it this morning."

They went outside again and found that the bus stop was just by the station entrance. The No. 88 bus barely stopped at the stop. They jumped onto the rear platform, climbed the winding stairs, and found two vacant seats at the front of the top deck. "This is bliss," said Fred. His alarm had subsided. "We have a wonderful view. So much better than being underground. And look, the rain is stopping."

The conductor came. "Let me do it," Mabel said to Fred. "Two to Balham High Road, please," she said to the conductor.

"That will be tenpence, ma'am." He pulled out two tickets marked with a large 5d from a rack in his hand and clipped them using a ma-chine on a belt around his neck. He took a shilling piece from Mabel, and gave her two large pennies from a pouch at his side. This was all done while he kept an eye on the road ahead and, via a convex mirror at the top of the stairs, on the bus platform below. When the bus stopped, and passengers had boarded or alighted, he gave the signal to move. He did it here – they were just above the operator – by banging twice with his foot on the floor. Elsewhere he pressed twice on one of several buttons that rang a bell in the operator's compartment.

"The man has quite a job to do," said Fred. "I guess it frees up the operator of the bus to concentrate on the traffic." He'd noticed the congestion on Oxford Street. He thought he was a competent driver but he wasn't sure he'd feel comfortable navigating this road. Vehicles moved too close to each other for his comfort. Also, the sidewalks – he knew they were called pavements here – were so crowded people were spilling into the road traffic. It was chaos. He asked, "What brings so many people here?"

"It's nothing special, just Saturday afternoon shoppers. I'm along here often. Oxford Street is the home of several of the department stores I must keep an eye on: Selfridges, Marshall & Snelgrove, John Lewis, Peter Robinson, and a few others. I don't work here on a Saturday. It's always too busy. We're going to turn right here and go down Regent Street. This is another of my haunts, especially Liberty's, which you can see ahead on the right. Then we'll see Piccadilly Circus, Trafalgar Square, the Houses of Parliament, and – you will recognize it – the Tate Gallery."

"What a wonderful tour, and an excellent guide. I saw some of this when I walked to the Tate this morning. I'm glad to see it again from a different vantage point."

Just after the Tate Gallery, the bus turned left to go over Vauxhall Bridge. "You're now entering South London," said Mabel. "It's a different world, or at least a different city from just north of the river." The buildings were smaller, grimier, and evidently less well maintained. Every now and then there were commercial establishments: stores – shops they were called here – offices and low-level industry. After a while, she said, "We're now passing through Clapham, the district before Balham. Clapham has the reputation of being the most ordinary place in England. There's a turn of phrase here: 'the man on the Clapham omnibus.' It means an entirely ordinary man. Where it comes from, I've no idea. But you are now a man on a Clapham omnibus."

"I guess we'd say the man in the street. We'd also say Clapham, which may sound odd to you." Fred sounded the 'h' and put equal emphasis on each syllable rather than only on the first. "As for omnibus, I guess it's just the original word for bus."

They passed a large park to the right. The houses on the left seemed larger than others south of the river, but modest compared with what Fred had seen north of the Thames. "We're now entering Balham," Mabel said, saying it as Fred would. He smiled at her American pronunciation. She added, "There's a very popular author here and in South Africa, at least among children. His name is Arthur Ransome. He also wrote a book for adults about London. In it, he described Balham as something like 'the ugliest and most abominable of London's unpleasing suburbs.' I'll not allow my children to read his books."

"It looks OK to me," said Fred, as the bus went down a gentle hill into an active commercial district. The street was lined with numerous stores, pubs, and other businesses.

"There's the Underground station we would have gone to," said Mabel. "We get off at the next stop."

They climbed down the stairs. Mabel went first and while Fred was still on the stairs she had an altercation with the bus conductor. When they were on the sidewalk, Mabel explained that their fivepenny fare had ended at the Tube station and next time she should pay sixpence from Marble Arch. She said she had asked for Balham High Road, which they were still on. It was the conductor's job to go into such details. Fred was impressed that the conductor had remembered where they had boarded and what they had paid. He wondered why she sometimes said Underground and sometimes Tube.

"That's where I live," said Mabel, pointing across the road to a large apartment complex, eight stories high and out of scale with its surroundings. The sign at the entrance to the driveway said Du Cane Court. Beside it was a smaller sign announcing flats and maisonettes to rent from £70 a year or 26/- a week. She deciphered the sign for Fred. A maisonette was a flat – apartment in America – with its own entrance from the outside. The weekly rate was in shillings and could have been written as one pound and six shillings, but 26 shillings was easier to write and read, if you knew what it meant. She said the design of the complex was typical Art Deco style, although she wasn't sure what that meant.

Inside the elegant foyer, a uniformed doorman said "Good afternoon, Miss Miller."

"This is like a hotel," said Fred, when they were in the elevator.

"A little," said Mabel. "There's a not bad restaurant on the premises as well as a games room, bar and other amenities. There are even guest rooms that can be rented by the night when your flat is not large enough. I like that there's a grocer's shop on the premises and even a place to buy wine."

"Why are you here, so far out, rather than near the department stores you have to spend time in?"

"I can rent a small furnished flat here by the week much more cheaply than staying in a hotel or a furnished flat in central London, even allowing for bus and tube fares. The air is better here and the people are nice. It takes me under half an hour to get to anywhere in central London. This is the cleverest thing here," she said, pointing to a letter chute just outside the elevator. "There's one on every floor. They lead down to a box on the ground floor from which the Post Office makes collections twice a day, once on Sunday. There's a telephone kiosk on each floor. As well, each flat has a chute for rubbish. We have every modern convenience"

They arrived at her apartment on the fourth floor of E Block. She said it was spacious by British standards, although Fred found it small. She did too, but flats in Central London were smaller and cost twice as much. She offered him a drink. They both had vodka tonics.

"Now you've got me here, what are you going to do with me?" said Fred.

"I thought that when we've had a drink, and perhaps another one, we could have dinner at the Indian restaurant across the road. The Du Cane Court restaurant is good for breakfast and lunch, but not so good for dinner. After a nice meal, I would walk you to the Tube station and tell you how to get back to your hotel. It's very easy."

Fred was puzzled. He'd imagined she'd brought him all the way to her apartment so he would spend the night with her. Perhaps she wanted him to ask that. He'd see how things went. Perhaps she'll suggest it later. And he must always remember that she might be different from what she seems. She was probably South African, but her talk of fashion work might be a cover for something else. But why the subterfuge, if there was subterfuge?

"A penny for your thoughts," she said. This is how she'd greeted him at the Tate. It must be an old English idiom, thought Fred, in use on both sides of the Atlantic and elsewhere where English is spoken. But one of the big heavy pennies here must have twice the value of the little American cent. Were thoughts worth more here?

"Forgive me," said Fred, "I was being rude and thinking about my meeting with Sigmund Freud on Monday."

"You're not rude at all, just being relaxed. What are you hoping to get out of the meeting?"

"I've read a lot of what he's written and I'm mostly impressed. It'll be enough just to be able to associate all those written words with a real person. I know he's old and sick. He may no longer be the stimulating person who wrote those startling things many decades ago. But he has agreed to talk with me, so he must still have some interest in these matters – and the energy to pursue them. If I have a particular goal, it's to share with him some of my thinking about evolution and get his response to what I say."

"Do you mean evolution as in Darwin and how we were all once apes and even amoebae? Is that the right word?"

"I do mean that kind of evolution. And Americans often say amoebas – and spell it with 'e' rather than 'oe.' What do you, and other South Africans, think about evolution?"

"I really don't know. What odd questions you ask. Let me think.

You know, when I was at school there was a lot of excitement about the 'missing link,' which had been discovered in South Africa. We were told to be proud that humans originally came from Africa, from South Africa in particular. This pride came along with the idea that whites were more evolved than other races. I never bought that, but I had to keep quiet about it. I knew that Blacks and Coloreds were just as smart as us, maybe more so, but they didn't have the guns and ammunition that we had."

Fred was impressed again. She said she knew little but she actually had a lot to say. She said Blacks like she said Africa, with the 'a' sounding like an 'e.'

"Let me visit what I think you call the ladies room. Then I'll get us each another of these nice refreshments, and listen to you say something interesting about evolution."

While she was in the bathroom, Fred walked around the small living room and quietly opened what turned out to be the door to the bedroom. He just had time to notice the room's tidiness when he heard the toilet flush. He quickly returned to his chair.

When they were both settled with refills, he said, "Do you think that all the complexity of life that we see about us could have happened in the way Darwin suggested? He said it was through the simple processes of variation and selection acting over very long periods of time – perhaps billions of years?"

"Oh-oh, another hard question. I can't imagine a thousand years, let alone a million, and a billion years seems a ridiculously long time. What is a billion, a million millions?"

"It's a thousand millions," said Fred.

"No, I think you're wrong about that. But maybe it's another difference between American English and British – and South African – English."

"If it is, someone should wave a big red warning flag whenever the word billion is used."

"To answer your question," Mabel said, "the only other idea I know is the one that says God made everything six thousand years ago. I don't believe that for a moment. I don't believe in God. But I do have difficulty accepting that there's nothing more than blind chance in the way things have happened. As I understand Darwin, we are as we are because some feature of our ancestors made them more successful than rivals who didn't have the feature – multiplied a million or more times. I don't think that's enough."

"Well, you have a very good idea of Darwin's basic insight. I'm impressed. It's like animal breeding. You might have a litter of puppies and allow only the ones of a certain color or with long ears to survive or at least to breed."

"But there's an intelligence guiding that: the animal breeder's goal to improve his breed. Are you saying there's a purpose guiding Darwin's process?"

"Far from it. What I'm saying is that over millions or billions – my billions – of years, the Earth has changed and the changes have produced conditions that do what animal breeders do. They make some features more likely than others to survive to later generations. For example, when there were Ice Ages, features such as thick fur were more likely to survive, but not when it warmed up again."

"And the changing environment of a particular species also included other living things," continued Fred. "It included plants and animals that could also have been changing."

"This seems to have moved far from my original question about Freud," said Mabel. But, before you get back to him, I think we should make a start for the restaurant. It closes at eight o'clock. We're not in central London where places stay open late."

"My apologies," said Fred. "It's part of my job to explain things, and sometime I forget that not everyone is a student of mine."

They left the building after spending a little time in the foyer, where Fred admired the black and white decorated marble floor, the elegant pillars and the splendid staircases.

An advertisement for Du Cane Court prepared during construction early in 1936 with an artist's impression of the finished building. In the late 1930s, Du Cane Court may have been the largest apartment building in Europe. Hitler was said to have chosen it as his British headquarters for use following a successful invasion. The surrounding area was one of London's most heavily bombed during World War Two. Du Cane Court was unscathed.

SIXTEEN

Unresolved Intimacies

London, Saturday May 27, 1939

Fred hadn't eaten in an Indian restaurant before. He was pleased he'd followed Mabel's advice and chosen the mildest of the lamb curries. Even that was too fiery for him, although a few glasses of the warmish beer helped him get used to it. Mabel's curry was more fiery. She explained that in both South Africa and Britain some of the best cooking was done in Indian restaurants. She was used to the spicier dishes.

When they were well into their curries, Fred launched again into the topic of evolution. He tried this time to link it to Mabel's question about Freud. In the way Darwin had taken some of the mystery out of evolution, he said, Freud wanted to take some of the mystery out of human behavior. Freud had often been brilliant, when dealing with slips of the tongue, for example. However, he'd complicated things by appealing to internal entities for which there was little firm evidence: the ego, super-ego, and id.

Darwin had located the main driving force of evolution in the interplay between life forms and their environments. He, Fred, wanted to do the same for the behavior of humans and other creatures. He believed that humans behave as they do in large measure because of their interactions with their environments during their lifetimes. These interactions are the causes of their behavior, not ids, minds, souls and other supposed internal entities. He wanted to discuss that with Freud.

"This is a bit deep for me," said Mabel. "I told you I don't like the idea of there being no purpose in evolution. Now you're saying there may be no purpose in what we do. I like that even less. We make plans and act on them. We are agents of our own fortune and misfortune. It's not just a matter of what we have been exposed to."

"You know, Mabel, you're smart, smarter than many of my students, and they've had the benefit of formal instruction about these matters. There's no doubt we make plans, and often act on them. My questions are these. How do we get to be making plans? And, what are we doing exactly when we follow, or don't follow, a plan?"

"Thank you for the compliment. Would this be a good time to stop discussing Freud and learn about the other reason you are here – something to do with Cambridge, I believe?"

Fred was quickly on his guard. Had he mentioned to her the meeting with Wittgenstein? Yes, just very briefly at the start of the meal on the *Coronation Scot*. Should he be surprised and even concerned that she'd remembered about Cambridge and even Wittgenstein? He saw that she was watching him closely. He said, "I can't remember how much I told you about my plans for next week."

"Don't be alarmed," she said, "I'm just making polite conversation. You said you were going to Cambridge to meet someone called Ludwig, a very ugly name to my ears. I forget his last name."

Fred noted that she had pronounced Ludwig phonetically as an English-speaking person would say it. She didn't say Loodveeg, as a German person would, and as he had said it on the train, showing off his German competence. She must have already known the name. "It's Ludwig Wittgenstein," he said, again using what he believed to be the German pronunciation.

"Is Wittgenstein a psychologist, like Freud?"

"Freud would call himself a psychoanalyst rather than a psychologist, or perhaps a psychiatrist or even a neurologist because that was his original training. Wittgenstein is a philosopher."

"Forgive my ignorance, but what does a philosopher do?"

"I guess there are two main kinds of philosopher. One is concerned with matters considered to be beyond science, such as values, ethics, and how we should live our lives. Another kind of philosopher is concerned with how words are used. Wittgenstein belongs to the second type. He must be good at it because he's just being appointed to a top philosophy job at Cambridge University."

"Why are you going to see a philosopher?"

Fred told Mabel about the invitation to the Cambridge ceremony. He suspected it was because A.N. Whitehead – at Harvard, but well-known at Cambridge University – knew he was writing a book on verbal behavior. This was behavior involving words; it included talking, listening and reading. Fred now thought he and Wittgenstein might be saying similar things but from different perspectives. Whitehead probably felt it would be useful for them to get together and so had engineered the invitation. Fred didn't mention Bertrand Russell.

"So, you've come all this way on the chance you'll have a discussion with this person Wittgenstein?"

"I'll get to talk with him. I'll be in Cambridge for a few days. He has to be there, and I can't imagine that he won't spend an hour or two with me. Remember too that I'm here to see Freud, and that looks as though it's going to happen."

"I've come all the way from South Africa to do a few drawings, so it's not so much different. But my company is paying for me, because they want the drawings. Who's paying for you to come here?"

Fred was convinced these weren't idle questions. Mabel, or someone pulling her strings, seemed a little too interested in his meeting with Wittgenstein. He had a truthful answer to her last question. "We professors get grants for things like this. Most of my trip is being paid for by a small grant from the Carnegie Foundation. It believes meetings such as I'll have are worth supporting. I'm paying some of it myself."

"Mabel," Fred continued, "what's your real interest here? You seemed to know already that I was going to meet Wittgenstein, and your questions have become quite searching."

"I don't know what you mean." Her usually pallid skin had gained some color. "I'm a naturally nosy person. I wouldn't know your Wittgenstein person from the man in the street, or should I say the man on the Clapham omnibus."

"Sorry to be accusatory. I just felt you were pumping me for information. I couldn't figure out why."

Fred had ordered an ice cream dessert to cool down his tongue after the curry. Mabel asked for a glass of white wine, but they had none by the glass so she had a whisky and soda.

"I'm on an expense account, so I'll pay for my own meal," said Mabel. "If I could represent you as being useful to Stuttafords I could pay for yours too. I don't think I can do that. Let's split the bill down the middle and pay half each, and I'll help you with the money. Then I'll help you find the Tube station."

When they were outside, Fred said, "I know where the station is, just past the bridge." He pointed north along Balham High Road. "But, before I find my way there, I want to be a gentleman and escort you across the road to your apartment building."

In the building's foyer, she said, "Now you're here, I suppose I should invite you up for a drink."

Fred was quite unsure what to do. He could be walking into a trap, but what kind of trap? He could find out more about the reason for her questions, but did he want to know? There were the other factors. Did he want to be intimate with Mabel? Perhaps he did, but he was also concerned about his marriage – although that seemed far away. He felt the packet of Trojans in his pocket.

While Fred was doing all this thinking, she'd summoned the elevator. She led him into it and pushed the button for the fourth floor.

When she'd fixed them vodka and tonics, she sat on the couch. Fred was in the armchair. "Come and sit on the sofa with me," she said. "We can be friendly, but I should warn you I don't do sex."

Fred joined her on the couch, but with a little distance between them. "Mabel," he said, "what's your game? Why have you invited me up here? Why have you spent so much time with me today? And, if I may say so, why, once we were back here, did you straight away start talking about sex?"

"Now *you* are asking *me* a lot of questions. I have no game. I like you and enjoy your company. I'm a bit lonely here in England. I don't have sex because I am frightened of being penetrated. When I said my husband divorced me for malicious desertion, I was saying politely that he got a divorce because I wouldn't have sex with him."

Fred was taken aback by her frankness. He wondered if it was a diversion to distract him from pursuing the reason for her interest in his meeting with Wittgenstein. Nevertheless, he was interested in her condition. "Do you want to talk more about that?"

"I forgot for a moment that you are a psychologist."

"I'm not that kind of psychologist. But I know that talking about difficulties can often help."

"I saw someone about my problem in South Africa. I believe he was a disciple of your friend Dr. Freud. He wanted to know about my childhood sexual experiences. I couldn't remember having any, not until I was a teenager anyway. I don't know if my problem is in my head or lower down. I do know that penetration is painful, sometimes very painful. We've had Tampax in South Africa for a few years, but I

217

can't use them. I have to keep on using sanitary towels – sanitary napkins of pads they're sometimes called."

Fred was taken aback again. Her candor, if it was that and not a diversion, was truly unusual. Perhaps she was talking to him as she would talk to a therapist. He played along and said "Are there times you don't feel pain?"

"Not really, if you are talking about penetration." She paused, and then said, "Since we've come so far, can I be very intimate?"

Fred wondered what more she could say. If her confidences were a ploy to divert the conversation away from Wittgenstein, she was certainly pushing the ploy to an extreme. He said, "Please go ahead. I don't think you will embarrass me more than you have already."

"If I masturbate in a certain way and reach an orgasm, I've found that I can then explore my vagina with much less pain, sometimes none at all. What do you think?"

"Well, now you *have* embarrassed me more. I'm impressed with all these technical words you use: orgasm, masturbation, and so on."

"I've been doing some reading about my condition. I thought, talking to a professional, I'd use what seem to be the proper words. We have our own words for these things. They may be English or American words too. Some of the slang words we use are Afrikaans rather than English, like the word 'doos' for vagina, which means box in Afrikaans. But tell me, what do you think about my condition?" She pronounced 'doos' as though it rhymed with Suez.

Fred could not remember ever having had such an explicit conversation, particularly with a woman he hardly knew and had not been intimate with. "The only thing I can think of is that the orgasm relaxes you. This suggests that the pain from penetration results from some kind of tension. Do alcoholic beverages relax you, enough to help with the pain."

She paused before replying. "I don't know. You've noticed that I

218

drink a lot. I've never associated my drinking with my pain problem, negatively or positively. I must think about it."

Fred stood up. He wasn't sure why he did that just then. As he stood, he felt a compulsion to leave. He said, "I've enjoyed having this extra drink with you, Mabel, and I'm honored to have been able to share your confidences, but I really think I should go now and find my way back to Euston station and my hotel."

"Please don't go yet." She held his hand and pulled him gently back onto the couch, this time closer to her.

"If I stay, you must tell me why you are so interested in me and in my meeting with Ludwig Wittgenstein."

"My, you are persistent. All I can do is repeat what I said before: I like talking with you. For that reason alone, I'm interested in what you're doing. Why do you keep on about this?"

"In the restaurant, I sensed you already knew I was here to see Wittgenstein, even before I told you that on the train."

"I didn't, and I can't imagine how you got that impression."

"In the train, I pronounced Ludwig as a German would say it, or as I think a German would. In the restaurant, you pronounced it as an English-speaking person would. You must have already known the name and the two ways of saying it."

"But I did. There was a Ludwig in my year at secondary school. He was from Germany. He pronounced his name much as you did. But we British called him Ludwig, as I have just said it. So I was familiar with both ways of saying it. When you said Loodveeg on the train, I thought of Ludwig."

"Instead of sleuthing an imaginary preoccupation of mine with your Ludwig man," she continued, "perhaps you could apply your skills to figuring out what to do about my condition. I've just remembered the name the psychiatrist gave it. It was vaginismus."

"I don't know that word. I'll accept what you say about Ludwig Wittgenstein. However, apart from talking about your condition in a general way, I don't think I can help you. But if there is something more you want to tell me, I'll offer an understanding ear."

"There's not a lot more to tell. If there's a move to have something inside me, or if I just think about it, the whole works seem to clamp up. Trying to push through it can seem like – like what? – like trying to push a finger into your thigh when you have a bruise there." She pushed a finger into his thigh.

Fred said, "The kind of psychology I do leads me to think that Dr. Freud may be right about the origins of your condition. I think Freud would say that you can't remember the incident responsible for your condition because the painful memory of it has been repressed."

"Here's how I differ from Freud," Fred continued. "He'd say that the incident that caused your problem must be uncovered through psychoanalysis for a cure to be possible. I'd prefer to deal with whatever it is in the present that maintains your problem."

"I'm not sure what you mean."

"Well, before the event that caused your problem, the tightening was an inherited reflexive response to pain in the area. Let's say that the event included touching the area and then pain. Because the two occurred together, in that order, touching gained the power to produce the response to pain. It's a little bit like Pavlov's dogs, which you may have heard of."

"I think I followed you until you got to the dogs."

"Pavlov was a Russian scientist who presented dogs with a sound just ahead of food. He found that after some pairings the sound alone made the dogs salivate. The sound stood in for the food. In your case, touching stands in for whatever caused pain in the area."

Mabel said, "For how long did the sound alone – with no food – continue to make the dogs salivate?"

"That's a good question. You're a smart lady, Mabel. It would take about a dozen pairings to establish the sound as what we call a conditioned stimulus. It would take about the same number of solitary presentations of the sound to undo the effect of the pairing. The technical expression is to extinguish the conditioned reflex."

"Do you mean I had repeated pairings of touching and pain?"

"Not necessarily. With an unpleasant stimulus, conditioning usually requires fewer pairings, perhaps only one. But extinction can require more solitary presentations. Let me say this another way: when a tone is sounded just before rats are given an electric shock, they show a fear response to the tone very quickly, and then it's hard stop the tone producing the fear response."

"That seems cruel. I'm glad rats are used for that and not dogs." Mabel continued, "Are you saying hat in my case if there is enough touching without pain, eventually there will be no tightening."

"I think so. But you have to understand that this is theoretical. I've no formal experience in helping people with such problems."

"What you're saying makes more sense than trying to remember whether I had a bad experience when I was three years old."

"Let me add something," continued Fred, as though she hadn't spoken. "In humans, thoughts can stand in for actual happenings. So, thinking about being touched can have the same effect as being touched. And it may not be touching that is the conditioned stimulus producing the tightening. It could be an odor, or the thought of an odor, or something else. I would guess that touching must be at least part of the conditioned stimulus."

"Sorry to go on," Fred added, "but can I say one more thing? If you move too fast, so that penetration is attempted before extinction has occurred, the penetration could be painful and there will be reconditioning of the stimulus."

"I think I get that too: a lot of touching, and hold off on the penetration until I'm sure there is no tightening."

"Perhaps you can help things along by taking advantage of situations in which touching the sensitive area doesn't produce the tightening. I can think of three ways of doing this. We've touched on two ways: orgasm and alcohol. They may need to be tested more. The third way would be to approach touching the area slowly and gently, in the hope that the tightening doesn't happen."

"With all three methods," Fred continued, "the aim is produce touching, and even some penetration, without tightening."

"Well, Dr. Skinner, you said you're not that kind of psychologist, but I think you could go far as a therapist. I like all three methods. Perhaps they could be used in combination. Would it help if someone else were to do the touching as well as me? Would you help me?" She looked at him intently, gently pulling on his arm.

Fred looked beyond her. "I like your forthrightness, and I would like to be able to say yes." Standing up, he said, "But I think I really am going to go back to my hotel. I've said too much. I don't know enough to be your therapist. As well, even though you've shared intimacies with me, we're not close enough for me to be the kind of friend you may need to help you."

She was still looking intently at him. He could see that her eyes had become moist. She said, "I can't really disagree with you, although it must be no secret to you that I'd begun to hope for more." She paused and then said, "Can I see you tomorrow?"

"Tomorrow? I must do more preparation for my meetings. Perhaps it's better if we part now."

"I'd be pleased to sit with you while you do what you have to, and eat with you when you are hungry. Nothing more. You could do your preparation here or I could come to your hotel room, or we could go somewhere else, to a park if the weather is good."

Fred was about to say no, as politely as possible, when she said,

"I'll tell you what. Let me telephone you in the morning to see how you are. Perhaps one of us will have changed our minds."

He didn't answer and left quickly, before any opportunity for a goodbye hug or kiss. As he walked along Balham High Road to the Underground station he wondered whether he'd done the best thing. He'd declined spending the night with a congenial and fairly attractive woman. But, assuming her vaginismus actually existed and was not a diversionary tactic, it would have been a night with complications, although not necessarily unpleasant complications. And if her vaginismus was a ploy then he could have uncovered the reason for the ploy. Would he have wanted to do that? If she were trying to find out more about the purpose of his trip to England, did he really want to know why? If he asked too many questions, or got too involved, he might reveal things he should not reveal.

He had arrived at Balham Underground Station. Even though it was almost ten thirty on a Saturday evening, a man was selling newspapers outside. Fred bought two to read during the trip to Euston Station. When the train arrived, he was surprised by how small it was. There was room for him to stand only along the center line of each car. This was not a problem because there were many vacant seats at each side, but he imagined that when crowded such small cars would be very claustrophobic, particularly when stalled in a tunnel deep underground between stations.

Each newspaper had the same two main stories, but gave them different emphases. The *Evening Standard's* main headline was "Fare Shock" with the sub-head "No more ha'pennies." On the train to Euston, Fred read that bus, tram, Tube, and railway fares were to increase in two weeks, chiefly to round up fares that contained a halfpenny. The rounding up was being done to make it easier to mechanize the issue of tickets.

The main headline in the *Evening News* was "Russian pact with West against Axis?" That afternoon British and French diplomats had been to the Kremlin with a proposal for mutual assistance in the event of an attack by another European power, presumably Germany. Fred reflected on the second question he'd been asked to answer: Will the Soviet Union cooperate with Germany in an invasion of Poland? He knew there was an alliance between Britain, France and Poland. Would the proposed new alliance with Russia, if it happens, mean Germany would be less or more likely to invade Poland? Would Russia be less or more likely help Germany?

Fred couldn't puzzle out these matters. Until now, he'd not thought enough about international relations to realize how complex they could be. He wished his knowledgeable students were here to help him.

One thing was clear to Fred from the current overture towards Russia. The proposed alliance was an act of desperation on the part of Britain and France about the anticipated war with Germany. He'd read that in April the two countries had rejected a proposal by the Soviet government for an alliance. As far as Britain was concerned, the Soviet Union had been pariah state because of her treatment of the Russian royal family and her communism. Now, a little more than a month later, Britain and France were themselves proposing an alliance, presumably hoping it would deter Germany.

Fred was glad he was at least able to draw one conclusion from the political mess. War, provoked by Germany, could start soon unless extraordinary things happened. He wondered how Sophie and Anna were faring on their rail and sea journey to Germany. They would now be in their sleeping cabin in a train on a ship moving across the North Sea.

Which brought him back to the present reality of Mabel. She had been another complex encounter. If he was going to have dalliances, perhaps he should seek or accept only ones that were free from complexities. How could he do this? As he thought about Mabel, he couldn't put to rest his suspicion that she was hiding something. However, what concerned Fred more just now was the advice he'd given her and the behavioral analysis on which it had been based.

Fred's problem was that his analysis didn't include reference to behavior reinforced by its consequences. This was the kind of behavior he'd spent several years investigating, which he believed to be of profound importance for humans. Mabel said she had unwanted behavior: inconvenient muscle tightening. His analysis could have led him to identify an ongoing consequence of the tightening that was maintaining it. He could then have figured out a way of allowing the tightening to occur without its maintaining consequence. This would have extinguished the tightening, at least in the presence of the stimulus that set the occasion for it.

This line of thinking assumed that the muscle tightening was behavior that was not normally changed by reinforcement but could be. It was like the control of abdominal muscles illustrated in Kovoor Behanan's book on yoga, or the control of toe movement Behanan demonstrated on the deck of the *Duchess of York*. As Fred tried to imagine how a woman's involuntary pelvic muscles might be brought under explicit control, the train arrived at Euston Station and he had to find his way to his hotel.

Anna and Sigmund Freud early in the morning of June 5, 1938, arriving by train at the Gare de l'Est, Paris, in the course of moving with some of their family from Vienna to London.

SEVENTEEN

Anticipating Freud

London, Monday May 29, 1939

It was a beautiful afternoon. Fred was walking to Sigmund Freud's West Hampstead home. The hotel staff had plotted a good route. Much of it was through Regent's Park and over Primrose Hill. He now had a copy of the new *A to Z Atlas and Guide to London and Suburbs*. Using it made finding his way around the bewildering city a little easier. He surmised that being involved with the intricate street patterns *and* British money must give London children exceptional conceptual abilities. He'd allowed two hours for the walk, twice as much as he was told would be needed. He'd be able to savor some of the sights and avoid being late.

Mabel had called yesterday morning. She'd almost persuaded Fred to see her again. In the end he'd said no. She called again in the afternoon, but he was out and didn't call back. He was visiting the nearby Madame Tussauds wax museum. After that visit, he'd explored the Boating Lake, in a different part of Regent's Park from where he was now walking. Fred had enjoyed his own company yesterday and this morning. He'd accomplished much reading of Freud and Wittgenstein and had composed yet another letter to the other Fred. Apart from Mabel's call, he'd hardly exchanged a word since Saturday with anyone other than hotel staff.

The previous evening, Fred had had his first exposure to television. Samuel Brown had piqued his interest in this invention during their lunch in Glasgow. The Euston Hotel had what it called a television viewing room. Fred and a dozen other hotel guests had assembled there at nine o'clock for the live broadcast of a play, *First Stop North*, from a London theatre. The screen was small, about a foot from corner to corner, but large enough for Fred could see the expressions on the actors' faces from his chair ten feet away. The sound was good. The picture made it better than radio but much inferior to what could be experienced in a movie theatre. He'd been tired. The very British play seemed to be set in an auto repair shop somewhere north of London. It didn't hold his attention. After twenty minutes he left and went to bed.

Over leisurely breakfasts, yesterday and this morning, Fred had read the numerous newspapers in the hotel dining room. He scoured them for hints as to how he might answer Calvin Cooper's four questions. At the same time he wondered what this exercise could contribute. If British newspapers were useful sources of information, surely the White House would have someone better qualified than he to review and assess them? Perhaps not. He remembered Cooper's comments about Joe Kennedy, the untrustworthy ambassador to Britain. Because of Kennedy, the White House might give little credence to any information sent from the London embassy to Washington.

Fred read articles on air raid practices in schools and on the dispersal of industry. He read of an intensification of the military alliance between Germany and Italy. These were among many items that described preparations by both potential sides in an imminent war. As for which side the Soviet Union might take, there were reports that Vyacheslav Molotoff, the Soviet Prime Minister and Foreign Minister, had promised an early response to a British-French proposal for an alliance. David Lloyd George, British prime minister during the Great War and still a prominent politician, had said in the House of Commons that the alliance would avert war. One newspaper noted that Lloyd George had become a Hitler sympathizer. Fred was surprised by this statement. He tried to figure out how such sympathies would color a view about the British-French proposal.

It was a fine day for a walk. The sky was almost cloudless. The sun was hot but there was a cooling breeze. Regent's Park was beautiful, with elegant trees, lush lawns, and magnificent floral displays. Even more people were out than yesterday, strolling or sitting, or lying on the grass. At the hotel, he'd been told it was Whit Monday, a national holiday. A hotel guest at the reception desk had added for the benefit of an American that Whitsun was the English name for Pentecost, an important Sunday in the Christian calendar. The Whit Monday holiday had become an occasion to enjoy the good weather the day was usually blessed with. Pentecost was a special day for the Pennsylvania Dutch, people of German origin in the Susquehanna Valley where Fred grew up, but he recalled no holiday associated with it.

Now Fred was walking past the Regent's Park Zoo. He wondered what would happen to the animals in event of war. He crossed Prince Albert Road and walked up the rough grassy slopes of Primrose Hill, quite different from the manicured lawns of Regent's Park but still crowded with people. At the top he admired the view across London and then sat on the grass in a vacant spot in the shade of a tree. He was well ahead of schedule and could stop for at least half an hour. He pulled out the letter he'd written the day before and a pencil in case he wanted to change something.

Dear Fred,

I'm looking forward to meeting Sigmund Freud tomorrow afternoon. My fears that he hadn't received my letter – or that he had but wouldn't see me – were unfounded. I'm still thinking about what I'd most like to discuss with him. I'm hoping this letter will help me decide. He may have his own ideas as to what to talk about. What I've heard about his clinical technique positions him more as a listener than a talker. But that may not apply to discussions with people who are not his patients, especially other professionals. Even if he's inclined to dominate discussions with colleagues, there's also the reality that he's old and sick. What may be a general weakness – as well as the cancer in his jaw I've heard about – could well make him less of a talker. But I've encountered older people who are quite garrulous.

I hope he doesn't want to talk about his new book Moses and Monotheism. *The first two parts of it had already been published in German. The complete work, including a controversial third part, was published for the first time this month, in English. I know this because of a superb publication available at my hotel here in London,* The Times Literary Supplement. *The current issue has a review of the new book. The anonymous reviewer said the third part could be controversial because it argues that religion is a form of neurosis. I believe Freud had said as much in earlier books. I fear he'll want to talk about the book just as a father wants to talk about his newborn child.*

If I'm setting the agenda for our discussion, I'll want to start with matters we have in common. I may have touched on some of these in my last letter. With apologies for any repetition, here's what I think Freud and I both believe.

We believe that human behavior can, in principle, be explained. It's more complex than the behavior of other organisms. This is because humans speak and engage in other verbal behavior. We both believe that even the most complex behavior is amenable to scientific analysis.

We both believe too that the causes of behavior are often not evident to the person behaving or to observers. We locate the causes in different places, elaborated below.

Also, Freud and I both believe that evolution through natural selection is an important framework for understanding human behavior. We might both go further and say that this century is seeing a revolution in our understanding of the human predicament comparable to the revolution caused by Darwin and Wallace in the last century. That revolution destroyed, said Freud, "man's supposedly privileged place in creation." Freud and I have different ideas as to what this century's revolution in understanding human behavior actually consists of (again more below). Nevertheless, each of us is convinced that his approach has or will upend conventional thinking about what makes people do what they do.

The last matter of agreement is the shared belief that much can be gained from the detailed study of individuals. Freud's analytical strength is evident in his accounts of his individual case studies. As you know well, I've found that the results of detailed observation under controlled circumstances of a few organisms to be more compelling and fruitful than results teased out of large samples by statistical manipulation.

I guess the main difference between Freud and me concerns the importance of behavior. For Freud, what people do is a mere expression of more important inner activities. For me – and you – behavior is the central topic of our science. For Freud, behavior is caused by the putative inner activities. For you and me, behavior results chiefly from the history of interplay with a responsive environment. Inner events may themselves also be the result of such interplay.

Freud has elaborated a structure of mind to explain what people feel, say and otherwise do. In one of his introductory lectures there is even an "unassuming sketch" of the structural relations. The three main elements of his diagram are the ego, the id, and the less familiar super-ego. Behavior is the result of unremitting conflict among the three. It's a nice fabrication that leads to often-persuasive hints as to what may have

231

caused particular behavior. My problem with it is that the only evidence for it is the behavior that is being explained. It's a fabrication without a proper foundation.

Freud is an admirer of Darwin. He accepts the notion that the evolution of species has occurred largely through natural selection, through the favoring of particular features by the environment. I wonder what he would say to my suggestion that the development of human behavior within a lifetime occurs mostly through a similar mechanism of selection: the reinforcement of some rather than other features of behavior.

I wonder too about the evidence for Freud's developmental stages. The sequence of oral, anal, and genital preoccupations makes some sense. I wonder how determined its details are by our culture or, specifically, by the culture of turn-of-the-century Vienna. I've heard that Margaret Mead's two books point to considerable cultural difference in these matters. This wouldn't surprise me. Major cultural differences would be inconsistent with Freud's implicit position that the stages are universal and likely inherited.

Another issue is whether the unfolding of an individual's developmental stages determines the individual's personality type. Freud believes it does. What if the stages don't exist, or occur in a different order? That's another thing to raise.

Again, Fred, you have helped me greatly, even though you may never know it.

Your friend,

Burrhus

Fred didn't make any changes in this letter to the other Fred. Writing and now reading it had given him a better grasp of how he could begin a discussion with Freud. Would Freud take an initial focus on agreements as politeness or as an expression of fealty? He would like to have a productive discussion, but not one that merely gratified the old man's ego. Fred caught himself using a Freudian term. But it wasn't a Freudian term. Freud had used the German word for I, *ich*, and a translator had equated the Latin *ego* with *ich*. Similarly, the German word for it, *es*, had become id in English. Freud's *Über-ich* had become *super-ego*. Fred wondered if English-language psychoanalysis would have proceeded differently if the translator had used I, super-I, and it.

Ego was an odd word in English, thought Fred, a direct borrowing of the Latin for I, but serving as a noun rather than a pronoun. It seemed to have two meanings. One was self-importance. He has a big ego; she has a small one. The other was self, a more slippery concept. Bertrand Russell had written somewhere, "When I die I shall rot, and nothing of my ego will survive." What did he mean? That he would no longer behave? He might say it meant something more: that his essential being – his self, the aspects of him that made him distinctive – would not continue. But surely it's Russell's behavior that makes him distinctive? Weren't ego and self merely other words for personality, an equally imprecise notion? Russell, perhaps following Freud, might have been referring to his own consciousness. We know about the consciousness of others only through their behavior. We might also know about our own consciousness only through our own behavior. This would be because it's only through our behavior that we have words to describe our consciousness – through the process he'd described in his letter about Wittgenstein to the other Fred, the process of correctly reporting a toothache.

It helped to think about animals. Could an animal have an ego, in either of the above senses? If ego was a word for personality, then yes. Dogs certainly differed in their habitual behavior. Were they conscious? Were they self-aware? It would be interesting to devise ways of answering such questions experimentally.

Fred was aware of himself in a way that he was not aware of any other person. Was his ego this different awareness? Was this awareness what would not survive his death?

A breeze started. Fred began to feel chilly thinking about death in the shade of the tree. His watch said three fifteen. He walked on and was soon at the beginning of Maresfield Gardens, with half an hour to spare before his appointment. He went into St. Thomas More Church and learned a little about this advisor to the notorious King Henry the Eighth. He read that More was beheaded in 1535 for opposing the formation of a separate Church of England. Henry wanted release from the authority of the Pope so he could then decree that his second marriage, to Anne Boleyn, would be legitimate.

More was not canonized until 1935. Fred wondered why it took Catholics four hundred years to honor one if its martyrs. More had written the novel *Utopia*, and coined the word. It was about an ideal society that sounded a little like communism. In More's *Utopia* there was no private property and no unemployment. There was free medical care and distaste for warfare. Perhaps More had lost his head as much for these heretical proposals as for his defense of papal supremacy. His canonization might have had to wait until communism became fashionable, at least among intelligentsia. Writing a utopian novel, Fred mused, could be a good way of setting out ideas about how better understanding of human behavior could improve society.

Some minutes after the arrival shown in the photo before Chapter 17, Sigmund Freud walked along a platform at the Gare de l'Est with two of the well-wishers who greeted the family: Princess Marie Bonaparte of Greece and Denmark, a friend and benefactor, and William Bullitt, U.S. Ambassador to France.

EIGHTEEN

Meeting Freud

London, Monday May 29, 1939

A t four o'clock, Fred pressed the front door bell button at 20 Maresfield Gardens. For a few minutes before, he had waited on the sidewalk admiring the large house and its fine sash windows each with many small panes. He was reminded of the oldest building at Harvard, Massachusetts Hall, which he knew to date from the early eighteenth century. He wondered if Freud's house was that old. While admiring the house, he had noticed a movement at the drapes in the window just to the right of the front door. Someone was looking out for him.

The door was soon opened by a short, plain woman. Fred guessed she was about his age. She wore a long black dress and black stockings with open sandals. For a moment he took her to be a maid, but realized she could be Freud's daughter Anna.

"I am Anna Freud," she said, extending her hand. "You must be Professor Skinner." He recognized her voice as the one on the phone on Saturday. She spoke good English with a pleasant low voice and a German accent whose location he could not place. It was similar to that of the dentist Lucas Glaser but her words were more precisely articulated. Fred nodded and shook her cool hand.

"Please come this way," she continued. "You must understand that my father is frail and tires easily. He is in good spirits today, but when he is like this he goes on for longer than he should, and suffers later. I will interrupt you after about forty-five minutes. Please support me and bring your discussion to a close. He will resist, but please do as I ask."

"Of course," said Fred, "I appreciate your consideration for your father's welfare."

She led him to the door on the right side of the entrance hall. As it opened, Fred caught a mix of odors more often encountered in hospitals: disinfectant with an undercurrent of decaying flesh. They entered a room darkened by heavy velvet drapes across the windows to the right of the door. One if these windows must have been where Fred saw a movement when he was on the sidewalk. Most of the long room was to the left of the door. The far wall was a bay also covered by heavy, floor-length drapes. The only lamp in the room was on a desk in the bay. Figurines and statuettes occupied most of the desk's surface. A small work space remained. It held a text being edited and a mess of papers and books.

Sigmund Freud was sitting back from the desk. He stood as Anna and Fred approached. She said, "Professor Skinner, may I introduce you to my father, Professor Freud."

Fred said, "Professor Freud, it's my pleasure to meet you." He added, gesturing at the desk, "I hope I am not interrupting you unduly."

"My father sees few people these days," Anna said, "but he told me to make an exception for you."

"I'm grateful, Professor Freud," said Fred, "and I hope our discussion will be worth your while."

"*Danke*, Anna," said Freud. As she left, he pointed to a green tub chair beside the desk and said, "Please sit there, Professor Skinner. First, I want to tell you why I am pleased to see you."

Fred saw a chaise-longue behind the chair, adorned with oriental rugs. Could this be Freud's consulting couch, brought from Vienna? Could this be where countless patients had engaged in free associations about their childhoods? Could the chair Fred was lowering himself into, when turned away from the desk, be Freud's customary seat for his clinical sessions?

Before Fred could resolve whether to ask these questions, Freud, who had sat down, said, "You probably know that I am near my end. My frail body has become a burden. I tire easily. I am often in pain, although not just now. My daughter, my wife, her sister, my physician, and many friends have advised me to see as few people as possible. One friend said I should avoid Americans because they upset me. And yet, I am making an exception for a young American professor of psychology. Can you imagine why?"

Fred was still examining the room and only half listening. The question took him by surprise. He had a better view of Freud now that his eyes had become accustomed to the gloom. The man he saw was shrunken and old but not evidently at death's door. He spoke well-structured and well-phrased English with a strong accent, but very slowly and precisely, and thus clearly. His voice – pitched a little higher than average – could have been that of a younger man, although not a young man. Freud was sitting upright in his chair, facing the far end of the room. Fred saw less of the right side of his face, perhaps the side affected by cancer. He said, "I'm honored that you have agreed to see me, and eager to learn why."

Freud did not respond immediately. As Fred waited he noticed two other odors: cigar smoke and dog. He could see nothing associated with cigars on the desk. In the near-darkness beyond the desk he could just make out the source of the other odor. A large furry dog was lying half under the velvet drape, watching both men.

Freud turned a little towards Fred and said, "My body is near its end, but I like to think that my mind shows few signs of decay. Should I use the word mind when speaking to such a psychologist as I am told you are? We will come to that. I am very busy, with one book just published and two more in progress."

"I read about your newly published book, *Moses and Monotheism*, just this weekend. Many congratulations, Professor Freud."

"Thank you. It is a book that will be of interest mainly to Jews. I will be pleased to tell you what is in it, but I expect that with the name Skinner you are not a Jew?"

"I'm not a Jew, but that doesn't mean that I wouldn't be interested in your book. I've always found what you have written to be of great interest. Even if I haven't agreed with your ideas, I've found them thought-provoking."

"Thank you for your kind words, Professor Skinner. Let me tell you about my two unpublished books, both of which may interest you more than the book on Moses. One is unfinished. I was working on it when you arrived. I am writing it in German, of course. The working title is *Abriss der Psychoanalyse*. In English it could be 'Outline of Psychoanalysis.'"

"Could it also mean 'Demolition of Psychoanalysis'?"

"*Ach, ich verstehe dass Sie etwas Deutsch sprechen*," Freud said, chuckling. "Now I remember that your letter to me was in German. Let us continue in English for we are here in England. May I let your little joke pass and say something about my other book?"

"Please do, Professor Freud. I meant no offense."

Freud paused for minutes before continuing. Fred felt much more relaxed in Freud's presence than he had expected. Freud was still not facing him, perhaps to hide the right side of his face. Fred took the opportunity to look again around the room, which he could now see clearly. It was a comfortable and comforting space. He had become used to the strange mix of odors, although the hint of rotting flesh was sometimes disturbing. The dog had not moved.

"My other book is finished, but may not be published for a few years. Unlike almost everything else I have written, it is the result of a collaboration. My co-author – is that the word for *Mitverfasser*? – is a remarkable friend who was here earlier this month, on the day your letter arrived. His name is William Bullitt. He is now the ambassador of the United States to France. I asked Bullitt about you and he said he would make inquiries. A few days later he telephoned me from Paris and told me about you. He said that if I was feeling well enough and could find the time I should meet you."

"I'm amazed! I'm afraid I've never heard of Mr. Bullitt."

"He is a well-connected man. He has the ear of your president. He knows the president's personal secretary well. They were once engaged to be married. I believe they remain good friends. I owe Bullitt a large debt. He caused President Roosevelt to intervene on my behalf with the government in Berlin. Otherwise I would still be in Vienna. Bullitt also made much use of his protégé Mr. Wiley, the American Chargé d'Affaires in Austria, to facilitate the safe passage of me and my household. Bullitt and Wiley helped in other ways too, but they could not arrange passage for my four sisters."

Freud paused, again for a long time. He said, "I am seeing you because Bullitt said I should, but I think I shall enjoy our discussion. May I tell you about the book that Bullitt and I have written?"

Fred was surprised and curious. He had not mentioned his interest in Freud to Roosevelt's people, but now they had discovered it and even facilitated it. The idea that Freud had written a book with an American ambassador was extraordinary, to say the least. He said, "I'd very much like to hear about this book."

"It is a psychological study of an earlier American president, Thomas Woodrow Wilson. Bullitt proposed that we write about him. I was intrigued for four reasons. One is that Wilson interests me as a significant historical figure with evident defects of personality that call out for explanation. Another reason is that these defects contributed to his and to America's intrusion into European affairs during *des großen*

Krieges and, even more, to the disastrous settlement that followed. It was disastrous because it paved the way for the monstrous things that are happening in Germany today. A minor consequence of these monstrosities, but huge in its impact on my family, is my relocation here when I could be spending my last days in my beloved Vienna."

Freud paused. Fred was now used to the lengthy pauses. He waited for the other reasons. What Freud was saying was in any case so different from what he expected, he was unsure as to what he could say at this point. He reflected on the old man's remarkable lucidity. Apart from the slow expression and lengthy pauses, it was that of a younger person, not of someone in his eighties who was near death. Freud did speak remarkably slowly, more slowly as the conversation continued. Perhaps he was tiring. Perhaps he was in pain because of the cancer. Would he speak so slowly in German?

Before Fred could ask if he was content to continue, Freud said, "The third reason was that Bullitt knew Wilson personally. He was a member of Wilson's staff at the negotiations leading to the *Treaty of Versailles*, the disastrous settlement I have just mentioned. Moreover, he was prepared to undertake much of the research for a book. Bullitt speaks and writes excellent German, which made our collaboration easier. I am to be the first author, but more of the words in the final version – which is in English – are his. To avoid any doubt, we have indicated our agreement with every word of the study by putting our signatures to each of its thirty-five chapters. That is what we were doing when your letter arrived. There are other parts of the book that we have identified as having been written individually."

"The fourth reason may seem to you to be a trivial one, but it has some importance for me. Wilson and I were born in the same year, 1856. I don't believe that birthdate determines destiny, but I do believe that people born at about the same time can be subjected to similar influences. If you don't know of it, I commend the excellent novel *Jahrgang 1902* by Ernst Glaeser. It's about a group of boys born in that year. They were too young to fight *im Krieg* but old enough to experience it and its aftermath and become attracted to a fanatical leader. I believe it has been translated, but I don't know the English title, perhaps *Vintage 1902*."

"I commend Glaeser's writings to you for another reason. When the Nazis had their obscene book burning in May of 1933, soon after they took over the government, Glaeser's books were among those sent to the bonfires. They were sent with mine and those of many other writers, including Albert Einstein, Karl Marx, and your Ernest Hemmingway and Upton Sinclair. I remember what the person who consigned my books to the flames was reported to have said: *Gegen die Übertreibung der unbewußten Triebe basierend auf zerstörungsfreie Analyse der Psyche, für den Adel der menschlichen Seele, verpflichte ich in die Flammen das Schreiben von Sigmund Freud.* Did you understand that?

Fred said, "Not fully. It was something about unconscious drives, the psyche and the soul. I imagine it was not flattering. I hope you were not upset."

"Not at all. Sales of my books increased for a period, especially outside Germany. But I should have heeded the warning. At the time of the book-burning, I joked that this was progress. In the Middle Ages they would have burned *me*. I should have heeded the words of the great poet Heinrich Heine. A hundred years ago he said something like this – and I will use English this time – "Where books are burned, in the end people will be burned too.""

Fred said, "I'll read your book on President Wilson with great interest. Could you tell me now, in a few words what you and Ambassador Bullitt have written about him?"

"First let me say that Bullitt and I have agreed that our book will not be published until after the death of the second Mrs. Wilson. We want to avoid any discomfort on her part that may result from publication of our study. Mrs. Wilson is now almost seventy years old. You may not have to wait for a long time."

Freud continued, "In view of what I have just said, what I tell you now about our psychological study must remain in confidence. In our view, President Wilson provides a classic case of what I have called an unresolved Oedipus complex. By this I mean that at the stage of development when young people achieve some emotional separation from their parents, Wilson did not. He maintained an ambivalent attachment to his powerful father that persisted long after the father died in 1903. Wilson was already president of Princeton University."

Freud paused for more than a minute. Just as Fred was about to ask about the nature of the attachment, Freud said, "Wilson's ambivalence showed itself in his relationship with other men. He hated them, as he had hated his father. Or he loved them, as he had loved his father. His love took two forms. When challenged he was passive, as he had been passive when challenged by his father. At other times, he was idealistic, as his father had been. *Sein vater war ein protestantischer Pfarrer. Was is der englische Begriff?*"

"We would say protestant minister," said Fred, delighted that he had understood Freud's lapse into German.

"Thank you, Professor Skinner. Let me say a few words more. It was Wilson's idealism that led him to propose his Fourteen Points as a basis for terminating the war and securing peace. It was his passivity – as well as his distaste for the French and British leaders – that led him to abandon many of the fine sentiments he had held. The result was the disaster I mentioned earlier."

"So you and Ambassador Bullitt blame President Wilson for the present alarming state of affairs in Europe?"

"We do not go so far. But it would have been better if America had stayed out of the war. Then in Europe there would have been a deadlock. Is that the right word?" Fred nodded. Freud continued, "Then there could have been an honorable peace. Then Austro-Hungary could have survived. Then, above all, there would have been no basis for the humiliation of Germany that set the stage for her present despicable government."

"So, you say that Germany was unreasonably humiliated at the end of the war. If she had not been humiliated, the Nazis would not have become so powerful."

"Many bad things have happened during the last twenty years. I would not want to assign the blame for all of them to President Wilson or, indirectly, to his parents. I do believe that if Wilson had been helped to come to terms with his attachment to his father he would have been a more capable president. He would not have been responsible for so much harm."

There was a long silence. Freud seemed to have all that he wanted to say about the book on Wilson. Fred felt he could move the discussion toward matters he wanted to raise. He said, "Professor Freud, should I understand that the three stages of human development you have identified – oral, anal, and genital – are inherited."

"Yes, all children go through these stages." Freud was becoming animated. "To a degree, the stages reflect differing sensitivities of the sense receptors, and to this extent they are inherited. But what happens at the stages is important, and that depends on the child's interactions with its parents. If, for example, a boy has an overbearing father who becomes a rival for the mother's affection – as seemed to be the case of Wilson – the boy may not progress out of the third stage in a satisfactory manner. There would be resulting disturbances in personality. I am simplifying greatly, above all because I am saying nothing about the personality of the mother."

"Are such disturbances in personality inevitable?" asked Fred.

"There are processes – universal laws of psychic development – that psychoanalysis has found to be true for all human beings." Freud was becoming animated. "It is reasonable to presume that humans, through natural selection, have a brain that provides a foundation and a locus for these processes of mental and psychic development."

244

"I have two more questions," said Fred. "But if my questions burden you, please tell me."

"Please ask your questions, Professor Skinner. I am feeling tired but I am enjoying our discussion and would like it to continue. I fear that my daughter will arrive soon and make us stop."

"Thank you. My first question concerns the evolutionary advantage to humans of the phases of development you've elaborated. You are known to be an admirer of Charles Darwin. This great scientist taught us to see each feature of a species as the accumulation of advantages in relation to an environment that changed across eons. The beaks of finches he found on the Galapagos Islands differed in shape according to the food that was available. If the phases of development are an inherent feature of humans, what evolutionary advantage did they and do they provide?"

There was another long pause. "We need more research on such matters. I do not have an answer to your question, but I hope I have pointed the way towards an understanding of how the human mind evolved. I am indeed an admirer of Darwin. I believe too that there must be room for mechanisms in addition to natural selection. For example, we must allow for the inheritance of acquired characteristics such as proposed by Lamarck."

"We could discuss that more," said Fred. "Let me first ask my other question. What if the study of other cultures shows that children do not always go through your three developmental stages? What if in these other cultures, and even in our own, adult patterns of behavior are observed that bear little relation to childhood experience? If these things were found to be true, how could your arguments about the inheritance of developmental process and their impact be supported?"

"Professor Skinner, I am first and foremost a scientist. If I am convinced that essential facts have changed, or there is wholly new information, I change my formulation. I have made changes before. A significant change was the inclusion of *Todestriebe*, death drives, as a counterpoint to the sexual or survival instincts." Freud paused. He was clearly tiring. He continued, "On the matters of the universality of development stages and their effects on adult personality, I do not believe that the essential facts have changed."

Anna Freud came in. Her father said, "Anna, please leave us to talk for ten more minutes. Our discussion is at an interesting point."

Fred concluded that the main factor in her warm appearance was the deep-brown color of her eyes. He said, "I'd certainly be interested in talking more. But if that would tire you, Professor Freud, I would prefer to leave."

"Let me make a suggestion," said Freud, consulting a small book he took from his jacket pocket. "If you could return tomorrow morning, at eleven o'clock, we would be able to continue our discussion for another forty-five minutes. That is as long a visit as Anna will allow me to invite you for."

"I'd be delighted to return tomorrow morning," said Fred. He stood and remembered that they had not shaken hands when they had met. Perhaps it was not Freud's custom, or he did not now want people to come close to him.

"I have another request," said Freud. "Would you be able to accompany my daughter to a concert this evening?"

Fred took a moment to digest this unexpected question. He looked at Anna, who had not spoken since entering the room. She gave a slight nod. Fred said, "I'd be honored. What is the concert?"

"My good friend Pablo Casals is playing at the Royal Albert Hall. It is in aid of Spanish children. He has given me two tickets, which I believe are for good seats. I promised him I would attend if I could, but I cannot. Anna should go. It would be better if she had an escort." He paused and smiled. "I must return to my writing. Perhaps you could discuss your arrangements in another room."

As they left, Fred expressed his thanks for the meeting. Anna and her father exchanged words in German that Fred did not understand.

In the entrance hall, Anna beckoned Fred to enter what was obviously the dining room. They sat at the end of the dining table. She said, "I hope you did not feel trapped into accompanying me to the concert. It is not too late to say no. If we go to the concert, we should have dinner first."

"I meant it when I said I would be honored. And I'd be doubly honored if we were to have dinner together."

"You are very polite. In case you were to accept, I have reserved a table at the excellent restaurant in the Gore Hotel, a few minutes' walk from the concert hall. It will take us almost an hour to get there, perhaps longer because today is a holiday. We should leave soon. Please wait here for a few minutes. There is a toilet – is that the word in English? It is to the right as you return the entrance hall."

Fred rinsed his face and hands, combed his hair, and straightened his tie. He was dressed too casually to eat at a good restaurant and attend a concert, and perhaps not warmly enough to be out in the evening. His fears about being under-dressed were allayed a little when Anna returned. She had not changed out of her shapeless long black dress, or even her sandals. The only addition was a light raincoat, far from new, and she might have tidied her hair.

Flyer announcing a March 1939 concert at London's Royal Albert Hall, on which the concert described in Chapter 19 is based.

NINETEEN

Evening with Anna

London, Monday May 29, 1939

Fred and Anna arrived at the restaurant at a quarter past six, the time of the reservation. They had said little on the way, apart from exchanging pleasantries during the walk to Finchley Road Underground Station and from South Kensington Station to the Gore Hotel. The three subway trains they took were too crowded and noisy for conversation. When changing trains they were too intent on navigating the mazes of tunnels between platforms, some closed for construction, to talk about much else than finding their way. Fred was surprised by Anna's familiarity with the subway system. He had expected her to be less worldly. He was surprised too by her interest in the system. She'd pointed out that their arrival platform at Baker Street was the oldest in the world, dating from 1863.

At the restaurant, Fred's fear that they were under-dressed was confirmed. The other diners were smartly attired. Women wore fine dresses. Some men wore tuxedos. Another confirmation came from the disparaging look of the head waiter, who barely welcomed them. The man spoke to Fred, but Anna answered. She said their reservation was in the name of her father, Professor Sigmund Freud, who could not be there. She was with the professor's American guest.

They were seated in an out-of-sight alcove near the exit from the kitchen. Fred explained what he thought had happened. The head waiter was going to turn them away on account of their appearance until her father's name was mentioned. They did not get the prominent table assigned to him, but an undesirable one. Fred would have caused a fuss at home. Anna said that this kind of thing did not upset her. She was used to it because she refused to dress up. In any case, she was so pleased to be safely in England she tolerated London's silly expressions of class distinction. They were even more absurd than those of Vienna.

A waiter asked about cocktails and wine, which Anna and Fred both declined. They agreed that they wanted to remain awake during the concert. Another waiter arrived with bread, water, and menus in French. Anna ordered the roast chicken dish to be followed by a salad. Fred ordered the traditional English roast beef and Yorkshire pudding to be followed by *bagatelle à l'anglaise*. This dessert he took to be English trifle. He had tasted it for the first time on the *Duchess of York* and had enjoyed it immensely. Anna declined bread. Fred helped himself, hungry from missing lunch.

"If I could ask without being impolite or intrusive, I would very much like to know what you and my father talked about," said Anna.

Fred said, "Your father told me something of his recent and forthcoming books. He spoke a little about *Moses and Monotheism*, which I'd read about. He mentioned his new survey of psychoanalysis. The most time was spent on a book about our President Wilson he's written with William Bullitt, our ambassador to France. When you came back into his office, we'd just begun talking about the role of heredity in human behavior."

"The book with Bullitt is a mystery to me," said Anna. "It is a part of my father's work – perhaps the only part – that he kept from me. He has a high regard for Mr. Bullitt, the only person who may address him as Freud. His colleagues, even some of his friends and family, call him Professor or Professor Freud. Another indication of my father's esteem for Mr. Bullitt is that they seem to have written a book *together*. My father has rarely shared authorship. He wrote a book with the eminent Professor Breuer many years ago. More recently, there was a short pamphlet published with Professor Einstein. That is all. As you know, my father's *œuvre* is large. Is the book with Mr. Bullitt completed?"

"I believe so. It's a psychological study that's not to be published until the second Mrs. Wilson has died."

"I know my father and Mr. Bullitt share a dislike of Thomas Woodrow Wilson. I suspected they were working on something about him. Is the book in German or English?"

"Your father said that the book is written in English, but much of their collaboration occurred in German, in which Bullitt is fluent."

"He is indeed – quite remarkably so for an American, especially one who does not come from a German family. I have also heard him converse fluently in French, and I have been told that his Russian is serviceable. He was your ambassador in Moscow for several years."

"I didn't know that. I've not had the pleasure of meeting Ambassador Bullitt. How well do you know him?"

"I have met him often. He was here a few weeks ago, after my father's birthday, and a few months ago. Last year, he was on hand when we stayed in Paris, *en route* from Vienna to London. Several years ago, when they were working on what must be the book you refer to, Mr. Bullitt was often in Vienna. I felt especially excluded because the collaboration was giving my father much pleasure."

Their main courses arrived. They ate in silence for several minutes. Fred took quick glances at her, registering her fine skin and lips, devoid of make-up. She often sat hunched over her plate, which made her seem even smaller. Fred had his back to conversations at other tables. They were loud, with a jarring quality. He could not make out the words well because of the frequent noise of the nearby door being slammed open by waiters leaving the kitchen area.

He said, "How does your father know Pablo Casals?"

"They met in Vienna at the studio of Ferdinand Schmutzer. They were there for portrait sittings. Between the appointments – I forget who followed whom – they fell into discussion and remained friends. Their friendship was unusual because my father is almost entirely un-musical, as I am to a lesser extent. Perhaps you saw Schmutzer's por-trait in our entrance hall. My father likes it very much."

"I'll look at it tomorrow. Anna – may I call you Anna? – many things your father said today surprised me, but one thing above all, and it wasn't the fact of the book with Bullitt. It was his assertion that America should not have intervened in the war."

"You may call me Anna, but what should I call you?"

"Fred, if you will. It's my second name. My first name is an unu-sual one – Burrhus, spelled B-U-R-R-H-U-S – but only one person ever uses Burrhus. He's a friend who shares the name Fred."

"I imagine that Fred is short for Frederic?"

"In my case, yes, without a 'k' at the end; but I believe my friend has always been just plain Fred."

"Fred, my father is not normally a patriotic person. He strives to transcend everyday politics and allegiances. There is an exception to this. I remember that at the beginning of the war, in 1914, he experi-enced a surge of patriotism for Austro-Hungary. I was eighteen years old and strongly affected by my father's emotion."

"I feel strange calling you Fred rather than Professor Skinner," she continued, "even though I think you may be younger than I. Please reassure me that this is acceptable."

"You must remember that I'm an American, and that we are often informal. In America, it wouldn't be unusual for two people of about the same age to use first names soon after meeting."

"My father does not like your country, in part because you are so informal. But, Mr. Bullitt, an American, is among his closest acquaintances. And you, also an American, are almost the only person he has not known for decades whom he has allowed to visit him here in England. I believe Mr. Bullitt recommended that he see you."

Their plates were cleared. Her salad arrived, and then his dessert. After he had tasted a little of the trifle, Fred said, "I know you've followed your father in your interest in psychoanalysis. Are there ways in which you differ from him?"

"Not many. I can suggest two. One is expressed in my book *The Ego and the Mechanisms of Defense*. There, with my father's approval, I suggested that the ego has a stronger role than in his formulation. The other is my focus on children, particularly disturbed children. In his psychoanalytic practice, my father has seen only adults. He has dealt with childhood experiences from adult perspectives. I have focused my therapeutic work on children, on techniques for communicating with them and for earning their confidence."

They finished their courses. Anna asked, "What will you and my father talk about tomorrow?"

"I'll let him guide the discussion, to the extent he wants to. We may say more about the role of heredity. If possible, I'd like to focus on his masterly contribution to the study of what I call verbal behavior. I'm writing a book on this topic. His analyses of slips of the tongue, mishearing, forgetting, metaphor, symbolism and other features of speech are the most thought-provoking I've encountered. I'll suggest it's not as necessary as he thinks it is to look for explanations inside the speaker. I'd prefer to look for them in the speaker's interactions with the outside world. Is your interest in communicating with children a move away from concern about mental processes?"

"It is not a move away but a focus that builds on my father's work. Perhaps I shall try and join you for tomorrow morning's discussion.

You saw him at his best today, at least his best for several days. Tomorrow morning, he could have had a worse night than usual and be quite low in spirits."

"I hope he's as good as today. We now have twenty minutes or so before we should leave for the concert. Will you have coffee? If it's not too painful, may I ask you to say a little more about your last days in Vienna and your move to London? Several times this afternoon your father lamented having to move."

"Of course I will have coffee. I was brought up in Vienna. It is painful to talk about what happened during the past year. But it may help me to talk about it."

Fred ordered two coffees. Anna told him how the takeover of Austria by Germany in March last year had devastated her family. The takeover was expected. They should have left earlier, but there was hope until *der Anschluss,* the actual incorporation of Austria into Germany. Anna was so distressed she had wanted them all to commit suicide. Her father scorned this suggestion. He did not want to give the Nazis the satisfaction of finding him dead. Stormtroopers raided the apartment. She was arrested and interrogated by the Gestapo.

Meanwhile, Anna continued, an international effort had been launched to free them from the new Greater Germany. William Bullitt's efforts were the most significant. He caused President Roosevelt to intervene. Bullitt secured the strongest involvement by the representative of the American government in Vienna. Also important were the actions of her friend Dr. Ernest Jones. He knew members of the British cabinet and persuaded them to insure that residence permits were granted for the Freud household. The third important figure was her father's ever-present friend, Marie Bonaparte, Princess of Greece and Denmark, who has wealth beyond ordinary comprehension.

The Nazis seemed as interested in securing the assets of Austrian Jews as in persecuting them. The presence of the exotic princess, literally throwing money around, certainly helped. Almost all of her father's assets in Vienna were confiscated. The princess paid their way out, paid for their journey, paid for a stopover in Paris, and paid to settle them in London.

Anna's main fear was for the health of her father, but he endured the waits and the indignities well. He avoided despair by engrossing himself in his work, chiefly in writing *Moses and Monotheism*. During the horrific three months between *dem Anschluss* and their departure, Freud's only lapse into despondency was when he realized that his four sisters would be left behind. Her dear aunts are still there, barely surviving the harshness of the regime towards Jews.

Anna paused. She seemed tearful. Fred waited until he was sure she wouldn't continue. "Thank you for telling me that. It is a moving story that has told me more than I expected to know about the difficulties you've had." He paused and then said, "I should ask for the check, I mean the bill."

"You do not have to do that. It will be sent to my father."

"Well, thank you. The dinner was an unexpected pleasure, as will be the concert."

Anna said, "My father believed that he would return to Vienna. He gave a copy of his book *The Future of an Illusion* to a former patient and current benefactor. He wrote in it: 'To Mrs. Margaret Stonborough on the occasion of my temporary departure.' Mrs. Stonborough had been Gretl Wittgenstein, Ludwig Wittgenstein's sister. Decades earlier, she had married a wealthy American. The book and inscription were of course in German. It was not until my father settled in London that he realized he would never return."

Anna referred to Wittgenstein as if Fred knew who he was. Fred pondered whether this would be because of Wittgenstein's eminence, or because she knew that Fred was to see him in Cambridge. If the latter, Bullitt must have provided this information, having been given it by Roosevelt or his staff. If it came from Bullitt, what else did he know? What had been conveyed to Freud? Fred was tempted to quiz

Anna as to what she knew. He decided not to, in case his questions provoked concern about his motivation for meeting Freud.

Instead, he said, "Thank you again, for the information about your father's predicament. It must have upsetting beyond belief for your father, and also for you and your family." He looked at his watch and said it was perhaps time for them to leave for the concert.

After another disagreeable encounter with the head waiter – over retrieving Anna's raincoat – they walked up the hill towards Hyde Park. There they turned and saw the Royal Albert Hall, a huge dark domed edifice. Fred was surprised. He'd seen a painting of it when built decades earlier and had expected to see an elegant red brick building with extensive decoration in white stone. The smoke from London's millions of coal-burning fireplaces and thousands of factories, not to mention the vehicle fumes, had buried the Hall's extraordinary exterior in layer upon layer of grime.

Fred now realized that all London buildings must have suffered the same fate. They were not originally the dark gray they now appeared. He'd seen similar discoloration in American cities, and some in Europe, but nothing as extreme as this. He wondered about the impact of this air on the lungs of London residents. He'd learned a new word in London for this poisonous air: smog – a portmanteau of smoke and fog. Children here had a head-start on mapping and mental arithmetic, but they could go to their graves earlier succumbing to asthma, bronchitis, emphysema and worse.

The usher at Door 6 frowned at Anna and Fred when she presented their tickets. Fred suspected it was because of their attire. He said, "Where do we go, buddy?" in his strongest mid-West accent, and "Thanks a million!" when the usher reluctantly pointed them to a door marked "Orchestra Stalls." They found their way to their seats in the center of Row J. Everyone around them was finely dressed. Anna buried herself in her program. Fred did too, but only after looking around the huge hall. High above him, in galleries obscured a little by haze, he could see people dressed more casually. The haze was no doubt London smog that had found its way into the building.

As he scanned the program, Fred realized he'd been missing music during the trip – not as much as he'd been missing his family, but enough to make him feel content to be where he was. He said to Anna, "Thank you very much for this. It will be a splendid concert – just what I needed. I hope you'll enjoy it as much as I shall." As he spoke, he touched her on the arm. She flinched and moved her arm away. She said nothing and returned to her program.

Fred reflected that if he had not been feeling so sanguine he would have felt slighted and even disturbed by her rebuff. His good spirits allowed him to read the program in more detail. He saw that Casals was to play not one but three concertos. It would be a long concert. He knew four of the five pieces on the program, all except the cello concerto by Edward Elgar, a composer he associated with British imperialism.

The concert had been chosen to reflect the times. It was in aid of Spanish children, refugees from the fascistic regime installed at the end of the civil war. The first two pieces were by Austrians, Mozart and Haydn, perhaps in lament of the disappearance of Austria into Greater Germany. Then followed an excerpt by a French composer from an opera set in Spain. Elgar's concerto was the item before the interval. The one item after the interval was the longest on the program. It was the cello concerto by Antonin Dvořàk, in his time a passionate Czech nationalist. It had no doubt been included to lament the recent German takeover of Czech lands. This concerto, Fred knew well, had been completed in the United States at the same time as the composer's New World Symphony.

After the short overture, Pablo Casals came on to the stage to applause that was restrained in the orchestra stalls but rowdy high up in the galleries. Casals was short, not much taller than the cello he was carrying. He was almost bald with just a graying rim of hair, portly and yet delicate in movement. He mounted the low stand beside the conductor's podium and settled. Only his eyes, firm behind rimless gold spectacles, taking in the audience, gave any suggestion of a virtuoso. Otherwise his appearance was that of an aging clerk in an old-fashioned grocery store.

As the orchestra played the introduction to the Haydn concerto, the audience continued stirring, just a little. It stilled when Casals began playing. He was doing no more than elaborating the themes of the introduction, but for Fred these themes were being expressed at an emotional level he had rarely experienced before while listening to music. He sat entranced for the twenty-plus minutes of the concerto. Casals played with his eyes closed. He opened them only during the few parts of the work he was not playing, resuming his assessment of the audience. During these brief moments, he often appeared to look where Fred and Anna were sitting. This discomforted Fred, already resenting the interruptions to the beautifully fluid sounds coming from Casals' cello.

At the end of the Haydn concerto, Fred found that his and Anna's arms were against each other on the armrest. He was unsure how that had happened, and whether Anna had even noticed. He leaned a little towards her. "That was truly magnificent," he said.

She moved her arm away. "He is a most remarkable performer," she said. "Even a person as unmusical as I can see that."

"If you are so unmusical, why did you come to this concert?"

"Do not misunderstand me, but I liked the idea of an evening out with an intelligent American psychologist with quite a different perspective on the human condition from that held by my father and me. When I say do not misunderstand me, I want you to know that I have lost any interest I had in men as men."

Fred didn't know how to respond, or even if a response was expected. He didn't have to because the conductor was returning to the podium to conduct the brief Spanish element of the program. It was the potpourri of Andalusian themes that began the final act of the opera *Carmen* by George Bizet. Fred and Anna said nothing during the brief interval when the conductor left the stage to fetch Casals for the Elgar concerto. Again, there was much applause at the sight of Casals. Even the spectators in the stalls were more animated.

The audience stilled the moment the conductor lifted his baton. It was soon clear why. The piece began with Casals' cello producing the most sublime sounds from a musical instrument Fred had experienced. As the first movement continued, Fred realized that this was not the Elgar of reputation. This was not what Fred understood to be an English musical sensitivity. He was not sure what it was, other than it was sublime.

Fred was entranced by the concerto and Casals' playing all the way to the unexpectedly modest finale. As well as a complete revision of his opinion of the composer, this concerto – and the previous one – had changed his view of the cello. Before, he'd regarded the instrument as no more than part of the array of string instruments that provided the orchestra's base, dominated by the lofty, nimble violins. Casals had revealed the cello as the orchestra's emotional core. Fred reflected on what this might mean. Were certain arrangements of sounds intrinsically reinforcing? Or punishing? Should behavior related to music – for example, sight-reading – be regarded as part of verbal behavior, or something different? He should consider these matters. He realized that Anna was talking to him. She had turned to him and was smiling. He heard her say that they had ten or more minutes during which to stretch their legs. She might have said something before that.

Before they could stand up to join the few people who were walking to the rear of the Hall, a distinguished man in full tuxedo sporting a row of miniature medals went to the microphone. He introduced himself as the chairman of the organizing committee. He credited Casals with the idea of an occasion to build up a fund to help "his little countrymen and countrywomen without regard for political considerations." Casals had donated his time and extraordinary ability. The speaker hoped that the audience here and people elsewhere would be so generous. Collecting boxes would now be passed around.

Bills, even the large white five-pound banknotes, were being added to the boxes that Fred and Anna could see passed along the rows in front of them. "I have nothing to give," whispered Anna. Fred replied that he could spare only a few coins. As a box reached them, they passed it along without contributing, as Fred had seen done a few times by people in front of them.

"It's like being in a church," said Fred.

"Or a synagogue," said Anna.

The orchestra had returned and was warming up again. There was no time to walk. Fred wondered if he should ask Anna to explain her loss of interest in men. But this could amount to admitting that his earlier slight physical contact was deliberate. He decided to say nothing, reflecting that the adoring daughter of a man as powerful as Freud could be expected to have problems with other men, as Freud himself might agree.

The conductor led Casals back to the center of the stage and quickly launched the orchestra into the Dvořàk concerto. Casals again scrutinized the audience during the minutes before he was required to play. Then, as in the Haydn concerto, he transformed the orchestra's introductory theme into a transcendent experience.

Fred was transported by the performance. He reflected how this work, although in detail different from the New World Symphony, was evidently by the same composer. The common features were analogous to an author's distinctive style or even a speaker's accent. He'd produced analyses of literary styles, the latest being a study of alliteration in Shakespeare's sonnets. During this trip, he had already considered doing the same kind of thing for speakers' accents: how they are acquired, and how they persisted, or not. Perhaps musical styles should be added to the list.

Then, Fred became so absorbed in Casals' playing that the finale took him by surprise. He had rarely been so keen for a concert to continue. The applause lasted several minutes. Casals returned to the stage several times. Loud pleas of "Encore! Encore!" did not persuade the maestro to return with his cello. He seemed drained.

On the way out, Anna explained that he could get a bus to his hotel from the stop across Kensington Road. There was already a long line there and she suggested walking for ten minutes to Knightsbridge Underground station. They exchanged comments about the concert as they walked. Fred wanted to find out more about her emotional and intellectual interests, but did not venture there. Even more, he wanted to do nothing to jeopardize the meeting planned with her father for the next morning.

On the train, Anna explained that she would get off at Piccadilly Circus for her journey north. He should continue for another stop, changing at Leicester Square for a train to Euston. Fred offered to escort her home. She thanked him and declined the offer. She knew her way. It was safe. They were not in Vienna. And the journey there and back would make him very late in bed. Just before she alighted, she offered her hand formally and thanked him for an enjoyable evening. He shook it gently, said the pleasure was his, and watched her disappear into an exit from the station platform.

The 1926 photograph Ferdinand Schmutzer used to prepare the etching of Sigmund Freud mounted in the entrance hall of his London home, and several other etchings.

TWENTY

Freud's Caution

London and Cambridge, Tuesday May 30, 1939

At eleven the next morning, Anna answered the door greeting Fred with a soft smile. She showed him Schmutzer's portrait of her father. "I'm not sure why my father likes it so much. He used to have that look on his face when he chastised me as a child, although of course the face was younger."

"I see the sketch was done in 1926. He is noticeably older now, but I sense that his mind, as they say, is hardly diminished."

"That is true, and it is kind of you to say so. But there is an important qualification. He tires much more easily now, and when he is tired he is not so alert. As I did yesterday, I am going to attempt to stop your discussion after forty-five minutes, or even earlier. Again, I hope you will support me. My father has said I can remain in the room for your discussion. I shall say little, but if I address you it will be as Professor Skinner. Now, let us go in."

The same mix of odors struck Fred as he entered Sigmund Freud's room. What would he call it: study, office, library, consulting room? Whatever the name, it was now more familiar, even in the same low level of light as yesterday. Freud was standing and, as if to gainsay the severity of the hallway portrait, smiling. "My dear Professor Skinner, thank you so much for coming again, and for your courtesies to my daughter yesterday evening. She told me she much enjoyed the outing. Come and sit and let us continue our discussion."

There were now two chairs at the side of the desk. Fred was directed to the green tub chair. Anna sat on a high-backed chair between the two men. The dog was not under the drape.

"I'm the one who should thank you for giving me the opportunity to spend time with your daughter and to attend such a magnificent concert. Your friend Pablo Casals is a truly remarkable musician."

"So I am told." Freud paused. "My daughter said this morning that you think highly of my work on mistakes in speech and other psychopathologies of everyday life. That is pleasing to me. But, if you do not object, I would ask that we first continue our discussion about what in us is inherited and what is acquired. I said yesterday that I had difficulty with your two questions. Today, I have thought about them more. I will try to answer them in a better way."

Fred had to think a little to remember his questions. He said, "My questions were a little impertinent. You handled them well. I'm intrigued that you may have more to add."

"Your first question concerned the evolutionary advantages of the developmental phases that I have identified. I did not answer it directly. Let me try again. Each phase has its own evolutionary advantage. The advantages are almost obvious for the first two phases. The infant must initially suck or eat to thrive. Then it must control its elimination in order to remain appealing to its caregivers. The unfortunate infants who do not glide happily through these two phases may be presumed to be less fit in later life, if they reach later life."

Fred noted that Freud was speaking even more slowly than yesterday. Perhaps he had not had a good night. Or perhaps his jaw was bothering him.

"Difficulty remains only with the phallic phase at age four or five years," Freud continued after a long pause. "Then, young boys and girls explore their genitals and, perhaps coincidentally, see a parent as a rival for the other parent's affection. My conjecture is that this phase is necessary preparation for the real business of life, which is reproduction."

Fred said, "Yesterday, you linked two other matters to these developmental phases. One, I believe, was the development of an individual's mind. The other was the need to posit mechanisms other than natural selection."

"The new-born has no mind," said Freud. "Mind develops as the infant passes through its developmental stages. It is fashioned by conflicts over weaning, toilet training, and jealousy. These conflicts, and the architecture of the brain, form mind into the three-part structure I have identified. During this forming process, some experiences can be embodied in the brain – in the mind – as if they are part of its structure. As such, they are passed on to later generations."

"You are a follower of Lamarck?"

"*Vielleicht bin ich*. Perhaps I am. I do believe in the possibility of inherited memory. In *Moses and Monotheism*, which you kindly asked about yesterday, I wrote that the survival of Jewish tradition can be explained only if what may be called 'Jewish memory' is inherited."

Fred ventured, "Wouldn't it be simpler to avoid such hypothesizing, not only about Jewish memory but also about mind?"

"Do you dispute that you and I and other humans have minds?"

"We have minds," said Fred, "but they may not be what we think they are. Please allow me to approach these questions in another way. Darwin's revolution lay in showing how the miracle of human existence – and the existence of toads and daffodils – could be explained as the cumulative effect of countless interactions between organisms and their environments. The interactions were in the form of the process we know as natural selection. This process allows the persistence into future generations of some mostly small variations in form rather than others. Because of Darwin's great insight there is no need to invoke god-like creators or human specialness."

"I agree about not needing gods," said Freud, "but not that there is no human specialness."

"Be that as it may. Could we not take a leaf from Darwin's book and say that what a person does during his or her lifetime may also be determined above all by interactions between the person and the environment during the person's lifetime?"

"You are talking about experience," said Freud, "which of course has a role in development. But our task is to seek universal laws, and for these we need to know about the structure of the entity that underpins what a person does. The entity is mind."

Anna was enthralled, more than during the previous evening's concert. Fred saw her turn her gaze from Freud to him and from him to Freud, as if she were a spectator in a tennis match.

"Whatever we regard as the human mind, we are now at the nub of the issue," said Fred.

"What do you mean?" said Freud. He looked to Anna for help.

"*Der Kern der Sache*," said Anna. "It's another way of saying the heart of the matter."

"My apologies for using such an unusual English word," said Fred. "Your daughter is exactly right. The central question is how mind develops. The human mind seems to me to be mostly a by-product of language development, which is a social process. Children talk through interacting with others. They then acquire the skill of talking to themselves. Mind is mostly that private discussion."

"There is no doubt that what you say is part of the truth," said Freud. "But there is more to it than that. For example, there are the dark forces of emotions, which are found in the id."

"Equally, there is no doubt that what you say is also part of the truth," said Fred. "If we had more time ... " He paused, realizing he may be about to make a tactless reference to Freud's imminent death. He continued, "If we had more time this morning, we could begin a stimulating reconciliation of our perspectives."

"I am set in my ways of thinking, but I hope I have provoked you to try," said Freud. "May I ask one thing? Are you proposing that there is a mechanism analogous to natural selection that acts during a person's lifetime to produce the behavior that most fits the person's environment?"

Fred was taken aback. The old man had grasped almost instantly what he, Fred, had been stumbling toward for a year or more. "Yes, indeed I am. And if I may say so, Professor Freud, you are certainly *not* set in your ways of thinking."

"Reinforcement is the process concerning behavior," Fred continued. "A mother smiles more at elements of her baby's babbling that approximate her language. Those elements are thereby reinforced in that they are more likely to occur in subsequent babbling. This process is analogous to natural selection except that it occurs across minutes rather than across millennia. I believe that the selection of behavior by its consequences is as important for the evolution of a person's behavior within a lifetime as is natural selection for the evolution of species. Of course, we must – as with evolution – allow that there are other processes at play."

"If you are appealing to a process similar to natural selection," said Freud, "let me provide you with a caution. As an American, you may not appreciate how difficult things are in Europe. Part of the cause of our difficulties is misuse of Charles Darwin's remarkable insight. The phrase 'survival of the fittest' has become *der Wahlspruch* for many of the people in power here today. *Anna, wie soll ich sagen 'Wahlspruch' auf Englisch?*"

Fred noted that Freud did speak more quickly in German.

"I'm not sure, father. Perhaps one could say slogan or motto."

"*Ich habe verstanden,*" said Fred. "There is another word in English: watchword. Any one of the three words will do."

"Thank you, Professor Skinner," said Freud. "This is my caution to you. If you give prominence to an analogy of natural selection, you will risk being associated with those, such as Herr Hitler, who characterize human society as a racial struggle for existence."

Fred pondered whether he should reveal his interest in Hitler. Again, he wondered what Bullitt had been told; and if Bullitt knew of his mission for the White House, what had he told Freud? Fred decided to be cautious. "Please explain, Professor Freud, how Hitler's views are associated with those of Darwin. I can see that superficially a racial struggle for existence could be seen as a manifestation of something like natural selection. But I've read that the Nazis don't believe in evolution. They believe that God put Germans – Aryans – on this planet as the highest form of humanity."

"Hitler and his gang of criminals say many outrageous things to justify their outrageous actions. I can say only that they are believed to practice 'Social Darwinism' – I have now remembered the term – which involves removing the weak and undesirable."

"There could be another concern," continued Freud, "which may seem paradoxical to you. Let us assume that the development of human mind, personality, and behavior are as mechanistically determined as Darwin said the evolution of species has been determined. It would follow that mind, personality, and behavior could in principle be controlled by arranging the correct environmental conditions. It would be just as a farmer can selectively breed his cows to provide more milk. You could be accused of advocating such control and thereby condoning totalitarian excesses."

"With respect, Professor Freud," said Fred, "that is very far-fetched. Of course a science should be striving for control in an experimental situation as part of its process of validation. However, that does not mean that control is necessarily achieved or, if it can be achieved, is desirable."

"In your conception of human nature," said Freud, "you must leave room for free will, or people will not like what you are saying."

"Again with respect, sir, you seemed to say the opposite in one of your books. It was *Civilization and its Discontents*, I believe. You said something to the effect that people do not want freedom because freedom involves responsibility."

"That is true of most people, but not all. It is the few who want freedom who will criticize you. You have appealed to Darwin, but Darwin left room for God – as the architect of evolution by natural selection – and so you should leave room for free will."

"But you more than anyone have shown that humans often do not behave as if they had free will."

"That may be true," replied Freud. "But it is also true that psychoanalysis can be seen as an attempt to provide a measure of free will. That is where I have left some room for what I would agree is a difficult construct."

Freud paused, but seemed to want to continue, and so Fred did not respond. Freud then said, "Professor Skinner, perhaps that is enough of these philosophical matters? Could we change the topic of our discussion?"

"Of course."

"You may not be as familiar with Herr Hitler as we are in *Großdeutschland*, but no doubt even in the safety of the Americas you have heard much about him and the monstrous things he and the Nazis are doing. May I ask you, based on what you know, how you would explain his behavior? It would be of interest to me to compare our accounts."

"You, Professor Freud, are the expert in providing such explanations. My skill, if any, is the more limited one of absorbing and sometimes criticizing what great analysts such as you say. I would much prefer to hear what you have to say about Hitler."

"I have heard that my former associate Professor Jung of Zurich has met Adolf Hitler and made some observations about him. I have not had that opportunity, or spoken with someone who has met Hitler. Thus, I am reluctant to speak on the matter." He paused.

"Let me say just two things," Freud continued. "I underestimated Hitler. I have already mentioned that I did not heed the warning provided by the burning of my books. There is more to it than that. I saw a decade ago that he was a threat to me, to Jews, and to humanity. I fooled myself into believing that I was stronger than he. I believed that my vision of humanity would speak more loudly than his. This false belief kept me in Vienna when my family and many colleagues urged me to leave."

"The other thing I will say is that I believe Hitler to be mad, psychotic, and thus beyond the reach of psychoanalysis. He is mad in the way a shaman is mad, and he has the appeal of a shaman. He believes he is possessed by spirits. He conveys that possession in a way that is especially appealing to the German people. Nothing he says is new. Racial purity, anti-Semitism, fear of communism, the need for *Lebensraum*, distaste for the *Treaty of Versailles* – all these were threads of German consciousness before he came onto the scene. He has appropriated them as part of his emergence as the personification of the Germanic spirit. In every scientific endeavor, there are phenomena that are beyond today's means of explanation. We must put the study of them aside until we have better tools. Adolf Hitler is such a phenomenon."

Anna interrupted the discussion. "Father, you are becoming too excited and may be talking too much for the good of your health, not to mention the comfort of our guest. *Lieber Vater, sollten wir die Diskussion nicht abbrechen.*"

"*Wie du sagst*, Anna. As you say."

Fred stood and said, "Professor Freud, I must apologize for taking so much of your time. You've given me much to think about and I'm very grateful."

"Professor Skinner, the pleasure has been mine. You have been a very congenial conversationalist. If we were able to talk more, I would have to change my opinion of your country and its inhabitants. I have just remembered something. Ambassador Bullitt had a strange request. It was that I should not mention your visit here in my diary. He did not say why, but it is a request that is very easy to meet. These days, I rarely make entries and I am sure that when I do I overlook much of what has happened. Goodbye, Professor Skinner, and *bon voyage – gute Reise.*"

"*Herzlichen Dank, Professor Freud*," replied Fred. He would have stayed and talked to Anna. In the hallway she explained that she must prepare for another visitor who was expected soon. They parted with the same formal handshake they had exchanged on the subway train the previous evening.

As he walked back across Primrose Hill and through Regent Park to the Euston Hotel, Fred reflected on what Freud had said. He agreed it could well be the wrong time to emphasize the analogy between reinforcement and natural selection. Such a powerful idea could be his most important intellectual legacy, but he should put it aside for a while and return to it later. There was still time for him to be the Darwin of the twentieth century.

Fred didn't agree that room should be left for free will, even if it made his main ideas easier to accept. He wished they had been able to discuss their mutual dislike of negative reinforcement or punishment as means of controlling behavior. They seemed to agree that punishment's adverse side effects could outweigh any benefit. He, Fred, would add that punishment is ineffective compared with its alternatives. Would Freud agree that people feel freer when their behavior is changed or maintained by positive reinforcement than when they are controlled by punishment?

The unexpected bonus of the morning's encounter with Freud was the series of observations on Adolf Hitler. Freud's views about Hitler and evolution, about his sense of rivalry with Hitler, and about the particular form of Hitler's insanity could all contribute to the answers Fred must provide to Roosevelt's people. He would still like to know whether Freud had been prompted, via Bullitt, to talk about Hitler, and Anna about Wittgenstein.

Fred had lunch at the hotel, checked out, and took the Underground to Liverpool Street Station. He bought a return ticket to Cambridge and also a one-way ticket to Southampton for June the second. His memorized instructions about returning home were to pick up an envelope at the front desk of Southampton's Dolphin Hotel and meet a member of the *Clipper* crew there at eight in the evening. Perhaps hearing Fred's American accent, the ticket office clerk gave him first-class tickets. Fred wasn't sure he had enough British pounds to be able to afford this luxury, but paid the higher amount.

The three o'clock train to Cambridge steamed out of the station and passed through London's north-east suburbs. The sky was gray. The buildings needed attention. Fred saw broken windows, gutters hanging loose, and gaps in fencing. The vegetation seemed undernourished.

There was a brief stop at Tottenham Hale Station. He wondered whether the station name had any relation to Tottenham Hotspur, the football team – he would say soccer team – avidly supported by a boisterous group in the hotel bar on Sunday evening. There was also Tottenham Court Road, which he'd seen on subway maps and the destination signs of buses. The Hotspur part of the team's name – could that be to do with the valiant rebel depicted in a Shakespeare play? England offered many opportunities to reflect on language.

As the train steamed away from the station, Fred figured out from his *A to Z Guide* that the Essex countryside was not far ahead. He'd hoped for miles of verdant fields such as he had seen on the way to London. What he saw after a few unkempt fields startled him: a small airport was being readied for war. Its runway was being lengthened and another was being laid out. Fortified structures were being built around the perimeter. Existing hangers and other buildings were being covered in camouflage paint. New buildings were under construction. Non-military planes were still using the airport – one was landing as the train passed – but they were outnumbered by larger military planes lined up near the hangars with insignia he recognized as belonging to Britain's flying corps. He wondered about the distinctive bull's-eye pattern painted on the fuselages. It could help avoid fire from friendly forces, but could also provide a good target for an enemy.

Britain was readying for war. Fred was surprised this was obvious from a passing train. Perhaps it was more important that the Germans know about the preparations than they not know. And Britons might be reassured to understand that the country is not defenseless. Fred wondered how far this airport was from Germany – three hundred miles? – and about the ranges of the military aircraft he could see. Then he noticed something unexpected: an American flag. It was flying above the door of one of the smaller buildings. Fred could not make out what the building might be used for. Some of these airplanes may have come from America. There had been great debates in Washington about supplying England with arms, but Fred could not remember where things stood.

He reviewed the letter on Wittgenstein he'd written to Fred Keller on the *Duchess of York*. He realized why he thought Wittgenstein's only published work – *Tractatus Logico-Philosophicus* – was pretentious. It was because of its echoing of one of the founding works of modern philosophy: *Tractatus Theologico-Politicus* by the seventeenth-century Dutch philosopher Baruch Spinoza. This was an early critique of organized religion, a defense of democracy, and plea for rationality. There or in another book, the author had argued against the idea that mind and body are distinct entities that can affect one another. Spinoza had proposed that they are the same thing, spoken of in two different ways. This was a view consistent with the position Fred was developing. Spinoza's *Tractatus* was one of the seminal works of modern philosophy. Wittgenstein evidently believed his *Tractatus* to have a similar standing.

Fred looked again at *The Blue Book*, the type-written notes dictated by Wittgenstein in the early 1930s. Wittgenstein's self-regard had become even more grandiose. Not only had he solved all the problems of philosophy in his *Tractatus*, he now appeared to be replacing its analysis with something he regarded as better. Specifically, Wittgenstein seemed to be saying that language did not necessarily picture the world; this was not its primary function. The essential quality of language was that of a tool, with words having as many functions as their users put them to. Some might see the replacement of the analysis in *Tractatus Logico-Philosophicus* as an expression of intellectual humility. Fred had not detected this quality in Wittgenstein's writings.

He was reminded by the first few paragraphs of *The Blue Book* why he liked what Wittgenstein was now saying. He read that the question "What is length?" produces in us a mental cramp because we can't point to anything in reply. A few pages later, Wittgenstein declared that the "life" of a word – that it to say, its meaning – is in its *use*. Thus, Fred concluded, if we want to answer the question "What is length?" we need only to list the circumstances in which the word "length" is used, or make a general description of the circumstances. If there are two or more separate sets of circumstances, then "length" has more than one meaning.

The essential point for Fred was that Wittgenstein was beginning to see the use of language as *behavior* rather than as a manifestation of a mystical mental process. Some pages later, Wittgenstein had supported this notion by writing that a sentence gets its significance from the language to which it belongs. For Fred, this meant that the significance lies with the verbal behavior of the people who use the language, including the producer of the sentence. In his letter to the other Fred he had called the users of a language a verbal community because they engender and sustain each other's verbal behavior. Language is an aspect of *social* behavior, arising from the interactions among the people who comprise a verbal community.

Later still in *The Blue Book*, Wittgenstein suggested that we could advance our understanding of language by studying how children begin to talk: "When we look at such simple form of language the mental mist which seems to enshroud our ordinary use of language disappears. We see activities, reactions, which are clear-cut and transparent. On the other hand we recognize in these simple processes forms of language not separated by a break from our more complicated ones. We see that we can build up the complicated forms from the primitive ones by gradually adding new forms." Fred could not agree more.

He wished he had taken more opportunity to study exactly how Julie was understanding words and then saying them. Her comprehension was first noticeable when she was nine or ten months old. Her first recognizable words were uttered a month or two later. Fred was convinced that this language learning happened through the processes he had studied in the laboratory using rats. Understanding at Julie's age came about through the reinforcement of behavior appropriate to one sound pattern rather than another. When Fred said, "Come to Dada," her crawling towards him was reinforced by a hug. When he said, "Go to Mama," crawling in another direction was reinforced. Julie's understanding was her different behavior in response to the different instructions. Of course, stimuli other than the words could be involved too, such as beckoning.

Julie was babbling at about the same time, often for minutes without stop. Yvonne and Fred reinforced approximations to English words. Her first recognizable word – and her only one for several days – was "owl," uttered with remarkable clarity. For a time, these utterances were strongly reinforced with laughs and hugs. Then "owl" was superseded by more useful words.

Fred wished he'd been closer to the beginnings of Julie's verbal behavior and had been able to pin down more carefully the interactions with her environment that produced the behavior. When he got home, perhaps he should go beyond merely observing Julie and try some informal experimentation on her speech acquisition. He might be able to use light onset as a reinforcer, as he had discussed in the second letter of this trip to the other Fred. He could use the table lamp that had a switch on its cord.

Fred and Julie could be in the armchair with *The ABC Bunny*. He would point at the drawing of the rabbit, and perhaps say "bunny" or "who is that?" Unless she'd already begun to say "bunny" while he'd been away, she'd likely make another sound. At first, Fred would flash the light on whatever sound Julie made. Then, he'd do it only when the sound resembled "bunny," gradually requiring closer approximations to a recognizably correct utterance.

If successful, it would be much as he had molded the behavior of Pliny the rat to perform the complex chain of behavior involving marbles that had been reported in *Life* magazine. There'd be an important difference. In Pliny's case, differential reinforcement had been achieved by laboriously changing the details of the apparatus that contained the rat. It was rather one-sided. The rat responded to changes in the apparatus, but the apparatus did not respond to the rat, at least not immediately. In this case, if it worked, the process would be two-sided. Fred would control the lamp, which would reinforce particular utterances. But, Julie's movements would also be exerting control over Fred's behavior. What she did would determine when he operated the lamp. He would be controlling her behavior, but she would also be controlling his.

Of course, he could use another reinforcer instead of light onset. A hug could work, or saying "good." But light onset could be a more consistent reinforcer and could more easily be recorded, if he wanted to do that. Fred began devising a switch that would both turn the lamp on and off and made a record on a moving chart. As he was doing this, he realized that the important thing about the situation he had imagined with Julie was that it would be *social* behavior. Each of two actors, he and Julie, would be affecting the behavior of the other. The precision and immediacy with which each could control the other could make for rapid and effective behavioral change. This process of mutual control could be a model, thought Fred, not only for the acquisition of language but for verbal behavior generally, at least verbal behavior that involved more than one person.

But much verbal behavior involved only one person, including the thinking that Fred was doing now. Wittgenstein had written that thinking is not "mental activity" but "operating with words." Saying the mind is doing the thinking, he wrote, was to make use of a misleading metaphor. People invoked mind because they couldn't observe such operating with words in other people. Fred agreed up to a point, but felt dismissing the matter in this way to be unsatisfactory in a way he couldn't yet put his finger on. Perhaps clarity would come from a focus on how children begin to think.

And there is also the matter of non-verbal thinking. He had promised to write to the other Fred about this and must do so soon.

Wittgenstein had asked, "Is it possible for a machine to think?" He found the place in *The Blue Book* and looked for an answer. Wittgenstein did not provide one, except to say, cryptically, "We are up against trouble caused by our way of expression."

The train stopped and did not move again. Fred looked out the window and saw that he had arrived at Cambridge, and it was raining. He been so absorbed in re-reading parts of *The Blue Book* and thinking about thinking he had not noticed the stops and starts at the dozen or so stations since Tottenham Hale. If the train had not terminated at Cambridge he could now be well north of the city. He quickly took hold of his small suitcase, alighted from the train, and walked to the station exit. The larger suitcase was in the baggage check office at Liverpool Street Station. He was told that Trinity College, where he was heading, was a thirty-minute walk from the station. Because of the rain, he decided to treat himself to a ride in one of the London-style taxicabs lined up outside the station entrance.

The entrance to the College was magnificent, more splendid than any university building he'd seen, even at Harvard. Fred inquired at the porters' lodge and was told he would be staying in what sounded like Hewell's or Hughill's Court, on the other side of Trinity Street. Fred crossed the street in the rain and saw that the building there was Whewell's Court, which, he remembered, was where Wittgenstein had his office. He inquired at a smaller porters' lodge and figured out that the Ws in Whewell's were not pronounced. So, he might be staying close to Wittgenstein. This could be fortunate.

A young man was called from within the porters' lodge and told to take Fred to rooms on the first floor of Staircase J. Fred already knew that this meant the second floor. He asked where in the building he could find Professor Wittgenstein's office. He was told that the professor's rooms were close to the rooms he was to use, at the top of the tower at the far end of the Court.

The young man picked up Fred's small suitcase and led him across a small courtyard and a larger one – all in the rain – to a staircase marked J. He told Fred that the next staircase, K, led to Wittgenstein's rooms at the top of the tower. Bathroom facilities were in the basement. Meals could be taken in the Hall. This was in the main part of the College at the far side of the Great Court. He could dine informally there from five until seven thirty. Today being a Tuesday in term-time, there would be Formal Hall at eight o'clock. For this he would need a gown that could be provided at the Porter's Lodge. Fred thanked him for all his help, wondering whether to tip him, and if so, how much. The young man did not appear to expect a tip.

Formal Hall presumably meant a formal dinner, perhaps even more tradition-bound than he had experienced at Harvard. He should inquire about his meal privileges and the use of a gown. Meanwhile, he explored the two small adjoining rooms he had been allocated. One contained only a single bed, wardrobe and chest of drawers. It reminded Fred of his cabin on the *Duchess of York*. The other room had a desk and chair, bookcase, armchair and a functioning washbasin in a corner.

He wondered whether to pee in the washbasin but decided to explore the bathroom facilities below. He might even be able to have a shower to wash away the grime of the journey. He took the thin towel by the basin, used the key already in the door from the stairs, and ventured below.

There were no showers in the basement, only stalls containing bathtubs. Perhaps showers were uncommon in Britain – Fred could not remember from his last trip. His room at the Euston hotel had a shower head over the bath tub, perhaps an addition for American visitors. He filled a bath and soaked in it for a while, resuming his consideration of what to discuss with Wittgenstein. His thoughts were interrupted by the echoing sounds of men entering and leaving the bathroom area. He could not see them because his back was to the open end of the stall. He made no progress other than to resolve to try and make children's language learning a key topic of any discussion he and Wittgenstein might have.

Back in his rooms, refreshed by the visit to the basement, it occurred to Fred that Wittgenstein might well be nearby and he could introduce himself. He climbed to the top of K staircase and navigated around the dozen or so folding chairs stacked in untidy piles. As he went to knock on the single door on the landing, it opened. The noise from the creaky wooden stairs must have announced his visit. Fred found himself looking down at the glowering face of a shorter man of military bearing who seemed about his age.

"What do you want?" the man said. "You do not have an appointment." His eyes were a penetrating blue with unusually large areas of unblemished white. His stare made Fred uncomfortable.

"I'm Fred Skinner, an American psychologist from the University of Minnesota. I'm in rooms on J staircase and …"

"Skinner?" the man interrupted, almost shouting. He appeared taken aback. He slapped his hand on his forehead and continued more softly, "*Ja, ich hatte vergessen.* I had forgotten that Russell asked me to see you." He pronounced Russell as though it had an 'h' before the 'R.' He spoke English with an accent similar to Glaser the dentist and Anna Freud. It was Ludwig Wittgenstein. Fred had expected someone older.

"I cannot see you now, or tomorrow, or the next day," Wittgenstein continued, "Friday morning, here, promptly at ten o'clock, for no more than ninety minutes." Before Fred could reply, the door slammed in his face. Then it opened again. Wittgenstein's expression had softened a little. "I do not allow tourists at my lectures, but you have come a long way and I will make an exception. Will you come to my lecture in this room at five o'clock tomorrow? It is on the foundations of mathematics, but there may be something in it of interest to a psychologist." He smiled bleakly, "I may criticize Russell's view that logic is a necessary foundation for arithmetic."

Without thinking, Fred mumbled "Yes" to the invitation. The door slammed shut again. Fred returned to his rooms to recover from his first encounter with Wittgenstein. He needed the fortification that good food and wine could provide and went to explore the possibility of joining the formal dinner in Trinity College's dining hall.

Part IV

Cambridge

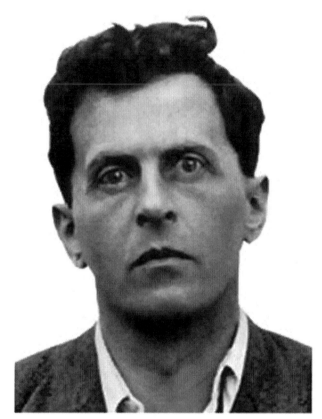

Ludwig Wittgenstein in 1929.

TWENTY-ONE

Wittgenstein and Turing

Cambridge, Wednesday May 31, 1939

Fred was in Wittgenstein's rooms, fascinated by what was around him but unable to concentrate on the topic of the lecture. There were fourteen men in the room. Fred had been among the first to arrive. He'd taken a folding chair from a stack on the landing and set it the corner farthest away from the chair in the center of the room. Wittgenstein was already sitting there, deep in thought, right elbow on left thigh, chin on bent left hand, the posture of Auguste Rodin's *The Thinker*. Occasionally he'd break pose by moving his left hand from his knee and passing it across his forehead. Fred had seen casts of this sculpture, which he knew to have been originally named *The Poet*. He'd seen one cast in Paris a decade earlier and the other more recently in Louisville, Kentucky, where he'd attended a conference. Thinker-poet might be an apt pose for Wittgenstein – agitated thinker-poet might be a better description.

As the room filled, Fred had noticed that many who came in were dressed as Wittgenstein was dressed. They wore buffed brown brogues, light gray flannel pants, an off-white flannel shirt open at the neck, and a brown leather jacket – all neatly put together. Were they imitating him, or were they all, including Wittgenstein, following a Cambridge style? Another thing he'd soon been aware of was the odor of stale sweat. Perhaps Englishmen did not wash as often as Americans, or wash their clothes as often, or both. Now, an hour into the session, he had become habituated to the smell.

Fred had also noticed that the windows were without drapes and had narrow strips of black paper along each vertical edge. There were a few books in a small bookcase, most with German titles he could not make out or understand. He recognized one book: William James' *Principles of Psychology*. It was not one he cared for, but its presence in Wittgenstein's sparse collection could help open discussion between them. Sparse was the word for the room too. There were no ornaments or photographs, just a few flowers in pots and some in a window box. Apart from the bookcase, he could see only a card table and a metal safe on the floor by the bookcase. Wittgenstein was sitting on an elegant upright chair, the only non-folding chair in the room. Fred imagined it was normally the only chair in the room, used by Wittgenstein to sit at the card table and read and write there. Only at the end of his survey did Fred notice what he now realized was the room's most conspicuous feature. It was an old-fashioned, unlit heating stove just behind Wittgenstein with a chimney pipe disappearing into the ceiling.

Wittgenstein had moved out of his pose at five o'clock. The room stilled as he sat upright and began moving his hands as though talking to someone. But he was not talking, except to himself. After a minute or two of occasional hand-waving, he did speak, saying that he wanted to talk about the relation between arithmetic and logic, in the sense that Russell and Frege used the term logic. Fred had heard of Gottlob Frege, a nineteenth-century German philosopher who was an intellectual antecedent of Bertrand Russell. Russell was again pronounced by Wittgenstein as though it began with an 'h.' Other than that and a few more Germanicisms, Wittgenstein spoke excellent English, with an accent closer to the English upper class than to his native Vienna. His high-pitched resonant voice was commanding. His face as he spoke was expressive, often fierce. His manner was more imperious than academic.

Fred had lost interest in the lecture. He thought about yesterday evening's enjoyable dinner in the Trinity College dining hall. He'd had stimulating discussions with neighbors at a long table, mostly about the Soviet Union, meanwhile enjoying good food and wine. He thought about what he had seen of Cambridge during his morning tour: splendid halls, chapels, and courtyards highlighted by a bright sun in a near cloudless sky. He'd enjoy spending more time here.

His attention was pulled back to the lecture by the sound of another voice. A man Fred had not noticed before had interrupted Wittgenstein with a question. He looked like a younger version of Wittgenstein but with a larger chin, dirty shoes, and unpressed black pants and dark sports jacket. He too had a high-pitched voice, but with an uncertain, often stammering delivery – the antithesis of Wittgenstein's overbearing certainty. Now, the man interrupted Wittgenstein several times. Polite questions were followed by polite comments that seemed to contradict Wittgenstein, although Fred had not followed enough to be sure of that.

Sometimes Wittgenstein waved away the interruptions. Sometimes he responded, politely but firmly. He said "No" to questions and "Yes, but ..." to comments, accompanied by what may have been a clear explanation. The lecture was nevertheless mostly a monologue, with Wittgenstein often appearing to be talking to himself rather than to his audience. Sometimes, speaking to the audience, he would say strange things: "I'm a fool today" "You have a terrible teacher" "I'm just too stupid to know how to proceed."

At close to seven o'clock, Wittgenstein stood abruptly and went into his other room, noisily shutting the door behind him. His parting words were, "For the moment I will leave you puzzled," but Fred could not recollect the particular reason for puzzlement. Members of the audience made moves to leave. Wittgenstein reappeared wearing a surprisingly dirty raincoat and carrying a light cane. He approached a man close by. Fred heard Wittgenstein ask, "Could you go to a flick?" The man nodded and they left together.

Now there were only two people in the room, Fred and the man who had interrupted Wittgenstein. The man asked if Fred would help stack the remaining chairs. "Each person is supposed to stack his own chair on the landing," he said, "but some people never do. My name is Alan Turing, by the way. I haven't seen you here before."

Fred introduced himself. He explained how – as an outcome of meeting Bertrand Russell – he had been invited to attend the inaugural lecture. Fred had come to avoid mentioning Russell's involvement, to stay away from his trip's political quest. But Wittgenstein had already mentioned him, in this very room. So Fred felt he had to, even though he felt qualms about doing so.

"You must be an important person," said Turing. "Wittgenstein has often said that his lectures are not for tourists. Let me be a cynic. You've been invited all the way from America to attend an inaugural lecture that is unlikely to happen. Wittgenstein, in a guilty moment, asked you to another lecture so your journey wouldn't be wasted."

"But," Fred protested, "I have a nicely embossed invitation to attend his inaugural lecture at four o'clock tomorrow at the Mill Lane Lecture Rooms. I passed by there this morning during a walk around this beautiful city."

"Wittgenstein can't stand such formal occasions, or set lectures. He'll be indisposed and won't turn up. Or, he'll be there, dressed as he's always dressed, with no concession to the formality of the event. He'll utter three or four sentences in his oracular manner. Then he'll leave saying that he has nothing more to say. I'd put five shillings on his not turning up."

"You appear to know him quite well. I'd like to know more about him. Can I buy you a drink?"

"I'm hungry. The pubs near here don't serve much in the way of food. There's an Indian restaurant along Trinity Street that has bottles of pleasant Indian beer. Could we eat there?"

"I'd be pleased to do that."

They stacked the chairs, tidied the room a little, and walked to the restaurant. Fred asked, "Could you say a little about yourself and your relation to Wittgenstein."

"I'm a mathematician, of sorts. I'm a fellow of another college, King's, where I also hold a minor lectureship. I also teach a course on the foundations of mathematics. I teach it from a maths rather than a philosophical perspective. I met Wittgenstein when I was in Cambridge a few years ago, interrupting an extended stay in America. He asked if I'd like to attend his lectures."

Fred asked, "Where were you in America, and why?"

"I was at Princeton, initially to sit at the feet of several distinguished mathematicians and eventually to submit a Ph.D. thesis."

"I'd like to know about your experience at Princeton and your thesis, but could I first ask a few questions about Wittgenstein."

"Yes, but only after you answer a few questions about yourself."

They ordered beers and their food. "I was brought up knowing about Indian food," said Turing. "My mother and brother were born there, and my father worked there. I was conceived there, but never returned. I resent the place because it took my parents away from me when I was young; but I acquired their taste for Indian food." Turing ordered a spicier Madras curry than Fred would ever eat. "You said you are a psychology professor. What does that mean?"

"As you'll know, we use the term professor liberally in America. I'm a junior person in the psychology department of a state university in the Midwest, recently promoted to assistant professor. The University of Minnesota is among the largest American universities. Its psychology department is moderately well known. My Ph.D. is from Harvard, an elite private university like Princeton. Harvard has only half as many students as Minnesota but many more graduate students. I hope to return there one day."

"What kind of psychologist are you that you might be interested in Wittgenstein's work?"

"I like to think of myself as a behaviorist with an interest in language. Wittgenstein seems to be becoming a behaviorist with an interest in language. I mentioned that the invitation here came out of a meeting with Bertrand Russell. He and A.N. Whitehead set it up perhaps because they thought I had been convinced by his arguments against behaviorism and could set Wittgenstein straight."

"So Russell thought Wittgenstein was becoming a behaviorist?"

"So it seems. But Russell got me wrong and he may have got Wittgenstein wrong. I'd been convinced by Russell's arguments *for* behaviorism. Indeed, it was reading Russell that mostly inspired me to become a behaviorist when I realized I wasn't good enough to be a poet or a writer of fiction. I'd not read Russell's arguments *against* behaviorism, which were at the end of the same book. When I did, after I met Russell, I didn't agree with them. I do happen to agree with some of what Wittgenstein has to say about language."

Fred noted that Turing rarely made eye contact and sometimes had odd facial expressions. Close up, he seemed more unkempt than before. His recent haircut suggested the work of an amateur. His irregular heavy stubble indicated hurried shaving. His shirt was unironed. Turing's voice was not as high-pitched as during the lecture, but the light stammer was still evident. His overall appearance was rough and out of place in the beautiful city, but his manner was gentle and attentive. Apart from the stammer, he was well-spoken.

"No one sets Wittgenstein straight except himself. And he's too much of a mystic and too anti-science to be a behaviorist. But I think I know what you mean. He believes the important thing about language is how it is used, which is a kind of behavior."

Fred said, "I'm afraid the discussion today was over my head. Can you explain in a few words how you differ from Wittgenstein?"

"First I have more questions of you. I can't believe you've come all the way from Minnesota just to meet Wittgenstein. What are your other reasons? Are you married? Do you have a family?"

"So many questions! I am married, with a fourteen-month-old daughter. They're with my wife's parents while I travel. My parents live in Pennsylvania, where I grew up. My main reason for taking advantage of the opportunity to travel to England was to meet Sigmund Freud, who is dying in London. I did meet him, twice."

"I'd like to hear more about Freud, but let's get back to Wittgenstein. What do you want to know, apart from how we disagree?"

"I'd expected an older man, but he's someone of our age."

"You may be wrong on both counts. He's fifty. I'm hardly more than half his age – I'll be twenty-seven in a few weeks. You are somewhere in the large gap between us. Thanks for the compliment of considering me to be more mature."

"You're welcome! I'm thirty-five. He seems about my age."

"He leads an ascetic life, and spends many months of each year in remote places. His manner can be that of a younger person – even a petulant adolescent."

"Is he married?"

"He's a homosexual – as I am. When he's not in his rooms he lives with a former student, Francis Skinner. Skinner was a brilliant mathematician but became a gardener, a mechanic, and the transcriber of Wittgenstein's dictation. I've been told he's the only person in Cambridge with whom Wittgenstein is on first-name terms."

Fred now understood why Wittgenstein was taken aback when he gave his name. He said, "Your frankness is remarkable. Could I ask if homosexual feelings of any kind underpinned the conflict you and

Wittgenstein were having today?"

"I can't say. I'm not attracted to him, I think because he is so evidently selfish and demanding of attention. But he's an unusual and compelling person. As for the conflict, that's working itself out. Wittgenstein is near the end of giving about thirty lectures on his concerns about the language of mathematics. At the beginning, we disagreed more, but I think we have each moved towards the other's position. I doubt you could have picked up much of that today."

"How did you disagree?"

"We still disagree on a couple of fundamental points. One may not be of interest to a psychologist. It concerns contradictions in mathematical logic. He's come to believe they are insignificant. I think he's quite wrongheaded on this. Bridges can fall down if there are errors in calculations. If the logical basis for the calculations is unsound there are likely to be errors."

"The difference that may be of more interest to you," continued Turing, "is that I consider humans as machines, amenable to scientific study. Wittgenstein believes we have souls, or at least some vital element that sets us apart from other creatures and inanimate things. This, he says, makes scientific study of humans difficult and, in some respects, impossible. However, we agree increasingly on two points. One is that some of our puzzlement about the world, including the part that can be described mathematically, results from how we use language. The other is that the important thing about language is how it is used, not what it is supposed to signify."

"I gathered the last point from reading the notes on his lectures known as *The Blue Book*. Russell gave me a copy."

Their food arrived. There was a pause in the discussion while they ate. A few minutes later Fred said, "May I ask a few trivial questions about Wittgenstein?" Turing nodded, his mouth full. "Why does he have strips of black paper at the edge of his windows?"

"That puzzled me. Someone, I forget who, told me it's a reflection of Wittgenstein's perfectionism. Windows, for him, must have certain ideal proportions. The black paper helps achieve that."

"Interesting. What else can you say about his perfectionism?"

"It's noticeable in his writing. He goes through draft after draft, eventually publishing very little."

"So he could have written a lot since *The Blue Book*. His ideas may have advanced considerably, but few people will know how his thinking has changed?"

"I've heard there's a later set of lecture notes in circulation called *The Brown Book*. I haven't seen it. I've been told it's also on language and other matters, picking up where *The Blue Book* left off. Enough about Wittgenstein. How do *you* view these matters, as a behaviorist?"

Fred paused and answered, "Use is, of course, behavior. I'm comfortable with saying, as Wittgenstein seems to say, that the meaning of the word 'length' lies in how the word is used. I'd go further. I'd say that speaking and writing, as well as listening and reading, are types of behavior subject to the basic laws that govern the behavior of living organisms."

"But don't behaviorists believe that human activity is no more than stimulus and response? Don't they believe that the brain – or mind – is some kind of irrelevant box, an inscrutable box, standing between stimulus and response, between input and output?"

"Some behaviorists may believe something like that for the good reason that scientific data should be observable. However, the behaviorist in front of you would add two important twists to the plot of that particular narrative."

"Do tell me about your twists," Turing said, making eye contact briefly, "but first let's order more beer. How was your curry?"

Fred noticed that Turing's eyes were a remarkable, almost translucent blue, not unlike Wittgenstein's. "Good, thank you," he replied, "mild enough for me. I saw that you ordered something stronger."

Turing ordered more beer. "I'm used to spicy curries, as I said."

Fred said, "One difference from the mechanistic behaviorism you refer to is a focus I have on events – stimuli – that occur *after* particular behavior and make occurrence of that behavior more likely in the future. It's a different kind of causation from bat hitting ball or food odor causing salivation. Let me use an example from my laboratory. A hungry rat presses a lever. It causes a food pellet to be delivered, making further lever-pressing more likely."

He paused to eat and drink and then continued, "It's as though the food delivery acts back on the lever-pressing. This is different from the forward direction of mechanical causation. It's as if the rat's environment selects lever pressing so as to make it happen more often. It's like natural selection, in which a particular environment, for example, leaves and twigs high on trees, selects some features, for example, long necks in giraffes, making them more likely to occur than other features, for example, short necks."

"I see, I see," said Turing. "I hadn't thought of natural selection as being a different kind of causation. At a basic level it must still be mechanical cause-and-effect but at a higher level it has the feel of causation acting backwards in time. It reminds me of an electrical feedback circuit in which an increase in amplitude adds power causing more gain. Am I being too technical?"

"Not at all, but I prefer to compare behavior change with what happens as a result of natural selection."

"So, are you saying that reward and punishment are the important processes in behavior?"

"Not quite. I use the term *reinforcement* rather than reward. People are rewarded. *Behavior* is reinforced."

"Negative reinforcement – punishment – is a more complex process," continued Fred. "I don't use different terms for punishing behavior and punishing people because I prefer not to employ punishment at all. Punishment often produces counterproductive effects. Say I'm trying to get a rat to press a lever with its right front paw. If I zap it with an electric current when it uses another paw, the rat may well stop pressing altogether."

"Your work is only with animals?"

"With humans too. As I said, I'm particularly interested in what I call verbal behavior."

"How do you get a rat to press a bar with a particular paw?

"Simple. You deprive it of food for a short while. Then you deliver a small pellet of food when the rat is near the lever. As a result, it spends more time near the lever. Then you deliver a pellet when it touches the lever; then only when the right front paw is used; then only when the lever is pressed. You could use the same process to get the rat to press only with a force of, say, fifty grams or more."

"And this, you believe, is how children learn to speak and adults learn to drive cars and solve crossword puzzles?"

"I think it's the key process in behavior change, just as natural selection is the key process in evolution. In both cases, there are other things at play too. We could go into that."

Turing said, "Perhaps we should. For the moment could we turn to the other way in which you differ from the usual behaviorists?"

"Can I elaborate a little more on the first way? If you think about it, there's really no logical alternative to natural selection but creation of species by some kind of deity. Similarly, there's really no logical alternative to reinforcement but control over complex behavior by some kind of internal agency such as mind. Positing such internal agencies merely shifts the problem to accounting for their actions. Only natural selection and reinforcement are consistent with scientific practice, which has mostly moved past the invention of inexplicable agencies."

"That's a lot to swallow. I agree that minds are a problem, but surely that is solved by talking about brains, which is where the actual control of complex behavior must occur?"

"I'll get to brains in a minute. Let me now explain the second way in which I might differ from other behaviorists. It's to do with what I call private behavior. By this I mean behavior that is not observable except to the behaver. And it's also to do with private stimuli – including sensations such as toothache – which are not directly available to observers."

Turing said, "Wittgenstein has a lot to say about toothaches."

"Yes. I saw that in *The Blue Book*. I can't say I fully understand what is in there. I do agree with his basic point that many of the puzzles about private events arise from how we use language."

"You spoke about private behavior. Do you mean thinking?"

"That's an important class of private behavior," said Fred. "It's something that each of us does that cannot be observed by others. The major puzzle for me is how, as children, we get to talk about private behavior such as thinking and about private stimuli such as toothache. I'm also interested in how thinking occurs. Thinking seems to consist mostly of interior monologues or even dialogues. Does that mean we don't think until we can speak?"

"How did I learn to say, correctly, that I have a toothache?"

"I'm glad you added correctly. I imagine it's something like this. A boy of about eighteen months gets his finger caught in a closing door and screams. The mother comforts the boy, noting the rapid discoloration of the finger nail. She says, 'Does your finger hurt?' He, used to answering questions by repeating parts of them, says 'Finger hurt.' Over subsequent hours and days, her comforting him becomes more and more dependent on his saying 'finger hurt.' When the discoloration subsides, 'finger hurt' becomes less likely to produce comfort. We can say that the boy has learned to use 'finger hurt' correctly. I'd prefer to say that the probability of saying 'finger hurt' correctly – when a finger hurts, and only then – has increased."

"A few days later," Fred continued, "the boy falls and grazes his knee. The phrase 'knee hurt' is already somewhat likely to occur because of the 'finger hurt' experience and the mother's asking 'Knee hurt?' The mother, seeing the graze, is quickly able to reinforce his saying 'knee hurt' with comfort. The extension of 'hurt' to other observable parts of the body follows quickly. Then the boy gets a toothache. The mother has a harder job distinguishing the source of 'hurt,' as may the boy, but they are both helped by distinctions made for observable parts of the body. They may be helped too by correlates such as a swollen cheek or a sensitive tooth."

"You've opened my eyes to the importance of understanding how these things get going. I can't yet agree with you that once a child learns to report on internal events external events continue to be so important."

"It's like evolution," said Fred. "Natural selection is not the only thing happening, but it's the most important thing. Similarly, reinforcement of behavior in the presence of particular stimuli may not be the only thing happening in complex behavior, but it could be the most important thing. In evolution, we attribute changes in the features of a species to changes in the environment. We no longer say the changes are the result of intervention by a deity. We no longer say they are the manifestation of some kind of life force in the creatures concerned."

Turing interrupted, "I'd always taken evolution to be a matter of survival of the fittest rather than of environmental change."

"They are two sides of the same coin," said Fred. "Loosely speaking, an animal's fitness is its ability to reproduce itself in a particular environment. However, thinking in terms of fitness suggests that it's something in the animal rather than a change in the environment that drives the process. Also, it suggests that environment is selecting a property of the whole animal rather than particular features, such as longer necks. It's better to view natural selection as a process driven by the environment, and it's better to view behavior in that way too."

"I've a problem with putting too much emphasis on natural selection. Wittgenstein has the same problem too, but for a different reason. Do you think we should have a third beer?"

"I'm enjoying this very much. Another beer would be welcome. What's your problem with natural selection?"

Turing called for more beer. He was told that the restaurant was to close in twenty minutes, at nine o'clock. He raised his eyebrows at Fred – who nodded – and ordered two more bottles. Turing also asked for the bill. "Let's drink what we've ordered," he said, "and, if we've more to say, retire to a nearby pub."

"You must let me pay," said Fred. "I've much enjoyed your company, and your insights into Wittgenstein."

"We'll split it, and you can pay for the first round in the pub."

"My problem with natural selection," said Turing, "arises from a wonderful book I read recently. It was *On Growth and Form*, written more than twenty years ago by a Scottish mathematical biologist named D'Arcy Thompson. Yes, D'Arcy – spelt D-apostrophe-A-R-C-Y – is the unusual first name."

Turing went on, "Thompson showed that the strongest factors in the evolution of features of animals are the constraints imposed by simple physical laws and mechanical processes. He used hundreds of examples to make his point." Turing's voice was getting higher as he became more excited. "Let me give just one. The eggs of different species of bird differ considerably in shape from spherical to elongate with one end more pointed than the other. Natural selection has been invoked to account for the different shapes. Thompson showed that the shapes are a by-product of the size of the egg relative to the size of the bird. Large eggs have a more 'streamlined' shape to facilitate passage through a relatively narrow oviduct."

"Thompson was not arguing against natural selection, "continued Turing, "but against its status as *the* guiding principle in the evolution of particular features. He thought the main role of natural selection could be to cause the *extinction* of features not their promotion."

Fred said, "I should look at Thompson's book. If he was saying that evolution occurred through self-organization resulting from simple chemical and physical processes, I can't agree with him. If he was saying that natural selection is constrained by what is possible, I couldn't agree more. We've talked about natural selection – and rein-forcement – but not about the variations in form or behavior that make it possible for these processes to work. Natural selection can produce longer necks only if neck lengths vary and longer ones can be inherit-ed.

Fred continued, "We had a well-known case in America of a baby chimpanzee reared with a human baby. I heard the child's father, a psychologist, report the results. For a while, the chimp understood what was said as well as the boy, but she didn't learn to speak. I sus-pect that an important reason was physical. The chimp's voice box and associated musculature were such that she could produce only a limited range of sounds. There was insufficient variation in sounds to allow reinforcement of approximations to language."

Turing said, "I'd like to teach a machine to speak, and perhaps to think. It would be a mechanical computer, more specifically an elec-tronic computer. I've played with the concept of a machine that would be capable of doing just about anything a human could do."

The waiter brought the bill. Fred invited the mathematician to cal-culate half the total. Turing seemed no more able to do this than Fred would have done. Turing suggested they go to the Eagle, an ancient pub on Benet Street, just off Trinity Street, which dated from the late seventeenth century. It was older than the United States of America, he said as they walked there. Fred replied that quite a bit of America was older than the U.S.A. Harvard University was founded *early* in the seventeenth century. Turing trumped this by pointing to a plaque in

297

front of St. Benet's Church, opposite the Eagle. It was the oldest building in Cambridge, England, dating from 1033. They laughed at their slightly drunken, slightly childish competitiveness.

In the pub, Turing guided Fred through the purchase of two pints of bitter and they found a small table in a quiet corner. Fred wondered whether to pursue the tantalizing line of discussion Turing had opened just before they left the restaurant – on intelligent robots – or to turn the conversation again towards Wittgenstein. He decided to attempt both, but Wittgenstein first if possible.

"You said that Wittgenstein has a problem with natural selection that differs from your problem. What is his problem?"

"Well, at heart he's a great nature lover. If you walk with him, he'll often comment on the beauty of the flowers and other plants he sees. I've heard him say that Darwin's theory – variation and natural selection – is too simplistic to account for the immense variety and complexity of life. It's the same kind of argument as he uses about humans. He seems to say that much human behavior is too complex to be usefully subjected to scientific scrutiny."

"How then does he explain evolution and human behavior?"

"He doesn't. He just criticizes others who try to do it."

"You, on the other hand, do seem to believe that science can address both sets of challenges. Your intriguing wish to teach a machine to think reflects that for human behavior."

Turing said, "I'm a long way from that goal. I do believe that in principle a properly designed machine could perform any intellectual feat of which a human is capable."

"Properly designed?"

"I mean 'properly instructed.' Let me explain. I have described what I call the 'universal machine.' For the moment this is a hypothetical machine. It differs from ordinary calculating machines in that it can accept instructions fed into it, as well as data to be acted on. It then provides results according to the instructions. Given the right instructions the machine could in theory do any calculation. Of course, the instructions and the data would have to be provided in the form acceptable to the machine."

"What form would that be?"

Turing answered, "I would use a long paper tape with a series of binary signs on it. They could be '1' and '0' or any pair that could be reliably distinguished by the device that reads the tape. Another necessary feature would be some kind of memory. This would store some of the instructions and parts of the calculation as it proceeds. There would also have to be some kind of output, which could be no more than a bank of lights. I've written a technical paper on the universal machine. I'll be pleased to give you an offprint."

"Thank you. How do you get from doing any calculation to performing any intellectual feat? I'd agree with Wittgenstein that verbal behavior – using words – requires more than what may be possible with a calculating machine, even one that can do any calculation."

"I think not. Set aside for the moment the practical considerations of speaking, reading text, etc., not to mention timing. If you have the right instructions it should in principle be possible to provide any particular output from any particular input. This assumes, of course, that the brain – or the mind – is a machine. If one or the other has extraphysical properties not amenable to physical instructions then the universal machine will not be able to do what humans do."

Fred said, "The most interesting thing about human behavior is not that it responds to instructions, but that it is remarkably capable of change, notably acquiring the ability to speak and write. How would your universal machine learn to speak?"

"In the way *we* learn to speak, through parental instruction, however casual. For the machine, the challenge would be providing the parental instruction in the precise form the machine could use."

"But children do not speak because their parents tell them to. They come to speak through a process such as I outlined in the restaurant, a process similar to natural selection. Could your universal machine accommodate such a process?"

Turing said, "I haven't thought of that, yet." He paused for more than a minute, occasionally moving as if to begin speaking again. Fred was reminded of Wittgenstein. Turing continued, "The machine would need features it doesn't now have. One would be provision a range of results, not just one. Another would be the ability to prioritize the results."

"In other words, aspects of the machine's behavior could be selectively reinforced."

"Indeed," said Turing. "Now that I think about it, I did touch on the possibility of such a machine in the technical paper I mentioned. I didn't pursue it. I called it a 'choice machine.' The choice would be made by an external operator from two or more courses of action that the machine could take. It could be reconfigured as a machine that learns according to the kind of process you described."

"That's interesting. Let's say you developed such a machine and its behavior – its outputs – were indistinguishable from those of a human. Would it have free will?"

"To all intents and purposes, yes," replied Turing, "even though we know its behavior is completely determined. This implies that humans have no more free will than such a machine, but I can't yet bring myself to that conclusion. What do you think?"

"I'm going to use your phrase," said Fred. "To all intents and purposes we do seem to have free will. But I believe it to be an illusion. A scientist must believe that what is being studied behaves lawfully or else there can be no prediction. Moreover, there'd be no discarding of failed predictions, the gold standard in determining what is going on around us. Ultimately the laws of physics have to apply, but there can be higher-order laws or processes that are potentially reducible to the laws of physics. Natural selection is one such process and I believe reinforcement is another. In practice, things may be so complicated that we can't – at least yet – explain things in terms of natural selection or reinforcement, let alone the laws of physics. That's in part where attributions of free will come in."

"In part?"

"Yes," continued Fred. "Although the main reason we attribute free will is because human behavior is so damned complicated, there's another reason. It is that our thinking does sometimes seem to be a cause of our behavior, although perhaps less often than usually supposed. And, thinking can be an even bigger mystery than behavior. We are even less able to identify the environmental factors in thinking than in overt behavior. Thus, we may be more inclined to invent an inner agent to account for thinking. This inner agent may be part of the source of the notion of free will." He paused.

Turing seemed immersed in thought, so Fred said, "You know, we'd really need another whole evening to make progress on this topic. Could we go back to your machine? What do you see as its possible practical applications, assuming one was constructed?"

"What interests me the most just now is the machine's possible use in cracking codes and ciphers. Oops! I shouldn't have said that. You're an American. I suppose I can trust you."

Turing was flustered. He continued, "Let me just say that I could have stayed at Princeton. It was very congenial there. But I wanted to contribute to the war effort, and so I came back to England."

Fred quickly understood from this that Turing could already be working for some part of the British government on German codes and ciphers. He said, "Don't let me pry into things I shouldn't know about. I'd be interested in learning whether you think there'll be a war in Europe, and when."

Turing became more relaxed. "I think my view is that of the majority of the British public. We've been expecting another war with Germany for several months."

"Would Wittgenstein share this view?"

"That's an interesting question, although I'm not sure why you would want to know. He's not just any member of the British public. He fought for the other side in the Great War, bravely I've been told. I've heard he's recently become a British citizen, but he's also an Austrian, presumably now a German. To be honest, I don't know whether he expects a war. I have heard he comes from a rich Jewish family, but went to the same secondary school as Adolf Hitler, at the same time. They are close in age. Like many things about Wittgenstein, his positions on Germany, Nazism, and the prospect of war could be unexpected and complex."

Fred wanted to think about the importance of being given this information by Turing, but felt he had to keep the conversation going to avoid suspicion, and divert it from Wittgenstein. He said, "I didn't pay much attention to these matters in America. In the few days I've been here, they've captured my interest. I saw preparations for war in and near London, but I've seen nothing of the kind in Cambridge."

"Here, we often live in the past, not the present. Also, the university is a hotbed of pacifism. Some of it is fueled by sympathy for communism, although I don't understand why. Pacifism seems to me to be playing into the hands of the Germans. Given that they and the Russians are ideological opposites, one might expect communists to be in favor of Britain's preparations for war. I've just remembered something else I've heard about Wittgenstein. He's an admirer of the Soviet system. He's been learning Russian, and has been to Russia more than once during the last few years."

Fred wanted to explore this new information but remembered that Turing had already questioned his interest in Wittgenstein's views. He said, "I've been puzzled by the attitudes here to the Soviet Union. Over the weekend I was reading that British and French diplomats went to

Moscow to try and sign an anti-German pact. I've lost track of what happened."

Turing said, "A headline in *The Times* this morning said the negotiations are continuing, but I didn't read the article. My limited sense of these things tells me that Russia is just as likely to sign a pact with Germany as with us." He yawned, revealing noticeably yellow teeth. Some teeth were missing, others were in need of a dentist's attention. "It's my bedtime, and this place will close soon."

Fred would have liked to pursue the discussion about the Soviet Union, but Turing was already standing. They paused when they reached Trinity Street. "My rooms are that way, and yours are that way," said Turing pointing in almost opposite directions. "Mine are nearby. Would you like to pick up the offprint?"

"I'm tired too," said Fred. "I think I'll take a rain check – meaning 'another time'– but you'll know that from your stay in America."

"If you're still in Cambridge on Friday, I could drop it off at Whewell's Court early in the morning. I'll be away tomorrow, and won't be at Wittgenstein's inaugural lecture"

"I leave on Friday afternoon, so many thanks in advance for that. And thank you too for a most enjoyable and interesting evening. I hope we meet again."

As Fred walked back to his rooms, he wondered if he'd just avoided a homosexual approach. He wondered too if Turing's absence from Cambridge the next day was planned to avoid the inaugural. Perhaps Turing's secret work for the government would be the cause of his absence. Turing's revelations about Wittgenstein's past and his wealth could well have been offered to divert attention from his indiscretion about codes and ciphers. Fred knew that he wasn't thinking clearly on account of the four beers he'd enjoyed. He resolved to be in bed and asleep as soon as possible.

The photo of Alan Turing used in connection with his admission to Princeton University's Graduate School in September 1936.

TWENTY-TWO

Inaugural Brevity

Cambridge, Thursday June 1, 1939

F red woke with a slight hangover. It had gone by the time he had eaten breakfast in the main Trinity complex and walked around Cambridge's narrow streets for an hour. He could have all his meals at the College until lunch on Friday. He'd expected to have to pay for his meals and accommodation but he was told he was a guest of the College. The problem caused by his over-spending in London had been resolved. He wasn't sure who was paying. Notes of gratitude to Russell and Whitehead would be due for setting things up.

After his walk, Fred noticed that he'd left the key in the door to his rooms. Someone had been in there. He assumed it was College staff, although the bed was unmade. He began a letter to the other Fred.

Dear Fred,

It's my second morning in Cambridge. I feel I've been here longer. I've encountered Wittgenstein twice, and will do so again this afternoon and tomorrow. He's strange, but perhaps I should hold back further comments on him until after tomor-

row. I had dinner last evening with a young man, Alan Turing, who's also strange but far more congenial than Wittgenstein.

Turing is a mathematician with broad range of intellectual interests. He was at a seminar given by Wittgenstein yesterday on the foundations of mathematics from the perspective of a philosopher. (Don't ask why I was there, or what I got out of it.) Turing, although only twenty-seven, also gives a course here on the same topic but from a math perspective. Wittgenstein – who is fifty, but seems thirty-five – doesn't attend Turing's classes. He dominated his seminar. The domination would have been complete if Turing had not challenged him several times. (Or appeared to challenge him – I wasn't entirely sure what was going on.) Turing and I were the last to leave the room and we finished up having an enjoyable dinner followed by a session in a pub.

Turing has devised what he calls a universal machine. It can accept automatically delivered instructions and, in principle, perform any intellectual feat you and I are capable of. He's going to give me an offprint of his paper on the machine. We were soon discussing whether the machine has free will. It does, at least to the extent humans have free will. We touched too on whether the machine's behavior could be reinforced. This has not been considered much by Turing but he said in principle yes. I suspect that Turing's remarkable abilities are already being snapped up by the British government for its codes and ciphers work. If there's a war he'll likely be so involved in it he'll forget we had our discussion. A war seems more likely each day I'm here.

Turing was helpful in deciphering Wittgenstein. Here are two things he led me to conclude: At first sight, Wittgenstein appears to be a behaviorist. He believes the important causes of verbal behavior are in the environment. He says the key thing about language is how it is used. However, Turing said he's too much of a mystic and too anti-science to be a behaviorist. Tu-ring added that Wittgenstein believes most human behavior is too complex to be usefully subjected to scientific scrutiny. My sense, which may change, is that Wittgenstein is a behaviorist who is anti-science. He may not care much for minds but may well believe in souls, perhaps of a non-religious variety.

The second thing was that Wittgenstein is a nature lover who believes Darwin's theory is too simplistic to account for the immense variety and complexity of life.

Turing said an interesting thing about natural selection. He thinks it's an important factor in evolution but doesn't shape as much structure as biologists believe. Often, he said, physical constraints on form are stronger factors. I suggested that these constraints limit the variation *that natural selection acts on. In the light of day, I believe the constraints may even strengthen arguments for natural selection. I must think more about this.*

Enough on Turing, and enough on Wittgenstein for the mo-ment. Let me pen a few words about a topic I promised to treat: non-verbal thinking. You and I agree that much but not all of the private behavior known as thinking is covert verbal behavior: silent talking to oneself. It follows that verbal think-ing has to develop with the acquisition of language. A six-month-old child can't engage in verbal thinking, nor can a rat. But child or rat may experience private non-verbal stimuli that enter into the control of private or public behavior.

Some non-verbal stimuli could be those involved in direction finding. You and I know from our early work with mazes that rats are good at this. Less sophisticated creatures are too. Bees are the classic example, but an ability to find one's way in the world and use that information could well have preceded the emergence of insects. The evolutionary advantage is obvious.

Let me say something that may or may not be related to direc-

tion finding. I'm intrigued by the strategies that people with especially efficient memories have used since Roman times to help with recalling long lists of items. Many of the strategies are like this. You imagine walking along a familiar street. You associate successive items in the list to be remembered with successive parts of the street. You recall the items by talking another walk along the street, making use of the associations as you proceed. A variation is the "memory palace." For this, the walk is through a familiar building.

Such spatially based mnemonic devices seem to be effective. Their effectiveness may exploit inherited mechanisms of spatial orientation and wayfinding.

What has this to do with non-verbal thinking? My hunch is that the private stimuli involved in spatial orientation and wayfinding may have been among the earliest to emerge in the evolution of animal life. They survive as an important element of human non-verbal thinking.

A question begged by the memory palace is how a location in the building becomes a signal for an item of the list, so that the second visit to a location prompts production of the image or word linked to the location. My next hunch is that organisms have evolved so that links with spatial locations occur with unusual readiness. This would be for obvious evolutionary reasons. It's good to be able to remember where the water is and what was encountered on the way.

Perhaps much or even all non-verbal thinking has its roots in mechanisms of spatial orientation and wayfinding. Other relatively primitive processes may be at play too.

A paradox could be that verbal thinking with its enormous complexity may be easier to account for than non-verbal thinking, which may be rooted in simpler, more primitive but less well understood functions.

Here's what I mean. Let's assume that verbal thinking is sub-vocal speech. Speech arises from interactions with the social environment, following basic laws of behavior. It's not hard to imagine how speech may lose its observable features, i.e., those available to other people. This could also be through the play of basic laws of behavior, including punishment for saying unacceptable things aloud. (In a deaf mute, verbal signing could become a similarly private process.)

Non-verbal thinking of the kind involved in the use of memory palaces could require the private formation of links between items and places. Usually links are formed through the pairing of external stimuli. I suggested that there may be an inherited predisposition to form such private links, but this speculation may not help unravel the specifics of their formation.

Moreover, in humans at least, most non-verbal thinking may be unrelated to spatial orientation and direction finding. When I imagine Julie's beaming smile, for example, or her calling out "Dada," these images are not related to particular places. When I imagine making a piece of apparatus, and go wordlessly over how parts may fit together, there is no reliance on the places in a building or street. What these non-verbal images do have *in common is a history of their actually happening. Julie did smile. The components of the apparatus exist. So the question becomes how external "seeing" becomes internalized and amenable to recall and even to manipulation.*

Your friend,

Burrhus

Later in the day, Fred was reviewing this letter while sitting near the front of one of the larger of the Mill Lane Lecture Rooms. He was waiting for the start of Wittgenstein's inaugural presentation. It was his least satisfactory letter, almost embarrassingly so. He resolved that even if the letters were sent – which seemed increasingly unlikely –

this one would not be among them. He wouldn't want to admit that he had engaged in such half-baked speculation, not even to the other Fred.

There were about twenty people in the audience. The room could have held two hundred. Fred looked around to see if Bertrand Russell was there. He was not. Fred recognized no one except Wittgenstein, who sat at one end of the front row of benches deep in thought. The proceedings began soon after four o'clock with two introductions. Professor C.D. Broad, the senior philosophy professor at Cambridge, introduced G.E. Moore the previous occupant of the position Wittgenstein had recently assumed. Then Moore introduced Wittgenstein. Broad and Moore each spoke for about ten minutes. Broad's dislike of Wittgenstein was clear, although he conceded that the appointment was deserved. He even said that to refuse the chair to Wittgenstein would have been like refusing Einstein a chair of physics, a comparison that greatly surprised Fred. Equally clear was Moore's admiration for Wittgenstein. The new professor was evidently a controversial figure within the university, or at least the part concerned with philosophy.

The end of Moore's introduction seemed unnoticed by Wittgenstein, who continued to sit in thought. After an uncomfortable pause, Broad and Moore both cleared their throats, almost in unison. Apparently spurred by the sound of the strange duet, Wittgenstein looked up. He looked around, as if slowly realizing where he was. He then walked briskly to the podium and began speaking. He said,

> I thank Professors Broad and Moore for their generous introductions. I thank the University for appointing me to the Chair of Mental Philosophy and Logic. This position has helped secure my British citizenship, which I prefer to use more than my Austrian, now German, citizenship. Apart from this welcome benefit, I can see no reason for appointing me. I believe that the word *mental* is invariably a source of confusion. I believe that *philosophy* is mostly a remedial activity more akin to nursing – nursing the linguistically wounded – than to the discernment of truth. I cannot imagine what *mental philosophy*

might be. I believe that *logic* is no more than one of many ways of using language. If I achieve anything in this position it will be to help practitioners of philosophy become less misguided in their use of words such as mental and logic. Thank you for your attention.

He then walked out of the lecture room. Turing had been almost right. Wittgenstein had behaved in one of the two ways he predicted, although not the way he thought more likely. If Fred had known Wittgenstein – and Turing – better he could have won five shillings.

Fred followed Wittgenstein, running to catch up with him as he strode along Trinity Street. Wittgenstein said, "I saw you in the audience. I was tempted to say that philosophy was like psychoanalysis."

"What do you mean?" said Fred, a little out of breath.

"Each is a kind of therapy." They were now striding together. "Each produces the same kind of result. Both philosophy and psychoanalysis allow us to eat from the tree of knowledge. They alter the way we see a part of the world. Neither solves problems."

"You may be right. I can't at the moment say." Fred hesitated to catch his breath. "Why would seeing me prompt that comparison?

"You are interested in Freud and have visited him recently."

"How could you know whether I am interested and what I have been doing?" Fred's near-paranoia about the other purpose of his trip had been in abeyance for a few days. His discussions in Cambridge – at the formal dinner and with Turing – had done nothing to arouse it, even though they might have done. Now Wittgenstein had set Fred's alarm bells ringing strongly.

Wittgenstein replied, "I was curious about you and went to your rooms this morning to ask you something. You were not there, but you had left the key in the door. I went in and looked around. I concluded from your notes and other items that you had an interest in Freud and had visited him on your way here. Am I correct?"

"That was extraordinarily intrusive and ill-mannered of you," said Fred, who had found a use for the word 'flabbergasted' but decided against it. "You are correct, Professor Wittgenstein, but that does not make your behavior any more excusable."

"What I discovered may not make your reason for visiting me excusable," said Wittgenstein. "Am I correct too in saying that you have an interest in Adolf Hitler? I saw that you have been reading an English translation of *Mein Kampf*. Are you to be visiting him too while you are on this side of the Atlantic?" They had reached Whewell's Court. "Don't answer now. We are to meet tomorrow morning. We will have much to talk about."

Wittgenstein sped up the staircase to his rooms. Fred thought of following him but decided to go to his own rooms to reflect on what Wittgenstein had just revealed. He needed to think more about this extraordinary man. The meeting the next morning was apparently still on. How it might proceed required more strategizing than Fred had so far engaged in.

Ludwig Wittgenstein in 1930.

TWENTY-THREE

Almost connecting

Cambridge, Friday June 2, 1939

F red had less sleep than he felt he needed before what promised to be the most eventful day of his trip. After the disturbing walk with Wittgenstein back to Whewell's Court, he'd examined his rooms carefully to figure out what the trespassing philosopher might have seen. He could have seen only the second notebook of the trip. Fred had begun this yesterday, continuing his notes on the morning meeting with Freud. The first notebook, now full, was locked in his small suitcase, which had not been tampered with. The notes Wittgenstein saw had just reached the discussion about Hitler. All mention of Bullitt and the book on Wilson was in the first notebook. He might still have to explain some things – the visit to Freud, the mention of Hitler, the presence of *Mein Kampf* in his room – but doing these things might not be difficult.

After a careful survey of his rooms and review of his notes, Fred went to the formal dinner in the Trinity Hall. He'd hoped to continue the discussion about Russia begun on his first night in Cambridge, or talk about something equally interesting. Instead, he ate and drank too much while listening to banter about university politics and the tedious love life of the recently deceased Irish poet W.B. Yeats.

The excess of food and alcohol had caused Fred to fall asleep quickly, and suffer some hours of wakefulness later in the night. He lay wondering why Wittgenstein had been to his rooms. What question had Wittgenstein come to ask – assuming he'd been there to ask a question? Did Wittgenstein come in the hope of exploring his rooms? Or was the search a spur-of-the-moment act prompted by Fred's absence and the key left in the door? Why the jibe about Hitler? Why did Wittgenstein *confess* to searching his rooms? Without the confession, Fred might never have suspected him of doing that.

Fred had an answer only to the last question. Wittgenstein could have told Fred about the search simply to provoke him. Their three encounters so far suggested that Wittgenstein made a habit of being provocative. Fred hoped it was no more than that. What else could it be? Could Wittgenstein have an inkling of Fred's other reason for meeting him? He thought not, but remained uncertain.

As Fred climbed K staircase to Wittgenstein's rooms, on time for the ten o'clock appointment, he was unusually anxious. He felt as if he were on his way to an oral exam for which he was not well prepared, or a court hearing. Wittgenstein once again opened the door before he was able to knock on it. This time, unlike two days ago, he was smiling. He appeared happy, even sunny. "Look at what I have," he said, pointing to a small dark blue stiff-covered booklet in the other hand. "It is my British passport! Do come in."

"Thank you," said Fred. As he entered the room, he looked more closely at the document held up by Wittgenstein. At the top of the cover, above indistinct words embossed in gold, was an inset containing the passport number. At the bottom was another inset bearing the handwritten name Mr. L. J. J. Wittgenstein. He was shown to a folding chair set up in the center of the room. Wittgenstein sat in the upright chair, which had been moved to the window. Wittgenstein's face was in shadow while Fred's was bathed in light. He felt the arrangement was more suited to an interrogation than a discussion.

Fred said, "I don't know enough about your situation and plans to understand why you are so pleased to have the British passport."

"I need to visit my family soon in Austria. I will not be detained there if I am travelling on this passport. Also, I may need then to visit America, again on family business. It is much easier to do that on a British passport. Otherwise I would have to use a German passport because Austria is now a part of Germany."

Fred wondered if Wittgenstein's good humor had brought on an unusual openness. He felt he could probe a little more and said, "They could detain you, just like that? Why would they do it?"

"It may be only a question of allowing me in and then not giving me a German passport. Without a British passport I would have to stay in Germany."

Fred wondered if Wittgenstein had misheard or misunderstood his questions, or was being evasive. He said, "Someone told me your family may be caught up in the terrible things happening to Jews in Germany and Austria."

Wittgenstein's facial expression – as far as Fred could see it – quickly changed from sunny to somber. It became the glower that had confronted Fred at their first encounter. "Who said that?" snapped Wittgenstein. "How would they know? Why are you interested in such things?"

"I'm not," replied Fred, as evenly as he could. "You introduced the topic when you showed me your new passport. I was trying to be friendly, even sympathetic. It was a way of moving beyond your egregious behavior yesterday when you trespassed into my rooms."

Wittgenstein did not respond immediately. He made some of the odd hand-waving gestures he'd made at the beginning of the lecture in this room two days ago. He said, "I do not understand moving beyond or egregious."

"Egregious means appalling, atrocious, outrageous. Perhaps the

German word is *ungeheuerlich*.

"Ach! Sie sprechen Deutsch!"

"Nur ein bisschen," Fred replied slowly. *"Ungeheuerlich ist einer der wenigen Worte die ich kenne."*

"In that case we must continue to speak English. When you said you were moving beyond *mein ungeheuerliches Verhalten* what did you mean?"

Fred was impressed by the way in which Wittgenstein sought and maintained control over the discussion. He said, "It's a polite way of saying recovering from or even forgetting about. I'm no longer upset by what you did."

"But I am still perturbed by what I saw in your rooms. I am assuming that your notes were not describing a fantasy. I assume they were reporting a meeting with Professor Freud that actually happened. The meeting is of interest to me. I am an admirer of Freud, even a disciple. I was intrigued your discussion with him about evolution and the development of mind. There are many ways in which I disagree with Freud – as you seem to do too – but these are two matters on which Freud and I may have some agreement."

Fred said, "I hope you and I will be able to discuss both topics this morning."

Wittgenstein continued as though Fred had not spoken, "I did not know that Freud is in London. Is it possible to visit him? One of my sisters knows him well. She could help to secure an introduction."

"He's not well. He's in his last weeks or even his last days."

"How were you able to meet with him? I will return to this question. First, I want to know why you spoke to Freud about Adolf Hitler. Why do you have Hitler's book in your rooms?"

"It's a coincidence. If I remember correctly, Freud introduced Hitler into our discussion. He was trying to caution me against promoting an analogy to natural selection. He said that Hitler's racial policies could be sullying the name of Darwin."

"Sullying?"

"Dirtying, damaging the integrity of."

"And *Mein Kampf*?"

"A colleague gave it to me for the sea voyage. He said I should read some of it to understand what is happening in Europe. Why are you so concerned about my possible interest in Hitler?"

"I do not want to go into that."

Fred thought for a moment and decided to be persistent. "I've been told you were at a secondary school with Hitler. *Realschule* is it called? Could that be true?"

Wittgenstein made more of his hand-waving movements and then said, "Who told you that? It is true. But I did not know him. He was some years behind me even though he is six days older. Our paths did not cross. How could you have heard that we were at the same school? I think you are not what you seem, Professor Skinner. Are you an American spy?"

"That notion is as preposterous as your intrusion into my rooms. How could you imagine that the American government might be interested in you, or in me? I heard about your being at school with Hitler while I have been in Cambridge. You seem to be the subject of much discussion, likely the subject of many unfounded rumors."

"That is one reason I dislike this university so much. There are too many people here with too little to do. The result is too much gossip."

"I've heard too that you are an admirer of the Soviet Union. You have taken Russian lessons and have been there several times."

"Who has been telling you these things? I see Russell's hand at play here. He is fond of meddling in politics and in other people's affairs. Russell asked me to see you, did he not? You confirmed that to me, did you not?"

"I didn't, but it's true that Russell's behind my visit to Cambridge for the purpose of meeting with you. My being here is the result of a discussion he and I had during the past winter, when he was visiting the University of Minnesota."

"Yes, he is still in America. He is there to avoid the coming war. He wants to avoid another jail term for his pacifist views. Why did he want you to talk with me?"

"Not about the war, nor about Hitler. He seemed concerned that you were becoming an ally of behaviorism and that this was ruining your promise as a great philosopher. Our discussion led him to believe, incorrectly, that I *had* been a behaviorist and I had seen the error of my ways. So, just as recovered alcoholics can help alcoholics recover, he seems to have thought that a recovered behaviorist may be good at showing another behaviorist the errors of his ways."

"Was that a joke?" said Wittgenstein, "I do not understand. Your notes suggest you continue to be a behaviorist."

"That is mostly true," said Fred, "but Russell was convinced enough – not directly by me – to believe that I was an ideal person to steer you back to the paths of logical analysis that you and he trod together many years ago."

"You speak poetically about the fanciful activities of a fading philosopher who is ripe for retirement," said Wittgenstein. "*Ach so*, you *are* a behaviorist. I am not." He paused, and was soon hand-waving again. "So, *your* real reason for meeting me may be to convert me *to* rather than *from* behaviorism. That *is* a joke. You will not be successful."

Fred understood the joke but did not compliment Wittgenstein on his attempt at humor. He said, "Turing told me that you don't think that natural selection is an adequate explanation for the evolution of species. You are not a Darwinian."

"Turing!" Wittgenstein exclaimed. "So it is Turing you have been speaking to. He knows nothing about me."

"Is it true that you believe there is more to evolution than natural selection acting on variations in the features of animals and plants?"

"I walk in the fields and woods," said Wittgenstein, "There I am struck by the awesome variety of what is before my eyes, and my ears, and my nose. Natural selection does not have the explanatory power to account for this variety. It cannot explain the ways in which the different species have come to occupy their places within the extraordinary panoply of life."

"Now that's a rare English word: panoply," said Fred. "I know of course what it means, but I'm surprised that a non-native speaker would use it. Your English is remarkably good."

Wittgenstein did not respond. Fred wondered whether his compliment had been misplaced. Then Wittgenstein said, "I have a friend, an acquaintance, who often uses the term 'panoply of life.' I borrowed the phrase from him."

"I have a friend, Willard Van Orman Quine – I know him as Van – who often uses a cruder phrase, 'the passing show,' to refer to the same thing as 'the panoply of life.' I have come to use it."

"I know of Mr. Quine, an American. I met him briefly when he visited here a few years ago. I would like to know why 'the passing show' is considered crude." From what Fred could see in the shadow, Wittgenstein's face had relaxed. His voice had become less high-pitched. Perhaps he was even enjoying the discussion.

Fred used the possible gap in Wittgenstein's armor to see if the session could be extended. "I'd tell you if we had more time," he said. "First, I'd like to talk about more important matters. Can I ask you this? If natural selection is insufficiently powerful, which other mechanisms are also needed to account for evolution?"

Wittgenstein tensed again. "I do not have an answer to this ques-

319

tion," he said. "I do believe that a focus on natural selection trivializes the complexity of nature. Equally, a focus on behavior trivializes the richness of human existence."

"How is human existence trivialized?"

"Don't interrupt me with so many questions," said Wittgenstein. He continued, "Science is a simplistic way of viewing the world. It is adequate for identifying basic relationships. It is inadequate for appreciating art and music. It cannot account for the richness of human experience and activity."

Fred ignored the arrogant plea for less interruption. He said, "Dog breeders can do amazing things with the artificial version of natural selection. The variety among dog breeds is remarkable. It's difficult to imagine that a four-pound Chihuahua and a sixty-pound golden retriever are members of the same species. The difference between them seems greater than the difference between many species, such as between crows and ravens. They're often confused, but they *are* different species. They don't normally interbreed."

"Many extraordinary things do not occur in the wild," said Wittgenstein, "including radios and rockets. That does not mean that what occurs in the wild is the result of the same processes that produce radios and rockets."

Fred wondered whether he should censure Wittgenstein for interrupting, but shied away from responding in kind to Wittgenstein's petulance. He said, "The interactions with a changing environment over geological time have been the main process in producing the multiplicity of plants and animals. Similarly, interactions with the environment during a lifetime – often involving parents, teachers, colleagues, and others –are the chief cause of human excellence in the arts, sciences, and every other endeavor."

"As well as the poverty of scientific description," Wittgenstein said, again as though Fred had not spoken, "I object to the attempts by scientists to explain things by reference to something else, rather than in their own terms. Music is more than a collection of sounds as ana-lyzed by physicists. A painting is more than blobs of oil as analyzed by chemists."

"I agree that things should be described or explained in appropriate terms," said Fred. "For me, the appropriate terms usually involve the environment of what is being explained rather than something inside the organisms. If we look inside animals for their origins – at their physiology or vital spirit or whatever – we are apt to overlook what may be the most significant contribution. What is the most significant is the history of interactions with the environment."

"What do you mean by interactions? I know what the word means. It is *Interaktion* in German. What is not clear to me is how you are using the word."

Fred considered whether Wittgenstein's question might mark the beginning of a useful dialogue. He replied, "Could I, for the moment, replace the word 'interaction' with the word 'encounter,' meaning to come into contact with? I'll explain why later. In the case of the origin of species, the significant encounters are those involved in natural se-lection. They are the encounters between a population and its environ-ment. Other explanations of the origin of species involve mystical entities inside the organisms – life force, for example – or outside na-ture, such as the hand of God."

Fred continued, "If we look in the mind – whatever that means – or in the brain for an understanding of musical composition we are apt to overlook what may be the most significant contribution. This would be the history of encounters between the behavior and the environment. In this case I mean the hours, days, years spent acquiring musical exper-tise and engaging in composition."

"How can this learning and practice be usefully described as inter-actions or even encounters with the environment?"

Fred was pleased to be now setting the pace of the discussion. He answered, "Improvement during hours of piano practice comes from the effects of consequences of the playing. There are several kinds of consequence, including a teacher's praise and a satisfying sound from the piano. The first of these is clearly an interaction. The teacher and the student affect each other's behavior. The teacher reinforces progressively refined approximations to good performance on the part of the student. The student's improved performance sustains the teacher's tutoring."

Fred added, "Merely behaving does not necessarily result in improvement. A well-known American psychologist, Edward Thorndike, demonstrated this. He tried to draw a four-inch line while blindfold. Without information about correctness, he was no better after three thousand attempts than when he started. I would say that the sight of a result of correct length reinforces the behavior of drawing a four-inch line, as opposed to drawing a five-inch line."

"Reinforces?"

"Strengthens. I believe the process of reinforcement of behavior is analogous to selection by the environment of one rather than another characteristic within a population, for example, white fur in an Arctic climate."

"But this is not a case of an *interaction* with the environment," said Wittgenstein. "The environment does not change. What changes is the prevalence of members of a population with white fur."

"Causality in natural selection is indeed often more one-sided than in the piano instruction example. However, Darwin showed too that many instances of natural selection involve interactions. In *The Origin of Species*, he wrote that the structure of every animal is related to the other animals with which they compete or prey on or escapes from. Tigers' claws are selected for their ability to damage prey. They depend for their shape and size, at least a little, on the ease with which the prey's skin can be penetrated. The claws also depend on the prey's running speed. If prey animals are speedy, tigers with heavy or even overly sharp claws may not be able to keep up. Similarly, prey may be selected for toughness of skin. However, skin that's too tough may impede running and thus the ability to escape. Natural selection acts both ways. Each species, prey and predator, is part of the environment for the other species. Each species is changed by its environment and changes that environment."

"I have not yet finished," said Fred as Wittgenstein signaled that he was to speak. The man was unusually discomforted by not being the only speaker. "The interactions between participants in verbal exchanges are, in my view, similar. Speaking is reinforced by a listener, whose speaking is then reinforced by the first speaker. Perhaps more than most other mammals the behavior of humans involves interactions. The interactions are chiefly with other humans, but they can also be with environments that are changed by human activity. The activities involved in construction of a bridge are selected by properties of the materials used. They are also selected by the laws of physics, notably those concerning gravity."

"So," said Wittgenstein, "you are proposing that just as natural selection may be the prime factor in the evolution of species, so may reinforcement be the prime factor in changing behavior during the lifetime of a species."

"You are perceptive," said Fred, immediately wondering if his comment was a little patronizing.

"Don't interrupt me," said Wittgenstein fiercely. "I must go and think about this." He stood and quickly walked over to the bedroom, shutting the door behind him with a bang.

Fred wondered whether to stay. The man was bizarrely rude. He was strange enough, thought Fred, to be a candidate for therapeutic interventions that could help normalize his social behavior. Fred spent a few minutes pondering how he might begin to change the way the philosopher interacted with people. He remembered Freud's observations about Hitler. The German leader could be too mad to benefit from psychoanalysis. Hitler's madness was similar to that of a shaman. Perhaps Wittgenstein's behavior was too bizarre to benefit from any known intervention, behavioral or psychoanalytic.

In any case, a more important concern about Hitler was whether any useful information about him could be extracted from Wittgenstein. Fred concluded he had nothing to gain by leaving, and stayed.

Some thirty minutes later, Wittgenstein resumed his seat under the window. He provided no explanation as to why he'd retreated into his bedroom. He didn't apologize for leaving Fred alone. He said, "Superficial is the word. There is a superficial resemblance between what you call reinforcement and natural selection. Both are superficial ways of accounting for complex phenomena."

Fred was tempted to comment on the man's absence. Instead he said, "If reinforcement and natural selection are superficial, what for you would be satisfactory accounts of evolution and human behavior?"

"You have already posed this question as it applies to natural selection. I repeat, I do not have an answer except to say that I find an account dominated by natural selection to be trivial. I find your reinforcement theory to be even more trivial because it takes no account of thoughts, desires, intentions, and feelings."

"Could we discuss how thoughts, etc., arise? Could we discuss the related question of how children learn to use words?" said Fred.

Fred was beginning to feel again that they could be relaxing into a dialogue when Wittgenstein continued, "Intention and other such matters have been occupying me. I am not ready to discuss them. I do not think a discussion with a psychologist, especially a behaviorist, could be useful."

"Thank you for your frankness," said Fred. "What are your concerns about psychologists?"

"I am concerned about their conceptual confusion. They are especially confused when they talk or write about minds and brains. From the time of the Ancient Greeks, we have been presumed to have inner entities – mind is the main one – that govern what we do. Descartes and other reputed sages have supported this view. It permeates popular culture. Psychologists, who should know better, have continued this way of thinking. It provides little more than circular explanations and reliance on immaterial entities or forces. Human behavior is said to flow from non-physical mental activity. The only evidence for this may be the human behavior that is being explained. More recently, the brain has often been substituted for mind. This does not resolve the conceptual and logical confusion. I have some sympathy for behaviorists. They have tried to avoid the circularity by ignoring the unobservable. In doing so, however, as I said before, they – *you?* – trivialize human experience and action."

"Psychology has become a sterile enterprise," continued Wittgenstein. "With few exceptions – at the moment I can think only of Professor Freud – its practitioners have provided little enlightenment as to the human condition."

Fred could see that, in spite of Wittgenstein's earlier protest about questions, they might be for him the most tolerable form of interruption, as long as the questions can be ignored. He was about to ask about the enlightenment Freud had provided when Wittgenstein said, "Freud must be praised for his cleverness in drawing attention to obscure connections between events in a person's life. He must be criticized for claiming that his speculations about mental phenomena have a scientific basis. In the end, his notions provide support for the popular view of the role of mental phenomena."

Fred could now see that he would be lectured at interminably unless he could resume control over their interaction. He said, "You and I may have more in common that you seem to suppose. I am indeed a behaviorist in that I focus on what is observable. As important, as I said before, I look for causes in the individual's interactions with the environment. But I also hold that people are influenced by happenings inside their skin that others cannot observe."

"Of course they are," said Wittgenstein

Fred continued, "Mr. Russell, in the course of arranging for my visit here, kindly gave me a copy of some of your lecture notes, which I believe are known as *The Blue Book*. I was impressed by what these notes say about toothache."

Wittgenstein interrupted again. "Russell had no right to give you those notes. They represent my analysis of language at a particular point in time. They were for my students only. My analysis is not for anyone else to make use of. I insist that you give me the copy that you have."

"I don't have the document with me." Fred hoped that Wittgenstein took this to mean that it was in Minneapolis and not in his suitcase. He added, "From memory, you made some excellent points and posed some good questions. You asked whether a machine can have a toothache. You asked too whether it makes sense to speak of an unconscious toothache. You raised the question as to how we learned as children to say correctly 'I have a toothache.' You asked whether one person can feel another's toothache."

"I was using the example of toothache to show my students the way out of some of the traps set by everyday language."

"I gathered that. You spent the least amount of time in *The Blue Book* on what I consider to be the most important point. It is how we learn to use the word 'toothache.' I believe I may have something to contribute on this matter."

"I doubt it," said Wittgenstein. "I agree it is an important point. I have considered the matter in some detail and have resolved it to my satisfaction. It is a question of identifying the criteria for using the word." He stood, turned, and began walking towards the bedroom.

"If you are going to hide in there for another half hour, I will thank you now for this discussion and say goodbye." Wittgenstein stopped. He turned toward Fred and gave him the darkest of looks, just as a sulking child might give when chastised. Fred continued, "Please sit down and let me provide a perspective on how a child comes to say 'I have a toothache' in a way that is useful to the child and to those he or she talks with." Wittgenstein sat down. He continued to glower. Fred was elated at what he had achieved. He worked hard to avoid smiling at his success.

Fred said, "Before I say something about how a child comes to use the word 'toothache,' let me say that in *The Blue Book* I found the treatment of criteria and symptoms to be especially confusing." Wittgenstein moved as if he would interrupt again. Fred cut him off, saying, "Let that be for the moment. I want to tell you how this behaviorist, how *I* account for the learning of words spoken in response to something that only the speaker has access to."

"First," Fred continued, "we must consider how a child learns to say 'red' in an appropriate manner. It's a simple matter of reinforcement of the use of the word 'red' only in the presence of red objects. The reinforcement most often consists of the verbal or other behavior of what might be called the child's verbal community. This community is initially the mother and other members of the child's family. Additional factors can be involved. These include imitation, pointing, and refinement of the pronunciation of the word. However, differential reinforcement – reinforcing the utterance of 'red' in the presence of a red thing and not in its absence – is the core process leading to appropriate use."

"Next," said Fred, noting that Wittgenstein's face had softened, "consider ways in which a child's verbal community can differentially reinforce specific verbal behavior – e.g., 'tooth hurts' – in relation to something to which the community has no direct access, in this case a toothache. Here are three ways – and there may be more:

1. Saying 'tooth hurts' is reinforced only in the presence of publicly available accompaniments, such as a swollen jaw.

2. Instead of inferring the private stimulus (the toothache) from accompanying public stimuli (such as a swollen jaw), the verbal community infers it from nonverbal behavior, such as

327

touching the jaw or tooth, grimacing and groaning.

3. The child already says 'knee hurts' or some such expression appropriately. In that case, the publicly available accompaniment (a bloody graze) is strongly correlated with the private stimulus (a painful knee). Through differential reinforcement of similar verbal behavior, versions of this expression become used correctly for other accessible parts of the body, for example, 'finger hurts.' Finally, likely in combination with the first or the second way, perhaps both, the verbal community can reinforce 'tooth hurts,' although never with the precision of 'knee hurts.'"

"Are you finished?" said Wittgenstein irritably. Without waiting for an answer he continued, "Perhaps such training based on reward plays a role in getting children to say things, but the way you put it makes the children seem like machines, or circus animals. Is there not a place for thinking in your formulation, even in a child?"

"I'm not finished, said Fred. "My formulation, as you describe it, is really no more than an elaboration of your position, as I understood it from *The Blue Book*. You said that the use of a word *in practice* is its meaning. I agree. I'd elaborate the position to say that the meaning of a word is its use together with *the circumstances* of its use. This elaboration positions the use of words as a form of behavior, as verbal behavior. Verbal behavior is subject to the same relations to the environment, to its circumstances, as any behavior. I also agree with something else in *The Blue Book*, if I understood it correctly. It's that there's no clear break between the simple processes of language acquisition and the sophisticated use of language."

Wittgenstein began the hand-waving routine that indicated he was about to speak. Fred said, "I'm still not finished. In verbal behavior, other people are the environment that counts. Verbal behavior is social behavior. We acquire verbal behavior as part of a verbal community. A child reared without a verbal community will not speak. I'm finished now, for the moment."

Wittgenstein seemed to be in torment, perhaps because Fred had been talking more than he had, perhaps because he disagreed with what Fred had been saying. Wittgenstein said, "I will admit that you have interesting things to say, even though I cannot accept the crudeness of your analysis in terms of reinforcement." He paused.

Fred began to speak but Wittgenstein stood. He gestured to Fred as a conductor would do when quieting an orchestra, or a speaker quieting an audience. Wittgenstein smiled weakly and continued, "We seem to be in agreement that the use of language is a social matter. Russell could be disappointed in you. He believes – or did believe – that a person could have a personal language, a language that only the person could understand. I favored such a notion twenty years ago. It flowed from the kind of mentalism that Russell and I espoused then, and he may still do. It holds, for example, that conversation is between minds, mediated by publicly expressed words that are translations from and to internal mental vocabularies."

Fred interrupted, "I like what you are saying even though I don't understand how a private language implies mentalism. Twins can have a private language, intelligible only to themselves. I have been told this by Ella Day, who conducts research into twins at my university. Such a twin language would probably be acquired by the same process of differential reinforcement I described earlier. In this case, the verbal community would be a total of two persons. It would be a private language acquired in a public way."

"I must think about twins," said Wittgenstein, evidently uncomfortable that Fred was talking again.

"Please don't think about it now," said Fred, "and certainly not in your bedroom. We may not have much time left. Could we talk about thinking? Before we do, can I thank you for one thing? Our discussion has clarified for me the difference between verbal behavior and language. Verbal behavior is what a person does. It is developed and maintained by the reinforcement practices of the person's verbal community. A language is a set of those practices. When a verbal community's practices constitute the English language, saying *bed* is reinforced in connection with a sleeping place. When the verbal community's practices are the German language, *Bett* is reinforced, and so on. Where there is no verbal community there is no language. This clarification will help me a lot. Let's now move on to thinking."

"What is there to say about thinking?" said Wittgenstein.

Fred surmised that Wittgenstein had not understood – or even listened to – the distinction he had just elaborated. He replied, "In *The Blue Book* you asked, 'Is it possible for a machine to think?'" I believe your answer was no. Your reason was that this isn't how we use the word think. But what if, as Dr. Turing believes, it will be possible to build a computing machine able to undertake every intellectual activity a human can engage in? When we talked about such a machine, would we use the word 'think'?"

"Perhaps, although I would resist using this word for a machine because I do not believe that human beings are machines. There is a word for giving human qualities to non-human entities. In German it is *Anthropomorphismus*. I believe the English word is similar."

"Anthropomorphism," said Fred. "It means the attribution of human characteristics to animals."

"Can animals think? That is an interesting question."

Fred was pleased that Wittgenstein was again asking the questions, although he feared that a question might be put in German that he could not understand. He could not remember taking part in such a competitive discussion. He said, "An American researcher, Winthrop Kellogg, and his wife raised a chimpanzee named Gua with their son Donald. Gua was about seven months old. Donald was a few months older. At first, Gua showed more comprehension of words than Donald. Then Donald began to speak, and surpassed Gua in comprehension. The sounds made by Gua changed relatively little, even though she had much the same environment as Donald. The 'experiment' was terminated after nine months when Donald began to imitate Gua's sounds."

"Ah! Imitation," interrupted Wittgenstein. "That must have been the important factor. Perhaps chimpanzees do not inherit a disposition to imitate."

"Young chimpanzees imitate many actions they are capable of," Fred continued. "They don't appear to imitate sounds. I don't know whether imitation is an acquired or an inherited ability. More likely it's a combination of the two. I suspect that imitation played a role. I suspect that the stronger factor was differential reinforcement of Donald's sounds according to their similarity to appropriate words. Because of the nature of her voice box, Gua could not make a range of sounds sufficient for differential reinforcement to have an effect."

"Another factor," said Wittgenstein, "could have been that the boy had more intimate relations with his parents, making the acquisition of speech easier."

Fred was delighted. Wittgenstein had moved from dismissing the centrality of reinforcement in the acquisition of speech to exploring its possibility. He said, "You are perceptive to raise that point. Kellogg highlighted two things relevant to it. One was that Gua seemed more dependent on human interaction than Donald. This argues against your point. The other thing he said could support it. Donald showed more interest in human faces. Gua tended to distinguish people more by their clothes and smell. Thus, Donald could have been attending more to the mouth, the source of sounds and also of movements correlated with sounds. Perhaps human children are genetically disposed to pay more attention to faces."

Wittgenstein said, "I can accept that animal research can help address basic questions about the acquisition of language. However, I presumed you were going to use this story of the chimpanzee to answer my question as to whether animals think, which I intended to be rhetorical. Nothing in your story provides an answer."

"I'm sorry. I was carried away by my account of Gua and Donald.

I believe the simple answer to your question is that animals may think, but not in the way humans do. Humans think mostly in words. Thus, Gua would not think as humans do. Donald was likely not thinking with words then. His thinking with words would have emerged later, as he acquired the ability to speak sub-vocally."

"I understand 'speaking sub-vocally' and would agree that much thought appears to be talking to oneself. But what about thinking that does not involve words? Much of my thinking is in images. Some of my communication is in images. I have a correspondent with whom I exchange only pictures and diagrams. A lion, if it thinks, must surely think in images of prey, lionesses and packs of hyenas."

Fred said, "I have a hunch that non-verbal thinking is closely integrated with navigation. This is a skill possessed by many creatures much simpler than the lion."

"I could concede that some animals, and even some machines – perhaps decades from now – may usefully be considered to be engaged in thinking. *Intention* may be a more difficult matter. I have some sympathy for the view of Max Weber. Do you know of him? He wrote that intention is the distinguishing feature of human activity. And he might well have said that intention distinguishes humans from machines as well as from animals."

Fred said, "What is an intention?" He waved away Wittgenstein's moves to continue. "Let me focus on this question for a moment. The conventional view is that an intention is somehow formed as a mental event. This mental event guides or even causes behavior. I believe that you, Professor Wittgenstein, have difficulty with this view of intention. I conclude this from your discussion of painting a portrait set out in *The Blue Book*. If I remember correctly, your view was that a portrait is a portrait only if the artist had an intention to create a likeness of the subject. Your difficulty lay in working out what might be the evidence for the intention to create a likeness."

"You have no right to assume what I think about such matters," said Wittgenstein, almost shouting. "I dictated those notes several years ago and my conception of intention has changed."

Wittgenstein paused. Did he have nothing more to say on the topic? Did he expect to be asked about his current view of intention?

Fred resumed his own explanation, as calmly as he could. "Let's think about an extreme case: a murder. This offense usually requires evidence of intention for conviction. There are two kinds of evidence. One is what the alleged murderer might have said. She might have said, for example, 'I'm going to kill my husband one day.' The other is associated behavior such as discovering the husband's affair, procuring the weapon, and creating an alibi. Although the verbal behavior may be a literal expression of intention, the other, mostly non-verbal behavior may well be given more weight, even though it could reasonably be viewed as a lesser expression of intention. This kind of consideration confirms your point. What is proper evidence of intention may be a slippery question. I would like to take a very different approach to intention."

"Before you do," Wittgenstein burst in again, "what about unconscious intention, which Professor Freud has been so imaginative about? Would that not obviate your first kind of evidence?"

The battle is going my way, thought Fred. "I'll deal with that too. What I want to say – and I think you may agree – is that it's not useful to consider that a mental act, whatever that may be, causes a physical act such as a murder."

Wittgenstein stood and waved his hands. Fred continued, "Please sit down and be still. You are making it hard for me to talk about these difficult matters." Wittgenstein sat. Fred relaxed and smiled a little. He said, "A woman who says she intends to kill her husband is not revealing a mental state so much as making a prediction about her behavior in the light of known circumstances. Can we move away from murder for a moment and talk about a more familiar intention – for example, to eat lunch at a particular restaurant? A person who says 'I intend to eat lunch in the Lyons Tea House' could be pointing among other things to the time since breakfast. He or she could be referring to the availability of that eating place, a history of being satisfied there, and prior observations that a particular young lady, or man, lunches there. Also important could be the immediate context of the utterance. This would include, for example, whether, it was a response to a question."

"Consider one of my experimental rats," Fred continued. "It can press one lever and receive a food pellet. It can press another lever and receive a drop of water at the end of a tube. Should we say that when it presses the first lever it intends to eat and when it presses the second lever it intends to drink?"

Fred added, "I doubt whether a person would be convicted of murder, or anything else, on the strength of an unconscious intention. My question is this. Let's assume that a person knows his own behavior including its controlling circumstances well enough to make a fairly accurate prediction of what he will do. Does the mental state of intention need to be added as a cause of the behavior? Surely this is an empirical question?"

Wittgenstein spoke. The words tumbled out. "The word 'intention' is not usually used in connection with trivial matters such as you describe. It is usually used for conscious acts, not for routine or mechanically performed acts. However, it has just occurred to me that Professor Freud's notion of unconscious intentions complicates the analysis of this word. What would you say about that?"

As if realizing that he had given Fred an unwelcome opening, he quickly continued, "You – like me – want to overturn much of philosophy. You want to overturn the part of it that is rooted in the notion of intention as the feature that distinguishes humans."

Fred said, not quite sure what he was replying to but seeing an opening, "It's an empirical matter. If we define intention and find that the behavior of non-humans, even machines, qualifies, then intention cannot be the distinguishing feature."

"I would agree," said Wittgenstein, "and I could agree again that animal research in this respect could be of interest. I would want to question whether we have a useful definition of intention."

"The distinguishing feature of humans," Fred continued, wondering if Wittgenstein had ever expressed agreement with anyone before, "must be only a matter of degree. To believe otherwise could be to suggest that humans are chosen creatures created in the image of a god, or some such thing? I'd say that the main distinguishing feature of humans is the richness of our verbal behavior."

"Now I must disagree," said Wittgenstein. He stopped speaking as the sound of someone climbing the stairs to his room became audible. The steps were being climbed one at a time. Wittgenstein rushed past Fred, opened the door and called out, "Francis, you must not come here just now."

The noise of climbing stairs stopped. Fred remembered what Turing had said about Francis Skinner, Wittgenstein's live-in companion and amanuensis. He remembered that – unusually for Wittgenstein – they were on first-name terms.

A young man's voice called up from the stairwell, "Ludwig" – he said it as 'Loodveeg' – "I want you to come back to our home. I need you, and I think you need me."

"We cannot talk about this now," said Wittgenstein in an even odder manner than usual. He spoke slowly, in a voice that was both clear and hushed – as though talking with patient affection to a child. "Go back downstairs and wait on the ground floor. I will be there shortly. I have my British passport."

"I don't care about your passport. Do you have Adam Church up there? Is that why I cannot come up? Is that why you have stopped staying at our home?"

"Don't be silly, Francis. There is a visitor from America here. I am coming down in a minute. Please go back and wait on the ground floor.

We will walk and talk."

Fred heard the sound of stairs being descended, one step at a time. Francis Skinner must have some kind of infirmity.

Wittgenstein returned. He gathered up his passport and the papers on his desk and pushed them into the safe, slowing down only to lock the safe door with care. He took his raincoat and walking stick and sped out of the room without a word to Fred. The noise of his bounding down the steps drowned out the already dwindling sound of the other man's descent.

Fred was less surprised by the abrupt ending to the discussion than he would have been if he had not already experienced much of Wittgenstein's bizarre behavior. What was to have been the main feature of Fred's long odyssey had turned out to be flat and inconsequential. He had learned nothing about Hitler from Wittgenstein, or about the Soviet Union. The quest to move the philosopher away from suspected behavioristic leanings seemed to have been pointless. It would probably take another letter to the other Fred to figure out whether progress of any kind had been made on the last matter. On Hitler and Russia, he could say already that whatever he might report about them would have to be based on other sources. He shut the door to Wittgenstein's rooms and returned to his own.

Part V

Cambridge
to
New York

Sebastian

Geschichte eines
Deutschen Haffner

Die Erinnerungen 1914–1933

DVA

The book Raimund Pretzel was writing in June 1939, not published until after his death in 1999 when the manuscript was found among his papers.It appeared first in the original German; a translation of the title is *Story of a German: Memories 1914-1933*. It was translated into English by the author's son, Oliver Pretzel, and published under the title *Defying Hitler: A Memoir*. The penname Sebastian Haffner was adopted in 1940 to avoid recriminations against Pretzel's family. The photo of the author dates from the early 1930s.

TWENTY-FOUR

German Wisdom

Cambridge and London, Friday June 2, 1939

As Fred reached the landing of J staircase where his rooms were, he found a bent figure pushing a document under his door. Alan Turing stood and said, "I'm delivering the offprint of the article I mentioned. I hope you will find it of interest. How did you fare with Professor Wittgenstein?"

"I'm glad to see you," said Fred, opening the door and picking up the offprint. "Please come in. Two hours with Wittgenstein is not good for one's sanity. It's hard to say how I fared. I guess I held my own. It was constant jousting for control over the discussion."

"That's exactly how I feel after a bout with him. I usually start strong and give up. You may have fared better."

"He's a bully," said Fred, "intellectually and perhaps physically too. Like other bullies, he backs down when confronted. Thanks for the article. I'll read it with interest. Would you like comments on it?"

"I wouldn't want you to take your time to do that. Circumstances beyond my control have pushed my interest and work in another direction. I hope to be able to return to the more exciting matter of intelligent machines later but I can't work on them now."

Fred remembered Turing's slip about codes and ciphers. He said nothing in response, but invited Turing to sit.

Turing continued, "Wittgenstein is certainly capable of making one a little unhinged. He does that to me, although I may be especially responsive to his provocations. Wittgenstein is only the strangest of many strange people here at Cambridge. I'm one of them."

Fred had noticed before that Turing was a little odd. He was untidy and awkward. He rarely made eye contact and sometimes had unusual facial expressions. But he was ordinary compared with Wittgenstein. He said, "Whatever you feel about yourself, compared with Wittgenstein you personify normality."

"It's encouraging to hear a psychologist say that. Do tell me a little more about Wittgenstein's presentation yesterday and your discussion with him this morning."

Fred explained that he had a train to catch at two-thirty and needed to have lunch. They agreed to eat at a café on Trinity Street. Walking there, Fred related the inaugural lecture, or lack of one, and Wittgenstein's confession about reading his notes. He told Turing about the philosopher's delight at having received his British passport, and the abrupt change in mood when Fred had probed a little about his status in Austria. He didn't mention Wittgenstein's dismissal of Turing as a source of information.

When they were settled with lunch, Turing said, "The man is experiencing more stress than usual. I think it's to do with happenings in Austria. Perhaps there's also an aspect concerning the Soviet Union. I've not discussed such matters with him, but I talk a little with people who are closer to him. I've heard he's involved in negotiations with the German government to change his family's racial status, so they can avoid the growing dreadfulness of being Jewish in that country. I've heard too that he's been in negotiations with the Russian government about moving there, I'm not sure why. These high-level intrigues are far beyond what Cambridge dons are normally involved in, especially

340

a don as unworldly as Wittgenstein."

"Do you know if he has political views?"

"I've had no indication of any. There are rumors he's spent time – and maybe still does – with people who are inclined towards communism. Apparently, the same people are inclined towards homosexual behavior too. I must add that I've had no direct experience of a homosexual who is a communist. Wittgenstein is a bundle of paradoxes. If he has communist leanings they'd have to coexist with his elitism, evident in statements such as 'philosophy is not for the common man.' And his elitism coexists with his evident dislike for university life. This must be reconciled with the fact that he stays here and seems to live for his work as a philosopher."

"Don't we all house inconsistencies?" said Fred. "Although I'd have to agree that Wittgenstein's contradictions could be unusually extreme."

"You told me that you were here because Russell wanted to set Wittgenstein straight on certain matters to do with logic and language. Were you successful?"

"I think you know already that I was not. After a bout of paranoia concerning his Jewishness – he even accused me of being an American spy – we had what may prove to be a useful discussion about language matters. The discussion was unfocused and inconclusive. It could take me some time to figure out whether either of us said anything of importance. His view about natural selection as a major cause of speciation was just as you described. He believes it to be an inadequate explanation."

Turing ate much of his lunch before responding. He then said, "Forgive me for intruding, but I suggested before that setting Wittgenstein straight was a pretty thin reason for coming all this way. Are you here for other reasons too? Could there be some truth to Wittgenstein's allegation? You don't have to answer these questions. Just consider them to be a warning that you may not be entirely credible."

Fred was much alarmed by Turing's observation. He endeavored to hide his alarm by responding promptly and calmly. "Thank you for your concern. Perhaps better knowledge of Bertrand Russell's large ego is required for a full understanding as to why he set this visit in motion. As I explained, I went along with it – in spite of opposition from my family – to be able to meet Sigmund Freud. I can't deny that the trip has heightened my interest in the fateful things happening these days in Europe, but that's the extent of my 'spying.'"

"I'm sorry if I've misrepresented your motives." Turing stood, and continued, "I've enjoyed our times together. I'd help you to the station but I regret I have an appointment at my college quite soon."

"I'm sorry you have to go. I was hoping to discuss thinking machines with you a little more. I'll read your paper."

They said their goodbyes. Fred wondered whether Turing's sudden departure reflected a real need to be somewhere else. Was an aspect of Turing's slightly odd behavior? Was it both? Fred could have said something that upset him, but he could not think what. More plausible would be the possibility that Turing suspected that Fred's trip had non-academic purposes. He could have seen the need to protect his own top-secret work from whatever Fred was up to.

Fred returned to his Trinity College rooms and packed his few belongings in his small suitcase. At the porter's lodge, he asked for the route to the station. It was a thirty-minute walk, most of it along a straight road with little chance of getting lost.

At the station, he was told that the first-class car at the front of the two-thirty train could not be used. He was invited to sit in a third-class car (there appeared to be no second class). He could receive a refund of the fare difference – the ticket collector would give him a form – or wait an hour for the next train. He took the former option to be sure of catching his train to Southampton later in the day. Alone in a much less comfortable third-class compartment, he began composing what could be the trip's last letter to the other Fred. It would be unsent, along with the others.

Dear Fred,

I'm now on the train back to London, with my head still reeling from a long session this morning with Ludwig Wittgenstein. He's a VERY difficult person to talk with. Prickly understates his manner. Paranoid may be more appropriate. At one point he left the room without warning and spent thirty minutes away. He returned with no apology or even a comment on his absence. He merely resumed the discussion where he had interrupted it with his departure. Talking with him is a relentless battle. He's constantly trying to control the discussion. If you let him he'll talk all the time. He's evidently distressed when another person talks, except perhaps to ask him a question, which he often ignores.

In spite of all of this we did cover some ground.

A man of about his age entered the compartment, shut the sliding door with a slam, and sat on the middle of the bench opposite Fred. The man seemed flustered, as if he'd been chased. Three younger men in laborer's clothes opened the door with another slam and filled its space.

"'ere's the 'un," one said. "A Jewboy too, if yer arsk me," said another, reaching out and knocking the sitting man's hat off.

"Please leave me alone," said the man, retrieving his hat and holding it in his lap, speaking in a high voice with a heavy accent.

"Please leave me alone," parroted one of the younger men, imitating the accent in an even higher pitch, as though a woman had spoken. "Who's 'e fink 'e is?" he continued in what was likely his normal voice.

Fred was inclined to stay out of such situations but the sitting man had a pleading expression and the louts – two were now fully in the compartment – were obnoxious. They appeared not to have noticed

Fred. He stood, hooked his thumbs in the top of his pants, and in his best Texan drawl said, "If you punks wanna get off this train alive you'd better scram real quick."

"A cowboy!" cried one as they left the compartment and disappeared along the corridor. Fred congratulated himself on his performance. Then what might have been the real cause of the rapid departure entered the compartment: a pair of burly ticket inspectors.

The man opposite must have put his ticket in his hatband. He felt around for it and then gestured to the inspectors that he could not find it. Fred saw the ticket at the end of the bench opposite him and handed it to one of the inspectors with his own ticket.

"This is a first-class ticket," said the inspector holding up Fred's ticket. He continued as though reciting rehearsed words, "Sir, we've been asked by the company to apologize for any inconvenience caused by the first-class carriage's unavailability and to give you this form and stamped addressed envelope for you to use to claim a refund." He then addressed Fred in a more normal voice, "If this man or the young men who were in here just now are giving you any kind of trouble, let us know."

They left, and the man opposite said, "I thank you for your help with the punks, as you called them, and with the officials." He offered a hand and continued, "My name is Raimund Pretzel." Even when calmer, his voice was still a little on the high side, as had been Freud's, Turing's and Wittgenstein's. What was happening here? Pretzel's voice remained strongly accented. Fred noted too that his suit and hat seemed of a continental rather than an English style. Was his odd name real? Perhaps it was common in Germany.

Fred said, "I'm Fred Skinner, and you are welcome." He shook Pretzel's hand and continued, "I take it that, like me, you are not from this part of the world. We foreigners must help each other." Fred had now had time to examine the man more carefully. He saw a face that was wider than usual, with staring, sunken eyes set far apart. It was not the face of a thin man but Pretzel was evidently slim. Fred remembered that when standing he was of medium height.

"I am a Hun, as the punk said, if he meant German, but I am not Jewish. My wife is a Jew, which is the main reason we are here and not in Germany. Please forgive my English, especially my accent. My English learning was at high school. It is now mostly from newspapers and books. I understand much of what I read, but not so much of what I hear. I need more practice in writing and speaking, and particularly in listening."

Pretzel's heavy accent was more like Freud's way of speaking English than that of Wittgenstein or Glaser the dentist. Fred guessed he was not another émigré from Vienna. He said, "I understand you well, and I will try to speak more clearly than I sometimes do. Which part of Germany are you from?"

"Berlin. And you are American? From a place where there are cowboys, such as Texas?"

"No. No. A good guess but I was pretending. I'm from Pennsylvania, but I live in Minnesota, in the middle of the country up against the Canadian border."

"I know nothing of American geography, except that your country is very large."

Fred's thoughts were racing. Was this encounter a happenstance event or planned? Should he be on his guard? He looked forward to soon being free of such concerns. He concluded that the arrival of Pretzel in his compartment could not have been staged. He said, "I'd be interested to know the story of your departure from Germany and what is happening to you in England."

Pretzel explained in slowly expressed, sometimes almost incomprehensible sentences that he had been a lawyer and trainee judge in Berlin. Then, when he did not like how the judicial system was evolving under the Nazi government, he became a journalist who wrote inoffensive articles about daily life. His future wife – a Jew as he had mentioned – and her eight-year old son had left a year ago to live with her brother in Cambridge. He had joined them some months later. Ostensibly he was making a temporary visit to do research for articles about the British car industry and British ways of living. In reality, he was here to stay, if he could.

As he had said, he and his wife – they were married soon after his arrival – were here because being a Jew in Germany had become intolerable for her. Being there had also become intolerable for him. This was not only because of her plight. It was also because he saw increasingly less hope of opposition to the Nazi regime from within Germany. And he saw hardly more hope for opposition from outside the country. Now, a London publisher was supporting him – all the family, including their new son, just seven months old – while he wrote a book on what has happened in Germany. He was on his way to his monthly meeting with the publisher. He would also explore moving his family to London.

This account made Fred more but not completely comfortable about talking with Pretzel. He explained the reason for his trip to England. Bearing Turing's comments in mind, he exaggerated the trip's academic importance in the hope of making that reason more plausible. He said that, in spite of his academic preoccupations, it was hard to be on this side of the Atlantic at this time without taking an interest in European politics. What was happening in Germany in particular seemed extraordinary. Would there be a war between England and Germany?

"Yes," was Pretzel's clear answer. After much trouble, he had secured a one-year residence permit. He was convinced he would not need another permit. There would be a war before the current one expired. He would not be deported during a war, although he would surely be a candidate for internment. His plan was to write a book that would help with Britain's *psychologische Krieg* against Germany and thus make him too useful to be interned. He apologized for the lapse into German.

"I understand a little German, and I am a psychology professor," said Fred. "The English expression could be psychological war or psychological warfare, but I have not heard it used before. Do you mean propaganda? I believe it is the same word in German."

"It is. But please let us speak English, for my practice. And your knowledge of German can be useful, and your knowledge of psychology too." Pretzel went on to say that by psychological warfare he meant something deeper than mere distribution of persuasive information. Propaganda is a tool of psychological warfare, but propaganda must be based on good understanding of its target population. Above all, the propaganda must express the *Kriegsziel* of the propagandist in a way that appeals to at least some of the target population.

Fred understood *Kriegsziel* to mean war-aim: the reason for fighting. He wondered if Pretzel could be a source of information that might help with answering the questions Roosevelt's man had posed. What were they? Was there a question he could put soon – during the hour left of the train trip – that flowed from their discussion so far? He said, "I'm very interested in your views on psychological warfare. But could I first go back to my question about whether there will be a war. You answered very clearly that there will be. *How* do you think it will happen?"

Pretzel replied that Germany would invade Poland, as she had invaded Austria and Czechoslovakia, although there would be more military resistance from Poland. An invasion would trigger declarations of war by England and France, bound by treaties to support Poland. Pretzel stressed that an invasion of Poland would not be *only* a matter of seeking *Lebensraum*. It would not just be a matter of moving Germany's borders eastward to provide more space and resources for the German people. Poland would be invaded because Germans did not like Poles. Another clear enemy was needed to shore up the waning support for the Nazi government. The invasion of Czechoslovakia had been unpopular within Germany. An invasion of Poland could be supported.

This was certainly different from what Fred had come to believe. He would have liked to probe more about Pretzel's views on the popularity of the Nazis and on *Lebensraum*. As the dentist Lukas Glaser had highlighted, securing *Lebensraum* was an important goal set out in *Mein Kampf*. However, Fred wanted to move on to his other questions, remembering too that he should bring the discussion back to psychological warfare. He said, "If Germany invades Poland, for whatever reason, surely Russia will be concerned."

"*Ach*, so you know something of European geography." Pretzel then said that Germans and Russians shared a dislike of Poles. The two larger countries had become so much like each other, it would not surprise him if they were to strike a deal about Poland. Each would take half of that country. Hitler's eventual aim was mastery of Europe, and more. A pact with Russia would be a tactical matter, to be cast aside when Hitler is ready to push the Russians back beyond the Urals.

Fred said, "Your analysis is very interesting. It seems different from what I have read in the newspapers here and in America before I left. Before we return to the fascinating subject of psychological warfare, could I ask you one more question? It's about the Jews. Why are Nazis so much against them, and how far will Nazis go in dehumanizing them? Sorry, I promised one question and I have asked two, but they may deserve just one answer."

Pretzel said that his wife's background made him especially sensitive to the plight of the Jews in Germany. Germans are not particularly anti-Semitic, unlike Austrians, Hungarians, and Eastern Europeans generally. It must be understood that Hitler is an Austrian, as are many of his closest disciples. Moreover, he had spent formative years in Vienna, the most anti-Semitic of German-speaking cities. People should understand too, he said, that the Nazis had even more support in Austria than in Germany. In the S.S. – the *Schutzstaffel*, the most extreme of the Nazi organizations – there were proportionately more Austrians than Germans.

348

Pretzel said that, in Germany at least, it was not anti-Semitism that impelled the cruelty towards Jews and other unfortunate people such as homosexuals. It was the sadistic impulses of the people attracted to Nazism and particularly to the *Schutzstaffel*. Few in the S.S. have been moved by what Hitler wrote in *Mein Kampf* – and what he still preached on occasion – about the need to keep the German race pure and to stop the Jewish world conspiracy. For the S.S., beating up Jews was more a sport used to test candidates for the organization. The candidates could show they have sufficient lack of scruple to participate in what has become a permanent sadistic orgy.

How far would it go? Pretzel answered by saying that in Germany proper the Nazis have gone just about as far as they can in humiliating the Jews. To do more would risk further unpopularity in the population at large. What the Nazis will do outside Germany is another matter. In countries to the south and east of Germany, anti-Semitism has historically had more of a murderous aspect.

Fred said, "You've twice mentioned the Nazi government's concern for its popularity within Germany. Is there much opposition there? If there is, could these opponents be the target of a program of psychological warfare by Britain or another adversary of the Nazi government?"

Pretzel had been staring at Fred while he spoke, and his staring now seemed to become more intense. He said he believed that a third or more of Germany's adult population was opposed to the regime, although very few have taken any action and almost no one has made his opposition clear. The sadistic impulses of the S.S. and other Nazi groups were directed against suspected opponents as much as against Jews, homosexuals, and other outcasts. In Germany, opponents as much as supporters gave the Nazi salute and hanged Nazi flags out of their windows. It was a regime of terror, but most Germans were not concerned by the terror. They have ignored the regime's distressing features and applauded Hitler's defiance of world opinion. They have liked how he and the Nazis have thrown off the chains of the *Treaty of*

Versailles. Germany was again a country to be concerned about in world affairs. Also important for the government's popularity were the high employment levels in every part of Germany.

Fred asked, "What would appeal to opponents and potential opponents of the Nazis?"

Pretzel replied, "First, I must add something. Most opponents – I cannot give a number – are not people I want to support. Most are Prussians from the north of Germany. They are Prussians who have been in favor of the restoration of Germany as a significant power within Europe. They do not want Adolf Hitler and his gang to be leading that power. Nazism is almost the opposite of what they have been brought up to admire. It is noisy, undisciplined, and *pompös* – what is the word in English"

"It's almost the same: pompous. You could instead say ostentatious or grandiose or vainglorious. As always, there are many English words."

"That is one of my troubles with your language," Pretzel continued, "For these Prussians, Nazism's leader is a half-educated, posturing foreigner. They see the Nazification of Germany as the means by which a person from the rabble has become ranked as an equal with the King of England and the President of the United States of America. Many, many Prussians are appalled and embarrassed."

"You've lost me," said Fred. "If Prussians despise Hitler more than other Germans despise him, why not make them the targets of your psychological warfare?"

"Because Prussians are to blame for Hitler. They would replace this Hitler with another."

"Are you saying that the problem is Germany and not Hitler?" Fred asked. "I'm confused. If the problem is Germany, how can any psychological warfare produce an acceptable result?"

Pretzel replied by outlining some German history. In 1871, the

Prussian politician Otto von Bismarck unified most German-speaking peoples under Wilhelm I of Prussia. This created a large, powerful state that was too big for Europe to live with. It brought to the fore some disastrous patterns of German behavior, mainly Prussian behavior. These included arrogance, expansionism, and the worship of force. This behavior was a major, but not the only, factor contributing to the start of *des großen Krieges*. It would be the main cause of the coming war. Hitler took advantage of Germany's humiliation after *dem letzen Krieg*, when her opponents ignored the terms of an armistice and starved Germany into admitting defeat. Prussians, who form the core of Germany's military, have uneasily sustained Hitler. If he were to go, a Prussian could replace him. There would less noise, but Germany's arrogance and expansionism would persist.

The next largest group of opponents, continued Pretzel, was on the political left. It included Communists who look to Moscow for guidance. It also included Social Democrats who thought there was merit in the writings of Karl Marx but not in Lenin's and Stalin's interpretations of them. The political left was a much smaller group within Germany because the organs of the Nazi state have worked hard to suppress this kind of opposition to the regime. Many of the left were in custody. More have emigrated, to the East or to the West. This group, if in control, could produce a necessary result – the disintegration of Germany – but it could also move a large part of Europe into Russia's embrace. That could be as disastrous as a continuation of Prussian dominance.

Fred cleared his throat as if he were about to ask a question. Pretzel averted his eyes and asked to be allowed to say one more thing, to which Fred gestured agreement. Then, staring at Fred again, Pretzel said he believed that Hitler had to go, to be killed if necessary. The man was a psychopath. He was a unique case whose political career continued to be the expression of fantasies developed during the humiliations of his youth, fantasies of megalomania and revenge. But killing Hitler would be pointless without a dismantling of the German state as it was now.

"So," said Fred, asking his question at last. "What is your solution, and where does psychological warfare come into it?"

"My recipe for Germany has many elements. It is based on the analysis I have just outlined. I have talked too much already. I must be brief. First, other countries – in Europe, the Americas, elsewhere – must open doors wide to immigrants from Germany. This will result in an exodus of millions who would be among Germany's best. Such an exodus would benefit the receiving countries. It would seriously harm Germany, although the Nazis may not see it that way. Among the benefits would be access to excellent advice about the reconstruction of Germany after the war that is sure to come."

"Second," continued Pretzel, "make sure that when the war comes Germany is crushed. This will require strong military force supported by what you and I have called psychological warfare. This warfare should undermine the will to fight rather than promote futile insurrection."

"Third, aim for an alternative Germany that is not a strong unitary state built on military values. It should be a number of loosely linked entities bound by a common cultural history. Ideally these entities would be part of a formal European economic association."

Fred recognized the outer edge of London's suburbs where he had passed a few days earlier. He said, "Herr Pretzel, I am very glad to have met you. You have given me much to think about. You have certainly broadened my understanding of what is happening and could happen on this side of the Atlantic. I would like to ask you some specific questions about what you have told me, but I see our journey is nearing its end. A final question: Do you think people in Britain and France will provide the strong military force you consider necessary?"

"Would you have time to continue our discussion when the train arrives?"

"I'm sorry but I can't," said Fred. "I must reclaim my suitcase at Liverpool Street Station and then find my way to Waterloo Station to catch another train to Southampton." He then regretted he'd been so forthright about his plans.

"I do not know if Britain or France will fight in earnest. Is that the right phrase?" Fred nodded. Pretzel continued by saying that a large element of the upper classes in Britain and elsewhere see Germany more as a bulwark against communism than as a potential enemy. Attitudes to the Olympic Games have been a good indicator of upper-class thinking. The International Olympic Committee awarded the winter and summer games for 1936 to Germany to boost her international standing. Another enemy of the Soviet Union, Japan, was awarded the winter and summer games for 1940. Japan has now declined holding the winter games because of her war with China, and will likely do the same for the summer games. The IOC meets next week here in London to pick a new venue for the 1940 winter games. The Committee will be very happy to hold them again in Germany, in Garmisch-Partenkirchen, he said, but he doubted they would be held at all.

The year 1936 was when Pretzel became convinced that action to stop Hitler would be inadequate, from within German and from outside. Hitler's first major item of international defiance was the remilitarization of the Rhineland in that year. This was done a few weeks after the successful winter Olympic Games. There was hardly a protest from America or Britain, or even from France, for which the Rhineland has been demilitarized as a buffer zone. Everything seemed to work in the Nazis' favor in that fateful year, with the summer Olympic Games providing the pinnacle of international respectability. As well, other countries seemed caught up in their particular distractions. America had its coldest winter and hottest summer on record, exacerbating the effects of the economic depression. Britain had a new king who was increasingly preoccupied by his American paramour. France was gripped by a financial crisis. In the Soviet Union, what became known as Stalin's Great Purge was getting under way in earnest, reaching into the highest ranks of the Communist Party and the Red Army.

Pretzel concluded by saying, "Thank you for the opportunity to

353

give you my thoughts about my country and about other matters. I apologize for talking too much. I'm sorry because I would like to have asked you many questions about America."

When the train stopped, they said their goodbyes. Fred went to retrieve his larger suitcase. At the baggage check counter he asked what would be the best way to Waterloo Station. He was advised to go by Underground to Bank Station, which was connected by a walkway to City Station. There, he should pay a small additional fare and take the Waterloo and City line to Waterloo Station. This would avoid a long, roundabout journey involving a change at Charing Cross. Each train journey was only a few minutes, although he had a downhill walk of several minutes between Bank and City stations.

Fred had allowed an hour and fifteen minutes to get from one London rail terminus to the other. The trip took hardly more than fifteen minutes. To pass the time, he settled himself with a pint of bitter at the crowded window of a station pub. Fred kept his suitcases within sight, under the ledge that held his beer. He asked a fellow drinker whether the pub was usually so busy. "It's Friday," he was told, "the end of the work week for most of us who work in the City. It's good to see a Yank here. Can I get you another? It's a bitter, right?" Before Fred could answer, his slightly flushed but well-dressed and well-spoken benefactor had taken his own glass and Fred's to the bar for refills. Fred had hoped to use the time before the train departure to begin to get his thoughts in order, about Wittgenstein, about Pretzel, and about his trip generally, but that was not to happen. He had given hardly any thought to the next stage of his trip – the *Clipper* flight to Lisbon, the Azores, and New York – but that too would have to wait.

Fred thanked his neighbor for the refill. He was about to ask whether the prospect of war was having a dampening effect on these Friday afternoon sessions or the opposite effect. A group in a far corner started singing loudly, making conversation impossible. When the song was over, Fred was told it was a Great War song: "It's a Long Way to Tipperary." These songs were becoming more popular; they don't sing much else now. Then a young woman in the center of the group sang alone. "This is a new one," said the neighbor. Fred made out the words of the chorus as the group bellowed it out: "There'll always be an England, and England shall be free, if England means as much to you as England means to me." Fred wondered how Samuel Brown and other Scots might feel about this song. He reflected on the corrosive effects of chauvinism. He turned to the window and saw that the train for Southampton was arriving and would leave in ten minutes. The group began another, even louder song. Fred mimed his thanks, gathered his suitcases, and went off to find his seat.

The *Yankee Clipper*, sister flying boat of the *Atlantic Clipper*, in 1939.

TWENTY-FIVE

Revelations and Evasions

London and Southampton, June 2, 1939

Which was more important, Fred wondered as the train left Waterloo Station, finishing the letter to the other Fred about Wittgenstein or writing notes on what Raimund Pretzel had said? He was in a first-class compartment with two other men. Walking to the train, he'd noticed that the train leaving the other side of the platform, for Portsmouth, had no locomotive. He figured out it had electric motors under the passenger cars, drawing its power from a third rail. He knew that subway systems were electrified – here in London and in Boston and New York – and the elevated system in Chicago, but he'd not come across electrification of intercity trains. He wondered about trespassers on the tracks who might come into contact with the third rail's high voltage. Perhaps they used an overhead cable. Chicago made him think about Julie and Yvonne. With these thoughts, and reflecting that he had drunk one beer too many, he dozed off.

When he woke, his train – propelled by an old-fashioned steam locomotive – was moving through English farmland, idyllic in the evening sun. The scene through the window could have been a painting.

Then he saw Mabel Miller sitting opposite him. The two men were no longer there. Fred wondered if he was dreaming.

"You're not dreaming, Fred," she said with a brief smile, "it really is me. I'm sorry to surprise you like this, but I really had to talk to you again." She was elegantly dressed and made up as before, but her voice had an edge to it. She seemed stressed.

"What are *you* doing here? How did you find me?"

"I'd like to be able to say that I'm here through a happy accident, but you wouldn't believe me. In any case, it's not true. I've been following you. Now I need to talk with you."

Fred was alarmed and fearful. He attempted to hide this by asking, "What happened to the two men who were in here at Waterloo?"

"They left the train at Woking. I wasn't supposed to talk with you again, but when I saw you were alone, I couldn't resist."

"How do you mean 'not supposed to'?" For a moment Fred had thought she was under the grip of some kind of infatuation with him. Then he remembered his earlier suspicions about her. The 'not supposed to' suggested she was following someone's orders.

"I need to do some explaining. When we met on the *Coronation Scot*, you were right to suspect that the meeting was something other than a quirk of fate. I'd travelled to Carlisle that morning to get on your train and make your acquaintance. They have a hold over me."

"Who has a hold over you?"

"The Germans. I can give you details later. For the moment, let me just say that my mother's parents are Jewish. They live in Linz, in Austria. My grandparents want to leave for South Africa. I've been told this can happen if I get information about you. I'm not completely sure how the link was made between me and my grandparents, Herr und Frau Weisskopf. I do know it's been made. I've been told that if I don't cooperate they'll be sent to the nearby concentration camp at Mauthausen or to the one at Dachau near Munich."

Mabel Miller blew her nose and continued, "I don't know my grandparents. My mother went to what was then the British Cape Colony with her aunt when she was quite young, in 1904. A few years later she married my father there and had me. Her aunt died and my mother became very much a part of my father's British family. As far as I know, my mother's never been back to Austria. I've thought of telephoning her about what's going on, but decided not to worry her. My mother's not in a position to look after my grandparents. I believe they're in their seventies. So far, I've gone along with what I've been told to do, but now I've had enough and I want to be far away from this mess. I'm not very good at this spying business."

Fred interrupted, "So you found me on the *Coronation Scot* – how? – and everything followed from there. Did you track me all the way to Cambridge and back, and then across London. I didn't see you in Cambridge."

"I was given a ticket for a seat in your compartment in the *Coronation Scot* and I had a snapshot of you so that I'd be sure. I'd been told you were going to Cambridge to talk with Ludwig Wittgenstein. My job was to find out why, and who sent you. I found out nothing that they wanted, so I was sent to Cambridge, where I wasn't able to add to the little I already knew. Then I was told to keep on following you because it wasn't clear what you were going to do next."

"Who told you what to do?" said Fred. "Who gave you the ticket for the *Coronation Scot*? Who issued the promise and the threat about your grandparents? How could you have followed me to Cambridge and back, and now to Southampton, without my knowing about it until now?"

"So many questions, Fred. The answers really don't matter. The important thing is that I've had enough. I want to change my life. I'm assuming you're going to Southampton to join a ship sailing for America or Canada tomorrow. I want to come with you and I want you to help me do it. Which ship are you on? I have my passport and if I'm with you there will be no problem."

359

She did not know how he was returning across the Atlantic. Which ship could he say he would be on? He said, "Mabel, this is too much to absorb. I don't know the name of the ship. I came here on a Canadian Pacific ship and that's how I'm to make the return trip, to Montreal, but perhaps not on the same ship. My papers for the passage should be at the hotel."

"So, you'll sail on CP's *Empress of Britain*. I've remembered all tomorrow's sailings from Southampton. She leaves at ten o'clock in the morning from the Empress dock. Can we meet there at eight o'clock? Where are you staying? I'll be at the Star Hotel."

It was stroke of luck, thought Fred, that a CP ship was to sail to-morrow. And she hadn't asked why his boarding documents would be at the hotel. He told her he was staying at the Dolphin Hotel. The actu-al arrangement was that Fred would meet a member of the *Clipper* crew there at eight o'clock, an hour after his arrival in Southampton. This was where *Clipper* crews stayed the night between flights.

"Both hotels are on the High Street, almost next door. Perhaps we can get a taxi to the dock together in the morning? Maybe you want to meet up this evening?"

"I'm still tired and I have business to do this evening, or else I'd be pleased to see you. Your proposal for the morning makes sense."

"I'll be in the lobby of your hotel at seven thirty in the morning. Don't you want to know about the mechanics of my involvement with the Germans? Surely you have to report back to someone? Surely this would be useful information?"

"You imagine I'm more than I am," said Fred. "I'm no more than an insignificant professor trying to make sense of the world."

"Then why were you talking so intently to Raimund Pretzel, a known agitator against the German regime?"

Whose side is she really on, Fred asked himself. He said, "My en-counter with Pretzel was entirely happenstance. He stumbled into my compartment when he was chased by hooligans. He had interesting things to say about European politics."

"I know longer know what to believe," she said. "I just want to get lost in a large space much bigger than I am."

"I am curious as to what you describe as the mechanics of your involvement with the Germans – even though there's no one I'll be telling it to."

"It's all to do with Du Cane Court. You were in my flat there. The building is a hotbed of German activity in London. It's the second time I've rented there for my three weeks in London. Last year, I had no idea about this, although I did go out once with another tenant who could have been German. This year, on my second day there, a man asked to sit with me while I was having a mid-morning coffee in the restaurant there. I was planning the visits I would make to department stores during the week ahead."

She blew her nose again. Fred could see that she did this when she needed to figure out what she was going to say next. She continued, "His name was Arnold Littman. He said he lived in the building and was a reporter for a German newspaper. He was in touch with the authorities in Germany and knew that my grandparents in Linz were in difficulty. If I could help him get some information that the German authorities needed, he'd be able to guarantee they could leave for South Africa. Otherwise, they'd have to be taken into protective custody for their own good because of the strong feelings in Linz against Jews."

She said, "I was shocked. I can only imagine I'd said something I should regret to the man I went out with last year. I can't even remember his name. Also, you have to understand that these grandparents were not part of my life like my father's parents in Cape Town. I'd do anything for them. In any case, I've always had the feeling that my mother and her aunt – my grandmother's sister – left Linz and their family there because they were keen to get away."

"So," Fred interrupted, to give her time to catch her breath, "if you have little feeling for your grandparents in Austria, why did you allow the man Littman to use their fate to get you to spy on me?"

"I don't know. I was a little bored. I didn't need all the time I had to do my work for Stuttafords. And saving my grandparents seemed like a good cause. It was only when it was too late that it struck me that my mother wouldn't want to have them in South Africa."

"What were you told to do?"

"As I said, I was told to find out why you were going to see Ludwig Wittgenstein – she pronounced the names in the German manner – and who sent you. I was told that Professor Wittgenstein was a person of great interest to the German government. Every bit of information about him, including possible links with the American government, could be of value. It seemed pretty harmless to me, and that was another reason for going along with it."

Fred's thoughts were racing. Before Mabel, the only person he had mentioned Wittgenstein too had been Sophie Graydon. Was she also not what she seemed too? This was unlikely, but perhaps anything was possible in these times. Lukas Glaser may have hinted that he knew Fred was to see Wittgenstein. But how would he have known? Fred asked Mabel, "Did you find anything out?"

"I got no information out of you on the *Coronation Scot* or during our time together the day after. This may have been partly because I was falling in love with you, at least just a little. I'd resolved not to take you back to my flat after our lovely meal because – because what? – because I didn't want you ever to think that I was seducing you to get information out of you. Arnold Littman was in the lobby. When your back was to him, he signed me to take you upstairs. He was quite menacing."

"So, we went up to your flat," said Fred, "and then your behavior was truly strange: all this talk of vaginismus and not doing sex."

"I exaggerated. I do have a small problem of that kind, but not the big problem I made it into. I was in a state of great confusion. Frankly, I was pleased when you decided to leave, but then I very much wanted to see you again."

"Was Herr Littman angry when he learned that you'd discovered nothing?"

"No. He was patient but firm. He knew you were to go to Cambridge on Tuesday, I don't know how. I had to go too, and find out what I could. I told you, I'm not good at this. I stayed so far in the background – in case you were to see me – I didn't even discover the name of the person you had dinner with on Wednesday. The only thing I learned was that Wittgenstein is a very strange person, but Littman knew that already. I had to return to London on Thursday evening to see Littman, who was now despairing of me. He gave me one more job: to find out when and how you'd be returning to America. I must telephone him about that this evening or tomorrow."

"When did you decide that now was the time for you to go to America? I remember that almost the first thing you said to me, back on the *Coronation Scot*, was that you'd like to go to America, even quite soon."

"Yes, I'd thought about it before. And I thought about it more this week when things were becoming difficult with Littman. That's when I decided to carry my passport around with me and more than enough money for the fare. But I didn't actually decide to go until I saw you alone here this evening. This must sound very impetuous. I'm not usually like that. But I do now have a strong urge to get away. If you can help me do that I'll be very grateful. I'm not expecting that I'll be a part of your life in America, although I'd like that to happen. In any case, I expect I'll have more chance of being admitted to Canada, because South Africa and Canada are both part of the British Empire, or the British Commonwealth as we're now supposed to call it."

Fred said, "You tell a good story, Mabel, but you know well that you can't just turn up and buy a ticket for a trans-Atlantic steamer as if you were going on a bus or a train. Besides, you have no baggage, which is sure to raise questions. And I don't believe you wouldn't be trying to help your grandparents. I don't believe you would condemn them to a concentration camp. What are your real plans?"

Mabel became tearful. "Fred, my story, as you call it, may sound pathetic, and cruel as far as my grandparents are concerned. But I swear it's the truth. What will convince you? I could show you my money and passport. Oh, and the baggage. I've thought of that. Perhaps my hotel could help. Perhaps I could say that one of your suitcases is mine."

Fred's thoughts were racing again. Should he put some effort into figuring her out more, perhaps by going to her hotel with her and listening to the call to Littman, if she made the call? He might find out something of use to the White House. Or should he get away from her as quickly as possible and avoid compromising himself further? He said, "Let's see how things go in the morning. Look, I think the train is arriving at Southampton. If our hotels are close to each other and not to the station we can get a cab."

"We'll need a taxi," she said, dabbing at her tears. "Thank you, Fred, for your understanding." When the taxi reached High Street, she said, "Let's stop at the Dolphin as you have luggage and I don't. I'll walk to the Star." She paid the driver.

"Are you sure you'll be OK?" he said. She nodded. "Sleep well, and I'll see you here at seven thirty in the morning."

At the Dolphin Hotel, Fred picked up the envelope left at the reception desk for him. It contained his instructions for getting aboard the *Clipper*. As well, it had details of what he was to do in New York and of his flights from there to Minneapolis. He asked for a room for the night. Mabel would likely telephone or even come to the hotel. Her suspicions would be aroused if he had not checked in. He paid in advance for the room, explaining that he might want to check out early in the morning. He said he'd be out for most of the evening. Instead of taking his suitcases to his room he asked the bellhop to store them near the lobby. He had forty-five minutes until he was to meet up with the member of the Pan Am flight crew. He left his suitcases with the bellman, went up to his room and then back down to the bar, ordering a much needed vodka and tonic.

A man in Pan Am uniform, about Fred's age, was sitting alone looking through files, nursing what appeared to be a non-alcoholic drink. Fred introduced himself and confirmed that the man was Tom Salinsky, the *Clipper's* third officer. He explained his predicament. A woman was after him. When they left for the *Clipper*, he needed to leave the hotel by a back door.

Salinsky said he understood completely. When Fred had finished his drink, he would call for a cab and take it around to the back door of the hotel, which he had used before. The challenge would be getting Fred's baggage there without arousing attention. Better, he should take Fred's baggage out of the front door and into the cab. Fred could then move inconspicuously to the back door.

The cab came. The suitcases were retrieved. As Salinsky took them out to the cab, Mabel came in through the main entrance, not noticing what she was passing. Fred greeted her, explaining that he was waiting for the associate with whom he was to have dinner. Perhaps she could come back later, say at ten o'clock. She wanted to talk now, about their plans for tomorrow and other things. He said he couldn't; he was to meet someone in a few minutes. Moreover, he needed to go to the washroom badly. The vodka and tonic he had drunk just now on an empty stomach had gone right through him.

The washroom door was out of sight from the hotel lobby. Fred walked past it to the back of the hotel where Salinsky was holding open the door of the waiting cab. As the cab turned on to the street, he looked back and saw Mabel standing at the back door.

A cut-away view of a Pan Am *Clipper*. A floor-plan appears before Chapter 27.

TWENTY-SIX

Breakfast Ashore

By the Atlantic Clipper to Lisbon, June 2-3, 1939

Tom Salinsky said, "That seemed to go well: no tears, at least none I saw. Y'know, I've done the same thing: left a babe at that very door, left her wondering what was happening."

"Thanks for your help," said Fred. He'd many misgivings about what he'd just done. Mostly he felt relief to be on his way home. "So, we're flying to Lisbon. What's your role on the flight?"

"I'm the third officer, which means I'm the fourth in line of the six pilots on this ship. Ahead of me is the captain, Harold Gray. Then there's the first officer, who is the co-pilot. Then the second officer, another pilot but he's mostly concerned with navigation. Then me, and a fourth officer and a trainee pilot."

"You need five pilots? I'm not counting the trainee."

"No. Legally we need just two. Pan Am says we must have a full relief crew on these long flights over water. And on this flight we have one more for additional safety, and to give another pilot the experience.

Extra pilots relieve the captain to schmooze with the passengers, when we have them. To be honest, the automatic pilot does most of the flying. So, it's a cinch of a job, until something goes wrong, which it does."

"I like the word schmooze. I haven't heard it before but I can guess its meaning. Are there other crew? Why do you call it a ship?"

"There's a flight engineer and a radio operator, each with an assistant or a relief. They're ranked differently. As on a ship, the flight engineer reports only to the captain, but he can't take over as captain. Only a pilot can do that. More than on a real ship, however, we can all do each other's jobs. It's a team, a real team. And I haven't got to the stewards, who in some ways are the most important people on a passenger-carrying flight."

"Oh, and why a ship?" Salinsky continued. "I guess one reason is that Pam Am's boss, Mr. Trippe, called flying boats *Clippers* after the early ocean liners. Another is that these craft spend quite a bit of time on the water, although almost all their movement is in the air. I suppose we keep the nautical terms going because we like to be a bit different from the crews of other Pan Am aircraft."

"You were going to mention the stewards."

"Yes. The *Clippers* are different in another way: the cabin crew are almost all men, known as stewards. On our regular planes they're now mostly women, usually known as air hostesses. With no passengers, we don't need cabin crew for this flight, but we do have one – Ruthie – as part of our testing. Ruthie, of course, is a she and just about the company's most experienced air hostess and one of the few women with *Clipper* experience. If she flies with us across the Atlantic when we have passengers she'll be known as a stewardess. Ruthie's been assigned to look after you during the flight, as well as get all of us meals and so on."

The taxi passed through the guarded entrance to Southampton Docks and drew up beside a quay where stevedores were carrying mailbags and boxes from a train to a barge.

Salinsky said, "On this flight we'll be carrying several hundred pounds of mail and several dozen boxes and bags of high-value cargo. I have to sign for it all when they've finished loading the barge. Then we'll go and load it on to the *Atlantic Clipper*. We'll take on more mail and perhaps other cargo in Lisbon."

"Can I help with the loading?"

"Not just now. Here it's union work only. But you can at the *Clipper*. In fact you should, because technically you're a Pan Am hire for this flight. We're not yet licenced to carry anyone else. You're here making expert observations for our head office."

"I'll be pleased to help," said Fred. "May I ask why the *Clipper* is not at the dock? It would make it easier to load and unload."

"The *Clipper* is moored in the middle of the river just past the end of the quay. You'll see her as soon as we move away. We're still waiting for the Brits to give us permission to use their new flying boat terminal, at the far end of the new docks over there." He pointed along the shoreline to a place a couple of miles away where a large airplane was floating in the water alongside a jetty. "That's one of Imperial Airways' flying boats. They've a normal range of only about seven hundred miles, which is OK for hopping from port to port to Australia. They can't cross the Atlantic unless they are refuelled in the air or fitted with so many extra fuel tanks there's little space for passengers. Neither makes financial sense. The *Atlantic Clipper* is more than twice as large. You'll see."

"This is our first mail flight here, to Southampton," Salinsky added. "It's our fourth across the Atlantic. Pan Am's been hopping across the Pacific and down to South America for several years. The Brits and the French have been holding things up for Atlantic crossings because they didn't want us Yanks to have a monopoly. The French now have a flying boat that can do it. Like us it's doing mail service only. It goes between New York and somewhere on France's Atlantic coast. We've been providing mail service to Lisbon and Marseilles for a couple of weeks. The French have allowed us to start passenger service to Marseilles this month if the mail flights work out. We're still waiting on the Brits. They're nowhere near having a plane that can cross the Atlantic economically. We've heard that the prospect of war is now getting in the way of developing one. We're hoping they'll swallow their pride and let us go ahead with passenger service – and use their terminal over there." He pointed again. "It's next to a railroad station with trains going directly to London."

Fred said, "So a couple of months from now, if all goes well, flying across the Atlantic will become quite commonplace."

"Not exactly," said Salinsky. "The fare will be too much for you and me. It'll be three fifty to four hundred dollars each way."

At that rate, thought Fred, a round trip would cost more than a quarter of his annual salary. The flying boat fare was almost four times what he had paid to cross on the *Duchess of York*.

"Another thing," said Salinsky. "In the summer and fall, flights to England may be by a shorter northern route via Newfoundland and Ireland, not the one we're doing. That's still being looked into."

"What's the prospect for land-based planes flying the Atlantic?"

"Flying boats are only a phase. Land-based planes make more sense. The Germans already have a passenger plane that's flown from Berlin to New York non-stop and then back non-stop. Boeing is developing one that can fly the Atlantic and so is Douglas. The American planes will be pressurized. They'll be able to fly well above ten thousand feet and use less fuel as a result."

Fred had many more questions, but the loading was now complete. Salinsky checked the mailbags and other cargo items against documents and signed for them. They boarded the barge, which moved slowly out into the river. Fred could soon see the rear of the *Atlantic Clipper*. It looked more like a plane than a boat, even though it was floating in the river. It was much larger than any plane Fred had seen, but small compared with *the Duchess of York*.

The barge pulled up under the flying boat's enormous wing, and was tied to rings embedded in a stubby fin that stuck out from the flying boat's hull at water level. Salinsky said the technical name for the fin was 'sponson' but everyone called it a sea-wing. He was not sure how 'sponson' was spelled. As well as serving as boarding platforms, the sea-wings on each side helped balance the craft when it was on the water. They also provided some lift in the air and contained the flying boat's main fuel tanks.

Fred became part of a human chain moving mailbags and boxes from the barge into the plane's small door. He passed the time reflecting unsuccessfully on the possible origin of 'sponson.' Fred's two suitcases and some others were the last items moved along the chain. He and Salinsky were the last to go through the door.

"We're not leaving for another hour," Salinsky said. "Captain Gray is very fussy about having everything just so, including how the cargo is distributed throughout the craft. As well, there's an inspection by British authorities to make sure we're not taking away anything or anybody we're not entitled to. It's a boring part of the trip, so just find a seat and a magazine and relax. If you're lucky, Ruthie will bring you something to eat and drink."

Fred walked around the passenger level of the flying boat, noting the two compartments and galley in front of the lounge and the five behind. The front and rear compartments seemed ready for passengers, as did the lounge. The other five compartments had no seats. They contained the mailbags and boxes. Fred was told that more cargo could be fitted into a hold in the level above, but that space wasn't needed for this trip.

A short woman with blond hair, perhaps in her late twenties, was working in the small galley. "I'm Ruth Williams," she said. "Please call me Ruthie. You must be Professor Skinner, our special passenger masquerading as an observer for head office. Can I get you anything? I'm not supposed to serve alcoholic beverages. Crew are not allowed to drink them during a flight."

"I am he, to be sure. Nice to know you, Ruthie. Please call me Fred. I'd love a vodka and tonic, but if I must I'll go for the tonic alone and imagine the vodka."

He watched from behind while she expertly prepared a vodka and tonic. She was short enough for Fred to be looking down at her scalp and even to see her eyebrows. He could see she wasn't a natural blond. She smelled nice. Her hands were beautiful. He'd not yet had a good look at her face.

"Sometimes it's necessary to put the mask aside," she said, turning and handing him the drink with an appealing wink.

"I didn't expect to find a woman crew member on board, and certainly not one as engaging as you." Fred could now see that her face was entirely appealing.

"Thank you, sir, or Fred I should say. Back home, nearly all flight attendants are now women, and we're taking over on the *Clipper* flights to Asia and South America. The flights across the Atlantic have longer legs in the air and they could be more dangerous for other reasons too: weather, war, whatever. So, I'm part of the testing, chosen for this flight because I'm a tough old bird."

Fred thought of a few responses that would continue the mildly flirtatious banter they'd started, but decided against them. He said, "I should get out of your way and find a place to read while you are all getting the plane ready to take off. Where's the best place for me to go, and where should I stow my large suitcase?"

"Stay the lounge for the moment, and leave your cases in the compartment just forward of the lounge. There's less cargo there."

Fred settled at a table in the corner of the lounge and attempted to read Turing's article. Often crew members passed through the lounge.

Less often there was passage through a door to the sea-wing, which opened out from the lounge. The two British officials gave him no problem, even though his passport listed his occupation as professor. The rest of their inspection was just as cursory. The officials seemed delighted to be on board the exotic *Clipper* and almost uninterested in the possibility of nefarious activity.

Fred found it hard to concentrate on the article. The after-effect of events earlier in the evening, the ongoing interruptions, and the prospect of flying out of the water were together keeping him in a state of tension, relieved only a little by his drink. He wondered whether he could ask Ruthie for another, and went to the galley. She said she used to be nervous before a flight too, but now it didn't bother her. She refilled his glass, adding what seemed to be twice as much vodka as before. He thanked her profusely. She responded with the nicest possible "Don't mention it!"

Back in the lounge, the article made no more sense. Fred skimmed though several sections of arcane mathematical formulas. He slowed down when he saw the phrase 'state of mind' in a section with fewer formulas, but he could not understand that section either. Why had Turing given him the offprint? He claimed to have devised a machine that could perform any intellectual feat a human was capable of. Perhaps the machine could think. Was this article supposed to prove that? Fred fell asleep. He was overcome by tiredness, the vodka, and a sense of inadequacy arising from exposure to what might be Turing's superior analytical ability.

When Fred awoke a few hours later, the *Atlantic Clipper* was in the air. He reached for the window blind and found that someone had fastened a seat belt around his waist, probably Ruthie. He was sorry to have missed the close encounter. It was pitch black outside. There was enough light in the lounge to see his watch. It was just after midnight. If take-off had been as scheduled, they would be about a third of the way through the six-hour flight, probably with the Bay of Biscay to the left and the Atlantic to the right. He went to the washroom and was surprised to find a urinal as well as a sit-down toilet. Ruthie was no-where to be seen.

He was hungry and made himself a cheese sandwich in the galley, making as little mess as he could. The door to the front compartment was closed. He walked to the back of the plane and found that the door to the last compartment was also shut. He was not sure where he was supposed to sleep. He thought of going up to the flight deck. He decid-ed against interrupting whoever was flying the plane with such a trivial request. He returned to the lounge. The chairs had arms that made it impossible to form a bed from them, but they also had cushions. Fred laid the cushions out on the floor and covered himself with his raincoat taken from his suitcase. He was soon lulled asleep by the engine noise.

When he woke again, another three hours had passed. He could hear Ruthie working in the galley. He crept behind her into the wash-room and greeted her when he came out. "I was just going to wake you," she said. "I need to arrange the lounge for anyone who wants breakfast before we set down in Lisbon. You were to sleep in the front cabin, but no one told you. You can stay in the lounge while I get it ready."

Fred reckoned that though it was only a little after three o'clock in the morning British time he wasn't going to get more sleep for a while. He put the cushions back on the seats, found his toilet bag and returned to the washroom to shave and spruce up. When he returned to the lounge, Ruthie had tidied up more and laid two of the tables for break-fast. She said, "We have a five-hour stopover in Lisbon. I'm allowed ashore for up to three of those hours. Unless you're really hungry – and I saw that you raided my galley – don't have breakfast here but come with me to a nice place on the square where our tender hits the shore. It will be open even so early in the morning."

Salinsky came in. He'd been flying the *Clipper* since just after the take-off at Southampton but Captain Gray was going to land her at Lisbon. The captain had been sleeping in the front compartment. Fred was glad he'd not gone in there at midnight. Salinsky was hungry and not in a mood to speak more. Fred nursed a coffee while the tired pilot ate ham, eggs, and hash browns that Ruthie had prepared.

After Salinsky had gone, three other crew members came, had breakfast and left. Few words were exchanged. When they'd gone, Ruthie explained that she was also serving breakfast to the crew members on duty on the flight deck, mostly only coffee. Up there, she said, she could see the sky just beginning to get light in the east.

Fred looked out of the window. He too could see a lightening of the sky along the eastern horizon. Below, he could just make out the coast of Portugal, or perhaps it was still the Spanish coast. He asked Ruthie where they were. She said they'd soon be passing Oporto, Portugal's second city. He'd be able to see lights on there. Fred first saw the wave-top reflections of the rotating light of a powerful lighthouse, and then a few dim lights scattered to the east.

Ruthie said, "Let me show you where you should have slept, and perhaps you can catch a few winks there before we land." She led him to the door of the front compartment and said, "I won't come in, but you're in the upper bunk on this side. Captain Gray was in the lower bunk. He's not there now."

When Fred woke, it was five thirty and still dark outside. He felt much better after the extra sleep. All was quiet except for a new soft hum. He'd now missed the landing as well as the take-off. He looked outside and saw that the *Atlantic Clipper* was about a hundred yards from a quay, and being refuelled from a tanker. This was the source of the hum. He tidied his bunk and went to find Ruthie. She was washing dishes in the galley. She said, "I hope you slept well. I had a nap too. We've been landed for more than an hour. There was a small problem with the landing – I know not what – and there's been a lot of talk about it upstairs. I think it's now solved, whatever the problem was. The launch for shore comes in about fifteen minutes so you've woken in good time."

They were left off at a large square with the shoreline on one side and impressive buildings on the other three sides, each with a colonnade. Dawn had begun to break. A sign in Portuguese and French suggested that the English name would be Commerce Square. They walked around the square. Ruthie led Fred to a part of the colonnade where tables were set out and a few people were already sitting. She said, "Someone from another crew told me about this place. He said the coffee was divine and the ham rolls were good enough to kill for. He recommended the traditional fish stew warmed up from the previous evening, but I don't fancy that."

They had the coffee and ham rolls, and watched the square brighten as the dawn progressed. Offshore, the *Atlantic Clipper's* silver hull glistened more as the sun rose. "This is bliss," said Fred, "thank you so much for bringing me here. Tell me how you were able to order our breakfasts in Portuguese."

"I had to learn some when I was on the run to Rio de Janeiro. Many Brazilian passengers expected it. Pan Am paid for the classes." She added, "We've almost an hour until the launch leaves for the *Clipper*. You know the only exotic thing about me, that I speak some Portuguese. Why don't you tell me about yourself and, if you can, why you are travelling with us."

Fred was startled. He should have expected this kind of question, but had no ready answer. He wondered whether to make up a story, but could not think of one. He said, "I'd be very pleased to know more about you. I'll be pleased to tell you about myself. I can't tell you exactly how I got to be on the *Atlantic Clipper* although I'm enormously pleased to be flying with you back to America."

Ruthie might have been told not to probe into their passenger's circumstances. She said, "Whatever you say will interest me. And I'll be pleased to answer your questions, although you should expect to be bored by my answers."

Fred explained who he was, and the academic purpose of his trip. He hinted that someone high up in Pan Am was returning an old favor.

His interest in flying had been sparked during his trip to Europe ten years ago. He'd flown in land planes a few times since, chiefly to conferences, but never in a flying boat. He couldn't figure out whether she accepted his hint as an allusion to the truth or as a subterfuge. He mentioned Yvonne and Julie.

Ruthie said she'd started with Pan Am nine years ago as one of the airline's first female flight attendants. She was hoping to move soon into a training position so she could settle down and have a family before it was too late. She was from Baltimore and wanted a position with the training school that Pan Am ran there. Her fear was that she'd be assigned to Pam Am's other school in San Francisco and have to decline or be separated from her fiancé.

"That doesn't sound like a good choice," said Fred. "I'll be pleased to talk to you more about this. But, just before we leave Europe, can I ask you what you think about the situation here?"

"You certainly can, but I know little about it. If I knew anything, my opinion wouldn't be of much interest. Why don't we ask these men what they think?" Ruthie gestured to two older men at a nearby table. Fred nodded. She spoke to them in Portuguese.

One of the men replied in English with an upper-class British accent, "It's very nice to hear an American woman speak Portuguese and to know two people who work on that magnificent machine." He pointed to the *Clipper*. "We both speak English. This is my young brother. We were sent to school in England, forty or more years ago." Fred could see the similarity in their noses and hairlines. The one who spoke was grayer and a little thinner.

"What do we Portuguese think about the European situation?" the man continued. "First let me say that we have a government that doesn't like political expression and wants to stay out of any war that might happen. The Portuguese people are not unhappy with these positions. Portugal declined an invitation to join the alliance of Germany, Italy and Japan. We also declined Hitler's request to break the Anglo-

Portuguese alliance, the oldest in the world. It dates back over five hundred years, perhaps over seven hundred."

"What about Spain?" asked Fred. He remembered the passion of the audience at the Casals' concert. He knew that the Germans had helped the fascists win the Spanish Civil War. The new government there and the Portuguese dictatorship could have much in common.

The other brother replied, "We have just signed a non-aggression pact with Spain. I think both our countries would want to be neutral if there is a war, we perhaps more than Spain. We still have an empire, more than Spain, and we don't have the means to defend it. The Azores – he pronounced it Assóreesh – where you are going next, are a special problem because of their location far out in the ocean and their potential importance for aviation, and also for naval activity including submarines."

"May I ask what you both do for a living?" said Fred.

"We work for the government," the younger, stouter man said. "Pedro is the head of this port's customs service and I, Miguel Cabral, am the harbormaster. We have breakfast here every morning except Sunday. We discuss our mutual problems in the port and the world situation. Most of all," he put his finger to his lips and lowered his voice, "most of all, we discuss our wives, who are sisters as we are brothers. Pedro and I – and we speak for our government – are very pleased that Pam Am is using our harbor."

Fred wanted to ask how it was they had been sent to England for some of their education, but Ruthie intervened first. "As you will know well, we must go now to our launch, to the *Atlantic Clipper*, and to the Azores. It's been a pleasure talking to you. We'll convey your warm welcome to our captain, our company's management and our government." She left a dollar bill on the table

The two men stood. The older one said, "*Boa viagem*, as we say in Portuguese. *Bon voyage*. We hope you will be back."

Fred and Ruthie said goodbye to the two men and walked towards the quayside. She said, "I've heard this is a more efficient stopover point for Pan Am than any other. I wonder if these regular early morning breakfast meetings are the secret. They could be the time and place where many of the problems get ironed out."

Fred said, "It could be having two well-connected and worldly brothers running things. Do you think they were on the level?"

"Whaddya mean?" said Ruthie, lapsing from her usual polished manner of speaking.

"Are they really brothers? If they have the jobs they say they have, how did they get them in a country like Portugal where everything must be controlled from the top? Is that really how people in Portugal feel, or were they just spouting what the government tells them to say to Americans? If they were having breakfast before starting work, why were they not wearing uniforms?"

"My, you are suspicious. What is your job again, Professor Skinner? Why are you here with us?"

"I'm sorry. I'm just a natural skeptic. I must have picked up some of the mistrust of things foreign I encountered in England. By the way, thank you for the enjoyable and interesting breakfast."

As they boarded the launch, Ruthie said, "Maybe they don't have to wear their uniforms on Saturdays. You're not wearing one either." It occurred to Fred that they had landed in and were leaving Portugal without intervention by any customs or other official. Perhaps they and the few mailbags that were unloaded and the larger number that were loaded were nevertheless being scrutinized.

In the *Atlantic Clipper*, Fred set himself up in the lounge, even though he could have done with more sleep. He wanted to experience the take-off. He also wanted to finish his letter to the other Fred and write notes about the discussion with Pretzel. More important, he needed to figure out how he was going to answer the questions about

379

Hitler and Germany. What Pretzel said might help.

The take-off was worth staying awake for. After some taxiing, the sudden roar of the engines was so loud Fred could not imagine how he slept though it before. The plane's steady acceleration pushed him back in his seat. Spray built up so that it covered the windows. In less than a minute, the spray stopped and the boat was flying. Then, the engines were throttled back enough to make conversation possible again. The plane had reached its cruising altitude, which Fred knew to be about eight thousand feet – just below the height at which most people need supplementary oxygen. Looking back, through occasional clouds, he saw the Portuguese coast receding quickly. Soon, only the ocean was in sight.

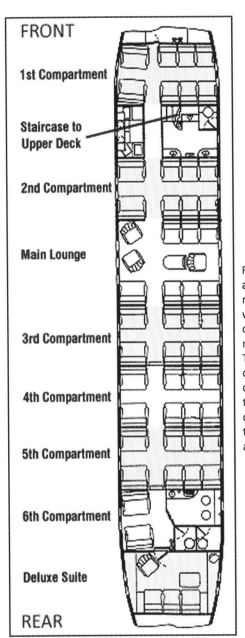

FRONT

1st Compartment

Staircase to
Upper Deck

2nd Compartment

Main Lounge

3rd Compartment

4th Compartment

5th Compartment

6th Compartment

Deluxe Suite

REAR

Floor plan of the lower deck of a Pan Am Clipper. Just to the rear of the first compartment were the galley on the left side of the flying boat and the men's washroom on the right. The women's washroom was opposite the small sixth compartment, to the front of the deluxe suite. Doors to the outside were on each side of the main lounge, which was also the dining room.

TWENTY-SEVEN

Variation and Selection

By the Atlantic Clipper to the Azores, Saturday June 3, 1939

Fred re-read his incomplete letter to Fred Keller, begun on the train from Cambridge to London. Should he now re-write the beginning to say that he was flying across the Atlantic? No, of course not. He *could* write that he was crossing the Atlantic. But why not write as if he were still on the train from Cambridge to London? He continued the letter.

Wittgenstein was dismissive when I steered the discussion to my topic of the moment: the parallel between reinforcement and natural selection. He already believed that interpretations in terms of natural selection trivialize the complexity of life. He now believes too that interpretations in terms of reinforcement trivialize the complexity of human activity. It was the newness of the latter idea that sent him out of the room. But he didn't come back with a better formulation.

I've been reflecting more on the parallel. I'm more and more convinced of its applicability and usefulness. It's even possible that there is a general principle at play here. All adaptive systems depend on variation and selection. It would be like Einstein's special and general theories of relativity. It's possible, for example, that variation and selection act to differentiate human cultures in the course of adapting them to particular environments. I'll be working on this more.

I still think it would be premature to pursue the parallel publicly. I'll pursue it when natural selection is better established as the key principle in biological change. I'll also wait until it no longer has unfortunate political associations – with Social Darwinism and fascism. I may wait too until I have a better understanding as to how cultures adapt, as well as individual organisms.

In a way that Wittgenstein may not have understood, our discussion helped me make an important distinction: between verbal behavior and language. Verbal behavior is what a person does, usually with words. It is developed and maintained by the reinforcement practices of the person's verbal community. A language is not the collection of words it is often thought to be. Rather, it's the collection of reinforcement practices of a particular verbal community. Put another way, a language corresponds to the behavior of a reinforcing community more than to the behavior of an individual speaker, writer or signer. (Yes, we must consider sign language as an important kind of verbal behavior.)

Wittgenstein believes he's concerned with language and how everyday language sets traps for philosophers. I believe he's concerned with verbal behavior and how some verbal behavior is controlled inconsistently, giving rise to confusion. He and I do agree that the important thing is what people actually say, not what they should be saying if they were speaking logically or unambiguously.

We touched on some interesting questions, including whether machines think or could be designed to think. His answer is that the everyday use of 'think' does not extend to machines and so machines cannot think. I have some sympathy with this. But what if you were to come across what is commonly regarded as thinking except that you couldn't tell whether the behavior in question was that of a man or a machine? Wouldn't the word 'thinking' still apply even if it were then discovered that it was a machine behaving and not a person? Wouldn't we have a thinking machine?

I got Wittgenstein to reflect on how verbal behavior is acquired, more than he may have done before. He conceded that differential reinforcement could get children going with speaking. He would likely argue that other unspecified processes then take over.

The discussion helped advance my thinking about how a child comes to say 'my tooth hurts' correctly. I figured out three ways in which the child's verbal community can engage in useful differential reinforcement: by reinforcing 'tooth hurts' only when (1) the jaw is swollen, (2) the jaw is touched or there is grimacing, or (3) 'knee hurts' or 'finger hurts' has been said appropriately. You can fill in the gaps here, and maybe add further means of managing behavior controlled by private stimuli such as a toothache.

Wittgenstein certainly believes that verbal behavior is a social phenomenon. But the importance of reinforcement eludes him. He can't comprehend how difficult it is for a verbal community to provide differential reinforcement with respect to private stimuli.

We touched on non-verbal thinking. He said that much of his own thinking is non-verbal. This is remarkable for a philosopher whose word games are at the center of his work. I offered my suggestion about the role of wayfinding in non-verbal thinking, but he didn't bite into that particular worm.

Finally, we discussed intention, which some people say is the distinguishing attribute of human behavior. I felt we were getting somewhere: on how we could say that machines and animals have intention. Then we were interrupted. Wittgenstein closed down our meeting as abruptly as when he disappeared earlier into his bedroom.

With more time, our discussion might have become more fruitful. Equally, he could have soon retreated into his paranoid shell. I'll never know.

My final thought on Wittgenstein is that someone should exploit his evident interest in nature to involve him in dog training or another exercise in the modification of behavior. If he and others concerned with words had more experience with how behavior can be changed, they might be more accepting of the role of the reinforcing environment. He did say at one point that animal work could be a source of useful insights into human behavior.

Your friend,

Burrhus

Fred didn't notice until he'd finished the letter that Salinsky had sat down opposite him, nursing a bottle of Coca Cola. He was trying to read what Fred had written. "It's nothing secret," said Fred when the other man averted his eyes and blushed. "It's a letter to an academic colleague describing a meeting I had with a professor in Cambridge. The letter may never be sent, but it's a good way of getting my thoughts together. How are things going upstairs?"

"Would you like a tour? Now would be a good time. We're not busy. Everything's nice and bright up there, and the captain's resting." Fred nodded. "Let me go and check with the first officer." A few minutes later he beckoned from the entrance to the lounge, "Let's go." Fred followed him up the spiral staircase.

The flight deck was quite unlike the cramped cockpits Fred had seen in movies. This space was the size of a living room with enough headroom for Fred to stand. Salinsky announced, "This is our mystery passenger, Professor Fred Skinner. You may have seen him help load the cargo. You may also have seen him laid out on the floor of the lounge last night. Ruthie didn't tell him where he could sleep."

Turning to Fred, Salinsky said, "I won't introduce you to them individually. They're busy. Briefly, the two guys at the front are the second and fourth officers. They're driving this bus." Then, pointing, he said, "he's the first officer, the main pilot after the captain but currently acting as the navigator." Pointing again he said "He's the radio operator and he's the assistant flight engineer. The rest of the flight crew, including the trainee pilot, are resting up because they'll be on duty for much of the coming night."

Fred said, "May I ask something?" Salinsky nodded. "What's the worst thing that can happen during a flight?"

"I guess bad weather or running out of fuel. We can usually fly above bad weather. We carry twenty per cent more fuel than we need, and watch fuel levels more carefully than anything else. But mistakes are made, and catastrophic leaks can happen."

"What about engine failure?" said Fred.

"That's not really a big problem. This crate can fly on two engines perfectly well. It needs all four only for take-off. The chance of three engines failing during a flight is pretty slim. In any case, our engineers have good access to the engines through walkways inside each wing. You'd be surprised what they're able to fix while we're in the air. We should go back down."

Fred thanked them. Downstairs he found that a plate of sandwiches had been put out together with coffee and soft drinks. This must have been done by Ruthie, although he'd not seen her since take-off at Lisbon. He took coffee and some sandwiches, resumed his place, and began to make notes on how he might answer Calvin Cooper's four questions. That telephone call was only a few weeks ago, but it seemed months in the past.

Wittgenstein was supposed to be Fred's main source of information, but he'd provided nothing of use. If Fred was going to answer Cooper's questions – and he believed he should – he'd have to make use of other sources. These could include his own reading of *Mein Kampf*, what Freud, Pretzel and others had said, and what he'd read in British newspapers. Presumably, the president had people mining sources such as newspapers for him. Or did he? Fred's best strategy might be to answer each question in the best way he could, give his sources, and leave it the president's advisers to sift out what would be useful. He was beginning to think that the whole venture was somewhat pointless. Perhaps the White House had shown an interest in Fred's trip just to placate Bertrand Russell.

Captain Gray came into the lounge. He greeted the two crew members present, and sat down at Fred's table. "Good to meet you, Professor Skinner," he said. "Glad you are well settled in. Can I come straight to the point?"

"Please do," said Fred, wondering what the point could be. Gray seemed younger than Fred, but imposing: tall, with blond hair, blue eyes and a piercing stare. Fred had the surreptitious thought that he could fare well in Germany as a model of the perfect Aryan man. His voice, however, was as mid-West American as could be imagined.

"We've been told to extend our flight to look at ice conditions at Botwood in Newfoundland and Shediac in New Brunswick, Canada. This will require a new flight plan from the Azores onward. I'd like to meet about this with the whole flight crew when we are at Horta, where we set down in the Azores. I'd like the stewardess to join us too. I don't think you should be at the meeting. The lounge is the best place to meet, and there's not really anywhere else for you on the *Clipper* unless you lie in your bunk. So we're asking that you leave us for a couple of hours when we land. You should take a walk about the pleasant small town of Horta."

"I'll be pleased to do that. But, won't that make our trip to New York much longer, going all the way to Newfoundland?"

"Not much. It's hard to explain without a map. Newfoundland sticks out quite far into the Atlantic. So, the Azores are actually much nearer Newfoundland than New York. It's fifteen hundred miles from Horta to Botwood, and then almost eleven hundred miles to New York via Shediac. The distance from Horta to New York is about twenty-four hundred miles. So going via Botwood will add only a few hundred miles to our trip, plus whatever we do in the air at those two places. We'll be flying for a couple of hours more at the most."

Fred found this hard to digest. He couldn't believe Newfoundland was that much nearer. However, he was pleased at the prospect of flying over Botwood and Shediac, and along much of the continent's east coast. Then he remembered that the *Atlantic Clipper* had been due to set down in Long Island's Manhasset Bay at seven in the morning. This would have given him plenty of time to get to the nearby New York World's Fair for his nine thirty meeting with Calvin Cooper. If the *Clipper* is to be a few hours late, he couldn't be there by nine thirty. Calvin Cooper should be told.

"I'm supposed to meet someone at the World's Fair at nine thirty tomorrow morning," Fred said to Captain Gray. "It's an important meeting. If we are going to be later than expected, I should reschedule it. Can I do that? And for what time?"

"If it's important, we'll have a radio message relayed. But we won't know our planned arrival time at New York until after we meet this afternoon and confirm it with our head office. We'll have several factors to take into account. For example, we don't want to arrive at Botwood before sunrise there. I'll arrange that you send a message before we take off from Horta."

Fred thanked him. The captain spoke with the other two crew members in the lounge and then left for the rear of the *Clipper*. He passed back through the lounge ten minutes later and climbed the staircase to the flight deck. Soon after, Ruthie came in and sat down. She buckled her seat belt, suggesting that Fred do the same. Captain Gray had just told her they'd be landing at Horta in twenty minutes. They'd had an unexpected tail wind and were an hour ahead of schedule. She'd been off-duty, asleep in her cabin until the captain banged on her door. She liked the idea of the detour to Botwood and Shediac and was delighted to be included in the meeting of the flight crew. This was an unusual honor for a stewardess, a word she didn't like. Including her was no doubt the captain's way of ensuring they got a good meal while they talked.

"I'll be spending a few hours in Horta," said Fred. "Any suggestions?"

"It's actually pronounced 'Orta,' not the way the captain says it. There's not much to do there except walk around and enjoy the fresh air. That's if it's not raining. If you want to just sit and look at the port and the huge volcano on the island opposite you can't do better than to walk up to the old fort. There's a nice restaurant there with tables on a balcony that overlooks the harbor. That'll be a good place to eat and read and write, if it's not raining."

Fred thanked her just as the engines changed pitch, presumably for the descent. He could see islands to the right, left and ahead. The one on the left was dominated by a large volcanic peak. As they descended past the peak, he could see the far wall of the volcano's crater. The sky was cloudless apart except for a fringe around the peak. They turned toward the sun and lost height rapidly. Fred could see what must be Horta to the right, with its busy bay where the *Clipper* was to land. The plane did a U-turn and approached Horta close to the water. There was a bump, much spray, and a change in engine noise. Half a minute later they were taxiing slowly through smooth water.

"We don't need a launch here," said Ruthie, who had already unfastened her seat belt and was replacing cushions that had fallen on the floor during the landing. The Portuguese have made a jetty just for flying boats. They are quite keen that we continue refueling here.

There's a flying boat jetty under construction at Lisbon too. There was no suitable tender here and Pam Am had just ordered one, but now I suppose it won't be needed."

They were drawing up at the jetty. Ruthie told him it was two o'clock local time. Their scheduled take-off was seven o'clock, but that could be delayed to avoid a too-early arrival at Botwood. The take-off was not going to be brought forward. She suggested he think of returning to the *Clipper* by six o'clock. He could come back earlier. The meeting would not last more than a few hours. Some of the crew might like to go ashore.

Fred could see the fort on a small rise to the south of the port. He walked up to it, surprised by the number of damaged, abandoned buildings he saw on the way. The restaurant was just as Ruthie said. He chose a table on the balcony with good views of the harbor and the volcano. His knowledge of French was enough to understand the Portuguese menu. He couldn't figure out the prices. He explained to the waiter he had some American dollars and one British pound. The waiter threw up his hands in puzzlement and fetched the manager. The manager said in English that the dollar was worth twenty-five escudos and the pound four or five times as much. The one pound bill would more than pay for a good meal with some good wine. Fred took this to be the offer of a transaction, which he accepted, knowing that he could be overpaying. He'd be making the most of a beautiful afternoon and a splendid view.

The manager said he would provide the fine American gentleman with the best meal that could be had *nas ilhas açorianas* – which Fred took to mean in the Azores. Was the gentleman with the *Clipper* that had just landed? In Horta, they were looking forward to many passengers arriving in this way, and staying long enough to enjoy Horta's hospitality.

Fred smiled politely. He had exposed himself a little too much at breakfast in Lisbon and he should be careful not to say anything that could arouse too much interest in him here. The manager saw that he didn't want to talk and walked away with the waiter. Fred hardly had time to open his notebook before the waiter returned to set his table and uncork two bottles of wine, one red and one white. Seven courses followed, one after the other. They included fish and meat dishes and ended with the best vanilla ice cream he'd tasted and a splendid cheese plate. Fred was in bliss. He drank most of the wine.

He became a little sleepy, the scenery was distracting. It was hard to turn his attention to figuring out how to answer the questions. The manager asked if all was well and beamed when Fred said the meal was perfect. Why were there so many damaged buildings, Fred asked. There was a major earthquake in 1926. It was better to build again on more solid land. The Azores experienced much geological activity, mostly minor earthquakes and under-water eruptions.

"One theory is that the Azores is geologically active because it is the true meeting place of Africa, Europe and America," continued the manager. "You do not have to be afraid, not does Pam Am. This is a safe and peaceful place."

"I'm impressed by your knowledge," said Fred. "What about that huge mountain there?" Fred pointed to the one the *Clipper* had flown by. "It looks like a volcano."

"It is," said the manager. "And, thank you for the compliment. *Montanha do Pico* has not erupted for more than two centuries, and is not expected to erupt again soon. We are proud of our mountain. It is the highest in Portugal and one of the highest in Europe. Sometimes in winter we see snow near the top."

The manager called the waiter to clear the table. Fred was left with the wine and splendid coffee and cookies. He spent some minutes surveying the scene, noting how the *Atlantic Clipper* dominated the harbor. It was larger than any of the boats there. A crowd had gathered on the quay and was being kept off the jetty by two policemen. He set out his pencils and notebooks and wondered what he had to say on whether German would invade Poland.

Then he saw a remarkable sight. A U-boat was moving into the bay riding high in the water. A red, white and black flag with a swastika in the center flew from a mast behind the conning tower. For a moment he thought he was hallucinating, the result of too much wine. But he was not. Small craft were making way for the submarine, which found a mooring. The U-boat was similar to the one he'd seen from the *Duchess of York* when they were passing north of Ireland, although that one didn't carry a flag. Then he saw the number, U-35, painted in white on the conning tower and realized it was the same submarine.

An official-looking launch was speeding to the U-boat. The manager approached and said this had happened before. A U-boat had arrived needing fuel, provisions or repairs. The people of Horta did not want them here. They were obliged by maritime convention to give help unless the countries were at war.

"Will there be a war?" Fred asked.

"Of course," said the manager, "Germany is looking for trouble. We could be involved even more than in the Great War when German submarines sank many Portuguese ships in this area. Portugal was neutral then and will be neutral again, but we will fear Germany as much as we did before. Also, we will have the Italians to watch out for too. A war will be very bad for flying boat travel. Will American join in, as she did before?"

"After the last war, many Americans feel strongly that we should not be involved in European affairs," Fred replied. "But this time we could have Japan to deal with too. If Japan, allied with Germany, shows too much strength in the Pacific, the feeling about American participation could change. In the meantime, we'll likely show support for Britain and France but not actually fight for them. I've been in Britain for a week and share your view that war seems to be coming." Fred realized he was talking too much – the wine again – and resolved to say less.

Fred was relieved when the manager then left him alone. He

looked through his notes, occasionally glancing at the U-boat. He had an hour before he should return to the *Clipper*. He should at least make progress with the question about Poland. He turned to the notes he had made on *the Duchess of York*. There he'd concluded, based on his reading of *Mein Kampf*, that there were three reasons to think Germany would invade Poland. They were: to gain living space and farmland for Germans, to redress the harm done to Germany in 1919 by the *Treaty of Versailles*, and to secure a stepping stone towards eventual conquest against the communists in Russia. To this should be added the view of the dentist Glaser: that Poland could be a good place in which Germany could make progress towards eliminating Jews from Europe.

What had Raimund Pretzel said? Fred found his notes on that encounter. He'd said that the Nazis would invade Poland because such an invasion would be popular among the German people, unlike the take-overs of Czechoslovakia and Austria. Germans did not like Poles. Fred surmised that the Nazis didn't seem to care that an invasion of Poland would cause Britain and France to declare war. They were obviously preparing for war. He had evidence in front of him: the U-boat being refueled in the harbor. The answer to the first question should be yes, Hitler will order an invasion of Poland.

Two or three questions to go. Fred felt reassured by having found his way to a clear answer to the first question, even though he wouldn't be able to say that Wittgenstein had made a contribution. It was time to return to the *Clipper*. He stood and beckoned the manager. "Here's my British pound. It seems a small amount for such a magnificent meal. I hope you'll get enough escudos for the pound to give a little extra to your helpful waiter and the excellent chef."

The manager smiled and expressed the hope again that he would see more guests from Pan Am's flights. Fred walked, unsteadily, down the hill to the harbor. The damage to the buildings was indeed not new. Now, more than the damage, Fred noticed flowers growing in every possible place. The crowd at the jetty was smaller. Fred still had to push a little to get to the front. There he showed his passport to one of the policemen and was allowed to walk along the jetty to the *Clipper*. The U-boat was still there, being refueled from a tender carrying a large tank and a primitive motorized pump.

In the lounge/dining room of a *Clipper* during passenger service.

TWENTY-EIGHT

Answering the Questions

By the Atlantic Clipper to New York, June 3-4, 1939

C aptain Gray sought out Fred and suggested they talk in one of the compartments containing cargo. There he explained that the original schedule involved leaving at seven o'clock local time – in about an hour's time – and arriving in New York at seven in the morning Eastern Daylight Time, sixteen hours later.

He said we now needed to be over Botwood in Newfoundland not earlier than five in the morning local time there, which would be three thirty in New York. It would be about ten minutes before sunrise at Botwood. There should be enough daylight to survey ice conditions. At the original speed, this would have meant delaying the departure from Horta by two hours. However, they were going conserve fuel by reducing speed and would be taking off at eight local time. This way, they'd run less risk of eating into the twenty-percent margin of extra fuel they normally carried.

Fred's head was spinning. In part it was the wine and in part the complexity of what he was being told. He still hadn't got used to the idea that Newfoundland was so much nearer the Azores. Then, it was hard to figure out all these local times. Could Botwood really be an hour and a half ahead of New York? That didn't make sense. Surely time zones were staggered by hours not half-hours?

The captain continued by saying that the flight from Botwood to New York would need six and a half hours. This would include some minutes at each of Botwood and Shediac for the ice surveys They'd set down in Manhasset Bay, just off Port Washington on Long Island, at ten thirty New York time. What message would Fred now like to send, and to whom?

Fred wished his head were a little clearer. The message should not go to the White House. U-boat crews may have the ability to intercept the *Clipper's* radio messages and even decipher them if they are coded. He said, "Please send a message to your president, Mr. Trippe. Ask him to convey that the meeting scheduled for nine-thirty will now have to occur at twelve-thirty. Ask him to secure a confirmation of this change." He hoped Trippe would have the wit to realize the message was for the White House and that it should reach Calvin Cooper, wherever he was.

"I'll do that. I must radio Mr. Trippe soon and I'll include this information. I assume you shouldn't be mentioned by name."

Fred nodded and expressed his thanks. They went back to the lounge and the captain continued to the flight deck. Fred was sleepy but he wanted to experience the exhilaration of the take-off again. Ruthie came in and asked about his afternoon. Fred described the enjoyable meal, apologized for being a little tipsy, and asked that Ruthie do what she could to keep him awake for the take-off.

He asked what she'd be doing during the long flight to Botwood. She said the crew had eaten well this afternoon. Some would want to eat again this evening and she'd have to have some breakfast ready before they reached Botwood. After take-off she was going to make up beds in the front compartment and in the crew's quarters upstairs, behind the flight deck. She'd then spruce up the lounge and the wash-rooms, and prepare a meal for those that wanted it. After that she'd be off-duty for about seven hours. Fred might want to retire to his bunk soon after take-off. She needn't disturb him there.

Fred could barely stay awake for the take-off but did, even experi-encing some of the exhilaration of the take-off at Lisbon. He then went quickly to his bunk and lay on it noting that the engines had a slightly lower tone than before, no doubt the slower cruising speed. He was asleep within a few minutes.

He woke two hours later, surprised he did not have a hangover. A Pan Am envelope with his name on it had been pushed through the curtains that enclosed his bunk. It contained a message from the cap-tain: "The event is confirmed at the original location, but at 11:30 a.m. (EDT)." Fred wondered how he could be there by then, but resolved to leave that problem until later.

No one was in the bunk below him, where the captain had slept. The curtains of both bunks opposite were closed, meaning that crew members were asleep in them. He climbed down taking care not to wake anyone else in the compartment, put on his shoes and crept into the washroom. Ruthie was washing dishes in the galley.

No one else was in the lounge. Fred began a new review of his notes relevant to Calvin Cooper's questions. Ruthie joined him and said, "It seems we're the only ones up on this deck. I'm off duty now. Would you like to join me in the rear cabin where we can have some refreshment without anyone knowing?"

Fred considered the wisdom of accepting this invitation. He said, "Do you think I should first arrange my bunk so it seems I'm asleep there?" Ruthie waited while Fred did that, leaving his notebooks and pencils in the bunk. They walked quietly to the compartment at the rear of the plane. Ruthie locked the door behind them.

She said, "This is the best room in the *Clipper*. It's known as the honeymoon suite, but don't let that give you ideas. You're married and

I'm engaged. All my precautions are because I don't want to be caught drinking alcohol on the plane."

"I'm in your hands, Ruthie. I won't drink a lot. I had too much wine this afternoon, although it must have been good wine because I'm feeling little after-effect. I'm pleased to keep you company."

Ruthie took ice from a bowl she had brought from the galley and added some to each of two tumblers with a measure of rye from a bottle she produced from a suitcase. They sat in the two chairs, which were more luxurious than the others he'd seen in the plane. "Cheers!" she said. "You understand I'm putting my life in your hands. You could easily report me and my lovely career with Pan Am would come to a swift end. From what I've seen of you so far, I like you and think I can trust you."

"Cheers to you!" said Fred. "I'm flattered that you trust me and want to spend time with me. I won't let you down. Is there something in particular you want to talk about?"

"Only my life. I don't know what to do. I'm not young anymore and I want to have children. I also want to keep this career if I can. As I said in Lisbon, I'm hoping for a position in our Baltimore training center. Baltimore is where I live and where my fiancé lives. How the baby thing would work out with Pam Am I don't know, but I think they like me and maybe even need me enough to accommodate me up to a point."

"You said your problem was that you might be reassigned to the west coast. Is that right?"

"In one way, yes. But my real problem is I'm not sure I want to spend my life with my fiancé. Going to the west coast could be a way out of that. He'll never leave Baltimore. But then I'd have to find a new father for the children I want. It would mean a new man to get to know, a new fiancé. And, as I said, I'm getting old."

"I don't know what to say. I'm guessing you're about thirty, not because you look it but because you told me you've been with Pam Am for nine years. I've heard about women having babies in their forties, so you could have lots of time."

"It's not only that, it's also that men prefer younger women."

"Many do. Speaking for myself, I'd say you are the perfect age."

"That's because you're an older married man. I may want a younger single man."

"Don't you have a lot of choice in the job you are in now? What about the captain? He seems a fine man, younger than me."

"He is a fine man, but he's also married with children. I met his wife, Exa. She's a lovely woman. In any case, Pan Am warns us strongly against fraternizing – as they call it – with members of flight crews. They found it causes too many problems. In my nine years, I've never done it."

Fred did not continue the conversation immediately. He then said, "I wouldn't worry too much about your uncertainty about your fiancé. That's pretty natural. Lots of people marry quite impulsively. They don't give it much thought and it seems to work out, more often than not. Marriage is much more than initial attraction, especially when parenting is involved."

"You should be writing an advice column," Ruthie said.

"I'll remember that if I'm ever out of a job," said Fred.

"You told me you were some kind of professor. Whaddya teach?" Ruthie was losing her polish again, likely the result of the rye she'd consumed. Fred had hardly touched his.

"Psychology. But not the kind that helps provide good advice about marriage. I teach about language, and about how to train animals to do things."

"That sounds like a good bashis for advish about marriage." She slurred some of her words. Had her drink been much larger than his?

She picked up the bottle, "Can I pour you another?"

"I think one is enough – for each of us. I'll have a little more of that ice in your bowl and suck on it."

"You're a lovely man, Fred. Can we lie on the bed together and hug, keeping our clothes on?"

"Ruthie, that's very nice of you to ask but I don't think we should. Forgive me for saying it, but the drink has clouded your judgement. In the morning you could regret anything you do now."

"My, you sure are a prude, Professor Skinner. All I wanted was a bit of comforting. Can you hold me on your lap? Would that be going too far for you?" She didn't wait for an answer but crossed the compartment, sat on his lap, and nestled her head into his neck.

Fred's first inclination was to push her away, but he didn't to avoid upsetting her. He held her stiffly at first, but softened as she nestled further into him. Then he could feel himself becoming aroused. She probably could too as his erection was being restrained by her thigh. She stood, steadied herself by holding his shoulder, grabbed both his hands and pulled him towards the lower bunk.

"We shouldn't do this," Fred said. "What if the captain were to come looking for you, as he did before? What if he or another crew member looks for me?"

"That was an unusual situation because we were arriving early and he wanted to tell me about the meeting. It's unlikely something like that will happen in this part of the flight unless there's a serious emergency – and we've never had one. We'll be fine." She was now on the bunk and trying to pull him beside her.

"OK," said Fred, "but let's just do what you said. Let's just hug, keeping our clothes on."

Fred climbed in beside her and put an arm over her. She kissed him on the chin and then on the lips. One of her arms was wedged between them and her hand sought his erection – unsuccessfully because Fred was no longer aroused. "I'm sorry. I've made you nervous," she said. He agreed, and gently moved her hand away. She put it back between them and began to undo his belt and fly. He could feel his penis stirring again and let her hand continue. She held his penis and said, "Please put this inside me."

"What about contraception?" Fred murmured. He remembered the rubbers he'd bought on the ship, but not where he'd put them. He hadn't expected this.

"I've nothing, but I'm at a safe time of the month. My period's due in two or three days." She undid her skirt and wriggled it off with what was underneath.

Fred was now beyond resisting. He felt her vagina, coated his penis with some of its wetness and slid into her. The engine noise changed, pulling him out of his sensual absorption. He became aware again of where he was and the ease of being discovered. His erection subsided a little.

"Don't worry about that," she whispered, "they're likely gaining altitude to fly over some turbulence. Do what you were doing."

"Can I make you come?" Fred said, slipping out of her. "I'm not sure I can just now."

"I take a long time. I'd love you to try."

She did take a long time, and when she did Fred put his hand gently over her mouth to reduce the sound. What she did, and his role in it, strongly aroused him. He pushed his very erect penis into her and came in a few seconds.

"That was wonderful," she said, "just what I needed."

"I think I needed it too," said Fred. "Thank you."

"The pleasure was mine, sir. Thank *you* very much."

Her tipsy demeanor seemed to have disappeared. Had it been an act or did sexual activity cure drunkenness? Fred said, "How can I put this to you? I don't want to stay. I want to go back to my bunk and fall asleep thinking about what we've just done."

"I'll go first and get something from the galley, to see if the coast is clear."

This, Fred thought, was further evidence that tipsiness had been neutralized. She, who had so much more to lose by being caught, had been rash before and was now a model of caution.

Ruthie returned saying there was no one about. Fred kissed her and went back to his bunk via the washroom, shaken by the violence of his behavior. Why had he been so aroused? Lack of sexual release? Ruthie's long but erotic road to orgasm? Her small, pliable body? He fell asleep puzzling the implications of the last possibility.

The next thing Fred remembered was being awoken by someone shaking his shoulder. It was Tom Salinsky. He said quietly that they'd be over Botwood in twenty minutes. Fred had forgotten that he'd asked to be woken. He looked at his watch. It was seven-thirty in the morning Azores time. He'd slept soundly for more than eight hours as well as the two hours soon after take-off. He felt rested.

Ruthie and he exchanged good mornings as he passed the galley. She'd set out coffee and sandwiches in the lounge. Through a window on the right side of the plane he could see the sky lightening behind them. They were descending over land.

Ruthie came in to the lounge carrying a map of Newfoundland. She said, "The captain is in good spirits this morning. He left this map for you to look at. He said that at Shediac you can join them on the flight deck."

Fred took her comment on the captain to mean that all was well. His visit to her compartment had not been noticed. The map showed that Botwood was thirty miles from Newfoundland's north shore, on the west side of the Bay of Exploits. The bay was much longer than its width, which was about two miles at that point. It was a large sheltered patch of water, perhaps ideal for flying boats. The plane was turning to the left. He could see what must be Botwood on the far side. They were close enough to make out individual houses, even though the sun wasn't yet providing good illumination.

The plane flew south for a few minutes and then did a U-turn and headed north along the bay toward the open sea. Fred had hoped he might see Canadian Pacific steamers as they passed Newfoundland, but they were at least two hundred miles north of Saint Pierre and Miquelon, which the *Duchess of York* had passed.

They were about the same distance south of the Strait of Belle Isle, which could now be ice-free and usable by the steamers. He hadn't realized Newfoundland was so large. He retrieved his small suitcase and pulled out his Canadian Pacific timetable. No steamer would be passing Newfoundland at this time.

The plane did another U-turn and headed south along the bay. The sun was now high enough for ice to be visible. Fred could see just a suggestion of it in some of the small bays but none in the open water. Just beyond Botwood the plane changed course again and headed south west, presumably towards Shediac.

Ruthie came in again and said they'd be over Shediac in about two and a half hours. It was now three fifty in the morning New York time and he might like to set his watch to that time. After Shediac she'd be making a real nice breakfast for everyone.

Fred turned to the second question he was to answer. Will the Soviet Union cooperate with Germany if she invades Poland? When he'd last thought seriously about this, on the *Duchess of York*, it was the question that had puzzled him the most. Again, Wittgenstein had provided nothing on which to base an answer.

He reviewed his notes. On the one hand, the Soviet Union – Russia – was a historic enemy of Germany, at least during the twentieth century, and was now also an ideological enemy. According to *Mein Kampf*, bolshevism (communism) was a scourge inspired by Jews. Moreover,

Russia and her satellite Ukraine offered the biggest opportunity for *Lebensraum.*

On the other hand, Germany and Russia had much in common. They were one-party totalitarian states. Both professed to be enemies of capitalism. Perhaps more to the point, each one had lost much territory to the Poland that was recreated at the end of the Great War. Fred saw the note to himself that Germany and Russia might agree to invade at the same time. They could meet at the 1914 boundary and eliminate Poland again. He read his notes on Raimund Pretzel's views. Pretzel had said that Germany would invade Poland not only for *Lebensraum* but also because Germans did not like Poles. An invasion could be popular.

The prospect of such a joint strategy involving Germany and Russia could be why talks about an alliance between England, France and Russia seemed to have stalled.

Why would the White House want to have information about this? Fred supposed it was all to do with the likelihood of war. Given current alliances, a German invasion of Poland would trigger a war with England and France. If Germany and Russia *both* invaded Poland, there might be less chance of a war because England and France would not want to take on Russia as well. If the West, rather than Germany, had an alliance with Russia the likelihood of war might also be lessened because Germany would not want to take on Russia as well.

Fred remembered that trying to think through these complexities had been beyond him when he had tried on the *Duchess of York.* It was still beyond him. He remembered too one more thing that Pretzel had said. Any pact with Russia would be a tactical matter on Germany's part, to be cast aside when Hitler is ready to push the Russians back beyond the Urals.

He decided to go with the knowledgeable Raimund Pretzel, whose rationality shone through the fog of his poor spoken English. Fred's answer would be this. Germany and Russian will strike an alliance to invade Poland at about the same time, meeting at the pre-war boundary. Later, Germany would take over the whole country, in the course of invading Russia. Would the double invasion of Poland mean war between Germany and England, and perhaps between Russia and England? Fred would have to admit strong uncertainty. He'd read that many right-wingers in Britain considered the Soviet Union to be a pariah state. Perhaps they'd welcome a war against Russia more than one against Germany.

What could America make of all this? There, Fred believed, the anti-communist sentiments were at least as strong as the anti-German sentiments. But the anti-war feeling – a plague on all your houses – was stronger. A lot of Americans would be pleased if Germany and Russia fought each other to the death and America stayed out of it.

Fred though he might have to return to Cooper's second question, and perhaps even reconsider his answer to the first question. This was turning out to be even more complex than he'd expected.

What about the third question: How far will Hitler go in ridding Greater Germany and German-controlled territory of Jews? What was the American interest here? Fred guessed it was related to the political weight of the Jewish community, which was strongly inclined to the president's party, the Democrats. But, if the Jewish influence was so strong, why were so few Jews allowed to immigrate?

Fred saw his note on Pretzel's view that Germans were not particularly anti-Semitic, at least compared with Austrians and others in central Europe. Pretzel had also said that the violence against Jews reflected more the sadistic impulses of the people who were attracted to Nazism. Fred was still more struck by the invective against Jews in *Mein Kampf*. There – he remembered the words well – Hitler described them as parasites, a type of bacillus, and public pests intent on polluting good Aryan stock with their racial inferiority. This was the kind of language that led to extermination.

Pretzel had argued that in Germany the regime would do no more

405

than expel Jews. Doing more would risk unpopularity among the German people at large. Outside Germany, the Nazis could well seek to exterminate Jews, if they have the opportunity. Fred found his note on the dentist Glaser's admission that thinking about what would happen to Polish Jews under Nazi rule made him sick.

Fred decided that his answer to the third question should be that inside Germany the Nazis will go only so far as expelling Jews. Outside Germany, if they have the chance, they will exterminate them. He should add Pretzel's plea. America and other countries should open their doors to refugees from Germany, Jews and others.

Cooper's fourth question was this: To what extent do British people accept the need for another war with Germany? It was the easiest to answer. Fred had concluded – from discussions, newspapers, and the strong evidence of preparations – that people in England for the most part now saw war as inevitable. They didn't welcome it, but were resigned to it, and seemed to understand the need for it. Germany had become ruled by a bunch of hoodlums who appeared to be acting with very little restraint. She'd become a menace to the good order of Europe and even the world. She had to be stopped even if Britain and possibly France were the only countries prepared to take Germany on.

It seemed that pacifism had prevailed in England as recently as six months ago. This was no longer true, especially since the German occupation of much of Czechoslovakia. However, while British people might accept the need for a war, they might not yet support the huge extent of mobilization needed to beat Germany. The same could apply to France.

Fred had the elements of a report. Was there anything else he had learned that might be useful to the White House? Yes, he could pass along more of Pretzel's opinions. Hitler should be assassinated. Germany should be crushed. Psychological warfare should be used to undermine Germans' will to fight. The German state should be reconstructed as several loosely linked entities, possibly within a European economic association. Pretzel's recipe for action against Germany could not be fitted easily into Fred's responses to the four questions. He would set it out separately, identifying its source.

Then Fred wondered if there was something else he might add, making use of his understanding of the mechanics of behavior. If you were trying to understand behavior, you should figure out what in the environment sustained the behavior, now and in the past.

What in Hitler's environment sustained his behavior? What sustained the behavior of the German people in supporting Hitler? To a degree, each set of behaviors reinforced the other. Hitler's behavior was reinforced, at least in part, by the adulation he received. What was the adulation sustained by? In part it was fear of being or appearing to be in opposition. But – here Fred consulted his notes – Pretzel had said that this applied to less than half of the German population. He'd suggested that what sustained support for Hitler and the Nazis was national pride, patriotism, even chauvinism. But how did patriotism – "the last refuge of a scoundrel," according to Samuel Johnson – serve as a reinforcer? Are the mechanics of the reinforcement associated with patriotism the same as those involved in support for sports teams? These and other questions should be addressed with some urgency by a science of human behavior.

Fred retrieved his copy of *Mein Kampf* to see if he could achieve more insight into Hitler's behavior. He read Chapter XI, headed "Race and People," more closely than before. He looked at other parts of the tedious and noxious manifesto, all the while taking care that no one saw what he was reading. When he'd done this reading he felt he had a better understanding of Hitler's *Weltanschauung*, his world-view. This world-view – at least at the time of writing *Mein Kampf* – was informed by a strange understanding of the human biological predicament. Human life, according to Hitler, was a matter of struggle. Hitler's own life was the focus of the first half of *Mein Kampf*, which Fred knew to mean "my fight" or "my struggle."

The primary human struggle, according to Hitler, was Darwinian. In *Mein Kampf* he wrote, "The struggle for the daily livelihood leaves behind everything that is weak or diseased or wavering … this struggle is a means of furthering the health or powers of resistance in the species." He believed the Aryans (the Germans) to be the superior race of humans, but they had to prove it. They could do this by subjugating neighboring races and using the neighbors' land to feed the growing population of the superior race. To stay superior, Aryans must breed only with Aryans.

Standing in the way of Aryans' manifest destiny, wrote Hitler, were Jews, a race of subhumans. Jews presented three problems. They denied the human biological predicament by arguing for reason over impulse. They did not seek their own land but lived as parasites within the territory of others, weakening their hosts. Although subhuman and unnatural, they bred with Aryans and lesser races, thereby infecting and weakening them.

Hitler's world-view, thought Fred, was more pernicious even than the "Social Darwinism" used a few decades ago to justify capitalism and racism in America. He should include a note about this world-view in his report. He could add that the President's advisers should study *Mein Kampf* carefully in order to understand the extremity and force of Hitler's ideology.

Freud had said that Hitler was so mad he was beyond the reach of psychoanalysis. Fred should include Freud's view in his report. It could make Pretzel's proposal for assassination seem less extreme. Freud had also suggested that Hitler was a phenomenon beyond today's means of explanation. Perhaps something of the same applied to any account of Hitler's behavior.

Fred decided his own behavioral insights, whatever they might be, would not be in the report.

The President's staff would also be interested in Fred's two encounters instigated by Germans or German interests: with Lukas Glaser and with Mabel Miller. He should give assurance that he'd provided not even a hint as to the role of the White House in his trip.

Finally, there were a few miscellaneous items that could be of interest and should be touched on briefly in the report. These included the U-boat sightings off Ireland and at the Azores, and the comments of the Portuguese officials.

Ruthie stood at the forward entrance to the lounge. She said, "It's now six-fifteen New York time and we'll be over Shediac in thirty minutes. We'll spend only a few minutes there. I've started to get the breakfast ready and I need to set these tables."

He moved past her, more closely than he would have done yesterday evening. Her hand brushed his thigh. That might be their last contact, he thought. He busied himself in the washroom and tidied his bunk. Ruthie, who was working the galley, said he'd be welcome on the flight deck. He climbed the spiral staircase. Salinsky welcomed him and gave him a chart. He said Fred was free to walk around the flight deck for a few minutes. Everyone was busy and questions would have to wait until breakfast back in the lounge when they'd left the Shediac area.

The *Atlantic Clipper* was over open water. From the chart, Fred could see that the land a few miles behind them must be part of Prince Edward Island. Ahead must be the coast of New Brunswick, Shediac Bay in particular. Fred assumed that flying boats would use the part of the bay sheltered by Shediac Island. He could see no hint of ice there. The *Clipper* circled the bay and continued in a south-westerly direction toward New York City. He went back downstairs.

Salinsky came into the lounge with three other members of the flight crew. Salinsky joined Fred and the other three sat at another table. Salinsky said he hoped Fred had enjoyed the flight. They were sticking to their new schedule. It would be a ten-thirty landing at Manhasset Bay.

Salinsky pointed to a flight crew member Fred had not noticed before – older than the others – and said, "Our engineer says we have plenty of fuel. Our radio officer, still upstairs, says the weather is good for the whole run except for cloud and rain in the New York City area. So, you can sit back and relax or do more of that writing you do a lot of."

"Forgive me if I've been unsociable," Fred replied. "I've got a deadline coming up for something I have to write. This flight's been a good opportunity to get on with it."

"Well, I won't pry any more. Tell me, how does this compare with crossing the Atlantic by ship?"

"It's been a great adventure. I'm grateful to Pan Am. Flying is the future of trans-Atlantic travel. Who'd not prefer a day and a half over six days at sea, even when the sailing is smooth?"

"Soon, as I said, it won't even be a day and a half. We'll have land-based airplanes that can hop the Atlantic and get you from New York to London in less than a day, perhaps via Newfoundland and Ireland. Engineers in Europe – and we have some too – are working on a new type of engine known as jet engines. They work like the rockets we set off on July the Fourth. Planes with jet engines could cross the Atlantic in a few hours."

Ruthie came in with eggs, bacon, sausages and home fries for everyone, and coffee too. She flirted gently with the flight crew members but was more formal with Fred.

"Exactly how are jet engines better?" Fred asked Salinsky after they had had a few mouthfuls.

"They put out much more power for a given weight of engine, a key thing for an airplane. They have many fewer moving parts – they don't need pistons or propellers, for example. Thus, they can be more reliable, another key requirement. This is mostly theory at the moment. The rocket scientists are having a hard job making them easy to control. The last thing you want is a plane powered by a rocket that's out of control."

"What will you guys do if there's a war?" Fred asked.

"Go and fly for Uncle Sam if we're involved. Otherwise, stay out of harm's way. Didya hear in England that there'll be a war?"

"I'm afraid I did, from several people. And I saw quite a few preparations for war."

"I guess it's that Hitler and his gang. I think we should stay out of it," said Salinsky, "but I know I'm biased." He paused. "My dad was training to a pilot for the Army Air Service in the last war and was killed in a flying accident in France in 1918. He never qualified. He never saw combat. He was only twenty-five. He was my buddy. I miss him today. I do this job because of him – over my mother's strong protests, I should add."

"I'm sorry. You must have been just a young boy. What a terrible thing to happen to you."

"I was eight, the oldest of three boys. Dad was our hero. We're all pilots now, I guess in memory of him. He always wanted to be a pilot. The war gave him a chance. Some chance! Our career choices drove our mother nuts – until she remarried, that is. Now, blessed with toddler twins in her mid-forties, she doesn't care so much."

"I can see why you, in particular, don't want a war."

"I might change my mind if I was given a good reason for our involvement. I'd like to hear more from you about what's happening over there but I've got to get back to work."

"Thanks for telling me about your family, and for your help in Southampton and here on the plane."

"You're very welcome."

"Could I ask you one more thing?" said Fred. "Would there be a fountain pen on board? I need to write something up to deliver soon after arrival and I have only pencils with me."

"We can't use pens. They leak because of the changes in air pressure. We use pencils. I've heard that a Hungarian has invented an ink pen that can work in the air. But he's sold the production rights to Britain's Royal Air Force. We've love to get out hands on one, or a dozen. Perhaps we will if there's a war and we're on the same side."

They finished eating. Salinsky poured himself more coffee and left for the flight deck. Fred was now alone in the lounge. Ruthie came in and asked with coy smile if there was anything she could get him. He said he was OK for the moment. Did she know Salinsky's mother had had twins in her forties. She didn't know that and thanked Fred for the information. She might talk to Salinsky about it.

After Ruthie had cleared and cleaned the tables, Fred settled down to write out his answers to Calvin Cooper's questions and the other matters he had decided to include. He wasn't sure if he was to make a written or oral report – or any report at all – but a written report might be asked for. Using his latest notes he wrote a report in handwriting that was clearer than his usual tight scrawl. Writing on one side only it covered twelve pages torn carefully from his notebook. There were ten pages of report, including coverage of Pretzel's views, Hitler's worldview, the German-instigated encounters, and the miscellaneous items. The final two pages were on his sources.

Fred had a brief qualm about including Pretzel's proposal that Hitler be assassinated. But that's what the man had said. It expressed the force of Pretzel's views and it might be the soundest recommendation in his report. He wondered whether it was conceivable that the American government would arrange for an assassination, and how it might be achieved.

Ruthie came in and told him they'd be landing in thirty minutes. Rather than fly straight to Manhasset Bay, they'd be making a detour. They were going to fly over the south end of Manhattan Island and then low over Flushing Meadows, the site of the World's Fair.

Fred regretted being preoccupied during this part of the flight and not seeing more of Canada, New England, and the east coast as they had flown down from Shediac. The *Atlantic Clipper* went into a steep turn to the left, almost a complete U-turn. As they straightened out, he could see ahead the Hudson River with extensive docks and piers on the far side. Behind were the towers of Manhattan with the distinctive spire of the Empire State Building rising above them. Soon they were over Manhattan. Fred could make out Fifth Avenue, which had unusually few pedestrians and cars moving in either direction. Then he remembered it was Sunday morning.

It had been raining. The streets and buildings were glistening in the sun. Fred was happy to be home, or almost home. Looking ahead, he could see the vast low-rise areas of Brooklyn and Queens. Visible in the distance were the white globe and spire of the World's Fair site, familiar from posters and from newspaper and magazine photos. Fred could now see that the Perisphere and Trylon – he'd remembered the structures' names – were at the center of a large concentration of light-colored buildings that stood out from the mostly grey suburban development. North of the Fair site a small plane was landing on the obviously new runway of an airport. Soon the *Atlantic Clipper* was over the site. They were so low they could see people waving to them. Fred wanted to wave back.

A few minutes later the *Clipper* turned again and landed on the smooth water of Manhasset Bay, coming to a stop pointing out of the bay. Salinksy came into to the lounge and said that a motorboat would be taking him to a jetty close to the World's Fair site. The *Clipper* would then taxi to its Port Washington berth.

Fred fetched his suitcases. He heard a motorboat draw up outside, then footsteps on the sea-wing and a knock on the door. Fred said goodbye to Salinsky, thanked him again for his help, and asked him to gives his thanks to the rest of the crew, particularly the captain and Ruthie.

The motorboat belonged to the United States Coast Guard. It must have been ordered by the President's staff. Fred felt important, but also embarrassed that so much trouble was being taken for him. Then he realized that it was more likely being taken for the people he had to meet, so they'd be delayed as little as possible. It was a speedy craft, but still took more than thirty minutes to reach a jetty in Flushing Bay, near the end of the runway that Fred had seen from the air. A car was waiting for him and he was sped to the Fair's Administration Building. His watch showed exactly eleven thirty.

Part VI

New York
to
Minneapolis

Edward Bernays, likely taken in the early 1930s.

TWENTY-NINE

Double Nephew

At the New York World's Fair, Sunday June 4, 1939

C alvin Cooper was waiting in the lobby of the World Fair's Administration Building. With barely a greeting he said, "You can leave your cases at the desk and retrieve them before nine this evening. Please come with me." Fred left his suitcases and followed him to a small room just off the lobby. Cooper said, "I'm sorry to be in a rush. There's an event in Washington this afternoon that I must attend. Please let me know your answers to the questions I posed."

"I wrote them out on the plane. They had to be in pencil, but I've tried to write as clearly as possible." Fred gave him the twelve pages torn from his notebook.

"I didn't expect a written report. I'm glad to have one as it will save time now. I'll read what you've written with care and convey the gist of it to the President and, if he asks, to Mr. James Roosevelt. Mr. Roosevelt was going to be here to meet you. When I told him yesterday about your delay he said he couldn't stay so late."

"Before I go," Cooper continued, "I must remind you that you and your wife are under oath to reveal nothing of the connection of President Roosevelt or his representatives to your recent trip, on pain of imprisonment. Soon after returning to your wife, you should both resolve never to mention this trip again, nor provide any indication that the trip was made. You'd be wise to tell her as little about the trip as you can get away with."

Fred's discomfort at this warning was quickly overwhelmed by the realization that he'd hardly thought about Yvonne or Julie since he left England, not even when Ruthie had been talking about marriage and children. He wanted very much to see his wife and daughter. He said, "Thanks for the cautionary reminder. Would it be possible to make a long-distance call just now?"

"Yes. I'll fix that on my way out. I've one more thing to say. Knowing your interest in Sigmund Freud, we've arranged that you have lunch here as the guest of his American nephew, Edward Bernays. Mr. Bernays played a part in getting the World's Fair going and knows it well. He may have time to show you around this afternoon. Please meet him in this building's restaurant at noon. He knows you're doing some work for us, but not that it was in connection with the trip you've just made. The only thing he knows about the trip is that you met his uncle. He doesn't know exactly when you met him, or anything else about the trip except that it was recent, during the last month or so. He'll be discrete, but you should be careful to say no more to him than you have to. Let's go to the front desk."

Fred followed Cooper to the reception desk, where the telephone call was arranged. Cooper said, "Goodbye and good luck," and went quickly through the front door. Fred followed him and saw him run down the steps and enter a waiting limousine.

At the desk, Fred was asked for the number to be called. He was directed to a small kiosk containing only a seat and a large shelf supporting a phone, a pad and a pencil. After a few minutes, the phone rang. It was the building's switchboard operator explaining that no one had answered at the number he had given. Would he like to try another number? Fred gave his home number. No one picked up the phone there either.

Fred wondered what to make of the upcoming encounter with Bernays. The name rang a bell, not for the link with Freud but for another reason that he couldn't pin down. What might be the purpose of the lunch? Could it be no more than the White House people telling him they knew about his visit with Freud? But Fred already had little doubt that they knew. Would Bernays be checking up on him, seeing if he would be indiscrete? Fred hadn't told the Freuds he'd be seeing Wittgenstein. He wouldn't mention Wittgenstein to Bernays – or any other specifics of his trip apart from a few of those concerning the Freuds.

At the restaurant, Fred asked for the table for two in Edward Bernays' name. Bernays was already there and rose to shake hands. He had a strong grip for a small man. Shortness seemed to be a trait of the Freud family but Fred couldn't readily see another resemblance. Bernays had the appearance of a man who had been thin and wiry but had gained weight. Fred guessed from his face and neck that he was in his mid-forties, but his hair and mustache were quite black. Perhaps they were dyed. He had a middle-European look about him, but his manner and speech were American.

"I was pleased when Calvin Cooper offered the opportunity to meet you," Bernays said. "He said that you recently met my uncle Professor Freud. I'm always delighted to have news about him and his family."

Fred realized he shouldn't reveal that he'd seen Freud only five days earlier, which would beg the question as to how he'd reached New York so quickly. He said, "I saw him at his home in London last month, and his daughter Anna. How are you related to them?"

"Quite strongly. He's my uncle in two ways. My mother is his sister Anna and my father is his wife's brother Eli. Siblings married each other."

Fred remembered the Lisbon brothers who were married to sisters. "What, then, is the relationship between you and Miss Anna Freud? Please forgive my impertinence but it must be closer than cousins usually are, perhaps as close as siblings?"

"The geneticists say that double first cousins, such as Anna and I are, have the same degree of consanguinity as half-siblings. Don't ask me for the logic of this. It involves some complicated math and the result is not intuitive. Anna and I share four grandparents, as siblings do. Half-siblings share only two grandparents, as regular first cousins do. Thus, we should be more like siblings than half-siblings, but apparently we are not."

"How do you and Miss Freud get on?" Fred asked. "Is your relationship like that of siblings or cousins?"

"We were reared apart, of course, she in Vienna and I in New York. I've lived here since I was one year old. We've seen each other often over the years, in spite of the ocean between us. We get on well. Cousins often like each other more than siblings do. How is she?" Bernays had become slightly flushed. His dark but pallid skin, accentuated by his jet-black hair and mustache, now featured a blotch of red on each cheek.

Fred wondered if Bernays' relationship with Anna was the cause of the flushing. Or was it more a by-product of the man's animated manner of speaking? He said, "She seemed in good spirits, although concerned about her father's condition. I had the good fortune to accompany her to a concert, at her father's request."

"I am envious. And how is my uncle?"

Fred replied, "He doesn't seem physically well, although I must say that intellectually he may have lost little of his sparkle. I met him for the first time last month and can only guess how he was before." While replying, he realized that Bernays' eyes were similar to Sigmund

Freud's. They were grayish blue and searching, the most expressive part of his face. Fred remembered too that Anna Freud had deep-brown eyes, her most appealing feature. He also noticed a difference between the uncle and nephew: Freud, even near death, was neatly dressed in well-cared-for clothes, albeit of an old-fashioned style. Bernays wore an ill-fitting more modern suit sorely in need of a dry-cleaner's attention.

Bernays said, "I do hope to see him before it's too late. May I ask what you and my uncle talked about?"

"Of course you may. Anna – which she allowed me to call her – was also curious. Professor Freud and I spoke of many things during our two encounters. During the first, the most time was spent on two books he was working on, especially one on President Woodrow Wilson written with William Bullitt. You may have heard of him. He is our ambassador to France."

Bernays said, "Did I hear you correctly: a book on Wilson written with Bullitt? Are you sure? My uncle is fond of making jokes."

"I'm quite sure. To be accurate, I should say that your uncle regards the book on Wilson as completed. However, the two authors have agreed it will not be published until after the death of the second Mrs. Wilson." He paused, and then said, "On reflection, I should not have mentioned this book and I ask you not to mention it again."

"Well, I'm astonished. Does Anna know about this book?"

A waiter asked for their orders. Bernays ordered a heavy lunch. It included an appetizer of stuffed shrimps, followed by lentil soup and steak and potatoes. Fred could see why he may have put on weight. Fred asked for the soup and the fish dish. Bernays suggested they have wine. He would like red wine and Fred might like white, so perhaps they should each have a half bottle. Fred demurred, saying he rarely drank alcohol at lunch.

Bernays asked again, "Does Anna know about the book?"

"She seems to have had only an inkling of it until I mentioned it. I now believe I shouldn't have told her. I may have caused a problem between father and daughter. That is another reason for you not to mention it again. Anna did tell me an interesting fact about the relationship between her father and Ambassador Bullitt. She said that Bullitt is the only person who may address him as 'Freud' rather than as 'Professor Freud' or 'Professor,' which is what other non-family members call him."

"I didn't know that surprising fact. I knew that Bullitt and my uncle were acquainted, and were even friends. I didn't know they had been collaborators. Ambassador Bullitt was helpful last year during the relocation of my uncle's household from Vienna to London. I wanted them to come here, but my uncle does not like this country and so that was not possible."

"Let me say quickly," Bernays continued, "I'm astonished in part because Bullitt and I participated in the American delegation at the peace conference in Paris in 1919, led by President Wilson. I had a role in the explanation of the American position. I resigned when the position became impossible to explain. Bullitt worked directly for the President. He resigned because of Wilson's acquiescence to the unjust and destructive *Treaty of Versailles*. Bullitt was also concerned about the way Russia was being treated. I remember his increasingly prescient statement that Wilson was giving the suffering peoples of the world a new century of war." He paused, and then asked abruptly, "What is this book about?"

"I know only what your uncle told me," Fred said, regretting again that he had mentioned the book. "He described it as a psychological study of President Wilson."

"Why would they write about him?"

"Your uncle said he was interested in a historical figure who had personality defects that contributed to the mess Europe is in now and that demanded explanation."

"Why write the book with Bullitt? My uncle has almost always been the sole author of his work."

"Bullitt knew Wilson personally, which your uncle did not. Bullitt seems to have had had a strong interest in psychoanalysis. He was prepared to do most of the research for the book. I should add that there's another, possibly trivial reason for your uncle's interest in President Wilson."

Bernays seemed not to have heard Fred's last sentence. He said, "I suspect it was a way for Bullitt to work off his anger about Wilson's performance in Paris. Is the book in English or German?"

"English, although your uncle said Ambassador Bullitt speaks and writes good German."

"Bullitt wrote it, to be sure. But my uncle is a co-author not just an adviser?"

"Professor Freud told me he was the first-named author of the book. Both authors have signed each of the book's chapters to indicate their agreement with the contents."

"You mentioned another reason for my uncle's interest."

"It was that he and Wilson were born in the same year."

Bernays snorted. "That's preposterous! As it happens, I know that Bullitt and I were born in the same year. I've not written a book about him, nor he about me."

Fred said, "Could we change the subject? I've been interrogated enough about an unpublished book I know little about. Your name is familiar to me and I can't pin down why. Could you help me?"

"I do apologize. I should have restrained my surprise on learning about the book. As to how you may know my name: I understand you are a psychology professor. Perhaps you have seen some of my books and academic articles? The most recent article is in the *Annals of the American Academy of Political Science*. Its title is 'Molding public opinion.'"

"So you are a professor too?"

"I do teach at universities, but I'm what's called a public relations counselor. I provide advice about public relations."

"You tell businesses how to advertise their products?"

"That's part of it, but I do more. I try to change people's circumstances so that more of them become potential customers. If that's not clear to you I can elaborate. I also represent people and businesses when things need to be explained and when they need to achieve something that's not as simple as an increase in sales."

"I'm not sure what you mean by any of this."

"Let me illustrate the second point first using the case of my uncle. I've been representing his interests here for many years. Some of this involves helping with the translation and sale of his books, which have provided him with essential income. Other things I do for him are more subtle. For example, later this month a team from *Time* magazine is to interview him in London for a cover article. I'm playing a part in moving that along."

Bernays had been doing most of the talking. He'd also been doing most of the eating. He'd almost finished his three courses while Fred was only part way into his second.

"You've helped me remember how your name is familiar. Just before I left Harvard for the University of Minnesota, a geology professor there, Kirtley Mather, asked me to subscribe to the bulletin of an organization he was getting going, the Institute for Propaganda Analysis." Bernays grimaced at the mention of Mather's name, and again when the Institute was mentioned. Fred continued, "I subscribed and have enjoyed reading it when it comes in the mail every month. The bulletins paint you as the Institute's archenemy. I read that your battles with the Institute have been notorious enough to have reached the pages of the *New York Times* and *Time*. Your mention of *Time* alerted me.

And I may have heard of you elsewhere."

"I'm not sure I've met Professor Mather, but the Institute – in the form of Mr. Clyde Miller – and I have had our differences. He believes that propaganda is undemocratic. I believe that effective public education is essential for the good functioning of democracy."

"But surely propaganda and public education mean different things? The first involves lying and the second should not."

"A decade or so ago, I wrote a book with the title *Propaganda*. I defined its subject as a consistent, enduring effort to create or shape events to influence the relations of a public to an enterprise, idea, or group. In an earlier book, *Crystallizing Public Opinion*, I'd written that the only difference between propaganda and public education is the point of view. I added that we tend to believe public education, but not propaganda."

"That's a cynical way of stating the difference," said Fred. "Surely the difference is whether the advocate is telling the truth?"

"Truth like beauty is in the eye of the beholder," said Bernays. "I don't remember where that comes from."

"I could agree that truth and meaning are what people agree on, and beauty is to some degree too. But surely the essence of what we mean by propaganda is the manipulation of public opinion for private or nefarious ends?"

"In the Great War, I was involved in the work of the Committee on Public Information, the first use of propaganda by our government. We sought to build morale in America, undermine morale in our enemies, and win over neutral countries. Our cause was good. We weren't in the business of serving private or nefarious ends."

"You've made a good point," said Fred. "I must think more about why I don't like propaganda. Could I go back to something you said earlier that I didn't fully understand? You spoke about changing people's circumstances so that more of them become potential customers.

Could that not be described as nefarious activity on the part of a business?"

Fred had now finished his fish dish. The waiter cleared their plates and asked if they would like desserts. Bernays asked for apple pie and ice cream, and coffee. Fred settled for coffee only.

"Nefarious activity?" Bernays replied. "What I was trying to explain was how I go about responding to a client's needs. I analyze the situation carefully to find ways in which the client's product can be made more appealing. This goes beyond simply shouting out the name of the product through advertising."

He continued, "Let me give you an example. A decade ago I was asked to help increase consumption of the bacon produced by the Beech-Nut Packing Company. I could have suggested the development of clever advertising that urged people to eat more of this particular brand of bacon. What I found was that during the previous twenty years Americans had come to make do with smaller breakfasts. This was not a good thing according to some members of the medical community. I drew the change in eating habits to the attention of physicians across America. They began recommending that Americans eat heartier breakfasts again. Sales of all brands of bacon increased. I had changed Americans' circumstances so that more of them became customers of my client."

"What if the physicians' advice wasn't sound?"

"I can't comment on that. I went with the best medical advice."

"Smoking cigarettes appears to be harmful to health," said Fred, "and yet physicians can be found who endorse smoking one brand over another."

"Sometimes things are complicated. I was asked to make it more possible for women to smoke in public. I'm an enemy of smoking. My wife smokes and I hate that she does it. I'm also an enemy of social practices that keep women down. The taboo against women smoking in the street was such a social practice. I weighed two evils. I favored the lesser of the two, and helped make women's smoking in public socially acceptable. Let me say too I'm proud that my wife was the first married woman in America to have her passport issued in her maiden name, the name she regularly uses." Bernays ice cream was melting. He attacked his apple pie with enthusiasm.

Fred reflected that Bernays probably went along with whatever satisfied the commercial interest. Tobacco companies are willing to pay for more sales. Physicians won't pay for fewer patients, although insurance companies might. Fred wondered what he could learn from Bernays about controlling behavior. He asked, "How would you summarize your approach toward changing people's behavior?"

There was a pause while Bernays spooned up the last morsels of pie and ice cream. "That was good," he said. "I see myself as an engineer. I'm not your usual engineer of materials, nor an engineer of opinion. I'm an engineer of consent."

"Engineers seek control over their materials," said Fred. "They design and manufacture a bridge that will work reliably for a hundred years. What are you trying to control?"

"Behavior, mass behavior, the behavior of large numbers of people. But I've moved away from the idea of control, and the goal of controlling behavior. I prefer to talk about persuading or suggesting rather than controlling. I use words such as attitudes, opinions, consent and support rather than the rather bleak word behavior."

"You don't have to be shy with me about controlling behavior," said Fred. "I too am in the business of understanding behavior, mostly individual behavior. In science, the best evidence of understanding is control – more precisely, accurate identification of a phenomenon's controlling variables. I'm trying to refashion psychology as a science of behavior."

"We can't control behavior in a democracy. That can happen only in dictatorships. In a democracy, we must persuade people, not control them."

"What's the difference?" Fred asked. "If you are a skilled engineer of consent, surely you seek to have as much control over your material as a civil engineer who is designing a bridge over a river? You seek one-hundred-percent reliability of effect."

"I doubt that such reliability could ever be achieved in the engineering of consent, even in a dictatorship. But there's a bigger challenge. In a democracy, there can be, and often should be, competing points of view. This means there can be rival engineers of consent. Opinions are fought over. Engineers do not fight over how their materials are to be transformed."

"They can do. There are competitions for the design of bridges."

"Not a good analogy," said Bernays. "Competition stops once bridge construction is started, but the molding of public opinion goes on and on."

"We haven't talked enough about what's wrong with propaganda. I suggested before that the defining feature of propaganda is that it involves lying, but I'm now not sure that is correct. The defining feature may be that it overwhelms with one point of view – often by exploiting emotional reactions – and doesn't admit to others."

Fred continued, "Targeted behavior may be brought under control through propaganda. But there can be a cost. The people, citizens, whose behavior is the target of propaganda may be less able to deal with complex situations. They have not been exposed to enough complexity and thus have had little experience of dealing with it. Propaganda may make it impossible to move towards a society that can do without propaganda."

"You've given me food for thought," said Bernays, "and I'd like to know more about your work. And about your trip to London. But I think we should leave now. Mr. Cooper asked that I show you some of the World's Fair. I have a few hours. By four, I must catch a train back to Manhattan to get ready for an engagement this evening."

As they stood to leave the restaurant, Fred asked how the meal was being paid for. Bernays said the check would be sent to his office and he'd take care of it. On their way out, Bernays stopped at three tables and chatted briefly with people there. He didn't introduce Fred who, each time, stood uncomfortably in the background. At the first two tables, Fred could find little more to do than figure out who Bernays might be talking to and who else might be at the table where Bernays had stopped and at other tables.

While waiting for Bernays for the third time, Fred found himself facing the restaurant's large bay window. To the right, through rain and across a busy road, he could see railroad trains on display, evidently part of the Fair. One of them was the *Coronation Scot,* the train in which he'd traveled several days ago from Glasgow to London, or its twin. A few dozen people, some with open umbrellas, were waiting to climb the temporary stairway giving access to the train's first car. As he watched, the rain stopped and the umbrellas were closed.

Bernays interrupted Fred's reverie and ushered him through a door in the glass bay. They then crossed a bridge over the road. Fred hoped they would go right, toward the *Coronation Scot,* but they headed to the building on the left. Bernays walked surprisingly quickly for a short stoutish man.

Spectators in moving chairs traveled a third of a mile while viewing the huge Futurama model. Here they were near the end of the tour, looking at the "City of the Future," the 1960 metropolis designed around the automobile.

THIRTY

Futurama and Democracity

At the New York World's Fair, Sunday June 4, 1939

B ernays said their first visit should be to the nearby General Motors pavilion, the Fair's most popular exhibit. He pointed to the long lines waiting to enter the pavilion and said he had a pass that allowed him to avoid waiting. He and his wife had been involved in developing the theme for the Fair. The pass was acknowledgement of their work.

They went to a door marked "Officials Only" at a level below the heads of the long lines that snaked up curving ramps to a high point in the futuristic building. Several people in the lines were wet from the rain, but seemed happy to be near their entrances. Bernays showed his pass to a guard who waved them through the door. Inside they took an elevator to a level where they joined regular visitors walking down a dimly lit ramp that turned into a large space dominated by a massive map.

The map floated above them as if suspended in an evening sky. The ramp continued gently downward in two long zig-zags, allowing visitors an extended view of the floating map. A soft intimate voice explained the map, which changed as they looked. It showed America's road traffic problems now: "today's traffic is moving on roadways designed for yesterday." It then showed how the problems would worsen by 1960, when "motor traffic on some of our main highways could increase by as much as one hundred percent." Then, green lines showed a network of "express motorways" that would relieve the congestion.

At the bottom of the ramp, visitors stepped on to a moving platform and into double-seated chairs. The chairs, said the voice, "will transport you into 1960." They were plush and comfortable, with high wings. The chair carrying Fred and Bernays moved slowly behind others into a short rising tunnel, turned a corner, and emerged above an enormous model – Futurama – that continued far into the distance.

The intimate, now more authoritative voice came from within the back of the chair. A commentary began on what they passed over, "Come tour the future with General Motors! A transcontinental flight over America in 1960. What will we see? What changes will transpire? … Since the beginning of civilization transportation and communication have been keys to Man's progress, his prosperity, his happiness. … Here we see one of our 1960 express motorways. …"

Fred realized that each chair must have its own commentary specific to the chair's position, a remarkable feat of presentation. He saw the purpose of the chair's wings, to direct his view to the particular part of the model described by the commentary. He saw how the visitors had been prepared for Futurama. The initial downward ramp allowed dark adaptation that enhanced the map experience. The map conveyed the exhibit's message: America needs a massive network of express motorways.

It was a similar strategy to what Bernays had described for the marketing of bacon. General Motors was not merely shouting out the message "buy our cars." The company sought to create conditions that facilitated, even stimulated the purchase of more automobiles.

Bernays seemed entranced. He may have seen it before and still be entranced.

The model was alive through changes in lighting and movements of clouds and aircraft. More than anything, it featured automobiles and trucks moving along a variety of roadways. The express motorways were the model's most conspicuous feature. The busiest had as many as fourteen lanes of traffic. Each lane had a designated speed, ranging from fifty to one hundred miles an hour. Vehicles joined and left the express motorways with ease. Through skillfully designed ramps, vehicles transferred safely between the motorways. "Automatic radio control" kept vehicles at safe distances from each other.

The vast model was a masterpiece of detail. It comprised hundreds of thousands if not millions of pieces: people, animals, trees, buildings and, above all, road, roads, and more roads. Many moving elements added to Futurama's powerful realism and vitality. Among them were moving tails of cows, a man throwing food to chickens, spray from a waterfall and shadows of flying aircraft on the ground.

For ten minutes visitors moved slowly across a mixed landscape of fields, woods, hills and rivers, viewed from the moving chairs as if from a low-flying aircraft. Then they tracked a motorway across a large suspension bridge into a city of two parts: the city of 1940 and the city of 1960. The latter mostly comprised skyscrapers along roads used only by vehicles. Sidewalks and storefronts were at a level above the road. Land uses – residential, commercial, industrial – were separated. Pedestrians and vehicles were separated. The voice said that instead of the city of 1940's "outmoded business sections and undesirable slum areas" the city of 1960 has "abundant sunshine, fresh air, fine green parkways, recreational and civic centers – all the results of thoughtful planning and design."

The end of the ride was spectacular. The voice had urged focus on a particular intersection in the model of the 1960 city. There, signal-controlled traffic moved well at ground level and pedestrians moved easily along walkways at the level above. "On the four corners," said the voice, "are an auditorium, a department store, and apartment house, and an automobile display salon." As Fred and Bernays left their seats they found themselves to be part of a life-sized representation of the same intersection, walking along the upper level. There were real vehicles in the street below. All were the latest General Motors' vehicles. They – and the vehicles in the automobile display salon – were the latest for 1939 and not for twenty-one years ahead.

"Wasn't that amazing?" said Bernays. "That was the third time I've see it, and I'm still amazed." They sat on a low wall outside the pavilion to gather their thoughts and plan the rest of their tour.

"It's not what I expected," said Fred. "I expected promotion of today's products – and there was some of that at the end – rather than a blatant political message. The exhibit must have cost a fortune. I expect General Motors wants these roads quite badly."

"It did cost a lot – more than seven million, I'm told – and GM does want more roads. But are you sure that was the main message? I think what this exhibit does is tell Americans that private business can provide for a prosperous future with lots of good jobs."

"Don't we know that already?" said Fred.

"Not enough. Our president and his New Deal are basically pro-government and anti-business. Unions are strong and also anti-business. State direction of business elsewhere – whether by communists in Russia or fascists in Germany – is gaining popularity. We see it more, even here."

"I'm confused. You seem strongly on the side of business and against our government. Yet I believe I heard Calvin Cooper say that you may be working for the president."

"We're in discussion. The president may need public relations advice. With my experience of business, I could help him."

"Another confusing thing," said Fred, "is that the anti-government message that you read into the GM exhibit is actually a plea for government to spend a lot of money building more roads so GM can sell more cars. To add to the paradox, aren't the express motorways GM wants already a feature of Nazi Germany, where – as you said – government directs business?"

"These are nice paradoxes," said Bernays. "They hadn't occurred to me. They'll have a place in any advice I give the president."

"I hope you remember where the thought came from and remind me to send you a bill."

"I've read that the Nazis have built a couple of thousand miles of their *Autobahnen*," said Bernays, "but that there are very few automobiles on them. Hitler is reputed to be a car fanatic – and has even inspired and contributed to the design of a *Volkswagen*, a people's car – but I think the *Autobahnen* are mainly for military use."

"Maybe GM should get together with the U.S. Army," Fred retorted. "If the coming war is to be a clash of civilizations, we should build on what the voice in our chair said: that the highways of a nation set the pace for advancing civilization." He wondered how Bernays would respond to the irony of war as progress.

Bernays appeared to have not heard. He stood and said, "We should plan how we spend the next hour or so. I'd like to take you to see another view of the future. It's known as Democracity. My wife came up with that name. It's in the Perisphere. You must know which building that is. We've time to fit in one stop on the way. We could go and see another automaker's display. Ford's and Chrysler's exhibits are close. Or we could see something else. Let me suggest the Westinghouse exhibit, a testimonial to our electrical future."

"I'm in your hands. I'm enjoying the Fair and your company. Let's hope the rain doesn't come back."

There was only a short line for the Westinghouse pavilion but Bernays used his pass to gain access at an "Officials Only" entrance. First, they examined the "time capsule" exhibit in the foyer. The capsule was a long copper-alloy long tube buried fifty feet down in front of the pavilion. It was designed to last five thousand years and to illustrate human life in 1939 to the people of 6939. The exhibit showed copies of the items including in the capsule. One was a newsreel featuring Jesse Owens winning the hundred-meter dash at the 1936 Berlin Olympics. Other items included several Westinghouse products as well as eleven hundred feet of microfilm containing ten million words and a thousand photos.

To help the people of 6939 find and use the capsule, details of its location and contents were noted in a fifty-two-page *Book of Record of the Time Capsule*. The *Book* was written in English as were almost all the microfilmed documents. It included a key to English: its sounds in relation to human anatomy and its grammar. Westinghouse had sent copies to several hundred institutions around the world.

Fred read the display of the opening text of the *Book of Record*: "… In our day it is difficult to conceive of a future less happy, less civilized than our own. Yet history teaches us that every culture passes through definite cycles of development, climax, and decay. … there will rise again a civilization of even vaster promise standing on our shoulders … The learned among that culture of the future may study with pleasure and profit things now in existence which are unique to our time … ." He wondered whether we would understand people of five thousand years ago better if they'd left a time capsule.

He wondered too whether any humans would be alive in 6939. If there were, how would they have changed, physically and culturally? What would they think of the pessimism of 1939, as expressed at the beginning of the *Book of Record*? Fred skimmed through a copy of the *Book*. The acknowledgements were all of men. The only mention of women was embarrassing: "Believing, as have the people of each age, that our women are the most beautiful, most intelligent, and best groomed of all the ages, we have enclosed in the Time Capsule specimens of modern cosmetics, and one of the singular clothing creations of our time, a woman's hat." Noted scientific achievements by 1939 included charting "the slow evolution of primal protoplasm into man.

There was no mention of natural selection or any other mechanism of evolution. If humans had become extinct or extinguished by 6939, what in the way of life forms would be left?

Bernays had already moved into the Hall of Electrical Living. He was gazing at a wall display showing the progress of housewives' chores through history. They ranged from the drudgery of previous centuries to the current freedom achieved through use of electrical appliances. Fred was about to interrupt him when a loud voice announced the next session with "Elektro, the Westinghouse Moto-man." Fred and Bernays joined the crowd around a small stage at the side of the hall. Elektro, a seven-foot metal humanoid, walked to the middle of the stage. In motion, Elektro sounded like one of Westinghouse's vacuum cleaners exhibited elsewhere in the hall. The humanoid was asked to tell his story, which he did in a sassy manner. He described his brain as being similar to a telephone switchboard and expressed interest in the women in the audience. Elektro showed that he could count, smoke, and even walk backward on command.

Fred remembered his discussions with Alan Turing in Cambridge, notably Turing's views that humans were machines, and that a properly designed machine could perform any intellectual feat of which a human is capable. Fred agreed in general with both points, but doubted whether such a properly designed machine could ever be realized. Elektro raised the question as to how much the properly designed machine had to look like a human. If the test was only of intellectual ability rather than, say, manual dexterity, its appearance wouldn't matter.

Bernays said, "I wonder if Westinghouse is going to come up with Elektra the all-purpose maid? Shall we go and find the demonstration of television. In 1936, I worked on television matters with James Skinner, head of Philco. Skinner lost his enthusiasm for the medium. I nevertheless thought that, with further development, it might become a major vehicle for advertising and public education. But I'm out of touch with developments."

"I saw television in Britain. It's been put out by the BBC for a few years. It wasn't very impressive."

"You mean there are actual television shows there, like we have radio shows here?"

"Yes. At my hotel I saw a live performance of a play, broadcast from a theatre. The sound was good but the small fuzzy picture was almost unwatchable." Fred cautioned himself not to reveal too much about his trip.

"I didn't know the Brits were so far advanced. I must look into that. I've heard that RCA has been broadcasting test television shows from the Empire State Building, but I haven't seen one."

At the demonstration, after a short wait, Bernays was invited to stand in front of the camera – about the size of a kitchen stove – and speak into a microphone. Fred saw the animated performance on a screen in another room. Bernays presented himself well. It was a much better picture than at the Euston Hotel. Fred imagined that a good picture was easier to achieve when the transmission was across a distance of a few tens of feet rather than several miles, and by a cable rather than over the air.

"We should move on," Bernays said when he had seen Fred perform in front of the camera. "I'd like to show you one more exhibit: Democracity, in the Perisphere."

As they walked past the Production and Distribution Zone, the buildings' geometric shapes and streamlining motifs reminded Fred of Du Cane Court, built in what Mabel Miller had described as Art Deco style. He wondered what had happened to her, feeling a twinge of guilt about the way he had left her and another twinge as to her possible fate and that of her grandparents.

"A penny for your thoughts?" said Bernays, walking quickly as before.

"I'm thinking about today's new experiences and also the architecture around us."

"What has impressed you the most so far?"

"Futurama. It was an extraordinary presentation. Whoever designed it is a genius. I didn't care much for the vision that was portrayed, but that may have been specified by General Motors."

"It was conceived and designed by Norman Bel Geddes," said Bernays. "He started out as a theatre designer, then turned to industrial design – radio cabinets and the like – and then to major presentations such as Futurama. I know him and his wife. I expect we'll see them this evening. Their married names are a composite of their names before marriage. He was originally Norman Geddes. She was Helen Belle Schneider"

Fred said, "I suppose that's an alternative to what you and your wife have done, one that also retains at least part of the wife's original name."

Bernays continued as though Fred had not interjected. "Futurama was his idea. A version of it was first proposed to the Goodyear Tire people as their Fair exhibit on highways of the future. General Motors was going to show a Chevrolet assembly line. When Goodyear decided not to participate in the Fair, Bel Geddes somehow persuaded GM to junk the assembly line and do something adventurous. The support of the chairman of the GM board was decisive; he wanted to use Futurama as an anti-Roosevelt, anti-New-Deal weapon."

Fred wondered again at the complexity of political maneuvers. He wondered whether his kind of analysis, focusing on variation and selection of behavior, could ever rise to accommodating such maneuvers let alone explaining them.

Bernays said, "In my family, there's been a more extreme case of assertion of the wife's name on marriage. When Murray Cohen married my sister Hella, he took her name. I forget why. It was confusing while he was part of the family. People thought he was my brother rather than my brother-in-law even though he looked nothing like me. He and Hella divorced years ago, but I've heard he continues to go by Murray Bernays. Of course, as I am a double nephew of Sigmund Freud, my two sisters are my uncle's double nieces."

They had reached the Perisphere. This time there was a long line. The speedy access with Bernays' pass was useful. Bernays said they also avoided paying the Perisphere's twenty-cent entrance fee, the only such charge at the Fair. As they walked up to the viewing gallery, he told Fred again that his wife had provided the name and the concept for the Democracity exhibit. They stood on one of two moving galleries that circled the model. It was a vision for an urban region in 2039. The region was about sixty miles across and had a population of about a million and a half. There was a commercial-institutional core known as Centerton where few people lived. The region's residents lived in two kinds of suburb. There were forty or so residential towns of ten thousand known as Pleasantvilles. There were also thirty or so industrial towns known as Millvilles, each with a population of about twenty-five thousand.

As a vision of the future, Democracity was less accomplished and less ambitious than Futurama. Fred nevertheless found it more engaging if only because the pitch for more roads was less blatant. Why should softer pressure be more acceptable than strident messages? Fred was uncertain. He chalked up the experience as yet another behavioral mystery to be explained.

When they were outside, he asked Bernays which he liked more, Democracity or Futurama? He then realized that Bernays' wife's involvement would color any answer, which it likely did. Fred skimmed through the Democracity booklet, noticing numerous typographical errors. Democracity seemed to be the institutional vision; it could even be the government's vision of America's future. It was less polished than the private-enterprise vision. He asked Bernays about the origin and purpose of Democracity, and the extent to which government was involved.

Bernays replied that Democracity reflected the Fair's theme. The Fair was the brainchild of a group of New York businessmen. Government was involved chiefly by providing the site: a massive ash dump to be turned into a park at the Fair's end. President Roosevelt had declared the Fair open on April the thirtieth, the one-hundred-and-fiftieth anniversary of George Washington's first inauguration.

"About a year ago," continued Bernays, "I was asked to make a presentation on the theme of the proposed Fair. It already had a theme: Building the World of Tomorrow. I recommended that democracy be the Fair's dominating motif. This led to the use of my wife's suggestion – Democracity – as the name for the model of the city of the future being designed for the Perisphere, which we've just seen. It also led to the muddled argument in the Democracity booklet that the world of tomorrow can only be built through the interdependent cooperation of men and nations."

Fred began to speak but Bernays spoke over him. "I must go now, but first I want to call in at the Jewish Palestine pavilion. It's on the way to the Fair's subway station. Like my uncle, I'm Jewish by culture and not by belief. Shall we part now, or at that pavilion?"

Fred was curious about the pavilion. "I'd be pleased to come with you. What interests you there?"

"Most immediately, they may have the latest news about the fate of the *St. Louis*. This is a ship carrying nine hundred Jewish refugees from Germany. They've been denied entry into Cuba, even though it had been promised. The ship is presently off the coast of Florida. A cousin on my father's side and her family are among the refugees."

They were walking quickly again, now into the Community Interests Zone of the Fair. They passed the YMCA's social center and the House of Jewels, a display of diamonds and other stones. "I can understand your concern," said Fred. "Tell me, what is the purpose of the Jewish Palestine pavilion?"

"It's a step towards the creation of a Jewish state. It portrays the accomplishments of Jewish settlers in Palestine, the Jews' Holy Land and ancient homeland. Beyond making a small financial contribution, I had no part in the development of the pavilion. I'm interested in how it's being received at the Fair."

"Do you support the creation of a Jewish state?"

"That's a difficult question to answer. I'm in two or more minds on this. Ideally I'd like Jews to be accepted everywhere. A Jewish state could be a reason to withhold acceptance of Jews elsewhere. On the other hand, given what is happening in Europe, and the almost world-wide resistance to accepting Jewish refugees, perhaps Jews need a place of their own to go. And having their own state could give Jews more status in the world."

"Whether the state should be a part of Palestine is another matter," Bernays continued. "Carving out a Jewish state from land mostly oc-cupied by Arabs would be a prescription for eternal trouble. The Brit-ish realize this. They formally control Palestine. Just two weeks ago their parliament confirmed Britain's World War pledge to foster the creation of a Jewish *national home* in Palestine, but not, it would ap-pear a Jewish state. The national home would be within a Palestinian state in which Arabs would remain in the majority."

Fred remembered something. He asked, "What do you think of the plan from within the federal government to open up Alaska to Jewish settlement?" Fred had had an interest in this proposal for an unrelated reason. It had been made by Harold Ickes, Secretary of the Interior and brother of the first wife of John B. Watson, known as "the father of behaviorism." The circumstances of the divorce, and Watson's dismis-sal from Johns Hopkins University, had made for the most salacious academic scandal of the century. Gossip about it, including Ickes' pos-sible orchestration of it, still reverberated around the halls of academia.

Bernays' replied, "I supported Ickes' plan at the time as being bet-ter than keeping refugees out. The American Jewish Congress opposed it – I don't know why – and it died. I was too busy last year to do much about it."

They arrived at the handsome Jewish Palestine pavilion. It was wedged between the pavilion for the Beech-Nut Packing Company – which Fred remembered had been a client of Bernays – and the huge Food North building. The Beech-Nut pavilion was billed as containing a miniature circus with five hundred performers. The Food North building featured "The World's Largest Store" with displays of cookies, ginger ale, junket, and olives, among numerous food items and beverages. The Jewish Palestine pavilion was clearly not part of the Government Zone, where numerous countries had their official pavilions. Inside, Bernays asked Fred to meet him at the entrance in ten minutes if they hadn't met up earlier.

Fred began reading the description of the items in the entrance hall, lined with Palestinian marble and dedicated to those who had lost their lives in the building of a Jewish national home. He read that everything in the pavilion was Palestinian, and wondered if that included even the basic construction materials. He saw that Albert Einstein had dedicated the pavilion just a week earlier. Einstein was just about the only person alive whom Fred unhesitatingly admired. He wished he'd been doing that today. He picked up a copy of the *Palestine Book*, lavishly produced for visitors to the pavilion and others. It was funded by what might have been the highest concentration of advertising he'd seen. Fred was reading President Roosevelt's letter – supporting the establishment of a "Homeland for the Jewish people" – when he heard Bernays beside him saying that he had to leave.

Outside, Fred asked whether Bernays had learned more about the situation of the *St. Louis*. The reply was drowned by an extraordinary noise from above. A huge airplane was passing over. Fred thought it might be a *Clipper* on its way to Manhasset Bay but its profile was more like that of a regular airplane. When it had passed, Bernays said it was probably Douglas's new DC-4, on test in the New York area. This aircraft, with some improvements, could be the first to carry fare-paying passengers non-stop across the United States and even across the Atlantic.

Fred resisted an urge to say something about his recent flying adventure. He resisted another urge to mention the German plane that had already flown between New York and Berlin. Instead he asked whether Bernays liked to fly. Bernays said he had a fear of flying since the death of a close friend in an aircraft crash. He avoided it as much as possible. Fred asked again about the *St. Louis*.

"There's no good news. Talks with the Cuban government have restarted, but I knew that. The *St. Louis* continues to move slowly up and down the Florida coast – sometimes in sight of Miami – perhaps hoping America will relent. But there's no word from the White House. The only response by the government is that a Coast Guard patrol boat is accompanying the *St. Louis* in case any of her passengers attempt suicide or swim for the shore. Also, the chief immigration inspector in Miami has confirmed that the *St. Louis* will not be allowed to dock there or at any American port."

"The way things are going," Bernays continued, "the *St. Louis* will have to return to Germany. Her passengers will go straight to concentrations camps. Now I must leave you. Nice to have met you."

"I do hope you have better news about your relatives. Thanks for the lunch and for your guidance around the Fair."

What an exhausting man thought Fred as Bernays' squat figure disappeared around a corner, and what an interesting mix of interpersonal insensitivity and likely sophistication about mass behavior. As he sat on a planter wall near the entrance to the Jewish Palestine pavilion to take stock, he reflected that Calvin Cooper might have told Bernays not to ask Fred too many questions. Perhaps Bernays had the impression that *his* discretion was being tested by Fred on behalf of the White House.

Fred would have liked to have spent time with Bernays comparing and reconciling their insights about behavior. Bernays' basic strategy seemed to be to create conditions under which desirable behavior would be more likely to occur, as in building more roads and getting physicians to endorse hearty breakfasts. This could reduce the range of likely behavior. But the required behavior – whether buying a particular brand of bacon or a particular manufacturer's automobiles – still needed to be reinforced. The reinforcement could be specific to the product: the taste of bacon or the virtues of an automobile. Or it could be whatever reinforcement arises from following the recommendation of an opinion leader. This begged questions about the nature of such reinforcement and how it might be used.

Bernays had also stimulated Fred's thinking about the role of government. Bernays had said that business, by creating taxable wealth, made government possible. Fred had retorted that perhaps government, by providing infrastructure and order, made business possible. Fred felt his political views were changing. He'd been a conservative with a weak allegiance to the Republican Party, a shadow of his father's strong ties. Now he was somewhat more in support of a government that did things. Was this a result of his trip to Britain? He couldn't figure out how. Indeed, the stronger exposure to the works of extreme government – that of Nazi Germany – could well have had the opposite effect.

Did Fred really favor stronger government? Surely, he felt, the best kind of society was one in which there was as little centralized control as possible. Centralized control was mostly aversive, maintaining order through fines, imprisonment, etc., or the threat of them. Could not society be arranged so that people experienced only positive reinforcement, mostly from parents and peers? Perhaps government would be needed to establish such a utopia. It would become unnecessary as people became free from threats and worse aversive events. This could be the "withering away of the state," to use the well-known words of Marx and Engels. Was he becoming a communist? No, certainly not if communism meant what he understood to be the unsavory system in place in the Soviet Union. Perhaps he was an anarchist, although certainly not of the bomb-throwing kind. Who was the appealing British thinker who advocated the replacement of government through a process of peaceful evolution? Goodwin? Godwin? He should check him out.

How would big things get done without big government? Well, this Fair was a big thing and, if Bernays was correct, it was being done without much input from government. General Motors and Westinghouse were big things, as was Pan Am, and they were not government. But, as he'd said to Bernays, GM needed the government to build roads. And what about the military? As he'd realized often during this trip, these matters were horribly complex. Would explaining them through processes of variation and selection of behavior make them more understandable? At the moment this didn't seem possible. Perhaps it would all become intellectually manageable if he thought and wrote more about them. Darwin was able to improve understanding of the inherited features of all organisms by interpreting them in terms of variation and selection of features by the environment. Perhaps one day he could do the same for the acquired features of organisms, for that part of their behavior that was not inherited.

In the meantime, he'd attend to more particular matters, not only to find an approach toward the complexity of human behavior but also to heed Sigmund Freud's warning that the present might not be a good time to promote analogies with Darwinism. For the moment, human verbal behavior was as big a challenge as he needed.

Fred pulled out his airplane tickets to Minneapolis, provided by Pam Am even though he was to travel by other airlines. His red-eye flight to Chicago was to leave Newark Metropolitan Airport at twenty minutes after midnight. When the airport being built near the Fair was completed passengers wouldn't have to go all the way to New Jersey to catch a plane. The flight was to arrive at Chicago Municipal Airport at five in the morning. He was to catch another flight there at five-thirty. He had to pick up his cases at the Administration Building before nine o'clock. That could fit in well with making his way across Manhattan to Newark Airport in good time for his flight. It was four o'clock now.

446

So he had four to five hours to spend at the Fair, which should include time to eat.

He wondered why Pan Am had not arranged for him to fly home earlier in the day, which could have been possible. Perhaps they wanted to give him a chance to see the Fair or spend time in Manhattan. More likely it was easier or cheaper for them to put him on a red-eye flight. No matter, he would make the best of what was possible for him to do. When Fred Keller moved last year from Colgate University in upstate New York to Manhattan's Columbia University, he'd promised to let him know whenever he'd be in town. But he shouldn't do that now. He'd have to make up a story that could raise unwanted suspicions. He'd do better to make the most of the Fair.

Fred decided to retrace his trip through the national pavilions – America, Canada, Ireland, Britain, and Portugal – with side trips to countries of interest: Germany, Poland, the USSR and possibly Cuba. Bernays had given him a copy of the Fair's *Official Guide*. All these countries had pavilions except Germany. The pavilions were nearby except Cuba's, which was in the Amusement Zone not the Government Zone. What an insult! Maybe worse than putting the Jewish Palestine pavilion in the Community Interests Zone. Germany didn't seem to have a pavilion, although its allies Italy and Japan did, and so did Czecho-Slovakia, which no longer existed as it had been incorporated into Greater Germany. What was the significance in the hyphen in Czecho-Slovakia? He hadn't seen one before. He'd have to ask about that, and about Germany's lack of a pavilion.

Looking west across the 1939 New York World's Fair, with the Manhattan skyline on the horizon. The Trylon and Perisphere are center left. The U.S. Government Building is bottom right, flanked by other national pavilions. To the left of the U.S. pavilion, below and a little to the right of the Trylon and Perisphere, is the U-shaped pavilion of the U.S.S.R., a photo of which is before Chapter 32.

THIRTY-
ONE

Recapitulation

At the New York World's Fair, Sunday June 4, 1939

T he national pavilions Fred had decided to visit were close together and just a short walk away. He began with the American
pavilion, as his almost-finished odyssey had begun in America.
This pavilion, he quickly discovered, consisted mostly of exhibits by
parts of the federal government on their services and accomplishments.
The first exhibit concerned transportation and communications, prepared for a dozen or so departments and agencies. He wondered if this
exhibit would have even a hint of the imagination and flair of Futurama and Democracity. It didn't; nor did any of the other exhibits in
the pavilion. Fred found them dull, of likely interest only to students of
government. Several state governments were exhibiting elsewhere in
this zone. Fred hoped their exhibits would be more interesting. He was
not disposed to find out.

The only animated feature of the federal pavilion was the young
woman at the information desk near the entrance. She seemed in need
of company and so Fred asked her why there was no German pavilion.
She said she wasn't supposed to answer questions about other pavil-

ions. She'd answer if he understood she'd have to change the topic quickly if another visitor or the pavilion manager came by. She had taken a special interest in the matter Fred was asking about. Her German-Jewish family had emigrated from what became part of Poland after the World War, when she was five years old.

The young lady said that, in spite of much local opposition, Germany had been invited to have a pavilion like every other country. Contracts had been signed for the erection of one of the Fair's major exhibits. Germany withdrew a few months later citing financing problems. Then there was a plan to have a locally provided "Freedom Pavilion." It would focus on Germany's past and future, not on the present Germany. The plan lasted only a few days before it was buried in controversy. There were threats from New York's powerful German Bund, which wanted a different exhibit, and from Jewish organizations, which wanted no exhibit at all. The Fair would be a place of very unwelcome conflict.

"Were there controversies about the pavilions of Germany's allies, Italian and Japan?" asked Fred. "I see there's a pavilion for Czecho-Slovakia, which has been taken over by Germany. What about that? And there's now a hyphen in Czecho-Slovakia? Why is that? Sorry for so many questions."

The young lady said she didn't know about the pavilions of Germany's allies, or exactly how the hyphen was added. She did know that Germany had incorporated Czechoslovakia into Greater Germany a few weeks before the Fair opened. The Nazi government had ordered that the pavilion not be used. He might know that New York's Jewish mayor, Fiorello La Guardia, was one of America's most vociferous opponents of the Nazis. The mayor urged several prominent businessmen put up the funds needed to finish the pavilion as far as possible and keep it open throughout the Fair. It opened a month late, just a week ago. It operated under the flag of the Czecho-Slovak republic that existed from the end of the World War until early this year. She believed the hyphen was there because New York's Slovak community wanted it, but she wasn't sure.

"You are impressively well informed," said Fred. May I take you to dinner this evening and tap more of your store of knowledge?"

"Thank you, sir, for your kind words and invitation," she said, blushing in a way that heightened Fred's interest in her. "I must decline. I have to be at this desk until nine o'clock. Then I must rush home to catch up with my sister's birthday party."

"What a pity," said Fred. "You are the best feature of this pavilion." He shook her warm hand and walked out of the almost empty pavilion into the sunlight.

The less monumental Canadian pavilion was nearby. Its focus was on depicting Canadian life and products. This was a more agreeable and interesting goal than illustrating the works of the Canadian government. Fred found two exhibits of particular interest. One was the huge illuminated map of Canada at the rear of the main hall, painted on burnished copper. It was a work of art and information. Fred learned that Canada was the second largest country in the world after the Soviet Union, and had the longest coastline. She was larger than the United States even including Alaska, and yet had less than a tenth of the population. Did this mean government had to be relatively larger in Canada, to hold the vast country together? Or did it mean that Canadians had more need to manage things themselves?

The other thing that caught Fred's attention was a small display on the North American tour of the English king and queen. After three weeks in Canada, they were to enter the United States two days from now and visit the Fair a few days later. He remembered the king smoking an early morning cigarette on their train's viewing platform a few weeks back. This seemed like several months ago. He had not seen the queen. The display seemed more about her than about him. Fred looked around for another source of information about the German and Czecho-Slovakian pavilions, and a potential dinner companion, but saw none.

The Irish pavilion was even duller than the federal government's. It was called the Irish Trade Promotion Pavilion but much of it was a display of pictures by Irish artists. They depicted what seemed to be scenes from the previous century or earlier. The Irish seemed more intent on celebrating the world of yesterday than on contributing to the Fair's theme of "Building the World of Tomorrow." Fred would have like to have seen explanations of Ireland's fraught relationship with Britain and its disposition towards Nazi Germany.

The British pavilion was logically next on Fred's tour, but was some minutes' walk away. The Soviet Union's pavilion was close by, next to that of Czecho-Slovakia, which was also next to Japan's. He decided on quick visits to all three. The Soviet pavilion was U-shaped. Between the U's arms was a spectacular statue of a workman, dominating the pavilion and the area around. It was easily the second highest structure in the Fair after the Trylon. The workman held a red star aloft and stood on a tall plinth of red marble. The marble was billed as being the same as used for Lenin's tomb. At the ends of the U were huge reliefs of Lenin and Stalin, facing each other. Fred now saw something he'd barely noticed before. Statues, carvings, murals and reliefs were everywhere in the Fair.

Inside the pavilion, Fred was intrigued by the full-scale model of part of a Moscow subway station. It was a palatial affair compared with its grimy counterparts in New York. The pavilion was clearly a strong effort by the Soviet government to display the achievements of communism. Fred's passage through it was often held up by the crowds of visitors. The pavilion was evidently one of the big attractions of the fair. He'd like to have spent more time there. He did pause at three remarkable works of art. Two were massive murals, positioned at each end of the route through the exhibit. The other was a map of the huge country mounted at the beginning of the tour. It was fashioned from diamonds, rubies, and other precious stones, and even outshone the copper map of Canada. It showed the locations of industrial development during the government's two five-year plans.

452

At the end of the path through the pavilion, visitors could help themselves from a large collection of booklets. Fred took some: *Across the North Pole to America*, *The Soviet Theatre*, *New People of the Soviet Countryside*, and *Soviet Youth at Work and Play*. He'd read them if he had no company for dinner. He must remember to leave them and other Fair materials behind. Otherwise there could be curiosity as to how and why he had been at the Fair. A sign directed visitors to another Soviet pavilion, the Pavilion of the Arctic. In front of that pavilion, visitors were told, was the Tupolev plane that, in 1937, had been flown non-stop from Moscow over the Arctic to Vancouver in Washington State. The Soviet Union government was treating the Fair very seriously.

Fred walked quickly through the Czecho-Slovak pavilion. He paused only at the exhibit on Zlin, a factory town built by the Bata company, the world's largest shoemaker. It was a workers' utopia as conceived by the Bata family. The Batas' successful industrial techniques appeared to be modeled on those of automaker Henry Ford. Ford and the Batas both recognized the need for contented workers. Ford felt it sufficient to pay them well, when they were working. The Batas did not pay so well but sought to achieve contentment in other ways. These included provision of adequate housing, agreeable factories, and reliable employment.

The Zlin model had been extended to Bata factory towns in several other countries including Canada, England and France. Perhaps this, rather than Futurama, was the corporate counterpart of Democracity. The Batavilles had a strong resemblance to Democracity's Millvilles. Much of the rest of the Czecho-Slovak pavilion was empty, a reminder of the Nazis' efforts to have this recently independent nation unrepresented the Fair.

The Japanese pavilion, modeled after an ancient Shinto shrine, was even more out of tune with the rest of the Fair than the American and Irish pavilions. It was nevertheless popular, perhaps because of the alien culture it portrayed. What Fred really wanted to know was how this small island nation could have defeated both China and Russia around the turn of the century. In the current conflict, Japan seemed to be defeating China again. The exhibits gave no clue.

Two attractive young women in kimonos were answering questions at an information desk. Fred had figured out that China had no pavilion and he asked one of them why. She waited for her colleague to finish with a visitor, consulted her at length, and then replied that he could inquire at the Administration Building. He thought of asking if she would be free for dinner, but did not want to endure another lengthy consultation and a non-committal response.

Fred walked past the huge American flag by the Lagoon of Nations, which sported an impressive fountain display. He saw the British Pavilion by the Lagoon but decided to stretch his legs and keep on walking to the Polish and Portuguese pavilions beyond. Both emphasized the links of their countries with America. The Polish pavilion focused on the contributions of Polish immigrants. The Portuguese pavilion focused on her contribution to early European settlement of the Americas. It suggested that Christopher Columbus might have been of Portuguese birth, and more certainly had a Portuguese wife and children. It suggested too that, a few years after 1492, Portuguese explorers were the first Europeans to remain in what is now the United States. They may have settled near today's Berkley, Massachusetts.

He returned via the Lagoon of Nations to the British pavilion, comprising two linked buildings. The smaller, nearer one housed the displays for Australia, New Zealand and the "British Colonial Empire." This phrase almost turned Fred away from the pavilion, but he persevered. The Colonial Empire display consisted of photos of people enjoying the benefits of colonial administration.

Fred went across the bridge to the larger section of the pavilion, which housed most of the British exhibit. It was a combination of two things. One was what Japan and Ireland had done, focus on history. The other was what the federal government had done, focus on the works of government. The highlight of the historical exhibits was an original copy of the *Magna Carta*, one of four that survived. It was described as a foundation document of both British and American democracies. In reality, it was an agreement forged in 1215 between the king of the day and twenty-five English barons who wanted some of his power. The American link was strengthened by a side display suggesting that George Washington was descended from nine of the English barons.

As Fred moved away from this display of questionable genealogy, he saw Fred Keller standing up after bending to look at the *Magna Carta*. There was no mistaking him. It was *his* genial, impish face, always with a mustache, rarely without a smile. It was *his* hair, rapidly graying even though he was hardly past forty. It was *his* tall trim body with a hint of a military bearing. He was talking in his usual animated manner to his much younger and very pretty second wife Frances and a couple that Fred Skinner did not recognize.

Fred's first impulse was to run across the Magna Carta Hall and say hello. Then he remembered the lies he would have to tell about being at the Fair and about what he had been doing recently. He resisted and quickly left the Hall. He walked around the English Garden and away from the pavilion. All the while he rued ever having gotten involved in a venture that had required him to go so far as to not say hello to Fred Keller. He wanted to put the whole trip behind him as soon as possible.

He decided to eat at the restaurant in the Administration Building. It was a good enough distance from Fred Keller and his companions, and wasn't the kind of place they'd consider eating at. His suitcases were there and it was a few steps from the Fair's Long Island Railroad Station. At the restaurant, he ordered the set dinner and a half bottle of wine. Then he read through the Russian booklets and other Fair material. As he read, he reflected on the contrast between the optimism about the human condition expressed at the Fair and the resignation about imminent war he had experienced in England. If the Fair had been held in Europe, say in Brussels or Zurich, could it have had a healing effect?

There was a hint of pessimism at the Fair. It was in the Westing-house Time Capsule's *Book of Record*. The usual message, however, was that things were quite good now. Through technology and through the unforced cooperation of people and nations, they would get even better. Technology would provide – was providing – an era of prosperi-ty that would overcome poverty, conflict, and ideological extremes. Was this American naivety or American wisdom?

Fred felt there was something missing from the focus on technolo-gy, attention to the technology of behavior. The engineering of consent that Bernays had talked about might be part of it. The insights of Dale Carnegie, Sigmund Freud and others might also be parts. The real chal-lenges concerned the raising of children. How could children be nur-tured with a minimum of aversive control? How could instruction at every age be personalized so that skills, knowledge, and understanding would be acquired with easy effectiveness? Improved child rearing would insure development of better citizens and a better society. The science of behavior must advance to the point of being able to make a contribution.

The science of behavior could also make important and useful philosophical contributions. These could be to topics as diverse as the nature of meaning and the nature of freedom. Fred had answers to these age-old problems. Meaning is how words are used. Freedom is not self-determined action but absence of aversive control. These no-tions, particularly the second, were far from everyday understanding. One of Fred's challenges would be to change that, particularly the no-tion about freedom. Wittgenstein had figured out the social nature of meaning, but his manner of presentation was not going to help people with their everyday lives. Freud had drawn attention to the long-lasting, often pathological effects of aversive experiences in childhood. He was not as interested as he might be in how the effects of such ex-periences can be minimized.

Fred's reverie was interrupted by a waiter saying that the restaurant would close in twenty minutes. It was time for last orders of beverages. Fred paid for his meal and retrieved his suitcases. Outside, the Fair looked quite different. It was a blaze of light against an almost dark sky, a spectacle in itself. His night vision was not as good as it used to be. He should wear his glasses more often.

He found the railroad station, and was at Penn Station in Manhattan by nine thirty. There he waited fifteen minutes for a train to the railroad station near the airport. The train was met by a shuttle bus that took him to the airport buildings. He arrived there at ten thirty, almost two hours before his flight for Chicago would depart.

The main pavilion of the U.S.S.R. was among the most popular national pavilions at the New York World's Fair in 1939. This photo was likely taken in May 1939, soon after the pavilion was completed but before the area in front of it was landscaped. After the August 1939 alliance between the U.S.S.R. and Germany, the pavilion did not continue into the Fair's 1940 season. Much of the building was shipped back to the Soviet Union. The site was razed and used in 1940 for an exhibit celebrating American racial diversity.

THIRTY-TWO

Home

Newark and Minneapolis, Monday June 5, 1939

T he baggage check-in was not until fifteen minutes before the twelve-twenty flight. The agreeable people at the American Airlines counter let Fred check his suitcases in early, and all the way to Minneapolis even though he would fly from Chicago by a different airline. He asked what would happen if the plane arrived late in Chicago. That would be unlikely given the good weather forecast, he was told. If it arrived late the Northwest Airlines plane would wait.

He had an hour and a half to kill. The only reading material he had were his two notebooks, removed before checking his suitcases so he knew where they were. But, unusually, he had little interest in reading what he had written. He looked around the airport building and learned that Newark Metropolitan Airport was the busiest in the world. At a newsstand he bought the early edition of the next day's *New York Times*.

He settled down with the newspaper. Many articles were about things he'd had contact with during his trip. A front-page article concerned a speech Hitler had given earlier in the day to a quarter of a million World War veterans. Hitler spoke "as a soldier to soldiers." Half the speech was about the unfairness to Germany of the *Treaty of Versailles*, the consequences of which Hitler had now "formally wiped out." Hitler said that the World War had been about the encirclement and diminution of Germany. This was still English and French policy. But now, Germany would defend itself adequately. To this end, any German leader who is not a "one-hundred-percent man and a soldier" would be dismissed from his post. Fred took Hitler's speech to be an exercise in rallying his nation for another war.

Another front-page article reported that Britain would have almost a million men under arms by the fall, the result of the recent reintroduction of conscription. Yet another article noted that this was a day of promotion of moral rearmament. President Roosevelt had endorsed it just this evening as an alternative or complement to military rearmament. Earlier in the day, there had been a live broadcast to "all parts of the world" of rallies in Washington and London linked by transatlantic telephone, an impressive demonstration of communications technology. The article had no clear account of what was meant by moral rearmament. The closest was a near-nonsensical statement about the needs "to acknowledge the sovereign authority of God in home and nation, to establish that liberty which rests upon the Christian responsibility to all one's fellow-men, and to build a national life based on unselfishness, unity and faith."

Also on the front page was a report on the fate of the *St. Louis*. It added nothing to what Bernays had told him earlier. Linked articles included more bad news for refugees. Some two hundred of them on another ship to Cuba were now back in Germany. The Costa Rican government had expelled numerous Jews who had arrived in the hope of becoming permanent residents there or in the United States. Possible good news for Jewish refugees was a report on discussions in Washington about settling thirty thousand of them in the Philippines to offset a growing Japanese influence. The government in Manila was in agreement, but the decision would be made in Washington. Fred was surprised to learn that the Philippines remained an American colony as far as external relations were concerned. He should review his distaste for the British Empire.

Inside, Fred found an item on the contribution of several thousand Portuguese volunteers to the Nationalist victory in the Spanish Civil War. A companion article addressed the support given the Nationalists by the German army and air force. The huge scale of the ongoing Spanish demobilization fitted with what the Lisbon brothers had said. Spain would likely remain neutral in the coming war.

Also inside was an article reporting progress toward the signing of a "pact of mutual defense against aggression" by Britain, France and the Soviet Union. While reading this, Fred realized he had become too interested in such matters and there were good reasons to wind down the interest. He couldn't be more than a passive spectator of politics without investing so much time it would interfere with his work. In any case, however strongly he became engaged, he'd likely have little impact. He could have more impact on the world by pursuing the science of behavior. Sales of *The Behavior of Organisms* were disappointing. Nevertheless, he felt the book provided a solid foundation on which to build. If he made progress with his book on verbal behavior, he could have a strong impact. Also, a sudden spurt in interest in foreign affairs would have to be explained to friends and colleagues, and he didn't have a good explanation.

Fred glanced at the weekend's baseball scores and standings and then back at several articles he found on the World's Fair. The current week was expected to be one of the Fair's busiest. It had begun today with the opening of the Greek pavilion. This ceremony had been attended by several thousand people but Fred had missed it. The week would culminate on Saturday with the three-hour visit of the British king and queen. This was to be commemorated with giant portraits of the couple placed at the Lagoon of Nations. Fred wondered what they would think of such bad taste.

461

He wondered too what else he had missed at the Fair. The article "At the Fair yesterday" could have been helpful but he now saw it was a regular humorous piece about quirky happenings rather than a serious account of events. He learned that one of the nudes who frolicked in a garden in the Amusement Zone had been laid low by poison ivy. Perhaps his time would have been better spent there than in the mostly tedious government pavilions.

It was time for his flight. Only three of the twenty or so seats were occupied. As well as for the low cost, he might have been put on the red-eye flight so that few people would see him. He fell asleep soon after take-off and woke only when told by the flight attendant that the plane was to be landing shortly in Chicago. She said he'd missed the nice meal she had prepared for him just after take-off. He regretted not having eaten her meal but said he must have needed the sleep. Half an hour later he was in the air again, now refreshed and looking forward to the breakfast he could hear being prepared behind him. This plane, another DC-3, was about one third full. The other passengers seemed to be Chicago men with business in the Twin Cities. No one got on or off at Milwaukee. The plane's brief stop there was presumably justified by carrying mail and other cargo.

He had forgotten how noisy and smelly land planes were, and how primitively furnished, and this DC-3 was one of the newest. He'd gotten used to the luxury of the *Atlantic Clipper*. The smell of fuel almost put him off his breakfast. He was hungry and ate what was put in front of him as they flew over Wisconsin's pastures, fields, lakes and woods. They were all lit beautifully by the sun rising behind the plane. He mused again about his trip, now more about his intellectual progress than the trip's impact on his political understanding. He read through several of his notes. With some exceptions it had not been a productive couple of weeks. He'd have made more progress, particularly on verbal behavior, if he'd stayed at home. Reading his unsent letters to Fred Keller caused a pit in his stomach about the near encounter yesterday evening.

The most important development during the trip concerned his thinking about the parallel between natural selection and reinforcement, set out in his first letter to Fred. The parallel's significance seemed greater each time he approached the matter. He wanted to explore it in more detail. If it survived the analysis, he could use it to help secure widespread understanding of the importance of reinforcement. There were two barriers. One was Freud's caution: behavior controlled by reinforcement smacked of a kind of Social Darwinism that could be anathema in the present political environment. The other was the uncertainty about natural selection in mainstream biology. The uncertainty seemed to be fading, but there was not yet a solid appreciation of natural selection's importance.

Even though he ought to hold off before emphasizing the analogy, he should not hesitate to consider its implications. One he liked was also set out in the first letter to Fred. It concerned what differentiated sciences. Biology was the domain of natural selection. Psychology – more precisely behavioral science – was the domain of reinforcement.

His third letter to Fred Keller had helped clarify his thinking about personal freedom. He now saw this more clearly than before as the condition of being under the control of positive reinforcement. People are free if what they are doing pleases them. Maybe the obverse of this was the more important thought. Lack of freedom is a condition of aversive control. There is no need to posit free will. If a person is behaving freely, the source of the behavior lies in his or her interactions with positive reinforcers and not in an inner agency.

He realized he hadn't written to Fred about his encounters with Freud, not that Fred would notice the omission. In truth, there wasn't much to report. Almost everything Freud said that touched on matters of concern to Fred was predictable. Freud's digressions about his book on Woodrow Wilson, Jewish racial memory, and his rivalry with Hitler were interesting, but Fred could remember nothing in them that contributed to the science of behavior. The caution about the analogy *was* valuable.

In Cambridge, Fred had gained more from Turing than from Wittgenstein. The latter had helped confirm his growing view that philosophers had little to contribute. He felt this even though Wittgenstein had figured out the social nature of meaning and the impossibility of private language. Turing, by contrast, was an intellectual gem. Fred would much like to have further discussion with him about thinking machines.

Wittgenstein had served one useful purpose. He had caused Fred to clarify his own thinking about the social nature of language. Anticipating the meetings with Wittgenstein had stimulated Fred to reflect more how Julie was acquiring verbal behavior. His big insight was that such acquisition – and much of verbal behavior more generally – was very much a two-way process. Fred would reinforce finer and finer approximations in Julie's utterances to acceptable verbal behavior. But what he was doing would be as much under the control of her behavior as her behavior would be under the control of his.

As well, the discussion with Wittgenstein had caused him to make a useful and perhaps important distinction between verbal behavior and language. Language was not a set of words but a set of reinforcement practices of a particular verbal community.

Thinking about Julie turned his thoughts to what would be waiting for him when he got home. Would there be no one there, or would Yvonne and Julie have returned from Chicago? Before he'd left he'd told Yvonne he would be in New York on Sunday June the fourth and returning home on the Monday. She might have expected him to call. He did call, both to Chicago and to home. If there was no one at home when he arrived he would call Chicago straight away and see what was happening. If Yvonne was still in Chicago, refusing to come home, he would get the overnight train there.

He remembered that he'd promised Julie a present. He hadn't bought one, or one for Yvonne. If they were not at home he'd still have a chance to get something. But he'd prefer they were at home.

The flight attendant said they'd be landing shortly and on time at Wold-Chamberlain Field, the Minneapolis airport. There was a bus from the terminal building to the city, but Fred treated himself to a cab to get home more quickly. Yvonne and Julie could be there, and in any case he'd avoid the transfer from bus to streetcar with his suitcases.

Less than an hour later, just before nine fifteen, he unlocked his front door and listened for signs of activity. From the kitchen he heard Julie making singing noises and saying "No more." He crept in and watched her for a few seconds as she was being fed in her highchair. She pushed the offered spoon away, said "No more" again, and resumed her tuneless singing. Then she saw Fred. Her eyes opened wide. "Dada," she called out, "Dada!" She struggled against the strap holding her in her chair. It was not Yvonne feeding Julie but Yvonne's mother. Fred said hello. He'd still not worked out what to call her. He unfastened Julie, lifted her up and smothered her with a big kiss. "Dada, show you my doll." She was indeed speaking in sentences.

Yvonne stood at the door still in her robe. "You're back," she said, smiling. Her mother left the kitchen. Fred walked over to Yvonne and embraced her with his free arm, pulling her head to his chest.

"Dada, Momma," said Julie, still held in Fred's other arm. Fred was tearful. Julie put an arm around each parent as best she could. "Dada cry," she said. "Momma cry too?"

465

Characters, as they were in May and June 1939

B.F. (Fred) Skinner (1904-1990) was an assistant professor of psychology at the University of Minnesota.

Calvin Cooper, aged about fifty-five, was a senior member of the staff of United States President Franklin D. Roosevelt.

James Roosevelt (1907-1991) was the eldest son of President Roosevelt. Now working in Hollywood, he had been Secretary to the President in 1937-1938.

Romelle Schneider (1916-2002) was James Roosevelt's nurse and companion [and later his wife].

Alfred North Whitehead (1861-1947) had taught math and physics at English universities, and then was a professor of philosophy at Harvard University until he retired in 1937.

Bertrand Russell (1872-1970) was a British mathematician and philosopher, and a former student of A.N. Whitehead. He was a visiting professor at the Universities of Chicago and California.

Yvonne Skinner (1911-1997) was Fred Skinner's wife. [She was later known as Eve.]

Julie Skinner (1938-) was Fred and Yvonne's daughter. [She is now Julie Vargas.]

Eustace Hopkins, aged about sixty, was a United States Federal Judge, District of Minnesota.

Lukas Glaser, aged about thirty-five, was a dentist who had moved from Vienna, Greater Germany, to St. Paul, Minnesota, early in 1939.

Marian Kruse (1920-2001), Fred Skinner's student and editorial assistant, occasionally looked after Julie Skinner. [She was later Marian Breland Bailey.]

Jean-Paul Tanguay, aged about fifty-five, was a cabin steward on the Canadian Pacific steamship Duchess of York.

Samuel Brown, aged about sixty-two, was a retired ship's engineer originally from Scotland but now resident in Montreal. He was a passenger on the Duchess of York.

Charles Richardson (c1885-c1955) was the ship's captain, *Duchess of York.*

Andrew Anderson, aged about sixty, was a Church of Scotland minister and a passenger on the Duchess of York.

Dolly MacDonald, aged about sixty-three, was a passenger on the Duchess of York.

Kovoor Behanan (1902-1960) was an Indian yoga scholar and instructor with a Ph.D. in psychology from Yale University. He was a passenger on the *Duchess of York.*

Anna Graydon, aged nineteen, and her mother Sophie Graydon were passengers on the Duchess of York.

Sophie Graydon, aged about forty-two, was a German-born widow and lecturer in philosophy at the University of Toronto who had married a Canadian soldier in 1919.

Fred Keller (1899-1996), Fred Skinner's closest academic colleague and personal friend, was an instructor in psychology at Columbia University in New York City.

Mabel Miller, aged about thirty-three, was a fashion buyer with Stuttafords, a South African department store, on assignment in Paris and London for her employer.

Sigmund Freud (1856-1939), founder of the psychoanalytic movement, had moved from Vienna to London in 1938 with many members of his family.

Anna Freud (1895-1982) was the youngest child and closest colleague of Sigmund Freud.

William Bullitt (1891-1967), United States Ambassador to France, and previously the Soviet Union, was co-author with Sigmund Freud of a forthcoming book on Woodrow Wilson.

Ludwig Wittgenstein (1899-1951), originally from Vienna, was appointed Professor of Mental Philosophy and Logic at the University of Cambridge early in 1939.

Alan Turing (1912-1954) was a fellow of King's College, University of Cambridge, and a lecturer in mathematics there.

Francis Skinner (1912-1941) was Ludwig Wittgenstein's acolyte, amanuensis and cohabiter.

Raimund Pretzel (1907-1999) had moved from Germany to England in 1938. [As Sebastian Haffner, he was later a well-known journalist in Britain and Germany.]

Ruth Williams, aged about thirty, was the flight attendant on the Pan American Airlines flying boat Atlantic Clipper.

Tom Salinsky, aged about twenty-eight, was third officer on the Atlantic Clipper.

Pedro Cabral, aged about fifty-seven, was the head of the Customs and Immigration Service, Port of Lisbon.

Manuel Cabral, aged about fifty-five, brother and brother-in-law of Pedro, was the Harbormaster, Port of Lisbon.

Harold Gray (1906-1972) was the captain of the *Atlantic Clipper*.

Edward Bernays (1891-1995), American double nephew of Sigmund Freud, was a public relations counselor and author of *Crystallizing Public Opinion* and *Propaganda*.

Illustration credits

Errors in this section are inadvertent. Corrections will be gratefully received and mistakes happily remedied.

The map across two pages of the front matter was adapted from the relief location map of the North Atlantic Ocean by Uwe Dedering by the addition of place names, route and legend. The file of the map is licensed under the Creative Commons Attribution-Share Alike 3.0 Unported licence, and is used with permission.

The photo of B.F. (Fred) Skinner before Chapter 1 is reproduced here with the permission of the B.F. Skinner Foundation.

The photo of James Roosevelt before Chapter 2 is from the Harris & Ewing collection at the U.S. Library of Congress and is in the public domain.

The image of the title page of B.F. Skinner's *Behavior of Organisms* before Chapter 3 is believed to be in the public domain.

The front cover of *The ABC Bunny* before Chapter 4 is reproduced here with the permission of the University of Minnesota Press.

The illustration of the "royal train" before Chapter 5 is believed to be in the public domain.

The painting of the *Duchess of York* before Chapter 6 is part of the collection of the New York Public Library and is in the public domain.

The photo of Fred Keller and Fred Skinner before Chapter 7 is reproduced here with the permission of John Keller, Fred Keller's son, on behalf of his mother, Frances Keller.

The illustrations from Kovoor T. Behanan's *Yoga: A Scientific Evaluation* before Chapter 8 are believed to be in the public domain.

The image of the passenger list cover before Chapter 9 is believed to be in the public domain.

The postcard picture of a whale at a St. Pierre whale-oil factory before Chapter 10 is believed to be in the public domain.

The image of the title page of *Mein Kampf* and the facing photograph before Chapter 11 is believed to be in the public domain.

The image of the title page of *Tractatus Logico-Philosophicus* before Chapter 11 is believed to be in the public domain.

The photo of U-boat 35 before Chapter 13 was taken from a website maintained by Hans Mair, a relative of the submarine's chief engineer. It appeared as a widely distributed official postcard first produced in 1936 and is in the public domain.

The poster of the *Coronation Scot* before Chapter 14 is believed to be in the public domain.

The photo of the main building at Bletchley Park before Chapter 15 was taken by Matt Crypto and is in the public domain.

The image of the advertisement for Du Cane Court before Chapter 16 is believed to be in the public domain.

The photo of Anna and Sigmund Freud before Chapter 17 is believed to be in the public domain.

The photo of Marie Bonaparte, Sigmund Freud, and William Bullitt before Chapter 18 is believed to be in the public domain.

The image of the poster for the Casals concert before Chapter 19 is believed to be in the public domain.

The photo of Sigmund Freud before Chapter 20 was taken by Ferdinand Schmutzer and is in the public domain.

The photo of Ludwig Wittgenstein before Chapter 21 is reproduced here with the permission of the Master and Fellows of Trinity College Cambridge.

The photo of Alan Turing before Chapter 22 is reproduced here with permission from Princeton University.

The photo of Ludwig Wittgenstein before Chapter 23 is part of the collection held by the Austrian National Library and is in the public domain.

The image of cover of *Geschichte eines Deutschen* by Sebastian Haffner (Raimund Pretzel) before Chapter 24 is reproduced here with the permission of the publisher (DVA, now Random House), the cover's designer, Jorge Schmidt of Kommunikationsdesign, Munich, and the late author's family (Sarah Haffner and Oliver Pretzel), who own the photo.

The photo of Pan American Airlines' *Yankee Clipper* before Chapter 25 is from the Harris and Ewing collection at the U.S. Library of Congress and is in the public domain.

The image of the cut-away sketch of a Pan Am *Clipper* before Chapter 26 is reproduced here with the permission of the Pam Am Historical Foundation.

The floor plan of a Pan Am *Clipper* before Chapter 27 was taken from *The Flying Clippers* website and is reproduced here with the permission of the site's operator, Michael McKinney.

The photo of the lounge/dining room of a Pan Am *Clipper* before Chapter 28 is reproduced here with the permission of the Pam Am Historical Foundation.

The photo of Edward Bernays before Chapter 29 is reproduced here with the permission of the Museum of Public Relations, New York.

The photo of the Futurama model before Chapter 30 may be owned by General Motors.

The aerial view of the 1939 New York World's Fair before Chapter 31 is part of the collection of the Franklin and Eleanor Roosevelt Institute and is in the public domain.

The photo of the pavilion of the U.S.S.R before Chapter 32 is part of the collection of the New York Public Library and is in the public domain.

About the author

Richard Gilbert with Isaac, his third-youngest grandchild, soon after Isaac's birth in 2012.

THIS IS RICHARD GILBERT'S FIRST NOVEL. He's produced many non-fiction books and several hundred articles on topics that reflect the many jobs he's had over a long working life.

The jobs have included high-school teacher and university professor, government scientist and elected politician, journalist and, most recently, consultant on transportation and urban issues with clients on five continents.

Richard's main formal qualifications are in psychology, although he's been doing other things for many years. He's a member of the Writers' Union of Canada.

Richard was born in London, England, in January 1940, some months after the period of this novel. He and Rosalind emigrated from Scotland to Canada in the late 1960s. They've lived in downtown Toronto for most of the time since. Their family includes many grandchildren ranging in age from newborn to early twenties.